Sweetnes

A NOVEL BY (

To Adam, For Reminding Me That I Can Still Do This

One

1994 was the maddest year of my life. I'd just started being able to get into pubs that summer, the World Cup was on in America, and Ireland were in it again, and I met Áine O'Shaughnessy. I didn't know it at the time, but meeting that girl changed the rest of my life. That might sound pure dramatic, but it was the truth. It happened in August, when I was fifteen - nearly sixteen. I remember my Ma saying it was the hottest summer since that year all that stuff happened in Thomondgate – with Paudie Collins, and those two boys, and everything else that went on. We were away on our holidays that week, but I remember my friend Richie talking about it a few times. Even though he didn't really like talking about it at all.

"SCATTER!"

I couldn't believe he actually done it. He was a headcase. I ran; Ian was already ahead of me. Harta was gonna be the slowest, cos he was holding onto the bottles. Ian headed down Roche's Street, he was way too fast for me. I was already nearly out of breath, but I wasn't stopping for no one. I could hear Harta behind me, clinking. He'd three Buckfast – two in one hand, one in the other. We were only messing when we dared him to rob them. It was him that came up with it anyway, we only egged him on. I nearly shit a brick when he came flying out the door, screaming at us to leg it.

I wanted to look back, but I didn't wanna slow down. I hadn't even seen anyone come out of Fine Wines after him, but they definitely had. That's why they always put two fellas working there – in case someone robbed something and ran out of the shop; they'd have one to stay back and the other to run after him. Otherwise people'd be doing it all the time.

I could hear Harta closer behind me now – sort of like he was crying or something. Then I copped on that it wasn't crying; it was laughing. He was seriously mental, that youngfella. Ian disappeared around the corner at the end of the road and turned off to the right. He was heading for Poorman's, or maybe under the bridge. I was still going – my lungs were pure dry – too much smoking. Harta was such a gowl; there was no need to rob anything, we'd all gave him money. I really wanted to look back now, but I couldn't slow down. The other fella in the shop had probably called the Gards already, and Ian had run down here – nearly in the same street as the Garda Station. He was another eejit. I barely got one foot on the grass of Poorman's when yer man from Fine Wines caught me. He either tripped me or pushed me, but I went face down in the grass with the weight of him on my back. My head banged into the ground and I got that feeling you get when you feel like you're gonna have a nosebleed. He was laughing now, on top of me, yer man. I couldn't turn over cos all the weight was on my back. Bloody Harta, stupid gowl, getting us in trouble for no reason, and now I was gonna get the face boxed off me. Or get arrested. Or both. He'd better hope the Gards caught him before I did, cos I was gonna –

"Get off him, you lala," said Ian.

"No! He's coming down the fucking cop shop!" said yer man on top of me, in a really bad, put-on voice, and I knew straight away it was Harta. I lifted myself up pure hard and he came flying off me onto the grass. I dived on top of him and started digging him in the ribs. Not serious, like, but hard enough so he'd remember it for a bit. Ian picked up one of the bottles from the grass next to us, and took the top off it. Buckfast was one of the wines with a twisty cap. You didn't need no opener for it. I rolled off Harta after making sure I'd got him back enough. Fair play, he'd got us good.

*****

There was no one down Poorman's, but it was early anyway, only about half seven. We'd been there about a half-hour since Harta's little joke. It was still bright, and sunny when the clouds weren't in the way. There'd be people along later. And we'd be going to Quin's anyway; we always did.

"Why's it called Poorman's Kilkee, anyway?" said Ian, not really to any of us.

"You serious?" Harta gave him a queer look.

"What? Yeah. Why's it called that? It's not even near Kilkee…" Ian shrugged at him, then looked at me.

"Jesus Christ. Ye don't know nothing about yeer history, do ye?" I said. He wasn't even messing. He didn't know.

"That's the upper classes for you, sham," said Harta. He took a swig of Bucky and passed it over to me.

"Fuck off, will you. My Dad's only an accountant, for fuck's sake. We're not upper class."

"*Only* an accountant, eh? You know what my Da does, shur?" I said, swallowing the wine down. It tasted rank, as usual.

"Well, no. I just-"

"He makes mock hips. In a factory, out the Dublin Road. Plastic hips, for auld biddies." He did as well. When they'd a party for all the fellas who worked there for ten years, they gave them all a glass paperweight thing, with a hip inside in the glass. My Ma put it on over the fireplace in the front room. Pure weird looking; a hip on the mantelpiece.

"Hips?" said Ian. He took the bottle off me and wiped the top, like I'd a disease or something. He probably washed his hands every time he went for a slash, that youngfella.

"Fucking hips, shur. Hips for the Queen Mother, and little black fellas in Africa who's after stepping on a landmine," said Harta, sparking up one of the fags from the new box he got in Fine Wines, when he was in there, *not* robbing stuff.

“What does your Dad do then?” said Ian. He’d a long-sleeve t-shirt under the Nirvana one. I could see the ‘Pearl Jam’ down the side of his arm, in red, faded away to pink nearly from being in the wash.

“My Dad? I dunno, pal. He walked out when I was three. Left my Mam to bring up four kids on her own. Wasn’t easy either, you know. Sometimes we didn’t have no dinner. Sometimes she had to… well, we’ll just say that she didn’t always make her money in a nice way, Ian. So, you mightn’t be upper class, like. And your auld fella might *only* be an accountant, and he might *only* drive a Beamer, and you might *only* live in some swanky fucking semi-detached up there in wherever it is you live, but you’re lucky. You know what I mean? You’re luckier than me, pal. Fucking appreciate it…” He’d the saddest look that I’d ever seen on anyone’s face.

“Jesus, man. I’m… sorry. I didn’t know. I’m… I’m sorry.” Ian’s face was nearly as sad as Harta’s.

“S’all right, pal. Was a long time ago. I’m over it. I even… some days I even think I forgive him. He’s still me Da, like. Blood is thicker than water, sham.” He took the bottle off me again. I spotted a little smile in the corner of his mouth, and then it was gone.

“Will you g’way outta that, you gowl,” I said. I punched him full force in the arm, and he nearly fell over onto the grass.

“Aaaagh, Jaysus fucking Christ, Jon.” He was holding in the giggles, biting on his tongue to keep a straight face. Ian looked confused.

“The fuck is…?”

"Him, the bollix. His Da didn't go nowhere. He owns Hartigan's out in Raheen. And he hasn't no brothers or sisters. You ever been round his house? Amiga 500, Atari ST, Super Nintendo, hi-fi stereo. Only child. Spoilt brat, so he is." It was true. His Ma and Da got him everything, and he still called them every name under the sun once they walked out of the room. I was an only child as well, but my Ma and Da hardly got me nothing, the gowls.

"Aw fuck, Harta. You prick, you. I thought he was serious and everything, lads. I was mortified." Ian leaned over to get the Bensons, and I chucked them into his hand. Harta had a big dirty sneer on him, with the fag hanging out the side of his mouth, so he looked like one of them auld fellas that does the gurning, over in England.

"Yeah, and anyway; Ian's Da doesn't drive a Beamer, either." I fiddled in the side pocket of my combats for a choongum, to get the taste of rank out of my mouth.

"Exactly. It's a Merc," said Ian, winking. He'd the fag all awkward in his fingers, like he wasn't used to it.

"Steamer!" said Harta, taking the cork off the second bottle. Ian threw the lighter at his head, but he ducked it.

*****

Me and Harta were doing our usual talking drunk shite about music later when Bríd and Ciara came along. Ciara was sort of a ride, sometimes. She'd a bit of a spotty face, but she was pretty as well. Massive chest on her too, but she wasn't fat. Bríd was rapid looking from the neck down. Face was a bit funny, but you could get over that. Few cans in you and you'd hardly notice. I just didn't like her hair; it was too curly. They were both sound out though. You could talk to them like they were lads.

"All right, men? What's the craic?" said Ciara. I tried not to look at her tits. Or not to let her catch me looking at them.

"Morning, gowls," said Bríd. She'd a skirt on, and trousers under it. I didn't understand women at all sometimes.

"Well, ladies? What you been up to, shur? Down the docks, selling your wares?" Harta gave them a wink. I was already a bit hammered, and most of it hadn't hit me yet, in fairness. Ian didn't even look up. He was away with the fairies.

"Yep. Your Mum said to say hi," said Bríd. Everyone done a *waaaaaa* at that.

"What ye drinking? Ooh, the fancy stuff, eh?" Ciara slid in between me and Harta, putting her hand on my leg, then taking it off.

"Only the best for us, Ceer. Hand distilled by the monks of Buckfast Abbey. 1995 too, a good year. No, hang on. That's next year, isn't it? Wine from the future, lads! They're spoiling us, they are." Harta offered over some of it to her, but she scrunched up her nose and shook her head at him.

"Do you distil wine then? Or do you brew it?" Ian had snapped out of his daze, probably cause Poorman's was suddenly full of women.

"You stamp on it. You stamp on the grapes, with your bare feet. And that's the sell by date, you mong, Harta," said Bríd. She sat herself down on the other side, next to Ian. Him and her lived near each other, Ciara lived up in Kileely, near me. She didn't look like she came from Kileely though. And she was born in England, but she moved over when she was five.

"Does Buckfast have grapes in it? I didn't think their budget stretched to it," said Ciara.

"Course it does. Grapes, water, sugar…" Harta was pretending to read ingredients off the back, but there was no ingredients on the back of wine.

"… speed, heroin, ecstasy…" Bríd must've done something weird to her hair. It was straighter than normal. It wasn't bad looking at all, but maybe I was drunk.

"I saw a fella punch a condom machine off a wall one night in Tropics, after drinking Bucky. It was mental, like. I remember the bouncers coming in looking for him. They ended up kicking the door of the cubicle in, and they found him sitting on the toilet, just wearing his jocks, hugging it like it was a teddy bear." I sparked up another fag. I'd only just put one out, but drink made me an animal for the cigarettes.

"Janey Mack! And how do you know he was drinking Buckfast?" said Ian.

"Oh, I dunno if he was. I just assumed."

Everyone cracked up. I didn't think it was that funny. Sometimes people laughed too hard at the things you said. Especially in school. Or when they were pissed. Ciara turned around to me. She'd lovely eyes. Greyish blue, nearly purple. She looked like a witch, but not in a bad way.

"How are you anyway, gorgeous?" she said. Her hand was on my leg again; this time she left it longer.

"Grand. How's you? Still single?" Me and her shifted once or twice before, when we were both drunk. I'd never really thought about having her as a girlfriend. I never really thought about having anyone as a girlfriend. I liked playing the field. Sticking with just one girl sounded pure boring. I didn't think Ciara would want to go out with me anyway, no matter how flirty she was with me. I didn't care. I didn't have no trouble shifting youngones. All the lads were pure jealous of me for it, probably. Lads never said 'well done' or anything to you. They just called you a jammy bastard, or tried to say there was something wrong with yer one. That was just the way it was.

"Me? When am I not? No one's going to tie me down, Jon. Well, not unless I ask them nicely." She gave me a wink, and I thought to myself maybe it was gonna be another one of those nights between us. Didn't seem like a bad idea. And it'd save me the effort of finding someone else.

"What's going on with the music anyway, Jonno?" Bríd had a naggin of Southern Comfort; she was drinking it straight out of the bottle.

"Ah, s'complicated, like." It wasn't that complicated, I just didn't wanna get into a big story.

"You doing Battle of the Bands?" Ciara robbed a fag out of our box, even though she'd her own ones.

"What, in the Glentworth?" I'd heard something about that one when we'd played up in the Pike Inn. Yer man who ran the bar showed us the poster.

"No, no. In the George." Bríd didn't smoke at all. She'd bad asthma.

“The George? Do they do gigs in the George now? Who’s playing this week, sham; 2 Unlimited?”

“No, you handicap. Not up in Tropics. Downstairs.” Ciara was well able for Harta. Tropics was the disco in the George. We didn’t go there, it was all rave and chart music. Nice looking women, but they were all tarts.

“Downstairs in the hotel bar?”

“No, no. *Downstairs* downstairs. In the Glory Hole. It’s for Paddy Expo,” said Bríd. I could see up her skirt from where I was sitting, but all I could see was trousers, in fairness.

“Oh right, yeah. Jaysus, where’ll they fit the stage in there? I’ll hop the back of my forehead off the ceiling when I’m singing. And they’ll have to cut a hole in the roof for Nailer.” Our bassist, Niall was even taller than me. He used to play rugby for Old Crescent until his broke his back popping out of a maul. He’d be out later.

“I dunno, but it looks good anyway. Better than the one in the Glentworth. Original bands only, like. No Fat Tuesday this time,” said Bríd. We went to see a Battle of the Bands a few months ago, to watch The DTs; the lads I used to do a bit of roadie-ing for, before our band got together properly. It was a joke. The band that won were good, but they didn’t play none of their own songs. All covers. Wasn’t fair at all. The lads were raging.

“Fat Tuesday can suck my mickey, sham. They’re only a bunch of steamers.” Harta wasn’t there on the night, but he knew them from doing gigs around town.

"I thought they were good, like. But they shouldn't have been in the competition… they were always gonna win with that crowd." Ian talked to one of their lads in the bar after; about guitars, probably.

"Yep. Playing *Summer of '69* to fucking langered people. Always a crowd pleaser." Harta had a little tin on his lap, full of Rizlas and dried up tobacco.

"Have ye hash, is it?" I wouldn't have minded a smoke.

"Will you g'way, I've only a nodge left."

"Ah, go on. Make a one-skinner, you Scrooge, you. Share the wealth." I couldn't see nothing in the tin besides papers, but he'd usually a bit of gear on him.

"Fuck off, will you. I haven't had a daycent puff in ages."

"You were smoking one when we met you a few hours ago, you gowl!"

"Exactly. Hours ago, sham. C'mere and I show you. Look. See? See that? Not even half a one-skin in that. Fuck off with ye." He showed us a tiny bit of Squidgy Black, between his thumb and his finger.

"Shupp and make the joint, will you? Or give it here and I'll do it. Stop acting the maggot." I wasn't any good at rolling spliffs; not like him, anyway. But a one skinner was just the same as a rollie, and I could do rollies fine.

"Acting the maggot? Who are you, like, my Da?"

"I am, yeah. Your Ma wanted to wait until you were eighteen to tell you, but like, I think the time is right."

"My Ma wouldn't give you the steam off her piss."

"Just roll the joint, you lala."

"Fuck off, you… *gay*."

"Good comeback, man."

"If you want your come back you can scrape it out of my hole, sham."

"Harta!" said Ciara, throwing a box of matches at his head.

"What's the story with the George though? All originals, no covers?" Ian sounded langered already. His eyes were all watery too.

"Yeah, I think you can do a mix. But you have to do one or two originals." Ciara wasn't in a band, but she played a bit of guitar, and she was always at gigs.

"One or two? How many songs do we get to do?"

"I think you get to do two, then come off and do another two later. It's for Paddy Expo, like I said, so it's big. Late bar and everything. Stop serving at half one; kicking out at two."

"Shit, out at two? Jaysus, I love culture, lads." The Expo was on every summer for the last few years. We weren't together last year, but The DTs done a few shows; I went along to see them, cos they were on in the daytime, and you could go into pubs underage as long as you didn't try buying booze.

"Yep. Hang on, who's this? Scobes?" Ciara nodded over to the other side; three lads with plastic bags of booze were sitting down. Two on the grass, one on the bench. Poorman's was only small. A little half circle of grass, hanging out over the river. Limerick Boat Club was across the water, and the old swing bridge bit of Sarsfield's on the right, people walking over it into town all the time, but they never looked down at you. It was out in the open, but at the same time, it wasn't.

"Waahs, is it? Knackers? Didicoys?" Harta was licking the gummy bits of the joint. I'd smelt him burning the hash. He was sort of from my place, well Woodview, so when he said stuff like that it sounded all right. If Ian said it, I'd be annoyed though, cos he was posh, and that made it sound like he was saying it about me too. It was hard to explain, but that's how it felt to me.

"Nah, they look sound," said Bríd, turning around to get a better look.

"You won't be saying that when they're over here raping the heart out of you," said Harta.

"Dominic Hartigan! Don't be so vulgar, please. There are ladies present." It was funny when anyone called Harta by his real name. He didn't look like a Dominic. He didn't even look like a Dom.

"Are there? Where? Where?"

"Right here, bitch. You're looking at 'em." Bríd stuck up her finger at him.

"If you're a lady, I'll eat my hat." Harta never seemed to get wrecked. He just got tipsy, and stayed like that all night. I'd only ever seen him off his face when there was drugs involved. Proper drugs.

"You haven't got a hat, you spa." Ciara raised her eyebrow, and I noticed the eyes again. The fellas over the other side laughed really loud at something, but nothing to do with us. They were too far away to hear us, and they probably hadn't even seen us.

"Exactly," Harta said, like that made sense. He lit the twisty end of the one-skinner. It was pure thin; there'd only be a few drags off it.

"O-kaaaaay. Anyway, Jon- if I were you I'd get signed up for it. I think ye could win it," said Ciara.

"Yeah? You know anyone else in it? Tank Boy? Deliverance? The DTs?"

"You worried about Eric's lot?" said Bríd. Eric was the guitarist from The DTs. He was the singer too, but he was terrible at that. Bríd was shifting him for a while, but they didn't get serious.

"No. Well, yeah. I mean, I dunno. We're not that ready… we need a proper drummer." We'd been using a few different lads. Tony from The DTs was probably the only drummer in Ardscoil or the Crescent we hadn't got to play with us.

"Neh. Drummers are fucking easy to find, sham. Just get some bollix with no brain and big arms that has a shed. A big shed", said Harta. He'd been playing guitar for years; he'd been in lots of people's bands, but he done more gigs on his own. They knew him in all the music pubs. He was older than us. He'd be eighteen next year.

“A shed, and a Dad who drives a van,” Bríd said. She was looking over at the other fellas again.

“Which one are you spotting, Bríd?” said Harta, passing me the joint; it was nearly all gone already.

“Piss off, you spa. No, I thought I knew one of them. I mean, I thought one of them was one of Steven’s friends. But he’s not. Don’t think so anyway.” Steven was her brother. He was sound enough, a bit quiet.

“Steven’s consorting with some low types these days, is he, Bridget?” Ciara was good at doing a snobby voice; probably cos her mother was from England.

‘What? Nah, no. Same Steven as ever.’

‘So, he’s still a virgin then?”, said Harta. He was eyeing the joint again already, but there was only the end of it left.

“Jesus, Harta. Did no one ever teach you how to talk to a woman?” Ciara gave him a thump in the back.

“Nope. I lets me mickey do the talking, sham.” He gave her a wink, rubbing himself where she’d hit him.

“I’m surprised anyone can hear him, the size of him.” She rolled her eyes and looked over at Bríd, who was sniggering into her hand.

“Never had any complaints, love.” He grabbed his crotch and gave it a squeeze.

"We don't complain to your face. We talk to our girlfriends about it, later. Talk, laugh, cry, whatever," Ciara said. Harta just gave her the finger and said:

"Right, are we going?"

He hopped up. No one else moved.

"Going where? We just got here." Bríd still had a bit of naggin left. I hadn't seen Ciara drink anything.

"I don't fucking know. Pub or something. I've to have a slash anyway." He'd a point. The drink had gone straight through me too.

"Go over there," said Bríd, pointing at the steps going down into the river.

"What? What do I look like, an animal?" Harta fixed his hair behind his ears, and it fell straight back down once he'd finished.

"Jesus, no. Animals have a bit of dignity." Ciara's hand was still on my leg. It'd been there for ages.

"Excuse me very much, Slattery; I've plenty of dignity."

"Harta, last week you spilt a naggin of Huzzar in the fridge, and when you saw what you done, you got a bit of bog roll, mopped it all up, and then you ate it." I'd nearly been impressed at the time, it was so disgusting. Ciara, Bríd, and Ian burst out laughing.

"Ah Jesus, he didn't," said Bríd, pretending to puke.

"I did! And I'd do it again, sham. Waste not, want not."

“You’re a vile creature, Dominic. Go to the toilet will you, before you spill something else. I don’t wanna watch you eat a ball of mopped up piss; I dunno about anyone else,” said Ciara, taking out a naggin of Power’s from her bag.

“Quin’s later is it? Termights?”

“What’s the other choices? We going to a dinner dance in the Two Mile Inn?” That was where my Ma and Da went. I didn’t even know what a dinner dance was. I’d picture them bopping away and eating a leg of chicken at the same time.

“Well, there’s Saints.”

“Saints? Nah. Full of jocks.” The first time I’d tried going out to a pub in town this year, it was Saints and Scholars, down near the market. We’d got served without anyone asking us for ID. I was drunk after two pints, but I couldn’t relax at all. My cousin Clodagh from next door went in there all the time, and she’d kill me for drinking or smoking, or she’d tell Mam, back then. I’d a pint of Foster’s in my hand under the table, and a glass of Coke in front of me, just in case. I’d keep the fag in the ashtray, and take sneaky puffs of it, looking at the door like a maniac, in case she came in. She knew I drank now, though. She was all right with me. That was months ago, like. Anyway, one night, we couldn’t get served. So, we tried Quin’s, and we’d gone there ever since.

“All right, all right. Just thought you might fancy a change. Doc’s?”

“Doc’s is worse, Ciara. Never any seats either. I’m not standing outside in the cold with my pint,” I said.

“Fair enough. I love your top; where’d you get it; Modesty?”

"Nah, The Edge."

"That was my next guess. What is it, anyway?"

"It's a cycling top. Belgian, that's why the black, red and yellow." I thought it was German when I got it, but the writing was in French.

"Yeah? It's nice. I mean it's a bit tight, but you're a skinny fucker anyway."

"Oi!"

"I meant it in a good way. I wouldn't mind being that skinny, trust me." She took a swig of her whiskey, and pulled a face cos of the taste. Bríd jumped in, doing the girl thing.

"Jesus Ceer, you're not fat."

"Thanks, like. But I am. It's mostly tits though… so, everybody wins."

I looked straight at them this time. I'd stopped caring about getting caught. It felt like I'd *permission* now anyway.

"Did someone say tits?" Harta was still doing up his belt. I looked at him funny. He didn't seem like the kind of person that'd own a belt.

"Nope. You imagined it. We going then?" Ciara got up from the grass, and Bríd did the same.

"Oh. We're going now, are we? Did I just take my langer out in public for no good reason?" Harta slipped his hands under my arms and lifted me up with a big grunt.

"Like you need a reason," said Bríd, throwing her empty naggin behind her onto the grass. The three lads across the way looked over at us for a second, then when back to their chat. One of them had a flagon of Linden; the other two were drinking cans of Carling.

"What can I say? My mickey is a national treasure, girls. It needs to be exhibited to the public."

"Well, if you need anyone to cut it off and put it in a jar, you've got my number, right?" said Ciara.

"Yep. Got it off the toilet wall in Termights."

"It pays to advertise, clearly." Ciara linked arms with me as we walked out towards Henry Street.

"You had to pay? Jaysus, I get my ads for free." He'd a fag in his hands for ages now without lighting it.

"Yeah, they don't charge for the gay ones."

"Yeah, your Da told me that."

"My Dad's dead."

"Yeah, the AIDS killed him."

"Well, you should've worn a condom."

"Couldn't. It's against my religion."

"Ah, right. Is having a shower against your religion too?"

"Only if I have one with your Dad, and he drops the soap."

*****

We were up town in no time. Monty on the door of Quin's was in fine form. He never ID'd us, and we let him take the piss out of us. That was the deal, even if no one ever said it. The pub was packed. There was three main bits. When you came in the door, on your right was the Vintage Club. That was a good name for it; it was full of auld ones. That first night we'd come in, after being ID'd in Saints, we'd sat in the Vintage Club. It was what my Da would call a *lounge bar*. All soft seats and nice lamps. We were trying to be clever, sitting in with the auld people, and no birds, so they didn't think we were underage. I was with other lads that night; Brian Quinn and John Conway. It was before the summer, cos I remember it being cold and it was dark outside. We drunk pints of Carling and told ghost stories. Rapid night, it was; even though we didn't do nothing really. Clodagh used to always say, messing, that I belonged in Quin's, down Ellen Street, with the other muppets. Turned out she was right.

After a week or two going there, we got the balls to go into the real bit, where all the cool looking people and art students went. By then it was Ian and Niall coming with me. Brian and John were more Doc's people. Harta was probably born in Quin's. He didn't need me to introduce him to it.

"Right, some of us need the facilities. Will you get me a drink, honey?" Ciara shoved a fiver into my hand.

"What you having?" I already knew, but I asked anyway.

"Pernod and black, duh." Pernod was harsh- tasted like gone-off Black Jacks, but my aunt Sarah called it a 'leg-opener' last Christmas, when we were watching Indiana Jones on the telly. I took that info straight on board, chalk it down.

"Duh. Anything else? Peanuts? Pack of Taytos? A straw?" I was wondering what to have myself. Probably Hudson Blue.

"Just the change, sweetie." She pinched my arse and walked away. I never understood that whole *sexual harassment* thing. When it happened to us lads, it was rapid altogether.

There was a third bit to Quin's as well: the back room. It was either where people watched a game of soccer during the World Cup, or where all the gays were. That wasn't official. People'd say things, like "Tuesday night is the Gay Night", but I'd never been there on a Tuesday night. People said the staff were gay there as well, and the owners, but I couldn't see it. I thought The White House was the gay pub in Limerick. Never seen any gays in Quin's. Unless I had, and they were just in disguise, maybe; acting not gay, so no one'd find out.

On the left as you came in was the big round table where the bikers or the metallers sat. I didn't know any of them, but Ciara saluted a few of them when we came in. She was always hanging out of older fellas with long hair. There was a few more tables like that, made out of wooden beer barrels, then you got to the end, and there was steps going up into the best bit- the loft, or the crow's nest, or whatever people called it. It was just some normal tables and stuff, but they were on a stage thing a few feet higher than the rest of the pub. If you sat up there you could see all down the pub, and see everyone coming in the door. Good place to hide too if you were too young looking to be in there, or you were barred and you sneaked in.

Them seats were already took. Friday night and all that. Looked like it was Nora's lot. Nora Ryan was an absolute handicap. Every time we went in there she was caught up in some shite or other between people. She loved the drama. Sometimes she'd be there, blathering away into my ear about who said what to who or who wasn't talking to someone else any more. Pain in the arse, she was.

"All right, Tone?" I always saluted the barmen; some of the lads were pure afraid to even go to the bar, but that's how you got them suspicious of ye. I'd just go straight in and up to get the drinks. Especially if I'd a few scoops in me already.

"How'rya?" Tony probably didn't know my name, but he'd know the face. I was in there every weekend, and we'd come in in the day too, for a glass of Mi-Wadi and a play of the jukebox. *Temple of Love* was on. That was always on. The gothy looking youngones in the corner, on the soft seats, were always playing it. Scary looking yokes, all of them.

"Grand, shur. Can I've a Pernod and black there, and… a pint of Hudson Blue." I didn't know what Harta and Ian were getting, and they'd given me no money, so they could come up and get their own. Bríd as well.

"Is that nice, is it?" He brought out one of the actual tulip glasses with 'Hudson Blue' on it, for the cider. I'd a few of them at home myself. Under the jacket and out the door.

"That one? Yeah. Lovely. Nicer than Bulmer's anyway. Cold filtered or something." I stopped talking then. You could talk too much to the barman. Made you sound nervous.

"Jesus, look at that. I'll do you another one, hang on." The pint looked green.

“What’s… what’s wrong with it?” My stomach went funny looking at it. There was rainbows on top of it too- like someone’d put washing up liquid in it.

“There’s your Pernod anyway. The Ribena’s there, you can put it in yourself. First one of the day after we cleaned the lines this morning, that’s all. Nothing wrong with it, like. Ye could still drink it. Just… I’ll do another one anyway, to be safe.”

“First one? It’s fecking half nine, like.” Pink Floyd were on now- *Comfortably Numb*. Harta done that one, busking.

“Ah, yeah. There’s no one fecking drinks it, see? It’s all Bulmer’s in here, usually. Cans especially.” Donie Lyons told me that they watered down the cider out of the tap in pubs; he’d always get a can and a glass instead.

“Mad. Cheers anyway.” I gave him Ciara’s fiver. I’d get her the next one.

“All right, cunt? Where’s mine, sham?” Harta was over my shoulder. His breath smelt like Bucky and Benson’s.

“Still in the tap, bud. Keeping it cold for you, I was.” I turned around to get past him, taking a swig out of the Hudson so’s it didn’t spill all over the place.

“Sound. All right, Tone? How’s the wife? Still pregnant? How many’s that now, hah? Three? Jaysus, you need to tie a fucking knot in the end of that, Tone. Or start riding her up the choccy whizzpipe.” Harta was going to Quin’s for years. He’d been to lock-ins and all.

Ian and the women nabbed a table in the back room, around the corner from the jacks. Niall was with them.

"There he is! Aboy the head, Muzzo. They for me?" Niall went to Ardscoil as well. I didn't pal round with him before I came into their band. He seemed like a bit of a swot before, and a rugger jock. Big bastard, but the glasses made him look quiet.

"No. They're for me. Well…" I handed Ciara hers. She forgot to ask for the change.

"Fine, fine. I'll get my own. Typical Muz. Sorting out the birds, and leaving your friends go thirsty…"

"She bought these, kid. And you're more of a colleague." I scooched in next to Ciara. Her leg felt pure warm.

"Ffffffs. I'll remember that. You all right for a drink, Bríd?"

"Ah, no. Harta's getting me a pint, thanks." She'd a tight top on, it made her tits look big against how skinny she was.

"A pint? What are ye, a docker? Want anything to go with it? A shot of something?" He opened a nice leather wallet and fingered through a few tens. I'd no idea where some of them got all their money. Rich Mas and Das, probably.

"Well, since you're offering, I'll have a jot o' Bacardi," says I, only half-messing, in case he said yes.

"You can have a jot o' *Fuck Off*, colleague. How about it, Bríd? My treat." He took a note out and rubbed it between his thumb and finger.

"Ah, go on then. Southern Comfort please. Ice, nothing else." She'd probably regret taking it later, when he was cornering her in Termights, trying to get his hole.

"That's more like it. Back in a bit." He got up and came past us, lanky and awkward. When he was standing on stage with his big bass, there wasn't hardly room for no one else. When he was gone, Ciara said:

"Told Niall about the Battle in the George thing too, anyway. He says ye should definitely do it."

Bríd nodded, Ian was away with the fairies again.

"Yeah, it sounds rapid. What you think, kid?" I looked over at him, but no sign of life. Bríd gave him a nudge with her shoulder.

"What? Huh? Sorry, what was that?"

"The Battle of the Bands, in the Glory Hole. Wanna do it?" I took a sip of the Hudson. There was no bad taste, but my brain was making me think it was off, cos I seen the green one a while ago.

"S'pose, yeah." He shrugged, as if he'd no idea why I'd be asking him.

"Jesus Christ, Ian. It's your band too. It's more your band than mine, in fairness." He'd started it- Him, Niall and Tim, who played the keyboards. Keyboards were a bit steamery all the same, but Tim did have a shed for us to practice in, and his Ma gave us lifts with our gear sometimes.

"Yeah, I know… *shop talk* though, bleh. We're supposed to be out on the tear. Oh, cheers, Dom." Harta was back from the bar; he'd slid a pint of Guinness over the table to Ian. Looked like Guinness anyway, might have been Murphy's.

"No probs, squire. Bríd? Budweiser pisswater, there you go. And a pint of porter for moi." He put the other stout down in front of himself. It was black and settled, and the head looked pure creamy. I couldn't manage Guinness at all. I didn't know how people drunk it; it was rank.

"Where's *Timothy* tonight anyway?" Ciara hadn't touched her Pernod yet. She'd a fag in her mouth, looking in her pockets for a light. I'd one somewhere on me, but I couldn't be arsed to find it.

"Ah, he doesn't really go out. His Mum and Dad are a bit strict," said Ian. Tim lived out by the Ennis Road, near Caherdavin way; so did Niall. Daycent place to live, all right; they'd a bowling alley and a Supermac's stuck together, between the Davin Arms and the 24-Hour garage. There was an Xtra-Vision attached to the garage shop, so you'd basically everything you needed in one bit of road- pub, fast food, bowling, arcade, shop, and somewhere to rent a video. All we'd got in Thomondgate was three shops and a rake of knacker pubs. Although there was a video shop, actually. It was just a shit one.

"They are, yeah. His Ma nearly had a stroke when she seen me having a smoke behind their shed." She'd been talking about phoning my house and everything. Mad cow.

"A *smoke* smoke?" Harta had a porter moustache on his lip, from the Guinness.

"Jesus, no. Just a fag."

"For fuck's sake. Aren't you sixteen, shur?" He pulled the big plastic ashtray over from our side of the table.

"Yeah. Nearly anyway. Fifteen and three quarters, like. As good as." I drunk a bit more of my drink. Should've asked for a glass of ice with it. Cider was better when you got it nice and cold. Especially in the summer; or in a packed pub, with everyone else's bodies making you too warm.

"And three quarters… you're a gas man, all the same, Jon. Cheers." He leaned over and clinked his glass off mine. Then everyone done it.

"Sláinte," said Ciara. She'd always gotta be different. She turned around to me, with her scary big purple eyes:

"Is your Cuz still working in Limerick Sports Store?"

"Clodagh? Yeah, she is. Why? Did you want a discount on some Nike-Aaayr-Jardens?" I said it in a scobey voice, cos only knackers went into that shop. Or culchies, looking to buy hurling jerseys. Clo hated it there, but it was money.

"Haha! No, I was wondering did they do Ireland rugby tops. My Mum wants to get one for her Dad, over in London." She said 'Mum' instead of 'Mam'. Posh people done that, although her Ma was English, so it could've been that as well. Some of the lads I hung around with in Ardscoil were posh, some of them were rich, some of them were farmers- so they'd money and everything, but they talked like huffmuckers. They'd say 'Mam', not 'Mum'. They'd probably say 'Mamma', in fairness.

"I'd say so all right. If they're not there, go into Lifestyle, in Arthur's Quay," I said, looking up to see what everyone was shuffling around for. Ian got up out of his seat, so did Bríd. I looked around and saw that it was Niall coming, with a tray. Ian leaned over and helped him put it down on the table. There was a rake of drinks on the thing.

"Right. Southern Comfort for you, Bríd. Pint of Heino for me. And here- no jot 'o Bacardi for Muzzo, you can have Southern Comfort like the rest of us; one for Ceer; Southern Comfort for Mister Lead Guitar; one for Harta, you cunt, you; anyone else? Oh yeah, one for me." He dished out the glasses to us; my jaw was nearly on the floor.

"Jesus Christ, Nailer- d'you win the Lotto or something? Cheers." I'd a little sniff; Southern Comfort smelt gorgeous and horrible- like rotten sweets.

"Nah, I made all that doing the rooms." When the exams were on in June, he got one of the jobs they gave, sitting at a desk outside the door to the hall; checking no one came in, and timing anyone who'd to go out to the jacks. You made a bomb out of it altogether.

"Jaysus. Nice littler earner for you, Del Boy. Sláinte, you jammy prick, you." I clinked my little tumbler against his, and knocked it back in one. The taste went up my nose and made me cough. *How Soon is Now?* came on the speakers over our heads. I loved the guitar on Smiths songs.

"Mawnge toot, Rodders." Niall sat down between Ian and Bríd, looking pure pleased with himself. Nothing like having enough cash to buy a round. One time, we were in Flannery's in Shannon Street, during the day- me and Ciara- and some fella bought a round for the house, cos he'd won big on the gee-gees. There was only about seven people in there, but it was still pure sound.

*****

Coming back out of the jacks later, I got cornered by Nora Ryan. I didn't even say hi to her; she just jumped me. She was going on about some shit I didn't care about.

"… and then Síle says to Taidgh- you know Taidgh, yeah? Saoirse's brother, goes to Clement's. Anyway, yeah, Síle says to him that she wasn't even going out with him anyway- they were just shifting, like. And he was like, we *were* going out, you don't shift someone for six months without it being going out. And Síle says to him, you never told anyone I was your girlfriend though, did you? And he was all, he didn't say anything to that, like. So, I dunno really. I mean, she says it wasn't cheating- and she only shifted the guy anyway, in a slow dance in Doc's- they didn't do anything else, like. But he says they're over now, so. And she's kind of like, well we were never really going out anyway, but I think really, she's heartbroken. She just doesn't want to show it." She barely took a breath. I was in a daze just listening to her.

"Yeah? Mad stuff altogether, Nor. Listen, I-"

"Have ye got a drummer yet? Are ye going to do the thing in the Glory Hole? Eric Broderick was telling me they're doing it. They're probably gonna do all originals. Are ye signed up for it yet? I heard Numb Fingers are breaking up. You should ask Terence to play with you. He's a fucking brilliant drummer. He used to be in Cold River, with Gary Conlan and them guys. You should ask him. I know his sister. Do you want me to-"?

"What's that? What? Sorry, Nora, love. Nailer's calling me. Terence, is it? Yeah, no, I'll ask around myself- see if he's interested. Cheers for that. See you later." I tore away before she'd a chance to say anything else. She could talk the cross off a donkey, that one.

Terence Madigan could piss off as well. Numb Fingers were a punk band- none of them could play a note.

"Where'd you disappear to?" Ciara moved in to let me sit down again. We were on our second round of pints; Bríd and Ian had gone up to the bar for them. I took a big slurp of mine; I'd got ice in it this time, the cubes were freezing against my teeth.

"Nora Ryan."

"Jesus. Are you okay? D'you want a few Disprins?" Harta was getting a plait put in his hair by Bríd, with a bit of coloured wool.

"God, that girl," Ciara said. She was still on the leg-openers. I could smell Ribena and Black Jacks off her breath. She usually just smelt like vanilla. She said her mother always bought her vanilla soap and shower gel from the Body Shop for Christmas, and cos everyone always smelt it off her, they'd buy her more vanilla stuff for every birthday and Christmas too. Harta called her *Ice Cream Fanny*, but only behind her back.

"I know, I know. I don't even *not* like her, you know? I just sort of can't stand her." That was the best way I could put it.

"No, I know exactly what you mean. What was she on about anyway?" Ciara took a fag out and done a lucky. She'd got a new box, from the machine. We'd all chipped in except Niall and Bríd. No one'd let him put his hand in his pocket after the round.

"Oh, God. The ins and outs of every relationship in Limerick. Oh, and she was picking drummers for us."

"Oh right. Anyone daycent?" said Harta, leaning over. He could play most instruments, but not the drums.

"Terry Madigan."

"Ten Thumbs Terry? Paha. Priceless!" Niall hated Numb Fingers. He was mad into his punk music, so any band who were saying they were punk, but were actually just shite, annoyed the tits off him. Me, Ian and Tim were all into the same kind of music. Niall done his own thing. He was good at playing the bass though, so it didn't matter.

"I know, I know. The Numb Fingers are splitting up, she says."

"Oh, fuck! How'll the music world recover from that? It's the Beatles all over again, sham," said Harta.

"Yeah, well. I think we might pass on Terry." I felt sloshed, but my words were coming out fine. To me, anyway.

"What about Rich?" Ciara offered the fag box to me, with one sticking out.

"Rich what?" I took one and lit it with a lighter that was on the table. No idea whose it was.

"Richie. Your Richie."

"Richie South? What about him?" Richie was in the year ahead of me in Ardscoil. He lived in Thomondgate, near me. Him and his brother Chris were the only fellas besides me from our place who went there.

"Why don't you ask him to play?" I could feel Ciara's toes rubbing off my ankle, under the table. She'd took off her shoes. She was very touchy-feely with me. I was definitely on for the shift. That was the leg openers for you.

"Richie doesn't play the drums; why am I asking him?"

"He does so. What does he do on a Saturday morning every week?" Ciara knew Rich through a girl from Salesian's he'd been going with. Dearbhla, her name was. He'd always a girlfriend, Richie. Ever since he was eleven and was shifting that ride from down our place. She was about two years older than him too. He got a good start. That was all you needed. When that was over with her, there was plenty of youngones wanting to ask him out. Women didn't really know what they wanted or they liked, sometimes. Sometimes they just liked you cos they saw other youngones liking you, so they just thought you must be worth liking then. Same way they'd all like a pop band if their friends liked the same one. We were nothing like that, us lads. We were more able to think for ourselves. A fella I knew from Ardscoil went past, wearing a Chelsea top. I hated Chelsea. I couldn't think of his name.

"I dunno. What does he do?" I turned back to Ciara again. She'd nice lips. Big, but not too big. And she'd always lipstick on, and that funny pencil thing that they drew around the edges.

"He goes to Sexton Street, for the marching band. My sister's in it with him; how do you not know that he does that? You're his best friend, aren't you?"

"Ah well, not anymore, really. I did know though, I think. Now that you say it. I just forgot. Anyway, what's that got to with anything?" I'd lost touch with Rich over the last few months. Hadn't seen him around much; I'd been busy practising with the lads, watching the

World Cup, and other stuff. We'd one night out, in the Henry Cecil, with Dearbhla, Ian, Ciara and Bríd. He wasn't able to stay out long though. Anyway, I was a bit old for best friends now.

"Well, he plays the fucking drums, doesn't he? Jesus, Jon. Put two and two together sometime, will you?" She knocked on my forehead with her fist.

"He does?" I was trying to picture how a drum kit'd work in a marching band, on St Patrick's Day.

"Well, he plays *a* drum. But it's all the same, isn't it? He can keep a beat, and whatever. I'd say he'd be up for it and all. And he has that big shed, doesn't he?" She was right. He'd a massive big long shed thing out the back. I'd been in there loads of times when we were younger, looking at magazines about fighter planes and all that.

"Yeah. No, yeah- you're right. But I mean, he'd still need a kit. Even to practice on. When is this Battle of the Bands thing?" I was trying to think how we'd get him a kit, but I couldn't think of nothing. 'Drain You' was playing on the jukebox, but you could hardly hear it cos Quin's was so busy.

"End of the month, start of next month. I'm not sure. At least four weeks though." Ciara gave a shrug. The rest of them stopped their own chats and were listening in to ours. Ian said:

"Four weeks isn't enough time to learn how to play. He'd be useless at it in four weeks."

"He'd be better than the drummer ye have now, sham. The invisible one. He's fucking shite, that lad. He needs to go." Harta's coloured plait was finished. Bríd put yellow, blue and purple threads in it.

"Exactly. Do ye know him as well, lads?" Bríd was asking Niall and Ian.

"Not really like. I know him cos Muz knows him… that's about it," said Niall, looking into his empty pint glass.

"Same, really. He came for a drink with us one night, didn't he? I didn't talk much to him, but he's sound, I think." Ian reached over for the new twenty box and rolled his eyes when he saw they were John Player Blue. He still took one though.

"Right then. You should talk to him about it, Jon." Ciara gave my ankle another little rub with her toe. I nodded at her, wondering if I'd actually ask Rich, or if all of this was drunk talk that we'd forget in the morning.

Two

There was a queue outside Termights going in. I never knew if that was a good thing or a bad thing when it came to the bouncers. I could see up ahead anyway that it was Jerry and Col. They were easy. Half the time if you didn't have no ID on you, they'd tell you to show them something anyway- a banklink card, or one for the library, like- so the cameras saw them asking you, in case the Gards looked at the tape. I knew Mike O'Gorman anyway, who owned Termights. I didn't know him properly, but I'd say "Aboy, Mike," when I'd go in, and he'd usually give me a salute. If Mike was on the door with them it'd be grand.

"Have ye something smuggled in? Show me. SHOW ME!" Harta was pretending to frisk me, like the doormen in the raves at the Theatre Royal did.

"No, boss. I've nattin' on me, sweartagod." The scobes were always trying to get drugs in with them. The bouncers at the Royal were honestly the worst - if there was some big DJ like Carl Cox playing. They'd get the knackers to take off their big knee-high boots - laces and all. Took about half an hour. Per boot.

"Open yeer mouts! Open dem!" Harta was tapped in the head sometimes. I opened up. That's where they hid their Es- under the tongue, or behind the back teeth- wrapped up in tin foil or tracing paper.

"G'waaaaay, will yuh? I'm innocent, boss. Like Nicky Kelly." I'd no idea who Nicky Kelly was, but you'd see 'Free Nicky Kelly' written on the wall sometimes. My cousin Clodagh said he was someone from the IRA. Dunno if she was only messing though.

“Free Nicky Kelly!” Harta was as happy as Larry. He’d been sinking pints all night in Quin’s, and we’d scobed a nodge off some Ardscoil lads in the jacks as well. The two of them looked like a strong fart’d blow them over.

“Free Nicky Kelly in every box of Coco Pops, sham.” People in the queue were throwing heads at us now, but I didn’t care. I was ossified drunk.

“Gift not available in Éire.” Niall was smoking some weird, skinny cigar - might have been a More. Made him look like a gay.

“Not available in Éire? The dirty Protestants! Balls to Kellogg’s! Up the RAH!” I looked around for the rest of them, cos they’d fell behind on the walk down. Ian was quiet most of the time, but sometimes if you got him drunk enough he was all talk, especially with the women. He was good looking, Ciara and them told me before, he just didn’t know it yet, so he gave off the wrong vibes. That’s what she said anyway, I couldn’t tell stuff like that. Not in lads, cos I wasn’t a gay. We’d left him straggling along with the women while we smoked the joint.

“Have ye flyers, lads?” Niall gave me a slap on the back that nearly panned me out.

“Christ’s sake, stop will you. Calm down.” It stinged like mad. He was a big galoot.

“I’m calm, man. I’ve that sweet, sweet ganja in me now. I’m calm as Bob Marley.”

“Bob Marley’s dead, you long streak of piss, you.” Harta was wearing a Hawaiian shirt and brown cords. He dressed like someone who robbed his clothes from the bags outside St. Vincent De Paul. He probably did too, in fairness.

“There you go. Can’t get calmer than that.”

"D'you know how Bob Marley died?" I was on my tippy toes, looking down the line for the other three of them.

"Yeah. He was playing soccer, and he stubbed his toe, right?" Niall had a Clash T-shirt on. I only knew a few of their ones - *London Calling*, and the one from the Levi's ad.

"Yep. And he got gangrene, and he didn't go to the doctor, cos that's against their religion, the Rastas. So, he died," I said. That was how I'd heard the story anyway. Harta looked at me like I was from Bawnmore.

"Died of gangrene, did he? You haaaaandicap, you."

"What? Yeah, he did. What are you now, an expert on Bob Marley?" I gave him a look.

"He died of cancer, you amadán, you. Died of gangrene after busting his toe… you're an awful steamer." He took out the Johnny Blues from his cords pocket.

"Smoke on that. And fuck off. That's how I heard it. Did you know him or something? Were you there?"

"At the soccer match? I was, sham. Up in the director's box, with Rita and Ziggy." He sparked up. We were nearly at the front; I could hear Jerry asking people for ID. Bollocks anyway.

"Oh right, so there *was* a soccer match then?" Niall had his ID out. A crappy looking UL one, with his brother's photo on it. He'd be all right anyway, the size of him.

“There was, yeah. Terrible fucking tragedy, sham. He went in for a fifty-fifty ball with the full-back - then, BANG! Cancer!” Harta made a slapping sound with his hands, and we all burst out laughing.

“Anyway, here, ye spas. I got these off Monty when we came out.” I gave them a Termights flyer each. It was four quid in the door, three with the flyer. I’d three more for the other lot, but I still hadn’t seen them.

“Souuuuuund”

“Souuuuuund”.

We were up the front. No Mike.

“Ye right, lads?” Jerry was the baldy one. I’d no idea what age he was, cos of thc bald.

“All right, Jer?” I was always cool as a breeze going in places. No point being anything else. They either let you in or they didn’t. You couldn’t ever argue with them or change their minds.

“Yep. Yeah, tipping away.” He gave the three of us a good look up and down. Niall kept his ID in his hand, but he didn’t show it. Then Col said:

“Go on in, lads.” Easy as that. We walked past them, pure casual, then tore up the stairs, laughing our heads off. Jerry and Col were gas. About a year ago, it was Junior Cert results night, when all the kids are out trying to get langers, and Jerry was on the door asking everyone “How’d ye get on, lads?” The amount of people who fell for it was something else-

"Six As and three Bs!"

"Yeah, fuck off home then."

"Ah, Jaysus."

Upstairs was nearly pitch black, as usual. Termights wasn't like any other disco in the world. Pure dark, with a few gammy lights on the ceiling. Sometimes they'd have a projector, showing a Manga film or something like that, onto the wall. You weren't supposed to watch it or anything (there was no sound anyway), it was just to make the place look cool. Sometimes there was no film in the thing, just big coloured blobs on the wall. All the acid-heads would stand there staring at the wall for two hours. They probably enjoyed the blobs more, in fairness.

"A drink or a piss?" Niall had to nearly shout into my ear; the moshing bit from *One* by Metallica was on. No one was on the dance floor yet. It was early.

"Drink your piss? Jesus, Nailer; buy me dinner first, at least."

"What?" He'd his fingers in his ears now, looking over me like a ginger skyscraper.

"Never mind. Go toilet. I'll get 'em. Heineken?"

"Heineken, yeah, souuuuuund. Get me a glass, will you?"

"A glass? Hark at Lady Muck," said Harta; still on the fag he hadn't given me a smoke off.

"Yeah, you bumbuster. Have a can like the rest of us. You're not in Doc's now." I fiddled around in my jeans for some money. I'd given most of my shrapnel to yer one in the ticket box.

"Fine, a can, whatever. I'm off for a slash."

"Have one for me too, will ya?" Harta passed me over the end of the fag- there was only a couple of drags left. I didn't even want it; I smoked too much when I was out. I took it anyway though.

"What you having yourself, Dom? Dominique. Dombo. Dominatrix…" I was wrecked.

"Ah, gimme a TNT, will you? Cheers, Jon-Boy, Jonnovox, Jon with the Wind."

"What the hell is Teen Tea?"

"No, T-N-T. It's white cider, sham. Comes in a stick, like dynamite. Pure strong. Seven and a half per cent. Put hairs on your chest, it will. And your cousin's." He was always going on about Clodagh, and wanting to ride her.

"Oh right. And it's 'T.N.T', yeah?"

"Yep. Like the bums."

"What?" I couldn't hear him properly; they were playing Rage Against the Machine. There was one crusty looking youngfella up on the floor, pogo-ing around on his own. Polluted, probably.

“Bombs! Like the bombs! Just go get the liquor, you handicap.”

There was hardly no one in there yet, but the couches were already covered in jackets. People didn’t give a shit, they threw their stuff down, went off, and came back at the end to find it. Half the time it’d have been robbed, or you’d take the wrong one home by accident. There was a lot of the same looking black combat jackets there. Sometimes you’d take the wrong one home, *not* by accident, but cos someone robbed yours. All’s fair in love and jackets, Harta said, one night.

The bar was only a tiny thing, mostly cans. That was what was great about Termights; if you snaked in a few cans, none of the bouncers could tell, cos everyone drunk cans anyway in there. You’d only to make sure it was Bud, Bulmer’s, Heineken or another one they sold in there. They done draught and spirits and all, but it wasn’t worth bothering with that. I heard Mike made them water down everything, the snakey man.

“Are ye right? Am… a can of Heineken. And… have ye TNT, is it?”

“We do, yeah. How many did ye want?” Yer one behind the bar had mad pink hair, and her face was full of studs. She’d have been a ride otherwise, probably. She looked like she was gonna be posh, but she sounded like she was from Moyross or somewhere like that.

“Ah, two of ‘em, cheers.” She took out two little tubes of glass from the fridge. They didn’t look like there was nothing in them. They were the right ones though; I could see the three letters written on them.

“There ye go. Four fifty altogether.” She didn’t say ‘please’ or ‘love’. She just looked at me with her miserable face, full of shiny metal. I liked her. She was too cool for school. Termights wasn’t like other nightclubs. The DJ didn’t say a word all night while he was playing the tunes, you could sit on the floor without the bouncers telling you to get up, and you could bring your can onto the dance floor and no one said nothing to you. Not your fag though. You'd take someone's eye out in a mosh with a fag in your hand.

"Keep the change," I said, handing her over a fiver. She nearly cracked a smile and everything. Just nearly though.

Termights was where the muppets went in town, as well as Quin's. It was the only club in town with no music from the charts, and no dress code on the door. Except maybe Costello's. Most places wanted you to have a collar, or to wear shoes. You could wear anything you liked in Termights, or in Quin's as well. The lads on the door were pure sound in both of them, usually. There was another few pubs to go to in town that were a bit like Quin's: Tom Collins was always full of hippies, but they were older fellas. Harta knew a good few of them from gigging and all that, but I didn't like it in there. There was only one place where you could sit comfortable. The rest of it, you'd to stand, or sit crushed up against the wall when people came through from the front door. Baker Place was all right sometimes as well, and Buddy's, but that was more for bikers. The bar of Costello's was nothing like the club upstairs. The bar was full of auld fellas. And Gards, sometimes. My Da told me it was a Gard's pub once.

"You right, Jonno?" Someone went past me in a black combat shirt, but I didn't recognise him. I gave him a nod anyhow. If they called me that, they'd be someone I knew from around. People from Ardscoil usually said 'Muzz' or 'Muzzo' or whatever, cos my last name was Musgrave. That was normally jocks anyway, and jocks wouldn't be seen dead in Termights.

Harta was over by the wall, with some muppety youngones I didn't know. They'd all coloured hair and white make up. Sometimes I couldn't even tell if half of them were rides or not, cos they'd so much slap on, as my Ma called it. They all dressed the same too: black everything and stripy tights. I said *muppet* all the time when I was talking about us and people who looked like us. It was something scobes or jocks called you, as a slag, but we started saying it about ourselves then. I'd still use it in the bad way about muppety people I didn't like, or I didn't know. The younger ones especially. Fourteen year olds, like. Kids.

"Nice one, Jon-Boy." Harta took the tube of cider off me. He didn't introduce me to none of the youngones. One or two of them looked up at me, but they didn't say nothing. Too cool, all of them.

"Where's himself?" I didn't know whether to sit down or not. One of the youngones gave me a look, her mouth hanging open like she was trying to catch flies.

"Still in the jacks, sham. He's having an orgy in there."

"An orgy?"

"Yeah. With Pam." He'd lost me now. I took a swig off my own cider. It was strong, all right.

"Yeah. Palm and her five sisters."

"Waaaaa."

The muppety ones didn't laugh. You'd swear they all had earphones on, the way they were sitting there, saying nothing. The DJ was playing *Love Will Tear Us Apart*, and there was people up dancing to it. It was a rapid song, but I didn't know any other Joy Division ones. They were from a good few years ago; like The Smiths.

"Room for a small one?" Niall was back from the jacks.

"The only thing small about you is your mickey, sham." Harta scooched over. I was still standing.

"Your Mum didn't think so last night."

"That's cos she had her magnifying glass with her."

"Yeah? She says to me she has to use a microscope to find yours."

"She's to use a telescope to find mine, sham. When I'm standing on the moon," said Harta. I laughed, even though it wasn't funny, and it made no sense. I was bladdered. I needed to sit down before I fell.

"So, you *do* let your Ma look at your mickey then, yeah? Ye must be a close family." I found a space on the ground for myself. My tackie hit one of them in the leg, and I wanted to say sorry to her, but she didn't even look at me.

"Well, sham. She has to wait her turn, after your Ma. And your Da." He grabbed himself in the crotch and jiggled himself at me. I was wondering where the other three of them had got to.

*****

The place filled up quick after that. It was always the way, about a half hour after Quin's threw everyone out. Most of them ended up going where we were going, when it was a Friday. Baker Place disco was all chart music and rave on the weekends. It was only studenty on a Tuesday and a Thursday. We moved away from the youngones after a bit; they were pure boring. One of them was a bit of a ride; she was all small and cute, and I recognised her from Salesian's; Michelle or something, she was.

We took a wander around the place, after getting another lot of drinks. The dance floor was full, metallers mostly. I couldn't be bothered with moshing, unless I was polluted. Them youngfellas loved it though. Pogoing and jumping on top of you when you were trying to enjoy some tunes. It was pure annoying. The amount of times someone nearly burned the eye out of me with a lit fag, even though you weren't allowed them on there… I wanted to belt them in the face sometimes, but that wasn't what you were supposed to do. People'd think you were a jock if you done something like that. You hardly never saw fights in Termights. Especially not over moshing. Most people were sound. It was only a laugh.

"What you think then, about the drums?" Niall threw his arm over my shoulder and was leaning in to me. He got pure touchy-feely sometimes when he was langers. You'd swear he was a steamer.

"What, like? Richie?"

"Yeah. Yeah, yer man from down your place. D'you think it's a plan or what?"

"I dunno. Yeah. I suppose." It sounded like a good idea. Richie was sound, and it'd be rapid to have someone from down my place in the band. I liked the lads and everything, but sometimes I felt like a right knacker when I was over their houses. Their Mas and Das were funny with me sometimes. If we were practicing in Richie's instead of Tim's sometimes, it'd feel better. For me, anyhow.

"It's a drummer, like. And you know him, and I kind of know him, so it's not like having to get a stranger… what's he into?"

"How d'you mean?" I closed the cap on my TNT. I'd been going way too fast. Probably should have got a water.

"Music, like? What does he like?"

"Oh right, yeah. Er, same as us, I suppose. Nirvana, Pearl Jam, Stone Roses, Oasis, Green Day…"

"I don't like any of those." He gave me a face.

"Right. Same as all the normal people then. Sorry I offended you, Johnny Rotten."

"I'm more of a Sid Vicious."

"Sid You Wish-ous, you steamer." I gave him a nudge with my shoulder, and he'd to hold onto me to stop falling over.

"Fuck off, will you? D'you know, actually, he couldn't even play the bass?"

I did know; it was about the fifteenth time he'd told me.

"Well then, you're halfway there already, man. Keep practising."

"You're a gowl, d'you know that?"

"Yep."

*****

We were over next to the DJ box. There was a little bit of a wooden stage next to it, where youngones got up and danced sometimes. Or us, if it was that kind of night. On the other side of the floor I spied the girls and Ian tumbling in the door, finally. I'd nearly given up on them three. But it was who they were with that made me give Niall a thump and point over. He squinted in the dark until he copped on who it was.

"Janey Mack! What's he doing here, like?"

"Aboy the head, Bono. And you, Adam Clayton. I ran into the Edge here outside, with some groupies. I hear ye've sorted the Larry Mullen Jr. situation, nearly?" Brian Collins was in school with us in Ardscoil. People called him 'Brillo', cos of his curly hair. He hated being called it, so he tried to make people call him 'Boxer', which was his older brother's nickname. No one listened to him about that though. You couldn't make up your own nickname, or we'd all have brilliant ones altogether.

"Jesus, Brillo. Did you get lost on the way to a Garryowen game?" Niall wasn't too fond of Brian, mostly cos he hung around when we were practising, or cos he told people he was our manager. I liked him, though; he was sound as a pound, most of the time.

"It's Boxer, big boy. And it's Shannon, not Garryowen. Garryowen? For fuck's sake, boss. What do I look like to you at all?"

"A fucking scouring pad."

"Shut up, you ginger prick. Anyway, Mister Lead Vocals, the L.V., what's the story? Thingy here was telling me you might be recruiting troops from the Sexton's marching band. Am I right?"

"Well, yeah. I dunno. I haven't even talked to him yet." At this stage, poor Richie was gonna hear about it before I'd a chance to ask him. But probably not, since it was the summer holidays.

"Well, d'you want me to talk to him? Give him the old spiel; give him the hard sell, etcetera? That's what I'm here for, guys." He really did probably think he was our manager, although in fairness to him, he'd got us a few gigs. And it wasn't like he was asking us to pay him.

"Ah, no it's all right. He only lives around the block. I'll catch him tomorrow myself."

"Oh right, yeah. Another blow-in from beyond the Treaty Stone, isn't he? Jaysus lads, ye might have some street cred yet."

"We have plenty of street cred, Brillo." Ian stayed with us while the other two went off to the bar.

"Ye do of course, yeah. Turning up for gigs in Tim Connolly's Mum's lovely blue Nissan people carrier. Run DMC have nothing on ye, lads. Chalk it down."

"You leave Marjorie alone, Brillo. She's a fine figure of a woman." Niall was always going on about riding Tim's Ma; it was pure funny as long as you weren't Tim.

"It's Boxer. You're right there, though. She looks like she does the Jane Fonda videos. She must have been about twelve when she had him, looking at her."

"Who's this we're talking about?" Ciara was back with the drinks, no Bríd with her.

"How'rya? Tim's Ma," I said. She looked much better than the last time I'd seen her; probably cos I was steamed.

"Marjorie? Jaysus, yeah. I wouldn't kick her out of bed for eating Taytos."

"Wahey! Do you swing both ways then, Ceer?"

"Any way that isn't swinging towards you, Niall."

"Ah, Jaysus. Always the bridesmaid, what?"

"You'd have a better chance if you were a bridesmaid, Nailer. She's only a dirty lezzer," said Harta, ducking out of the way when she went to box him on the nose.

*****

"Listen, listen, listen anyway. I've news for you." It was later on, and Brillo and me were sitting over on the soft seats. We'd robbed them off some yokes who'd run up to the floor when *Basket Case* came on.

"News, is it?" I was on the water, finally. There'd been loads of people at the bar; felt shite standing there just to ask for a bottle of Ballygowan. It was lukewarm as well, but she gave me a plastic glass with a bit of ice.

"Yeah. You know me, always wheeling and dealing, ducking and diving." I nodded at him. He was a strange yoke. He'd say things like *plates of meat*, and *trouble and strife*; Cockney rhyming stuff, even though I didn't think he'd ever even been to England.

"What's the scala then?" I said. One of the youngones came back over from dancing, but when she saw us, she went away again.

"I got ye an interview with the Leader. Well, I got you one. You're the L.V."

"The Limerick Leader? What?"

"No, the fucking Roscommon Leader. What d'you think, Maurice?" He done that as well: called people Maurice. No idea why. That was Brillo for you.

"All right, all right. Anyhow though, why's that? How d'you pull that off?" It was hardly the Sunday World, but still; we didn't even have a drummer yet. Or a name. People knew us a little, though. From playing around.

"I've got my contacts, you know. Friends in low places."

"Like Garth Brooks, yeah. Or the Taoiseach."

"Yeah, anyway. Well, do you know the O'Shaughnessy sisters? From Laurel Hill?"

"Aaaaaah, I dunno. Do I?" I knew a few ones who went to that school, but it wasn't ringing a bell.

"Pair of rides. Gorgeous looking, both of 'em. Caoimhe was doing a line with Danny Slattery. You know Danny, he plays out half for the Senior Cup team."

"I do, yeah, of course. Danny. Sound man." I'd never heard of him.

"Well anyway, yeah. Not her. The sister, Áine."

"Right. No, I don't know her."

"Ah, you must know her. Tanned, blonde hair, lovely diddies…"

"You're making me wish I did, Bril- Brian. No, though; can't place her. What about her anyway?" I'd no idea where he was going with the story. The DJ was playing *Live Forever*. I was nodding my head with the drums.

"Well now, she's mad into the English and the writing, yeah. Clever youngone altogether, even if she doesn't look it. Fair play. Brains and beauty, God help us."

"Right…"

"And she's got herself a summer job at the Leader, doing reports for the weekend edition, yeah. Music and gigs, most of it."

"I see. Right. Yeah." The weekend Leader was bigger, and it cost a pound. There was a load of pull-outs in it; about cars and houses and entertainment stuff.

"Yeah, so I was in Bewley's with the missus, having a pot of tea, and in comes yer one Áine. She sees Aisling, and sits down with us at the table."

"I getcha, yeah." His girlfriend was in Laurel Hill too.

"So… cut a long story short, squire: I wrangled you an interview for next weekend's one."

"Really? When is this then?"

"You're welcome, yeah."

"Sorry, man. Cheers! How'd you manage it, though? What did you say?"

"Well, she was going on about wanting to do a thing about new bands – like, ones no one's really heard of, but are good, and people should go see 'em. And I just brought ye up, like. Carpe diem, and all that jazz, squire."

"Oh, right. Sound. Did she know who we were, like?" Niall and Ian had a few friends from Laurel Hill that came to see us in the few gigs we'd done already. I didn't remember no one who looked like yer one he was going on about though.

"Ehhhhhhh, kind of, like. It's hard to describe ye, you know what I mean?"

"No." I wasn't sure what he was getting at.

"I mean cos ye've no name, like. Ye've no… *look*. She copped on when I said about the keyboards, though. She sort of knows who ye are. She says she knows you to see you."

"What, me myself, or all of us?"

"You yourself. I think she said you were tapping some youngone from their school one time. So she knows what you look like."

"Ah right. Well, yeah. That could be a lot of youngones, in fairness. You'll have to be more specific." I was only half joking. I'd shifted a fair few of them from that school.

“You’re some big-headed prick, Jon, you know that?” He was only messing with me. He knew I wasn’t really full of myself or anything. I hoped so anyway.

“I do, of course. When’s this thing, anyway, bud? The interview?”

“Wednesday in the week, there. You free?”

“When am I not free, like? Where’s she want me to meet her?” An interview with the paper, and I was getting to meet some ride of the girl too. It wasn’t even my birthday.

“The George, she said. Hotel bar, twelve o’clock. I’m assuming you have normal clothes, yeah?”

“Piss off. What’s wrong with my clothes?”

“Nothing, if you want to sell her some drugs. Have ye a pair of shoes that ye can wear at all? And a shirt, with a collar. No fucking grandfather bollocks, like.”

“What’s wrong with a grandfather shirt?”

“Nothing, if you want to look like a priest.”

“Ciara says I look like Liam Gallagher in mine.”

“Yeah, you keep telling yourself that, bud. Anyway, it’s the George Bar, Maurice. Gotta look respectable.”

“It’s an interview for the paper, Br- Boxer. I’m not going to mass…” I was ready for a real drink again. The Ballygowan was gone already.

"All right, all right. Just don't be wearing shades indoors, right? It looks cool when Stevie Wonder does it, yeah? Newsflash: You're not Stevie Wonder."

"Have you seen Stevie Wonder's new wife?"

"No."

"Neither has he."

"G'way and fuck off, you bollix, you."

"Waaaaa. Cheers though, Brian, man. Sound out for that."

*****

"Have ye any new songs anyway?" Ciara had come over to me later, after I was talking to Ger who done the cloakroom.

"What, like our own ones?"

"Yeah. And… whatever else." We walked over to a bit of floor to sit down on. It was packed now; well after twelve, probably, even though I'd no watch on me.

"One or two new ones, yeah. I've a chorus and a verse to one, but Ian hasn't done a bridge for me." I'd write most of the songs myself, with a few chords on an acoustic. He'd come along then and make them more fancy. I was able to play – not that good - but enough to come up with a tune, or to do a bit of rhythm if we really needed it on a song.

"Cool. What are they about?"

"About? Jesus, I dunno." Lyrics were the hard bit for me. I'd usually just put words in that fitted, or ones that sounded cool.

"Hah. All right, what are they called then?" She was close to me; her shoulder was rubbing against my arm. I didn't know if it meant anything. I could read the signs sometimes, some other times it was a mystery. It didn't matter. No point being shy about it, like some fellas were. Or putting them on a pedal stool, as my Uncle Frank called it. I usually just went for it. Worst they could say was no. And they usually didn't. Cos youngones went out looking for the shift as much as we did. They just pretended they didn't, cos people'd be calling them sluts.

"The first one has no name yet. And the other one, the heavy one, that's called *Nicotine Buzz*." I'd only written some of that one. It was really Niall's song. The bass on it was something else.

"*Nicotine Buzz*? Well that's the gayest thing I've ever heard. Well done."

"Oi, shut up. It's good!" I'd come up with that name; no one else'd said anything bad about it.

"It is, yeah. What's it about, like? The crazy high you get off a Silk Cut?" Obviously now it sounded stupid, when she said it like that.

"No. No, it's not about anything, really. It's just a song."

"About fags?"

"About… about nothing. You'd have to hear it. The bass line is rapid altogether."

"Another one about nothing? Leonard Cohen must be shitting himself."

"We're not… we're not the sort of band that- we're more about- we're more-" I didn't know how to put it.

"If you say *punk*, I will kick you in the balls, Jon."

"No, no, no. Not punk. We're… it's the tune that matters, isn't it? What's *Supersonic* about, like? Youngones taking Alka-Seltzer on a train? No, it's just a tune. You just have to write a tune that people like, or that they remember. Isn't that it?"

"Yeah, I suppose so. Like Burt Bacharach."

"Exactly, like." I'd no idea who he was.

"Well, fine. I'll have to listen to it next time you're having a practice. When's that anyway?"

"Tomorrow. Three o'clock."

"In Tim's, is it?"

"Yeah. Yeah, I was thinking of calling over for Rich. Get him to come along."

"Oh, cool. But he can't play though, can he? He doesn't have a kit."

"No, no. He can come over anyway though. Meet the lads, like. Have a listen to how we sound."

“Awesome. Come and dance. I like this one.”

“What is it?” I could hardly hear the music; my ears were all fuzzy.

“Elastica, come on.”

“Ah, Jesus…” They were bloody awful. But you had to get up and dance. Women liked it when you danced. Standing over by the wall with your can in your hand never got you nowhere with them. And anyway, I was langered. It was easier not to give a balls when you were steamed.

Three

My head was splitting in the morning. I'd forgot to take a glass of water to bed with me when I came in. I always forgot. I decided I'd go for a walk. I'd a few fags, and I robbed a cold can of Coke out of the fridge – good for a hangover. I was thinking I'd go out by Parteen, if the legs would take me. The Ma was in the shower for ages when I wanted to get in. A few sprays of Lynx was the closest I got to a wash. Her and the Da being up was the only reason I was out of the house. I could never have a lie-in after a night on the batter with them two hovering around; walking past my bedroom, and tutting. Not cos they thought I was drinking – they hadn't a clue, them two - just cos they didn't like me being lazy. I passed down Canon Breen Park and some youngfellas were knocking a soccer ball around. One of them missed the shot, and it rolled over the road to me. I flicked it up a few times, bounced it on my knee, and then I volleyed it in between the jumpers they had as the goals. A couple of them gave me a little cheer and everything, but they were probably taking the piss, the little gowls.

I kept going til I was out of Thomondgate, down the Barrack Lane way, and I could see the river. It was a good way to go, cos I wasn't gonna run into no one. No one I knew, anyway. I passed the bit where the swans usually are and I remembered the story Richie told me one night when he was langered, about him and that Marion girl, and what they got up to down there. He was going away with her for a good while, before it all went wrong. She was sound. Me and her had been pals for a bit, sort of. It was complicated. She'd to move away in the end. Not cos of him, cos of the other thing. She was always a bit too old for him. It didn't matter at the start, but youngones turned into women before youngfellas turned into men, my Uncle Frank said.

I went down the bushy part into the bit that was kind of like a forest. It was a mad place to go when we were kids – great for having stickyback wars or forksling fights. We'd go fishing too, down by the pipe, but all you'd catch there was eels or bream. No one'd eat bream, cos they ate the shit out of the sewerage pipe, and all the bog roll and jamrags too. It wasn't a real forest, just a few trees, next to a marshy bog bit, but it didn't feel like you were still in the city. You'd see a heron sometimes, or other things that didn't belong in Thomondgate. If you kept walking in a straight line you'd get out to the City Dump, and the Metal Bridge. There was lots of cool, weird places on the way too. I wasn't feeling too well – still hungover, but being out in the fresh air and walking through all the places we'd a laugh in when we were kids was making it better, a bit. There was a part of the path where someone'd dumped some old cars years ago, and someone else'd poured cement over them, so they were stuck there. Richie said they were like *fossils* of cars from the old days now. I called it the Car Graveyard. There was real fossils in the Quarry back in Thomondgate; little snail shells in the rocks, that came from millions of years ago, back from when dinosaurs were around. I couldn't imagine dinosaurs walking around where we lived, but they must have, sometime.

There was an old factory no one worked in anymore, but sometimes there was still a dog that barked in it when you went past. Only sometimes though. And no one'd actually ever seen him. There was a big old orange cement mixer truck that was all rusted away, and reminded me of the boxes off Yorkie Easter eggs. Richie told me one time that he used to have nightmares about that truck crashing through the wall of his bedroom, and it had a big evil face carved into the cement mixing bit, and it used to scare the shit out of him. I thought it was pure hilarious, and I told a few of the other lads. Richie got annoyed with me for that; didn't talk to me for ages. I sort of knew it was lousy to tell people his secret like that, but I didn't know it was a secret until it was too late and I'd already told everyone.

I was thinking about Richie and his dream when I heard someone talking up ahead. Two people. One of them sounded like a girl; she might have been crying. Or maybe just whinging, like a little kid. I was miles in now, where there should've been no one around. Too far away from Kileely to hear anyone, and not near enough the Dump. I was near the Dead Lake. We called it that when we were small, cos it was this creepy big pond thing, with one car sunk into it – one of the ones from the Car Graveyard, maybe – it looked like it was from around the same time. That was one reason to call it that, cos we thought maybe someone drove in there years ago and drowned – maybe a whole family. Probably not, but we liked scaring each other back then. Another reason was cos if you came down with fishing rods and cast out, you never caught nothing. Your line just got stuck in all the weeds and rubbish at the bottom, and the best you'd get would be a plastic bag or a sock. And one more reason was just that the water didn't move at all. It was just… dead. Sometimes it froze over in the winter, and we dared each other to walk across it, but no one ever did. Otherwise there might have been an even creepier reason to call it the Dead Lake. I was up the top of the slope now; the noises had come from down near the water. I put my hand over my eyes to block out the sun and see down. There was a tall youngfella standing down there with his back to me. He must have felt me looking, cos he turned around. It was Joe McNamara, from down our place.

"Well?" he said. I'd to squint to look at him, cos of the sun.

"How'rya?"

I didn't know him that well. He was part of that lot Richie used to hang around with, years ago, before we went to Ardscoil. Richie, Dara, Dermot, *Shane*. I hung around with him as well, for a little while, when I was small. That time of the cut grass in the Distillery. I smiled thinking about that. Carrie Lynch. You always remembered your first time doing stuff. The bushes next to Joe moved a bit, like there was something in them.

"I'm just here with my cousin," he said, even though I didn't ask him anything, and I didn't see no one else. It explained the talking though.

"Oh right, yeah."

The bushes moved again, and out came this little youngfella. Maybe about six or seven. He didn't look at me, and he was sniffling, like he'd a cold.

"That's him, there. Thomas. Aren't you, Thomas?"

The youngfella didn't say nothing. I didn't know what was going on. It was all pure awkward, for some reason. And I didn't care, anyway. I just wanted to get on.

"I said, aren't you?" He nearly shouted, and the little fella jumped with the fright of it.

"I am, yeah. I'm his brother," the kid said; he sounded posh – not like he was from around here.

"Cousin, you gowl!" said Joe. And then, to me, "Kids, hah? Fucking eejits. We're looking for eel fry, aren't we, Tom?"

"Yeah. But… I forgot my net," said Thomas. He sounded like he didn't know what he was saying. Or like he was reading out a poem in school.

"Forgot his net, like. And we all the way out here. He'd forget his head if it wasn't…"

I nodded. The whole thing was a bit strange, but it was none of my business, really. I felt a bit tired now, too. The walk over the bridge and out by Corbally was a bit long, now I was thinking about it. I'd probably just turn around and go back. I'd to call in to himself, still.

"Yeah, shur. Kids. Anyway, good luck." I turned away and started walking before he could say anything else. He was a bit slow when we were younger, Joe. Slow fellas sometimes hung around with little kids. So they could be smarter than them, or so they could boss them around. I left them to it anyway. I could hear him shouting a bit at the poor kid as I went back down the path. Hopefully he wasn't gonna be too hard on him, I thought. It was only a bloody fishing net.

It was boiling out when I got to Richie's. Their grass was always cut; the Da was mad into his gardening, now. The Ma was gonc years. I remembered my Ma and Da going on about it at the time. I gave the knocker a tap.

"Well? Jaysus, Jon. Haven't seen you in… a while? Aren't you after getting big? How'rya anyway?" Riche's Da hadn't aged at all since I first started coming over, years ago. He still had jet black hair, and it didn't look dyed.

"I'm grand, Mr South. Tipping away. Is himself about?"

"That lummox? Yeah, he's upstairs. Rough night, was it?"

"What? Yeah, something like that." I must've have looked like shit, still. My head was all right now, though, from the walk.

"Ah, feck it. Ye're only young once."

He cleared his throat.

"Er, Richard! You have a visitor!" He always done that when we called in - the silly posh voice, and calling him *Richard.* We thought he was gas, but Richie'd get pure annoyed with him. That was always the way.

"Was he out himself?" We hadn't seen him at all, but sometimes he went to Doc's, cos of his missus.

"Oh, I dunno. I never know anything with him, Jon; tells me nothing, so he does. Last week he comes in at three in the morning, no key, banging the door down. No explanation. A grunt is all I get most of the time." He was smiling. They got on all right, especially since the Ma had left. That was what Richie said anyway.

"Oh. All right, Jon?" Richie appeared behind him on the stairs, with a Gameboy in his hand.

"Well. The man himself. I wasn't sure if you were alive or dead up there, shur."

"What? G'way will you. I was up before you. I was down Sexton's at nine o'clock, like."

"Nine o'clock? God bless us and save us, Rich. What do you want, a medal?"

"Shut up, Dad. I'm going out." His Gameboy made the 'turning off' sound, and he put it on the stairs behind him, on top of a few books.

"Here, what are you doing there? Are they for the jumble sale?"

"What jumble sale?" He gave his Da the kind of look that said he was already sick of him. I was like that with my Ma sometimes.

"The one I'm having later; with all this stuff you're giving me for it. Should get enough for a few scoops down Frazer's."

"Will you g'way, Da. You don't even drink."

"How do you know I don't? I might be having parties here every Saturday, when you're down Sexton's, banging your drum." The two of them were gas to listen to. I was staying out of it.

"Yeah, right. You'd be on your back after two sherries."

"What do you know about two sherries, eh? Jon, he doesn't be drinking does he, when ye go into town? You can tell me; it's not squealing."

"G'way, Dad."

"Ah no, Mr South. He has a glass of red lemonade, same as me." I winked at the Da; Rich was holding in a laugh.

"Fecking red lemonade my arse, lads. Anyway, off out of my sight, you two. I've a party to plan."

"Yeah, have a nice party Dad. You and Rex." They'd that dog since we were about nine or ten. He was half blind now, Rich said.

"I will, I will. After the jumble sale."

We walked over by the White Wall. It was only about one o'clock. The practice wasn't for ages yet. I took out a box of fags and offered one to him.

"I don't smoke, Jon."

"Oh yeah. Keep forgetting that. Still, more for me." He'd given up about six months before, cos his Nana died of lung cancer.

"They'll kill you, man."

"Nothing worse than an ex-smoker, Rich."

"Well, there is. There's a dead smoker."

"Jesus, shut up will you? You're twisting my melon, man."

"*You know you talk so hip…* anyway, what's your problem?"

"My problem?"

"What do you want, I mean? Today?"

"Oh, right, yeah. Er, well you know the way you play the drum in that Sexton's thing?"

"Yup." He hopped up on the little red brick wall in front of the bungalows.

"Well, you ever thought about playing real drums?"

"I do play a real drum." He could nearly cut you with a look sometimes, Richie.

"You know what I mean; a real drum kit, in a band, like. D'you think you'd be any good at that?"

"Yeah, sure. I've had a go on them a few times, actually. No bother."

"Really?" It was the first I'd heard this.

"Yeah. Shur my Dad used to be a drummer in a Showband; did you not know that?"

"What? *Your* Da?"

"Yeah, man. They used to play out in the Jetland and everything. He still has them. Up in the loft. He brings them down at Christmas and they do an auld gig over in Thomond Rugby Club; him and my uncle. They're all right actually. Don't fucking tell him I said that, but yeah."

"Well, now. That's something."

"What?"

"Well, I was gonna ask you if you wanna come play with us. I mean, I didn't know if you'd be on for it or anything, and I'd no idea where we'd get you a kit, but now…"

"Me? Play with you and Ian? And Niall… isn't it?"

"Yeah, Ian Hurley and Niall O'Neill. And Tim. Tim Connolly as well."

"Haha, yeah. I forgot ye'd keyboards." He shaked his head and laughed.

"Yeah, yeah, yeah. I know. Anyway, will you?"

"Will I what? Play with ye? I dunno, Jon. I don't really know none of them."

"Ah, you do. They're all in Ardscoil."

"Yeah… I didn't know half the people in my year though, never mind yours."

"You met Ian and Nailer a few weeks ago."

"I know, yeah, for like five seconds."

"How about the kit?"

"My Dad's? You any good at pulling stuff out of people's cold dead hands?"

"Ah, it can't be that bad, shur. Will he not be delighted with you for following in his footsteps, like? Y'know, until you're old enough to drive a train, like?"

"*Crash* a train, more like. I'm old enough to do that now, shur. Well, look, I dunno. I'd have to ask him. When d'ye need to know by?"

"Well, there's practice today, over in Tim's. But… if you get him to give you the drums, I'll tell them we're having it here…"

"Having it where?"

"Well, at yours. In the shed. Ye still have the shed, don't ye?"

"What? Yeah. I mean, I didn't check this morning, but probably, yeah." Sarky little bastard, sometimes, he was.

"Rapid."

"Hang on a second now, Jon. So, you want me to get the drums off himself, give ye my shed to practice in, and what? Anything else, like? D'you want a pint of blood too?"

"Haha! Ah, go on though. It'd be rapid. We've a battle of the bands in four weeks. We might win it with a drummer." We wouldn't, but I was looking for ways to get him interested enough to say yes.

"Four weeks? Jesus, I'm not Ringo Starr yet, Jon. Hold yer horses there a minute."

"Go on. We'll ask him now. I'll come with you. He likes me."

"Does he? Who told you that?"

"He did, when I was riding him."

"Careful now…"

"I was careful, shur. I'm always careful with your Da. I dunno where he's been."

*****

Turned out we'd nothing to worry about. Richie's Da was delighted he wanted to borrow the kit. Helped us bring it out to the shed and set it up and everything. There was the usual messing between them, but he was pure proud. The kit was old, but he'd kept it in good nick, as Brillo would say. The parts that you hit with the sticks were all white, and the rest of it was yellow.

"What time are they coming then? How many of ye is there?" He was having a look for a double adapter for us, although Ian would probably have his four-way thing with him. I'd forgot that there mightn't be sockets out in the shed, but there was, anyway.

"Am, I gave 'em a ring a while ago. Well, I gave Tim a ring. He'll call the rest of them. I'd say about three o'clock, Mr South."

"Jesus, will you call me Mick, Jon. I'm not a teacher."

"Sorry, Mr Sou- Sorry, Mick." That felt weird. Next, he'd be giving me a can of Harp. Richie was sitting on a stool behind the bass drum, giving the pedal a few kicks, but quietly.

"Dad, have you any more sticks?"

"More sticks? Shur what do you need more for? Haven't you only two hands?"

"Yeah, but if I break one?"

"If you break one, I'll break you."

"Ha-ha. Seriously, like."

"Seriously I will. Now, do you know what you're doing there, or d'you want me to show you?"

"No, no. I can figure it out like. You're all right, Mick."

"Watch it, now. Or you'll be out in the Regional, getting the nurses to take them sticks out of your arse."

"Promises, promises."

"Go on, so. Give us a beat."

"What?"

"Tap out an auld rhythm for us there. Four-four tempo, yeah?"

"No idea what you're saying."

"Jaysus, give me strength. Here, start off with the pedal, right. Right, that's good. Now give me some snare. Good man yourself. Now, see the toms there? No, that one by you. Yeah, give us some of that too."

It was mad looking at them like that together. Richie was always slagging with his Da, but this was different. It reminded me of me and my own Da, when he gave me driving lessons; pretend ones, in the Escort out the back garden. I watched them for a bit, not saying nothing. I kind of wanted a fag, but I didn't think I'd get away with sparking up in front of the Da. Or Mick, as I called him these days.

*****

Ian was the first to get there. I wasn't worried about the poshies finding the house. I gave Tim good directions. Once you got to the boxing club on the corner, you could find your way easy. They couldn't drive past the bollards anyway, and Richie's was the second house after them, when you were walking. If they wanted to come in the back gate, they'd to find the alley, but the numbers were painted on the doors out there, so that was grand.

"Aboy the kid. How's the head?" He'd been langered when I'd left him down outside the taxi rank after Termights. Bríd was holding him up. They'd probably shifted, but I hadn't seen it myself. They'd disappeared for long enough anyway, so something probably happened.

"Ugh, don't talk to me about it. What were those things you were buying me again?"

"TNT? Yeah, blame Harta for that, man." He'd pulled as well, Harta. Some youngone from Salesian's, with long frizzy hair. She looked about twelve.

"Christ's sake. My mouth was like an Arab's tackie this morning." He'd a big rectangular case for his guitar, and a small Marshall amp. His Da must have helped him up the road with them, but he didn't come in himself.

"Chalk it down. I woke up thinking I must have given a lickout to someone with a sandpaper fanny."

"I'll tell Ciara that, she'll be delighted altogether."

"Ciara? What? No, Jesus no. I didn't go near her. At all, at all. Can't be getting into all that, d'you know what I mean? Not worth the hassle." I'd tried to put the moves on her at some point during the night, but she'd pushed me away, laughing. I was too langered to be offended.

"I believe you, yeah. Are the rest of them on their way?"

"They are, yeah. Here, you've met Rich before, have you?"

"I have, yeah. Sort of. How'rya?" He nodded at the other fella.

"How'rya. Yeah, we were all out a few weeks ago, 'member? I know your head from school anyway, like. You're Darren Hurley's brother."

"Yeah. That's the one." Ian opened the case. He'd a lovely looking guitar; a Les Paul copy, wooden looking, with gold pickups. There was a knock on the door.

"Come in, it's open," said Richie.

"Well, chaps. What's the story?" Niall nearly had to bend down to get in the door. He'd Richie's Da with him, lugging the big bass amp.

"It's the big man," I said. Richie's Da put the amp down and wandered away, whistling. There was one more to come, and we could get started. I heard a car beeping outside, behind the back gates. Probably Tim's Ma, shitting herself cos of all the poor people.

*****

Later, we were in Styx, for a few games of pool, and a mess. The practice was really good. Richie didn't know the exact drums for any of the songs, but he kept the beat, and threw in a few rolls. The lads couldn't believe he'd never played before, and I didn't believe it either. He must've had a fair few goes on his Da's kit before. or someone else's, cos he was well able. He was like that, though. Pure modest.

"Right, rack 'em up, buddy. I'm gonna take you to *Pool School*." Niall rubbed a bit of chalk on his cue. Him and Tim were first up. I was more interested in the video games myself.

"There's only one of us gonna get taught a lesson here, dude." I was shocked Tim said yes to coming along. Didn't seem like his kind of place.

“Yeah. You.” Niall blasted the balls all over the table, reds and yellows, like he really knew what he was doing. None of them went in.

“Shoot the chicken! Kill it! Kill it!” Me and Rich were on *Operation Thunderbolt*. He was better than me. He was better than me at most games. Video games, not sports or anything. Not any games in real life.

“I’m killing it, Rich. Look at it. Look at that little prick die.” I’d wanted to play one of the soccer games, but there was two lads already on it. Right pair of heads, too. Styx was in Nicholas Street, so we were nearly down the Island Field. Scobe central. You’d to be careful in there.

“Get the life! The extra life! Get it!”

“Where? What?” I couldn’t see any life. He pointed his gun over across my side of screen. Then I saw it; after he robbed it for himself.

“Haha! You snooze, you lose.”

“You gowl, you.”

*****

Tim had brought his Yamaha and the amp over to the shed, and he’d left them there as well. I wondered what his Ma was gonna say about it. I asked him what she thought of Thomondgate, but he didn't say nothing. Where they were from was way different. I was used to seeing piebald horses tied up in the green, and fellas drinking Linden Village on the small wall at half ten in the morning. If you were new though, it probably scared the crap out of you. I liked where I lived. Being around all that stuff, knowing pure hard lads, seeing fights all the time: it made you more streetwise. Whenever we were outside Supermac's after the clubs on a Saturday night, and there was a bit of bother, I'd see the lads get all tense, but I'd be cool as a breeze. No point being scared of a few heads; if they were having a scrap, it was usually nothing to do with you. Keep out of their way and you'd be fine. That was what my Da said.

Richie knew most of the songs we did; well, the covers anyway. I'd to give him a few pointers about our own ones, but he was grand with them as well. It wasn't like we were able to write anything too complicated yet. Tim was getting pure good at the keyboards, but he still played them like they were… keyboards. Big chords, string effects and all that. Worked brilliant when we were doing *Disarm*, or something like that that'd violins and stuff in it. But I wanted him to play normal piano too- so we could do a few Queen songs, or *Epic*, by Faith No More. He said he wasn't good enough at playing piano, but I'd no idea what the difference was, in that way.

*****

"Soccer's free." Rich nodded over to the *Football Champ* machine. The heads had gone away over to some birds over by the stairs. Fine looking ones as well; belly tops and cycling shorts. They'd knackerish hair, though. Perm at the sides, bump at the top. Smell the lacquer off them from a mile away. They hung around the jukebox and asked you what you were putting on, and tried to get you to put one of their songs on, like *Father and Son*, or *Two Out of Three Ain't Bad.* I usually told them to fuck off out of it, as long as they didn't look like they might stab you.

"Two player?" I liked playing a real person better. The computer always cheated on you, to take your money off you. Frank told me that; he said they programmed them to do it.

He didn't know nothing about arcade games though. He was ancient. He probably meant fruit machines.

"All right. Bags Germany."

"Bags them all you like; I'm being Argentina." The music on the jukebox was awful. They'd a few good LPs on there, but no one ever put them on. It was all 2 Unlimited and Technotronic. I hated Rave. Except the Prodigy. They were different. I still couldn't say I liked them in front of half the lads though. They didn't get it. None of them really took yokes or anything. Except Harta, and he wasn't part of them.

"Right, so. You be Maradona, and I'll be Rudi Voller." They didn't really have the proper names on it, but we pretended anyway.

"You're on. Time for the Hand of God."

"Not if I spit in your face first, boss." Voller was dirty as anything, in fairness. *Football Champ* was newish. The one we used to play before was called *Italia 90*, and it was shite, cos there was a cheat goal, and everyone knew it. So, the whole game'd be two people trying to get to the corner of the box and slide it in past the keeper. We didn't know any cheats for *Football Champ* yet.

"Right, you spa. Watch this." I took the ball and passed it fast up the pitch. You could do mad bicycle kicks and headers every time you hit the button. It was more like a cartoon than real soccer.

"Oof, not so fast, Diego." Richie's defender done a karate kick into my fella's face and sent him flying.

“Oh! You bollix, you.” There was only two buttons. If you were defending, the red one done a slide tackle that got you the ball clean. The blue one done a foul like a punch or a kick. You’d only get away with it if the ref wasn’t on screen and he was a big fat yoke that couldn’t keep up with ye when ye were running. Richie got the ball into my box.

“Are you ready? Are you ready for it? Are you?” He chipped it from one fella to the other, across the box, with my fellas sliding at him and getting nothing. The keeper came out and completely missed him.

“Ah, Jaysus!”

“Voller to Mattheus, Mattheus to… the other fella. Back to Voller. He shoots! He scores! Gooooooooooooooooooal-Laziooooooooooo!”

“You steamer, you.” He’d run rings around me, all the same.

*****

We’d tried the new songs out. The nicotine one Ciara thought was gay, and the one with no name. Ian had some lovely riffs for both of them. He was a decent enough guitarist. You wouldn’t think it to look at him. The lads from the DTs all looked the part: long hair, like Suede; cool clothes and everything. We just looked like normal people, really. “You’re too tall to be a rock star, Maurice,” Brillo always said to me. We tried *End of a Century* and *Live Forever*, and they sounded good. We could play *Parklife*, but I sounded stupid trying to do the Cockney bits. I’d never do that one at a gig; we’d be laughed off the stage. It was the same with Rage Against the Machine. Ian could do all the guitar bits perfect, and I knew all the words. But I wasn’t a black. I couldn’t pull it off.

*****

"Winner stays on then. Who's next?" Tim had whipped Niall. His family were pure rich altogether; he'd his own table and everything.

"Go on then," said Ian. He'd been playing some car racing game, on his own. Me and Richie were on our second match. He won the first one, then got knocked out by Brazil after two games. We were drawing one-all. That was no good, cos neither of us would get to play on against the computer if it finished like that.

"Here, go on. Let me score one. There's only twenty seconds left."

"No, you let *me* score one," I said. I spotted some lads coming in. More heads, but I knew a few of them to see them. Danny O'Neill, Mark O'Connor, and Shane Collopy, with his weird mouth. I didn't salute them. Richie didn't see them, he was looking at the screen.

"Feck off. I'm better than you; lemme score, and I'll beat the bollix off it." He was right, really. He was better than me, but then he was useless at real soccer, so.

"Go on then." I pulled the joystick down, so all my lads got out of his way. He took a shot, but the keeper caught it. Shane and them were over by the pool tables. I thought he sneered at me for second, when he was putting his 50p down, but it might have just been the way his mouth was. It was all scarred and deformed, from something that happened him when he was small. You heard all sorts of stories about it, but no one knew which one was true.

"For fuck's sake, man!"

"I didn't do nothing! It's automatic!" I hadn't pressed any buttons. Five seconds left. I'd still a half eye on the heads over at the table. They were on a different one to our lads, but they were right next to them. I got a funny feeling, like there might be some hassle in a minute.

"Jesus, you… let me, here, ah shite." The final whistle blew. Richie shook his head, and put in another twenty pence.

"Go on yourself, press the continue."

"Nah, I'll start again from the start," he said. I looked around. Tim was already four balls ahead of Ian. He went around to take his shot again, and nearly banged into the Mark fella. I held my breath for a second, when he said "Sorry", cos he sounded pure posh, and sometimes that was all you needed in here for someone to start something with you, but Mark just nodded at him, and went back to racking up the balls.

"Fine, go on. Listen, what are you doing tonight?"

"Me? Nothing yet. What have ye planned?" He picked Germany again. The computer picked France.

"Nothing. I'm not staying in though. Few cans or something, then out?"

"Yeah, sound. Where'll we- Gooooooooooooal-Laziooooooo!" He was good all right.

"We were in the Savoy last night. D'you go to Costello's?"

"Costello's? What's that?"

"Costello's nightclub. It's like Termights, only it's on a Saturday."

"They have a nightclub in Costello's? The Gards' pub?"

"Yeah. Upstairs. Two pound in, is all. It's all right, like. Bit small, but good tunes."

"Two pound? I'll buy that for a dollar."

"Sound. I'll see if the rest of 'em will come." I took one more sly look over at Shane and them, but they were talking to those youngones now, so it was grand.

*****

I was hammered when we got to the club. Couldn't remember half the night. We got a few bottles of 20/20 in Fine Wines; it was on offer. Rotten, but it got you polluted quick. We started off with Ian, Niall, Tim, Rich and myself. By the time we got to Costello's, Tim was gone home to his Mammy, Niall was in Doc's, and Richie went with him. Ian came with me, cos he was spotting some youngone from Salesian's who we met outside Quin's. We didn't even go inside the pub - we went down at eleven to see could we run into anyone we knew, and take them with us to the Costello's. I didn't really like it in Quin's on a Saturday anyway. It was a differentish crowd. Older. Not auld fellas, just older than us. People with jobs, probably.

The lights came on to tell us go home before I even had a chance to have a second pint. We must have only got there after twelve. Might have even been after half twelve, cos we'd stopped on the way back up from Quin's to finish our bottles. Yer one on the door only charged us a quid each; they done that when it was late, normally. I was destroyed; the 20/20 took a while to go through me, and by that stage I'd a pint of Bulmer's on top of it. And the drugs. That was the maddest part of the night.

I was in the jacks having a piss, when someone said my name. I turned around to look at whoever it was, and I didn't recognise him straight away.

"What's wrong Jon, sham? Cat got yeer tongue?" It was a blond fella. Red face. Pure Limerick accent on him.

"Eh, am, what?"

"It's Dara, you spa. Dara, 'member?"

"Jesus, yeah. Christ, what are you doing here, man?" He was one of the lads Richie used to pal around with from Thomondgate. He went to Sexton's school, in town.

"Here? With the muppets? Yeah, man. Not my usual scene all right, sham. Nice few birds though, yeah? No slappers like."

"Ah, yeah. Yeah, there's a few rides all the same." I only half knew him, but we'd always got on fine. His Da was a Gard.

"Yeah, yeah. Nice. Tell me anyway, what's the scala? You doing a few yokes?"

"Yokes? Nah, a few scoops like. We were bushing."

"Bush drinking? The Buckfast, is it?" His face was always red. It looked redder in the bathroom, might have been the lights. Some fella pushed past us to go for a slash. Dara gave him a big dopey smile.

"Nah. MD 20/20, like. The tequila one."

"20/20? The Mad Dog? Jaysus, that's awful piss altogether. Good times. Here, listen. Did ye want some yokes anyway?"

"Me, like? Ah nah, I haven't the cash, Dar." I looked at him and tried to blink myself a bit soberer. Selling drugs in a club, and his Da a policeman. Something else.

"Ah, I'll give it you on tick, shur. No bother. How many d'ye want?" He was whispering now, even though we were the only ones left in the jacks.

"Ah, when do I've to pay you, like?" I'd a bit of cash on me, but I didn't know if it was enough to pay him upfront. A yoke'd cost you a tenner in a club, if you were lucky.

"Pffft, don't worry about that, sham. Give it to me when ye've got it. Aren't we old pals, says you." His pupils were massive. He was off his face. That's why he was being so nice. Yokes done that to you.

"Sound. What are they?"

"Ah, they're Mitzis. Good ones, like. Not as good as pure white doves, like. But they're good. Strong, like. Trippy. I'm after doing three tonight, and I'm sorted, like. No bother."

I'd done Mitsubishis before, but someone told me that the name of them meant nothing anyway. Anyone could stamp the sign on a pill. You didn't know what you were getting really.

"Rapid. Okay, give us… two." I'd only have one, but Ian might do one with me. I wasn't doing yokes on my own. Not at that hour.

"There you go, sham. Listen. Have a good night, right? Feel the love, man. Feel the buzz. Techno, techno, techno, techno! Haha." He put his hand onto mine and passed them over without me seeing them. There was still only us in there, but he was acting like there was cameras on us.

"Cheers, Dara, man. I'll sort you out in the week, maybe."

"Jsssssssh, don't worry about it, bud." He turned around and walked out the door, dancing a little bit, even though the music wasn't on any more. I necked one of the pills, and took a drink off the tap to swallow it. Hopefully Ian would still be outside.

*****

It must have been an hour later when the E kicked in. I'd nearly forgotten I'd took it. Ian had disappeared with yer one, and I'd walked down town on my own, still langered, and worrying about coming up on a pill with no one to talk to or nothing. It was a bit chilly out, but I'd my Leeds jacket on me that was normally too warm for the summer, but grand for the night time any time of the year. I went and sat in Supermac's for a bit, upstairs, in front of a tray someone left there, half full of chips and a burger. I was hungry, but I wasn't that hungry. And eating something would make the pill work slower anyway. I was away with the fairies, watching all the youngones and lads come up the stairs to go to the jacks, or down the stairs to go out. I got bored after a while, and there was no music either.

There was a twenty-four-hour garage down in Henry Street, so I headed down there. When I got to the front of the queue of people buying sly bottles of wine, I asked for

Ballygowan. Six bottles of it. And two packs of Wrigley's. Yer one behind the counter didn't know what to say to me. She probably thought I was a mad auld junkie altogether. I'd enough money, cos I'd saved by bush drinking, and I'd only drunk the one pint above in Costello's. I was away out of there and down Catherine Street when I got the funny feeling.

I didn't know what it was, first, before I copped on. I'd only done yokes a few times before, and I'd always been listening to some tunes when I done it. When the music was pumping, and the blood started rushing, you knew you were up. It was the best feeling in the world while you were on it. The coming down was awful altogether though, and the next few days, you'd wanna kill yourself with the depression. That was why you couldn't do them all the time. And sometimes there was a bad batch, and people got killed off them. I was always reading about that in the papers, but I didn't know no one it'd happened to.

So, I was down a little street, still a bit langered, and coming up on an E, when I heard someone say something. I didn't know if I was imagining it first. Then it happened again.

"Hey."

I looked around, saw no one except this ride of a blonde standing in the alleyway, and then I heard it again.

"Hey. Hey… you."

My head wasn't spinning, but I felt strange anyway. My face was warm, and my fingers felt… different.

"Jon, isn't it? Jonathan?"

Now I was sure I was dreaming. It was the blonde one from the alley who was talking to me. Clear as day. I tried to find something to say back. I kept wanting to sniff the air, cos it felt brilliant when I took it in through my nose. And my jaw was going too. My teeth were grinding. It was time to have one of the choongums.

"Er, yeah. Jonathan. Jon, like. Who're you?" I tried looking at her. She looked like a model. Like a supermodel. Legs up to her neck, big cleavagy tits, no fat belly, and I couldn't see her arse, but that was probably rapid too. There was no one with her, but I still thought it was a trick. What if she'd some fella hiding down the lane, and they were gonna rob me? You heard about things like that.

"Heh. I thought so. I'm Áine. Áine Shaughnessy? I know your friend Brian?" She sounded posh. I'd no idea who she was, still. And I didn't know anyone called Brian.

"Oh right, yeah. Brian. Yeah. Brian who?" I couldn't stop gawping at her. I was on the horn and everything, just from looking at her. I wondered could she see it. I didn't even care. Let her see it. She's the one that done it to me.

"Brian Collins. He's going out with my friend."

"Oh. OH! Brillo, you mean." Of course. That Brian. The one nobody called Brian.

"Yeah, him. Did he tell you about me? About the interview?"

The penny dropped. Áine O'Shaughnessy.

"He did, yeah. Yeah, Wednesday, isn't it? For the Limerick Leader. Jesus, small world, hah?" I couldn't stop looking at her, but she didn't seem to be minding it. I was full of happy feelings. I still had one yoke left. I could give it to her. That'd be the nice thing to do. Share the wealth. And she might be grateful for it. I felt my langer twitch.

"Yeah, if that's all right. So, what are you doing down here on your own, Jon?"

"Huh? Oh right. I dunno, really. Ecstasy?" I just blurted it out. I didn't give a shit now.

"Ooh, cool. Got any spare, like?" She'd a gorgeous smile. She'd a gorgeous everything, from where I was looking.

"I do, I do. Want one?" I started to walk over to her a bit, so we weren't just shouting across the road at each other. I'd such a boner I was probably limping from it, but I didn't care.

"Ah no, I couldn't. I'm waiting for my friend anyway." She didn't look like she really meant it, saying no. She looked like she wanted to be… *persuaded*, I thought.

"Ah, go on. You don't want me doing yokes on my own, do you… *Áine*? God knows what might happen to me. It's a dangerous place, Limerick." I gave her a big smile. The corners of my mouth hurt from it, it was so big. I was fully up on the yoke now. It felt brilliant.

"Hmmmm, I don't know…" She did know though. She was just being polite. I could read her like a book already.

*****

The time passed pure quickly. She was up on her yoke dead soon. We'd gone down the alley, around the corner. There was a little car park, belonging to the place on the road at the front. I'd never been down there before, but I'd passed it some nights, thinking it'd be a good place to bring a girl down, for a bit of privacy. There was flats and stuff up above us, but they'd all got blinds or curtains, and most of them had no lights on, so no one was in. And no one would be looking out their windows that time of night, anyway. An alley carpark was hardly a great view. People had better things to be looking at. I was glad I'd bought all the water; cos I was gasping by the time we sat down. We were talking about everything and nothing. She was sound out, or it could've been the Es. Didn't really matter what it was, it was good.

"So, d'you know Brian long?" She'd a full pack of fags with her, I'd forgot about getting some more when I was at the garage. I'd given her free drugs though, so I wasn't gonna hold back on smoking her ciggies.

"Who's Brian Long?"

"Not Brian Long, you eejit. Brian. Brian Collins. Do you know him long?"

"Ah, yeah. We went to JFK together, man, but I didn't really hang around with him back then, you know?"

"Oh right. Why was that?" Her voice was very Laurel Hill. They were all nice girls in that school; well, all the ones I'd ever met. Being nice didn't mean they weren't a bit dirty too, though. You could be both; I'd met enough of them who were.

"Ah, he used to hang around with the lads from the year ahead. I dunno why, man."

"Hah. More mature, was he?" Even just smoking a fag was sexy when she done it. My eyes must have been on stalks, looking at her. I didn't care, though. You never cared about anything on yokes. No embarrassment. No shits to give.

'I dunno, like. Is he mature now, man?" I always said 'man' too much when I was off my face. My mouth was doing this closing thing, it was hard to get the words out. It'd go away and come back though.

"Couldn't tell you. Here, Jon. How am I going to pay you back, for the pill?" She smiled at me, with her nice teeth. I could think of a few ways she could pay me back, looking at her. I'd been thinking about her in all sorts of ways while she was talking. Picturing her naked, wondering how good it'd be to ride her. I wasn't even ashamed for thinking them either. It was all natural. It felt natural. It felt great.

"Ah, no. You're all right, ma- Áine." I wasn't gonna take a penny off her, even though I still had to get Dara back in the week.

I was full of this weird, warm happiness, as well as all the dirty thoughts. It was great. She was great. I was already in love with her, even though I wasn't really at all, and it was just the E. I'd never been in love with no one.

"No, no. I have to give you something. Hey! Have you ever done GBH?"

"GBH, man? What, like, beating someone up, like?" I wondered for a second if she wanted me to beat someone up for her. I would've, like. In a heartbeat.

"Haha! No, silly. The drug. GBH?" She'd a nice tan, it went great with the blonde hair. I didn't know if it was just the yokes making me think it, but she looked perfect to me. I really wanted to touch her now.

"What? No. What's that?"

"Oh, it's amazing. It's really called GHB – like, gamma hydra, something, but we call it GBH." Even her shoulders were gorgeous. I wanted to bite them. I was struggling to listen to her at the same time as having all these visions of riding her in my head.

"Cos it does a lot of damage?"

"Ah, no. I don't think so. It's just… well, it makes you feel kind of drunk. And loved up, like Es, you know?"

"Sounds cool. What is it, like? A pill?" I was already all loved up. And dying for the shift. I wondered was she gonna let me. And how long would it be until she did. Every bit of her looked good enough to eat now, and I'd a pain in my langer from being on the horn so long.

"No. No, it's a powder. Here, I'll show you." She reached down inside her top, into her bra, and pulled out a little plastic bag of powder. I was nearly more interested in what else was in the bra, never mind the drugs. My face felt like it was boiling, even though we were out in the cold.

"Jaysus, who are you, man? Scarface?"

"Haha. No, I got some earlier, for my friend. She's not fucking coming now though, is she? Left me in the bloody street, on a Saturday night in Limerick. I could have been raped, or worse." She was smiling, even saying that; we were both high as a kite.

"Yeah, pure lousy of her, man. Chalk it down. So, what do you do with it, like? Do you sniff it?"

"No, no I don't think so anyway. We usually put it in a cup of tea…"

"Tea? Haha! A cup of tea… Jaysus." Poshest thing I'd ever heard.

"Yeah, well. That's how I was told to do it anyway. But you can just take it."

"Take it like what?"

"Well, like when you take speed, but you don't want to sniff it? You just… put some on your finger, and rub it into your gums, or just swallow it." She knew loads about drugs for a nice girl from Laurel Hill. I was staring down her top now, and my breathing was gone pure deep – every breath I took in made me sort of come up again on the E, like a wave. It was getting hard to concentrate on what she was even saying. I just *wanted* her.

"Oh right, so. I'll have to give it a go sometime…" That was the right thing to say. Softly, softly. I knew what I was doing, even if I was off my face. I was having some of it, no doubt about that.

"Heh. Or we could have some now…"

"Really? Aw, thanks so much!" Bingo. I knew it.

"Have you somewhere you need to be?"

"No, man. I'm grand, no. I can stick around. I'm cool." I'd told my Ma I might be staying over in the North Circular Road with one of the lads. I usually said that, in case there was a party to go to, or a girl to take somewhere and get my iron. She didn't care anyway. As long as I came home at some point. I wanted to stay. I wanted to get off with her, and it looked like I was definitely on for it. Why else would she be down here with me, all by herself, where anything could've happened to her? She was up for it all right, it was just a matter of-

"Okay, cool. Me neither. Come over and put your arm around me though. I'm getting a bit cold…"

"Yeah? No probs." That was it, there. That was her giving me the green light. I'd been with enough youngones to know a sign when I saw one. I slid in beside her. My fingers touched the skin on her arm, and a rush went through me. I'd forgot how good it was, just touching someone, when you were buzzing.

"Right, now, Jonathan Musgrave, if that *is* your real name. There's only one more thing I must tell you, before we do this. There's something else that happens when you're on this stuff."

"Yeah?" I watched her lick her little finger, then open the bag. It was nearly the sexiest thing I'd ever seen. These pills were mad altogether.

"Yes. It makes you, well I don't know about you men, but it makes girls feel very… *frisky*." She dipped in and brought out some of the powder, then sucked it off her finger. I felt like I was watching a blue movie.

"Frisky?"

"Yeah. Frisky. *Horny*, Jon. Wanting some, er, *action*."

"Oh right, yeah." I felt like I was blushing, but my face was dead hot anyway, so it was hard to tell. I didn't ever blush really. If I wasn't on for it before, I definitely was now. I nearly spunked off in my jeans when she said 'horny', in her posh voice. I'd to nearly stop myself lepping onto her. Swear to God.

"So… you'll look after me, right? You won't let me get too crazy?" She smiled again and gave me a wink. My langer felt like it was gonna burst through my jeans. It felt like it was the size of a baseball bat.

"Oh yeah. Of course. Of course, Áine. I'd never do anything to hurt you. I lo- I like you, a lot." I didn't know where that came from. I tried to rewind the words back into my mouth, but it didn't work.

"Heh. Shush your big pilled-up face, you. You're too cute. Just… just keep an eye on me, yeah? Don't let anything bad happen to me?"

"Of course not!" I wanted lots of things to happen to her, and none of them were bad. Not bad for me, anyway.

"Promise?"

"Promise."

She'd more of the stuff on her finger. She held it out to me, and I leaned in and sucked it all off. The skin of her finger felt gorgeous in my mouth, and it tasted like I dunno what. The drugs were sort of salty and chemically, but I was more interested in her. I opened my eyes and saw her face really close to mine, and the next thing I knew, we were shifting.

Four

I woke up feeling awful. Guilty, like I'd done something really bad. I got like that after a night on the booze, sometimes. It felt like there was someone sitting on my chest. I looked around the bedroom. My clothes were all neat and tidy on the chair. I didn't remember putting them there. I didn't remember much at all. We'd gone bushing. And I went to Costello's. And I'd lost Ian. Dara- I'd met Dara from down our place. That was in Costello's too. Then I remembered yer one. Áine. Áine O'Shaughnessy. Then the guilty feeling happened again. I'd no idea why you'd feel guilty for shifting a girl that looked like her. I went back to sleep. Every part of me was sore.

The sleep was weird. It didn't feel like real sleep at all. It was like I was dreaming, but I was awake too. Lots of pictures I couldn't make out and forgot straight away. Lots of people I didn't recognise. Someone with a scar. Someone screaming. Me screaming too. Lots of colours and lights and scary music, and then I think I woke up properly, and straight away I forgot it all.

I could hear people in the house, talking. Real life people, not from dreams. I didn't know if they were talking about me, but once I got that idea in my head, I was sure that they were. The words came through my door all muffled and mixed up, and when they got to my ears, my brain turned them into cross, angry ones. About me. It felt like they were all on about me- my Ma, my Da, and Clodagh. Clo's voice was the loudest. She was *shrieking*, or it might have just been her laughing.

My Ma was making food in the kitchen when I went down. She gave me a nod when I came in, but she didn't say anything. I wasn't sure if that was good or bad, cos me and her never done big long chats or anything.

"D'ye want something to eat?"

"Ah, no; I'm grand, Ma." I'd no appetite yet. I was feeling weak though, and I knew I should have something.

"You sure? I'm making some oxtail soup, and a few sandwiches. For lunch, I mean. I can do you some too, Jon."

"Ah, no. No, shur I'm all right."

"Suit yourself." She was stirring something in a pot. It smelt like gravy, or the gravy you'd get in a stew.

The clock on the wall said it was nearly two. It didn't feel like it. It didn't feel like I'd slept either. The guilt was still there. It wasn't guilt; Harta called it *The Fear*. When you woke up after a night on the lash, and you couldn't remember how you got home. Then you start panicking about what you said to who, or what you did, and you still can't remember anything. Most of it comes back after a while, and it turns out you'd nothing to worry about. But, until that happens, you have the *Fear*.

I went out the back for some air. The sun was boiling again, but I wasn't trying to get a tan. The air always done a hangover good for me. Even better than water. I remembered all the water I'd bought in the garage. Yer one must have thought… God knows what she must have thought. Working that shift though, you'd meet all sorts. They weren't supposed to sell booze after eleven, but everyone went down there looking for it anyway, and everyone ended up getting served. You'd to beg a little bit, and that was easy when you were langered and gasping for more booze.

I tried to think a bit more about the night, and yer one. Not much was coming back though. Costello's was a blur altogether. The bit in the jacks, with Dara from down the road; that was mad. I didn't really see any of the lads from the old days anymore. The more time I spent hanging around with lads from Ardscoil, the less I wanted to be doing the stuff I used to do when I was twelve or thirteen. Cos that's all they done really, those lads; go to Styx, get a few cans, walk into town in the daytime, go robbing. Thinking about it then, I supposed it wasn't much different from what I was doing with the lads from my school, only apart from the robbing.

I knew Dara a bit when we were small, and Joe over the road too. And Richie, of course. I never hung around with Shane Collopy, or Danny or Mark; and I didn't know that Dermot guy at all, really. Richie was friends with most of them when he moved to Thomondgate first. Then, when he was about twelve, he didn't seem to be palling with none of them no more. Probably cos he'd gone to Ardscoil. He skipped a year when he was small, same as I did. His was cos his birthday was a funny time of year, mine was cos we moved house when I was six, half way through school, and there was no room in the younger class for me. He was pure clever, so it was fine for him. I wasn't that good at school, so it was harder for me.

Da's garden was gone to the dogs. He didn't care about it; My Ma was always telling him to get his act together about it. He was more interested in cars though. The one he drove himself, and the one out the back that he was always fixing. Yellow Ford Escort, pure

Seventies-looking. Me and Richie used to sit in it when we were small, and pretend we were the Dukes of Hazzard, or Starsky and Hutch.

"The head on you, you steamer. What time'd you get in last night?" It was Clodagh; she'd come out the back with a cuppa.

"Shag off. Am, I dunno. After three, I think?" It was probably even after four. I was guessing.

"Jesus Christ, does your Ma know?"

"Ah, I dunno. I suppose, like." I'd a key since my fifteenth. Most of the time they'd no clue when I came in, or how langered I'd be, as long as it wasn't a school night or nothing.

"You suppose? Jesus Christ, you've it easy. D'you know that?"

"What d'you mean?" I was looking at her tea, wanting one myself.

"Coming in at all hours, and you only fifteen, like."

"Nearly sixteen."

"Whatever, Jon. What-ever. Fucking… if I'd come in even after twelve when I was your age, my Da would've brained me. Mam too. Jesus Christ…"

"Ah, well."

"Ah, well, says you. Fucking hell, Jon. You dunno you're born, like. Spoilt rotten, ye are. Not fair."

"Jesus, it's not my fault they're mellow, Clo, compared to yours anyway. What d'you want me to do about it, like?"

"Pffft. Mellow. Mellow has nothing to do with it, like. It's cos I'm a girl."

"What d'you mean, cos you're a girl?"

"Think, Jon. Use your noggin. Mine didn't want me staying out all night, cos… well, in case I got…"

"Up the pole?"

"Exactly. Fucking shitty it was. You'd swear I was an eejit or something. I'm gonna go to hairdressing college, like. I've a future. I'm not gonna go out and get… get pregnant by some latchie, am I? I know how to be fucking careful, like."

"Ah, well. You're eighteen now, Clo. Doesn't matter anymore. You can get pregnant all you like now, and no one can say nothing to you."

"I don't wanna get pregnant, Jon!"

"Ah, you do. Go on, like. Lovely little babby to push round in a pram, shur. You'd be deligh-rah altogether, Clo."

"Fuck off, will you."

"Ah, Clo. C'mon now. Get out there and find a man, says you. Make some little grandkiddies for Auntie Mary and Uncle Paul."

“G’way you handicap, you. Go back down Poorman’s Kilkee and drink Club Shandy with your steamer friends from Caherdavin, yeah. All of ye listening to Neer-vahn-ah, yaw? You fucking social climber, you.” She said it with a smile. The older we got, the more I found out that she didn’t hate me at all; no matter what she’d said to me over the years. She was just being a teenager. I knew what that felt like now.

“Says you, and your hairdressing college.”

“Hairdressing’s a normal thing to wanna do, Jon. I’m not lickarsing no posh ones; I’m making my own way in the world.”

“Make your own way into the kitchen there and make us a cuppa, will you?” I gave her a wink.

“What did your last slave die of?”

“Ah, she got kicked to death. For not making me tea.”

“You couldn’t kick your way out of a Dunne’s Stores bag.” She gave me a push on the shoulder, and I’d to steady myself. My head was dizzy from the empty stomach.

“Jesus, don’t do that.” I felt a little sick come up my throat, but it went down again.

“Christ, you must have been polluted altogether. What are you like at all, Jon? You muppet, you. Listen, I’ll leave you go. I’ve to go over to Laura’s.” She got up.

“Ah, right. Tell her I says hi.” Laura Carey was a fine thing.

"I will in my hole. See ya." She went away off. I watched her for a bit, wearing her luminous green tackies, pink belly top and black cycling shorts. She looked like she was going to a rave. I'd no idea how we were related half the time.

*****

"All right, you bollix?" Harta came in the front gate and right up to me without me even seeing him or hearing him. I must have been spaced out.

"Eh? What're you doing here?" He didn't live near me, and my place wasn't really on the way to anywhere. Except town, maybe. But he'd still have to go out of his way a bit.

"Lovely to see you too, like." He'd a rollie in his mouth, not lit.

"You're the one calling people bollixes. Where you off to?"

"Me? Ah, I dunno. I've to go in and get me guitar from McDaid's."

"McDaid's?"

"Yeah, had an auld session last night, went on to a party."

"Why didn't you bring it with you then?" Harta was always in some room when there was a party, strumming away. He was the life and soul.

"Ah, it wasn't that sort of party, bud. Twas a party in my pants, and there was one lucky youngone invited, sham."

"You're an awful hound, all the same."

"Says him, the biggest whore in Limerick." He pulled on my sleeve, and everything hurted.

"What?"

"C'mon! Town, you gowl. The fresh air will do you good. What's wrong with you anyway?"

"Eh? Ah right. Am, nothing." I got up slow, my bones were aching me altogether. I slammed the door behind me, and followed him out the gate. I didn't know if I was hungry or not. Stomach was empty, but it wasn't wanting to be filled yet. No rumbles.

"Night on the sauce, was it? Two nights in a row? Jaysus, Jon. You're turning into an awful alko." He was dressed like he was in the circus or some other place where they had freaks. He was a one-off, as my Da would say.

"Turning into you, more like."

"You wish, you little gaylord."

"You're the little one, you half-steamer, you." I was about half a foot taller than him, nearly. He looked like he'd stopped growing already, too, at his age.

"Ah, but me bollix are big. Billy Big Bollix, that's what they call me, sham."

"Who calls you that?"

"People who've seen me bollix."

"Who else?"

"People who think my name is Billy."

*****

Town was empty, cos it was Sunday. Most places were closed, there was only a few people in Cruise's Street, wandering around. Half of them were probably tourists, even though you'd have no idea why people'd wanna come to Limerick for a holiday. I supposed if you lived somewhere shittier than Limerick though, our place was probably fancy.

"McDaid's is?" I'd forgotten which one it was. Head was too fuzzy.

"Denmark Street, down there."

"Grand." We weren't far from it.

"Stall on a minute." Harta was fiddling in his pocket for something.

"What's up?"

"What's up? Things, man. Things are looking up. Look at that, sham." He pulled a 20 pound note out, wrapped inside some dirty tissue.

"How'd you manage to have a score left on a Sunday morning?"

"Ah… no idea, bud. I think Seamie might've slipped me it after, for playing the gig, like."

"I thought you played for pints?"

"I did! And for twenty quid too, looks like. I'm not complaining, are you?"

"Nope."

"Pints or cans?"

"Ah no, man. I'm still bolloxed from last night." I got a jabbing feeling in my chest, around the heart. Dunno what that was. My face went a bit cold.

"Pffft, fuck off with you. Hair of the dog. We'll go to Fine Wines, see if they've any deals."

"I don't really-"

"Don't really, me bollix. You're not gonna let me drink on my own, are you?" He done a mock angry face. He looked a bit like the mouse off An American Tail. What the women saw in him was anyone's guess. Still, he done all right, so you couldn't knock him.

"What are you – Listen, all right so. No beer though. My stomach can't be having Dutch Gold now. Leave me alone with that shite." Dutch Gold was about five quid for six cans. Absolute poverty juice, but pure handy when you'd no money.

"Nah, we've twenty squid, shur. We can go exotic. Bit of Rosé, snifter of brandy, bottle of Listerine. The world's our lobster, shur." He'd spend it all, too. Harta was like that. Whenever he got a bit of cash, from busking or gigs or whatever, and you were with him, he'd treat ye all. No saving, no thinking about sensible things. You'd to remember that anytime you got money yourself and he was around. It was only fair. I got a funny feeling about the night before, when we headed up Catherine Street, to Fine Wines. Mad night, with yer one. Wished I could remember more of it though. I wondered should I tell Harta about her, or why I hadn't already. Something was holding me back. I didn't know what. It was nice out, a few drinks in the sun might be rapid all the same. Pubs on a Sunday afternoon were crap, and they closed them in the middle of it, cos of Holy Catholic Ireland. He'd forgotten about his guitar, but we were miles away from Denmark Street now, and I wasn't walking back just for that, so I didn't remind him.

*****

We were down by the big anchor thing under the New Bridge. It was good there, cos not as many people came there as came to Poorman's, and usually no scobes at all. It was worse sometimes too, cos when I was in Poorman's I'd never notice anyone going over Sarsfield, but here it was like everyone going over the other one was staring straight at you. I could see St. Michael's rowing club across the river. There was lads putting out boats, cos the tide was up. We'd got some new drink, called Pernod Hex. It mightn't have been new, I'd never drunk it before. It was on offer though, so it mustn't have been selling. Twelve bottles for eight pound. They weren't big ones, but that was a load of them. It was an alcopop, with Pernod, blackcurrant, and fizz. They were too warm, cos they hadn't been in the fridge.

"Cheers, anyway." I clinked my bottle off Harta's.

"Cheers. What you think of it?"

"Ehhhhhh," I said, making a face.

“Yeah, takes a bit of getting used to all right.”

"It tastes like hot sick."

"What do you want for that price, sham?"

"Cold sick, maybe?"

"You need to stop hanging around with them Ardscoil boys, man. You're getting airs and graces."

*****

Later, up town, we ran into some of Harta's friends from I dunno where. Adrian Buckley, and a fella called Emmet. He used to go to my school. Maybe he still did. They used to tell him he smelled, and throw tennis balls at him in class. It was a bit lousy, but I done that to fellas myself, just not to him. Didn't really know him enough to throw tennis balls at him. He didn't salute me anyway, so it didn't matter. Harta's friends were either all older or weirder than us. I dunno if all of them smelled, but if they did, they probably smelled like hash. That was one good thing at least; if you knew Harta you could get some gear easy. I was the one from Thomondgate and he was from Woodview, so it shoulda been the other 'round, but there you go.

"All right, ladies?' said Adrian, the snidey little one with the black eyes. He hadn't been in a scrap or nothing, his actual eyes were black, or really, really dark brown. Made him look like a snake, which was good, cos he was pure snakey altogether.

"Well, you little fucking mongoose weasel. What you upta?" said Harta.

"Up to my nuts in your Mam, you coss."

"Charming. She didn't say nothing about when I saw her this morning. You mustn't've been too good, like."

"I was so good she was lost for words, Harta."

"Ah no, I heard her say a few words during the night all right."

"Yeah?"

"Yeah. Like 'Is it in yet?', or 'does it get any bigger?' Just stuff like that, really."

"Gas man, all the same, Harta. What ye drinking, alcopops is it?" Emmet was talking now.

"Per-nod Hexagons, or something." Harta pronounced the D at the end, but he was only messing.

"Pernod? That's the leg opener. Which one's trying to ride who?" said Adrian, looking at me in a shnaily way. He needed a good box in the chops, that fella.

"No one. We're getting another slab of them and bringing them down to your Mam's. I'm grand like, but poor Jon here's gonna need about six more bottles to get up on auld Cathy."

I didn't know what to do, cos he'd brought me into his joke, and I didn't really know Adrian Buckley enough to be slagging off his Ma. He looked me up and down, shaked his head, and went:

"Pffft. Cathy'd eat him for breakfast, sham."

"Cathy needs to stop eating people for breakfast, man," said the Emmet fella. Harta sniggered and went:

"Cathy needs to stop eating, full stop. She's an arse on her like two rhinos tryin' to get out of a tent."

"Oi. Take it handy now, you,' said Adrian, looking a bit pissed off, with his little rat eyes.

"Oh. Here we go, scrap," said Emmet, scratching his dirty fringe.

"Ah now, he knows we're only messing, don'tcha?" Harta gave Adrian a friendly little dig with his weedy fist. He was pure skinny altogether.

"I'll give you messing in a minute, you handicap." Adrian spat a coughy snot spit onto the ground, not at anyone really, but it was near enough to my tackie. He might get a box yet.

"You will, shur. Course you will. Where ye off really, anyway?" Harta sparked up a rollie. I hadn't seen him make it.

"Quin's."

"Quin's? Bit early, sham. Half price drinks for steamers today, is it?" said Harta.

"Yeah. Your Da gave us the flyers. Sound man."

*****

Quins was full of metallers and goths. They looked mad dressed in all their gear in the daytime on a Sunday. Few rides all the same, but they wouldn't look at you twice. They liked fellas with long, combed hair, and drainpipe jeans. Most of them were called 'Mark' as well, for some reason. I went straight up and got served. I'd no balls for it in the daytime normally, unless Tony was working, but I'd drunk a fair few bottles of the Pernod stuff, so I was whizzing. It was grand anyway, cos Harta was a regular, and Emmet used to go down after school in a change of clothes nearly every day, so they must have thought he was in college.

"What's that fucking pisswater?" said Adrian to me.

"Hah? Oh, it's Hudson Blue."

"Hudson fucking yellow, more like. Smell off it, like. Smell a giggy off a rasher."

I'd no idea what he was going on about. I didn't know why Harta put up with him, he was an awful eejit altogether. Emmet was waiting for a Guinness, cos that's what studenty looking fellas with bum fluff moustaches drunk. You knew by looking at him that he drunk porter. You could nearly smell it off him, if it wasn't for the B.O. I'd never smelt B.O. off him actually. Probably something the jocks in school said about him, cos he was a bit different. That used to happen a lot, and nicknames stuck to you, if they were true or not.

Bits of the night were coming back to me, and other bits not coming back at all. Like how I got home, or what happened to yer one. She was some ride altogether, nearly a waste to be langered shifting her. I was more than langered though. It was drugs, more than anything. The booze was well gone by then. And that other stuff she had, the GBH. Jaysus, some rush. The bits I could remember, anyway. I got a little panic then, cos I couldn't remember if I'd said I'd meet her somewhere, or when it was. Like, I could've said to meet me outside Todd's today, and she could be waiting there now, like a gombeen. I probably hadn't though. But I didn't know. I'd see her Wednesday anyway, hopefully.

"S'rong with you?" Harta said, popping his pint down next to us.

"What?"

"Sitting there, staring into space, like you're dreaming of your prince or something. What's the scala?"

"Ah, nothing. Listen, did you ever do GBH?"

"What like, kick someone's head in?"

"No, you gowl. The drug." I said the last word as a whisper, on the sly.

"Oh! Oh right, yeah, no. GBH. That's a roofie, like."

"A what?"

"Date rape drug, sham."

"No it isn't."

"It is. Give that into some youngone's drink and she'll do anything with you. Won't remember it in the morning neither. Mad fucking shit."

"You're pulling my leg." The bit about not remembering stuff gave me a funny feeling, though. That was true. And the wanting to ride bit. But she'd given me it, not the other way around. I didn't rape no one. I couldn't even remember if we'd rode each other.

"Nope. Coleen Hickey got spiked with it one night in Docs. When the girls found her she was in the jacks, taking on three fellas at once."

"Jaysus." I sounded like I thought it was shocking, but thinking of it gave me the horn a bit.

"Yep. Like something out of a blue movie. But she'd no clue what she was doing, like. And she didn't remember nothing the next day."

"Who's this?" Adrian had been over at the bar, talking to some crusty looking youngone. He was back now. Emmet was I dunno where.

"Jonno's planning a rape."

"G'way will you, I'm not."

"A rape, is it? Who're you raping? Boy or a girl?" Adrian's eyes looked even blacker now we were inside.

"Shut up, the both of ye. Where's Emmet anyway?" I wanted to carry on asking Harta about the GBH, but I wasn't gonna do it with Adrian there.

“Eighteen leagues, bud. Four European cups. How long’s it took Man U to win that league? Pathetic. The ‘pool will be back next year, that’ll be the last one United win for another 27 years, trust me.”

You wouldn’t think Harta was into soccer, looking at him, but he was Liverpool through and through. Adrian was a Man Utd fan, the gowl.

“Go ‘way, you fucking steamer, you. Two leagues in a row. Who else is gonna win it next year? Fucking Blackburn? Gimme a break. Where’d ye finish, eighth? Sixth last year, sixth the year before that? Get used to it, man. Liverpool are over.”

“Eighteen leagues. Come back to me when ye’ve eighteen leagues.”

“I fucking will. And ye won’t have one another one since, either, cos we’ll be winning the lot of them.”

“You’re only talking through your arse now,” said Harta.

“Who d’you follow, Jon?”

“Hah?” Adrian woke me out of another little daze. I was trying to take it handy with the drink, but all the Pernods were after hitting me.

“He supports fucking Leeds, shur.” Harta rolled his eyes, like he was calling me a handicap. Leeds won the league a couple of years back. They nearly got relegated the year after, but they were getting good again now. I thought so, anyway. I’d still get a slagging sometimes though, just for wearing my jacket out. Soccer made people into right gowls, all the same.

"Leeds? Haha. Cheers for Cantona, man."

We'd sold Eric Cantona to United and he was their best player now. For only £1.2 million, as well. They won the league, and we came 17th after that. Then they won it again, the bastards.

"Yeah, you're welcome."

"Wasn't he riding Lee Chapman's wife?" said Harta, not really to anyone.

"What?" I hadn't heard nothing about this. Nirvana was on the jukebox – the end of *In Bloom*. Adrian answered him.

"Yeah, your one from Men Behaving Badly, the ride, not the fat one. He was riding her, I heard, and Chapman finds out, and he wants to fucking kill Cantona, so-"

"Ah, here. Cantona's a fucking beast, like. Lee Chapman's only a long streak of piss," said Harta.

"True, man. Anyway, shur, Howard Wilkinson's having none of it, so he phones up Fergie. Middle of the night, like."

"Middle of the night?" I really hadn't heard none of this before. Smashing Pumpkins was on– *Cherub Rock*. Someone was having rapid taste in there today.

"Middle of the night, swear to God. So, he says, listen, I've to get rid of Eric, d'ye want him or what?"

"He did in his hole. To United, like? Just like that? Their biggest rivals, like? Here ye go, have our best fucking player. Bollix he did." Harta rolled his eyes and popped open his little tobacco box.

"Look man, that's what I heard. Swear to God."

"Why didn't he ask for five million, like? Ten million? What did he cost Leeds, Jonno?"

"Ah, £900,000, I think."

"Exactly. Best player in England, wins the fucking league for you for the first time since, what, the Seventies?"

I nodded, even though I didn't really know. You'd have to ask my uncle Frank about that. He was who I got Leeds off in the first place. And he was around in the 70s, definitely.

"Look man, don't shoot the messenger. I'm just saying, Wilkinson phones up Fergie and he says-"

"He says, listen Alex. I'm the manager who brought this fella over from France, when no one'd touch him over there cos of his attitude, and no one knew him over here. Turned him into the best striker in the league, won the title for us, beat ye on the last day, fucking gutted ye were, everyone else in the country laughing at ye, all yeer fans probably hating yer man Eric, but… d'ye want him? For the price of a few bags of chips?"

I sniggered into my pint. Harta was gas.

"Ah fuck off then. Was only telling the story." Adrian lit up his fag, then threw the box of matches at Harta's head. It bounced off his forehead and landed on the cream of his pint.

Harta must have scobed some more money off someone, on top of the score he'd earlier, cos he was buying the drinks for me and him, and he didn't let me say nothing about it. The other two were buying their own. It must have been about five, I didn't have a watch, but it was starting to fill up a bit. Not night time full, but Sunday evening full, at least. I was well langered, and I knew I was, cos when I went down to the jacks a few times, the women were starting to look better, and I felt like talking to them, even though I didn't. I was going after every pint now; that was always the way- you could drink a load of drinks at the start without a piss, then you started pissing, and you'd to go after every drink. Then ye all wanted to go at the same time, and there was no one to mind the seats. *Animal Nitrate* by Suede came on the speakers. The guitar in that was brilliant.

Inside, having a piss, I looked at the head on me in the mirror. I was wrecked looking, probably. I felt good though. When you'd a harsh night, and then you went drinking the next day, you always felt better than moping around the house, feeling the Fear. No Fear now though, and no fear of me either. I was gonna crash out something awful later, cos two days drinking and all them drugs, but I was fine for now.

"There he is, himself."

When I got back to the table, Harta was sitting with two other fellas. I didn't know where Adrian and Emmet had gone. I looked around for a seat, cos one of the new fellas was in mine.

"How're ye?" I took Emmet's chair. He could argue about it when he got back, if he even was coming back. I looked over for my drink; it was still there.

"Listen, this is Jim, and Fearghal. Boys I has an auld jam with. This is Jon, lads." The two of them nodded to salute me. They were older than Harta; bit crusty looking. They looked like they were musicians, definitely. They'd clothes on you couldn't buy in Penney's. I nodded back at them, and reached over for my glass.

"Jon and a few boys from over Ardscoil have a bit of a band, see. Ye just got a new drummer, didn't ye?"

"Yep."

"They're doing the Battle in the George in a few weeks, like. Ye've played a few gigs already have ye though, Jon? With an auld spare wheel on drums, like."

"Yep." I felt like he was my Ma or something, telling her friends how much of a good little boy I was. The other two were looking at me like I was supposed to be giving real answers.

"Ye any good, like?" It was Jim who asked, or Fearghal. I'd already forgot which was which. Before I could say anything, Harta spoke, and I thought he was gonna slag us off, but he didn't.

"They're fairly fucking handy, like. Even if they do have a keyboard player, hahaha."

“A keyboard player, is it? What are ye, The Pet Shop Boys?”

Again, no idea if it was Féarghal or Jim. I done a little smile. No point in arguing, keyboards were a bit gay all the same.

“Ah now, he’s actually decent. No Brian Eno, like, but he’ll do.” Another compliment from Harta. Maybe he did actually get pissed.

“Ah yeah, nothing wrong with a bit of synths, man. The Floyd have a keyboard player. D’ye play any Floyd, man?”

“Just *Floyd the Barber*.” We weren’t good enough to be playing Pink Floyd, we could manage Nirvana, though. Just about.

“Haha, nice one. Bleach’s a fucking sweet album, man. Much prefer it to Nevermind,” said Jim/Fearghal. Of course he did, big pretentious head on him.

“Anyway, ye pricks, will we give ‘em a support for Thursday?” The two lads shrugged and nodded, and I didn’t know what Harta was talking about for a second cos I was slow with the drink, but then I realised he meant a gig.

“Oh right, what, this Thursday coming?” It was soon. We’d done one practice with Richie, but still, it was a gig. We needed gigs together.

“No, Jon. The fifth Thursday in November, in the year 2007.”

“Piss off, you. But yeah, sound. Thanks, lads.”

"No probs, kid," said Harta, like he wasn't only a year and a half older than me. Jim and Fearghal nodded and went on drinking their pints. I might have to get them to wear name tags on the night. I was sober enough when I went home later, cos we'd run out of money eventually. I gave Ian a quick ring to tell him about the gig, and to set up a practice. Tuesday was the next day everyone was free, he said. I didn't know how he knew that without asking everyone else, but I didn't care either, and I was tired, so I told him fine, and I'd see him then.

There was no one around when I woke up the next day. The Ma was off out somewhere, and he was at work, cos it was Monday. I put on the kettle for a cup of tea and read the back page of the paper that was on the table. More about bloody Gaelic, as usual. There was hardly any soccer in the sports pages in the summer. It'd be back soon though. The girl on Page 3 was nice looking. Small tits, but she'd a lovely arse. I wondered what their Mas and Das thought about them being in a newspaper with their clothes off. It was probably different if you were English, though. All their women were slags, Harta said. I was thinking about yer one from the other night. Áine. I wanted to give her a shout, to see if we were still on for Wednesday, but I hadn't her number. I'd looked in my jeans I'd been wearing, but there was no piece of paper or nothing. I couldn't remember taking it off her anyway, but I couldn't remember lots of things about that night, so that didn't mean anything. Then I remembered who it was that set the thing up in the first place. Brillo. He was bound to have her number, and if he didn't, his missus might. I went out to the phone with my cup of tea. I'd make myself some toast in a bit, my belly was rumbling.

Brillo picked up the phone himself. I'd been expecting his Ma to answer.

"Hello?"

"Hi, can I talk to – is that yourself?"

"It is, who else would it be?"

"Haha, yeah. True."

"Who's this, sorry?"

"It's Jon. Jon Musgrave, like. How's you?"

"Jaysus, that's weird. I was just gonna call you myself, Jon."

"You were?" He didn't usually phone me. We weren't really friends like that.

"Yeah, of course."

"About what, like?" The tea was just right. I'd needed it more than I realised. A fag would've been nice to go with it, but I couldn't spark up inside.

"About Áine!" That was weird.

"Hah? That's what I'm calling you about, like."

"Well, of course you are, like. You're the first person I thought of when I heard. Cos of, you know…that thing." He was losing me now, kind of.

"Yeah. Hang on, when you heard what?"

"The news, obviously."

"What news?" I'd no idea what he was on about now. And I'd a horrible feeling in my belly that wasn't the hunger.

"The news on the radio. I dunno if it's in the Leader too, I haven't-"

"You've lost me now, Bril- Brian."

"Have I? I thought you were calling me about it?"

"About what?"

"Áine!"

"I was!"

"Well then, you must know…"

"Know what?" I was getting frustrated now, I'd nearly forgotten what it was I'd actually phoned him for.

"That she's missing?"

"Missing?" That was a weird way for him to say it. I only didn't know her number. She hadn't disappeared into thin air.

"Yeah, squire. Missing. It's been on the news all day. She went out on Saturday night, she got split up from her friends, and she never came home."

"Oh, right. Yeah." My appetite was gone completely now. Brillo was saying something else, but I couldn't hear him. I was frozen to the spot, trying to understand what was happening.

"Listen I… I'll call you back later, okay?"

"Jon? Jon? Are you still there? Jon!"

I put the phone down. Something was really, really wrong. I needed to turn on the local station and listen for the news, but I couldn't get up yet. My legs weren't gonna work properly; I couldn't really feel them. I couldn't feel anything.

It was probably a half an hour before I got up from where I was sitting. The tea was cold in the cup; I threw it down the sink. The Ma was still out. I looked at the clock, and it was a minute to three. The news would be on in a second. I flicked the switch on the radio. It was already on Radio Limerick, cos that's what she listened to when she was doing stuff in the kitchen. Then I flicked it off again, before the news came on. I'd to go outside first, for a cigarette. Or upstairs. I remembered something that might help, and went up to my room to find it.

The Ma still wasn't back an hour later, when I was sitting out my bedroom window with the bottle of Power's. I'd hid it under my bed last Christmas. I didn't even like whiskey, but it was helping a bit. My room faced into the back garden, which was better than it looking out over the road, where everyone passing could see you. Them next door might be able to, and the houses across the way, but I'd the bottle still in a brown paper bag from when I'd robbed it out of the big liquor shopping the Ma had got before he Christmas party, and I was only taking it out from behind me whenever I took a swig out of it. The windowsills at the back were big; not exactly a balcony, but you could throw your legs over and sit fairly safely all right. Clodagh showed me when I was small, and everyone gave out to her for it, in case I tried it myself on my own, but it was okay. I hadn't died from it yet.

Áine was missing. She'd never come home Saturday night. Well, Sunday morning, anyway. I'd been with her Saturday night. I didn't get home til – I really couldn't remember, and now it was important to remember. Cos people'd be asking questions. Important people. Serious questions. I wasn't in trouble, though. She was fine last time I saw her. I thought. I couldn't picture it – saying goodbye or anything. Her getting a cab. Anything like that. We'd been wrecked though. You never remember the end of a night when you were wrecked. I could barely ever remember getting home most nights after being on the lash. That was normal. I wished this time was different though. Just the once. Cos it was important. I'd listened to the next news, an hour later, on the clock radio in the bedroom. They hadn't said any more than Brillo had told me, but it still sounded crazy, hearing them say her name on there. Made it way more real than him saying it.

I was trying to be calm, but it wasn't working. The whiskey was a good idea. It tasted rank, and I was used to there being red lemonade and ice to take away the taste whenever I drunk a bit, but I just wanted it to make shit easier to deal with now, and it was doing that. I wasn't happy drunk or anything. I was just sort of fizzling, like when you've a really bad headache, and you take some Disprins, and wait a small while, and then the Disprin starts to work. It was just like that – numbness, relief, something like that. I did wanna think straight, but I didn't wanna *be* straight, so there was a little battle going on in my head. And I kept having to tell myself to be careful up there, with the height and the drink, or they'd be scraping me off the concrete later. I thought about things that'd happened a few years ago in Thomondgate, and I got a little dizzy even though I was sitting down.

There was no real, actual bad feeling in me about that night. It was all nice memories and then no memories. I couldn't remember arguing or fighting, or her storming off, like in a movie. I just remembered waking up the next day, feeling like shit – but that was from drink and drugs, not something I'd done. Not that I could've done anything – not to her, that was stupid. She was missing though, like them kids in America on the side of milk cartons. She wasn't a kid, but she was maybe too young to be out for two nights without calling home, and her Ma and Da called the Gards. My Ma used to say that, if I didn't come home for hours without telling her where I was – she'd say "I was just about to ring the Gards." But she never did.

Áine could still come back though. She might already be back. If I went in and turned on the radio, the man on the news might be saying something about them finding her, and how it was all fine now, and everyone was happy and glad. I knew that wasn't gonna happen, though. I'd a feeling in my gut that it was only gonna get worse.

No one knew I'd met her. No one at all. All the time I'd been worrying and thinking about it, I'd forgot that bit. I hadn't even told Harta yesterday. I didn't know why, normally I'd be telling everyone about going away with some ride; especially when there was a mad story about drugs and all that to go with it. Richie always said a gentleman never kisses and tells, but we weren't gentlemen, we were lads. And lads have to have a bit of a boast and a brag. I didn't tell no one though. Maybe I nearly did, when I was asking Harta about GBH, and then they were all making jokes about raping someone, and then Adrian came over, so I didn't get to finish. Either way, it was good. No one knowing about it made it better, even though I obviously didn't do nothing to her or nothing. Someone off a movie saying 'The last person to see her alive' popped into my head just then, and it put the shivers up me. I shook the feeling out of me. She wasn't dead, she was just missing. People went missing all the time, if they all ended up dead, the world would be terrifying. They didn't, though. They came back. So would she. She'd probably be back today, and I'd see her Wednesday like the plan was, and we'd be laughing our heads off about all of it. I could hear the Ma moving around downstairs now, she was after coming in without me realising. I needed to go back inside the room and spray some Lynx around, so she didn't smell the fags. I'd been good though. I'd been keeping them outside on the ledge with me. Smoke comes back in sometimes though. And people who didn't smoke could smell it from miles away, cos their noses worked better than people who did smoke.

Five

Richie's Da was letting us in the back gate, Tuesday morning. The day before had been mental. I spent most of it hidden away up in my room, drinking the whiskey, listening to music on my earphones, and pretending stuff wasn't happening, so I didn't have to deal with it. I didn't have no dinner, just some Taytos and a few bars I robbed from the kitchen when I heard the Ma going down the shop. I must have passed out in bed about eight o'clock, still in my clothes. I just about remember her sticking her head in in the morning and tutting at me, but I'd hid the bottle away under the pillow before I went to sleep, so she didn't know.

"Back again already? Jaysus, ye'll be as good as The Who in no time, lads."

Richie gave the Da one of his looks.

"The who, Dad?"

"Yeah, The Who."

"No, I mean, the who? Like, *who*?"

"The Who, Richie." He squinted at Rich, and squashed his lips up, like he wasn't sure if he should be confused or annoyed.

"That's what I'm asking!" Richie couldn't keep the straight face.

"Feck off you, now. Before I tell them all about the bed wetting."

"Dad, I don't mind what you tell them about you wetting the bed. Honesty's the best policy, you always says."

"Ah now, ffff." He pretended he was gonna take a swing for Richie. They were gas altogether.

Once the rest of them were there, we got into it straight away. That was good for me, it took my mind off stuff. I couldn't believe how good Richie fitted in already. It was different to when we'd lads on the drums lads from other bands, and we didn't really know them, and it was all awkward between the songs and stuff. And them lads didn't really do it for free. We didn't pay them or nothing, but we'd get them a load of drinks on the night of the gig. Or we'd get them a new set of sticks or something, to say thanks. But they weren't our friends. They weren't in the band.

All the lads were doing great, I just couldn't concentrate, myself. They'd all been talking about Áine, I was expecting that. It was the talk of the town by now. None of them knew I'd met her Saturday night. I didn't even think any of them knew I was supposed to have the interview with her, cos none of them said anything about that. It was Friday night, in Termights, when Brillo told me. None of them were around to hear when he said about it. And at the practice the next day, I mustn't have said nothing, cos none of them knew. That was good, though. I didn't know why it was good, cos I didn't have nothing to hide, but it just felt… better that they didn't know about it. She still hadn't come home. They'd said on the news again in the morning. The Ma was about to switch over the station when I nearly shouted at her to leave it on. I thought she was gonna ask me a load of questions, but she just muttered something about me not usually caring about the news, and got on with her cleaning.

Ian and Niall were fighting about something, as usual. They got on grand; it was just the music stuff they'd get shitty with each other about. Pitches and keys or whatever. I never knew what they were blathering on about, I just tuned out whenever they were having one of their fights. It was over already anyway, and we started into *Breed*. Nirvana songs weren't hard to learn, and people always liked them. They tore the throat off me though, so I didn't give it the full whack when we were just practicing. The gig was in two days, and I'd still to ask Harta how many songs we were getting. I thought it'd be about eight, and that was another thing for the lads to argue about. Except Richie. I didn't think he thought he was in the band long enough to get to decide things. He was just chilled out anyway, and he'd play anything we picked, so it didn't matter to him.

We tried *Nicotine Buzz*, and Ian had a new guitar bit for it, to go with the mad bassline, and it sounded rapid. I didn't really move singing it, I never moved around in practice, but I was thinking of things to do on the stage in McDaid's, where the gig was gonna be on Thursday. I'd been in there before, I thought, but I couldn't picture where the stage was, if there was one at all. Sometimes the pub would just clear out a corner for ye, and throw up some speakers and a PA, if it wasn't already there for the DJ or whatever. We done *Promqueene* too, and one that didn't really have a name, but Ian wanted to call it *Encounter*. I thought it was a stupid name, but he'd wrote it, so there was no point in arguing with him.

McDaid's was dead, but I expected that. Just hangers on from Harta's band, and a few strays belonging to us. One or two lads who hung around school to watch practices when we were messing about, when we didn't really have a band. People'd just hear the guitars if they were around, mitching supervised study or something like that, and stick their heads in the door. If they played themselves they'd try borrow a guitar and join in a jam. Niall hated it, he was pure serious when he was practicing, but most of us didn't give a balls. We were only having a mess anyway, back then.

We'd a proper gig now though, the first one as the five of us. We didn't even know what we were called. They kept asking us for a name, the lads from the Battle, but we couldn't think of something we all agreed with. They'd us down as 'Ardscoil Band' so far, but we'd have to come up with something soon. I'd come in by myself, I didn't know no one there. I was looking round for Harta's head, but I couldn't see him. Someone was tuning a guitar over the speakers. Someone else was hitting the snare, and kicking the bass drum. People looked around from their tables when I walked in, then went back to their chats. Everyone was dressed like hippies or goths. We didn't have a look ourselves. Everyone was into the same music, except Niall, but we didn't look Grunge or Britpop. We just wore clothes, basically.

I didn't know where to go, or sit. I hated being in a pub on my own like this. It was grand if I was just mitching school and I'd go into the George and get a cup of tea or a glass of coke, and sit down looking at the paper. It was fine to be on your own like that. It was half seven though, so it was nearly the night time. You didn't go into pubs in the night time on your own, unless it was Quin's, and it was packed, and you knew you'd run into someone.

"All right, you bollix?" Harta was behind me; nearly scared the shit out of me.

“Jesus, where’d you come out of?”

“My mother’s fanny. How’s you?” He done a cough like he’d the Plague or something. Too much hash and rollies.

“Grand, grand. Who else is here?” I wanted a pint. Settle the nerves. I wasn’t nervous about playing, I was a bit on edge, since Monday. She was gone five days now – it was serious; I wasn’t sleeping very good, even though I hadn’t actually done nothing wrong. Keeping it to myself was probably what was messing me up, but I couldn’t tell no one. Not yet, anyway. One good pint or two, relax the shoulders, sort me out. I wasn’t getting pissed, I didn’t wanna forget the lyrics or anything.

“Ah, loads of people. You know Alex, yeah? And Don, Mary, Bazza, Aisling, Podge, all them.” He’d a pint of Guinness with about one sup gone out of it.

“Oh right, yeah.” I’d no idea who anyone of those people were. He always done that, acted like I knew all his mad friends who were all cool weirdos who went to college and looked at you funny in Quin’s, like you were a child. Harta was born cool, he’d make friends with anyone, and everyone in town knew who he was. Well, all the cool people anyway. He knew a few scobes too, maybe from buying hash so much. He never got jumped going through dodgy places or anything. They all knew his head from around. I didn’t know anyone who didn’t like him. He was sound.

“Wanna drink, so?”

“Does the Pope shit in the woods?”

We went over to the bar; I didn't know if he was offering, or I was paying, or we were getting free ones, but I didn't care as long as I got a drink.

Three pints in and I'd forgot about not getting pissed. All the lads were there now, all the Mas and Das dropping them off with the gear. I'd only my mic and my stand to bring. I'd be putting it through the PA, hopefully, I hadn't asked no one yet. Harta would know. I was dying to get up there now, I couldn't wait. Some yoke belonging to Harta was chatting away to me; no idea what her name was, cos I never listened when people told you who everyone was.

"So, yeah. I mean, in London they have some amazing places for gigs. Camden, like. It's amazing there. Really cool spots to go out. I miss it. I miss it a lot." She was boring me to death, but she'd nice tits.

"Mad. How long did you live there?"

"Two weeks."

Jaysus. I looked around for someone to save me. The lads were setting up over on the little stage, the two drummers looking at each other funny, cos Richie'd to use yer man's kit, and yer man didn't want him to hit it out of tune. I looked down into the end of my glass and wanted another one, but that'd be stupid of me, cos we were on soon, and the booze I'd drunk already wasn't even hitting me yet.

"How about you, babe?"

“What?” I didn’t know if she was coming on to me or what, or if she called everyone babe. I didn’t like her, but she was a ride, sort of. In that goth way, with all the makeup and the stripy tights.

“Have you ever been to London?”

“Oh. Ah, no.” My aunt lived over there, but my Ma wasn’t talking to her; hadn’t been talking to her for years. Ma was like that with her sisters. Always out with one of them and reading the hole off her to the others.

“You should go, babe. You’d like it there. It’s totally chilled. Lots of chilled people. Like-minded people. Groovy, like.”

“Yeah, sounds it all right.” The boring was winning against the tits now, I wanted to go over to the lads, just to get away.

“I’m thinking over going over again soon. Maybe to-”

“Whoops. Sorry, love. Sound check.” I got up, looking over at Ian like he was after saying something to me. He wasn’t.

“What? Oh. Oh, right, yeah. Groovy. Good luck, babe. Break a leg. Talk to you after!”

“Hehe, yeah.” Not if I could help it. A mad bit of feedback came out of one the speakers. It was Nailer, going too close to the amp.

It was still nearly empty when they told us to go up. I held off on another pint, but when I got to the mic, Harta brought over a tray of fresh ones for all of us, from the manager, no charge, so I took a gulp off mine and stuck it on the bass amp. *Here Comes Your Man* by the Pixies was first. Nice easy one to sing. I heard Richie tap us in with the sticks, and we were off. Ian and Niall hit the note together bang on, and I got a little jumpy waiting to come in with the first line. My voice came out all quiet at the start, but yer man on the PA shoved the volume up pure quickly, so it was grand.

We done *About a Girl* next, the version off Bleach, not the unplugged one everyone else did, and that went rapid. It was time to do one of our own now. The few people there'd turned around from their chats in the middle of the second one, so we'd an audience at least. I gave Niall a nod, and he came in with the bassline. It sounded rapid, what he'd done with the few chords I'd gave them. The words I'd wrote were pure bollocks, obviously, but it was Punk, Niall said, so it didn't matter.

"I'm in a dream, so it would seem, I'm in a mess, I can't confess"

They meant shag all to me, but *Supersonic*'s lyrics were all bollocks too, and that was a rapid tune.

"I'm in your head, feeling your dread, I can't explain, all of this pain"

I couldn't even tell if they could hear the words, but some heads were bopping to the tune anyway. The chorus was next.

"I... can't... survive; without... you in... myyyyyyy liiiiiiiiife. Kill... the need... in meeeeeee. Show... me how... you seeeeeeeee"

Ian stepped on the distortion pedal. If it was in a disco and I was hearing it, I'd probably have moshed to it. Richie was really smashing the drums. He'd come up with something more heavy and fancy since the last practice, but it was good. It was better. When we finished, with a load of drum rolls, cymbal smashes, and metal guitars, we even got a few claps. I wanted to smile, but I was trying to be a cool lead singer, so I just sank the rest of my Hudson.

Another cover next – one of Tim's ones. He loved REM, and this one was good, cos he'd been playing it for ages on his own, so he was rapid at it. It was all church organs on it, but he knew how do them with his keyboard, and it sounded pure good. There was a bit of lead guitar for Ian, but I played the rhythm for it, on acoustic. I'd borrowed Harta's cos he'd got pick-ups on it, to run through the amp. It was called *Sweetness Follows*, but we all called it The Sweetness Follows, even after Tim told us there was no 'The' in it. The crowd all looked up, cos most people knew it, and it sounded exactly like it, thanks to him. A thought went through my head that we should've saved it for last, but it was too late for that now. Halfway through the second verse, I saw her in the crowd, and I nearly forgot my words. *Áine*. She was okay. Everything was fine. I couldn't take my eyes off her, all the way to the end of the song. I swear she was looking at me too. It felt like I was singing it to her. For her. Like we were in a movie.

Another original next up, and I'd to go back to the sheet of paper over by Richie to know which one it was. *Promqueene*. One of the first ones I wrote myself, a pure rip-off of Nirvana. Same chords as *Rape Me*, but heavier and faster. I didn't even like it really, but the lads did, and they wanted to put it on our demo, when we could afford one. I let them off, cos no point in arguing, and anyway, it felt cool to think of my own song being on a tape, in a real studio. My nerves were all over the place now, but in a good way. I was pure delighted I'd seen her, and she'd been found, or come home, or whatever it was. Four bars of drums and bass, four bars of distortion.

"I don't have a date for tomorrow's prom. I don't have to wait, it'll take too long. If you hesitate, you might be wrong. I don't have a date for toMORROWS PROM"

[chorus] *"Ayyyyyyyyyy, I don't have a caaaaaaaare, meet you anywheeeeeere, don't care what you weeeeeear, I don't have a caaaaaaare."*

Absolute Kurt Cobain job, but it sounded good when I done the Seattle grunge voice, and people were coming in the door now, finally, and some of them were bopping and swaying away to it like it was a real song. I was high as a kite, from the beer, the singing, and seeing her. Another verse, another chorus, then the guitar dropped off and it got quiet, with just the bass and drums going. I looked down into the crowd for Áine's face again while Ian came in with his solo. It was good. It was much better than the first few times I heard him try it, months ago. He'd added new bits, and his pedal sounded rapid, like your man from Smashing Pumpkins. I stopped looking for her just in time to remember I'd one more bit.

"I don't have a caaaaaaaare, meet you anywheeeeeere, don't care what you weeeeeeear, I don't have a... care."

The last word was quiet and soft, and the end of the song. Bit of a gap, while everyone there realised it was actually over, then big whoops from the crowd, clapping, and I heard Harta's voice over the lot of them, shouting:

"Aboy the laaaaaaads!"

We were either actually good, or everyone in there was langered, but it didn't matter. I got an idea and turned around to the others:

"*Basket Case*!"

"It's not, that's not next. It's-"

Niall started arguing, but I cut him off. *Basket Case* was perfect, and cos it was me that started it – me and Ian. I turned around to the mic before any of them could argue with me more about it, gave Ian a wink to make sure he'd remember to hit the note with me when I said *"Do you have the time"*, and I stuck my hand up, like to say "Come in with me when I put it down." He hit it spot on.

Áine was back, right up the front now, pogoing like a lunatic. I tried to give her a smile, but she didn't see me. She looked the same, but a bit different. Probably cos she was wearing different clothes, or probably cos the school photo they were using in the papers was a bit old and I was used to that being what she looked like in my head, but there was something anyway. Then I figured it out – her hair was brown, instead of blonde. At least I thought it was, but it might just have been cos of the dark in there, and all the coloured lights. I couldn't really tell. I sang my arse off. Seeing her there took all the weight off me. I could talk to her in a bit. Might even get the shift off her, after I got the scala on where she'd been, and what'd happened to her. It was a pure good feeling, and I flew through our last three songs, high as a kite. I was enjoying it, but I couldn't wait til it was over too, cos I was dying to talk to her.

After we'd come off, and got all the cheers and the backslaps, I went looking for her. I'd lost her face again in the crowd, cos it was packed in there, and I wanted to get hold of her, in case she went off somewhere else. Harta's lads were already up doing their "One two, one two", but she mightn't have been staying to see them. She must have come to see us – to see me. If she did, she'd stick around to talk to me, definitely. It'd be stupid if she didn't. Unless she was angry at me. But if she was, why did she come here at all? I was just being stupid now. Our name wasn't even on the posters. We didn't even have a name yet. She must have just come in to listen to whatever band was on. She didn't know I'd be here.

Maybe she wanted to give out to me, though. Maybe I should be hiding from her, just in case. I dunno why she'd be angry with me, but I didn't remember everything from that night, I didn't remember saying goodbye to her, and I woke up feeling bad, I remembered, so who knows what the hell happened? Maybe there was a fight. Maybe I… I needed another drink, but I was too full of fizz and gas from pints. A Southern Comfort with ice'd be good. A bit more Dutch courage.

An hour later and there was no sign of her. She wasn't there. It was very weird. I was in the corner talking to the lads about how it'd went. They were all pure chuffed, anyway. There was even a few youngones over chatting with us. I seen Ciara and Bríd earlier, but God knows where they were now. It was easy to lose people in there when it was packed. Yer one with no name who'd been to London for two whole weeks was burning the ear off Ian now, so I was off the hook there. Brillo was there too somewhere – acting like a manager again, trying to impress some floozies. It wasn't working though; he was even more normal looking than me. Pure rugby jock, with hair like a black. He'd a girlfriend anyway. I hadn't talked to him yet, but I probably should have, cos I wanted to know if he'd seen her too.

I wanted to feel good about the gig, but the thing with her was bugging me. I wondered if anyone else'd seen her yet. If she just showed up at home today, and was out on the town already. Not even grounded. Maybe she hadn't been home yet though. Maybe she was still missing, as far as her Ma and Da knew. That was stupid though, cos why'd she be out in public like that, with everyone looking for her, and the Gards as well. Nah, everyone probably knew. I hadn't listened to the news since the morning. It didn't matter. She was back now.

Harta's lads were playing a blinder. He wasn't really a good singer, like I was, but he was rapid at working the crowd. All the years of busking, probably. He could play and sing at the same time, and he could really play, so him and the lads could bust out a jam in the middle of a tune, and it sounded rapid. I didn't know half the songs they were playing, but you could tell it was good stuff, cos you wanted to dance along or nod your head even if you didn't know what it was. The pub was packed, cos Harta and them were all cool people, and it was a cool people pub. It was good knowing Harta, all the same. Opened a few doors, as my Da would say.

I took a wander down to the jacks; down to outside the women's, just to see if I might catch her going in or going out. I'd a mad feeling, like I was nervous. It was probably just excitement. Frank always said being afraid or being nervous is the same as being excited, but I never really understood what he meant. There was a load of cool looking youngones around, all of them looked different, but they looked different in the same sort of way. They usually hung around with older fellas with long hair and tattoos and earrings and nose rings. I looked pure normal, so they didn't ever think I was their type. They took a bit of convincing, like. I was good at convincing them, though.

I looked at all the heads of the youngones coming through the little hall. It was outside a jacks, but it still smelt brilliant, all shampoo and perfume. Birds smelt rapid, I always forgot that until one was around. Herself next door even smelt good, but she was my cousin, so it didn't really give me the horn. It shouldn't have, anyway. A few blondes went past a few times, but I'd to remind myself that she'd brown hair now. Pure confusing. What'd she done? Gone off missing for a few days and went to the hairdresser's in between? Mad stuff. I reckoned she'd probably been at some friend's place, pissed off with her Ma and Da, trying to make them worried, and her pal done the hair for her. Maybe she was planning to go on the run, and the hair was a disguise, like in the movies. I saw someone about the same height as her, with brown hair, but when she turned around she was a rotten looking yoke. All spotty face, and cod eyes. I gave up and went back to the lads for a bit. Someone ran into me on the way.

"Hey, Jon." It was Eric Broderick, the guitarist from the DTs.

"Eric."

"Caught your set, man." He'd floppy hair that never looked too greasy, and he wore them skinny leather jackets from the 70s that you'd to buy second hand in The Edge or Modesty.

"Oh right." I didn't wanna be asking him what did he think; but he was probably gonna tell me anyway. He'd a look in his eye. I was half paying attention to him and half looking over his shoulder to see if I could see her.

"Yeah, man. Vocals were fucking sweet."

"Oh right. Cheers, thanks." Didn't know if it was that much of a compliment, cos he was tone deaf at singing himself, but it was better than him saying I was shit.

"Who's that dude on guitar?"

"Ian?"

"Is that his name? Yeah, that guy, man. I dunno." Should have known he was gonna slag something off. The DTs weren't really arseholes, but they were good - really good - and that made them cocky.

"Ah, Ian's grand. He's not as good as ye, like. But he's not playing that long." Didn't know why I was making excuses for Ian, but it was like he was slagging me off too when he was slagging him off. Like someone calling your Ma something. There was a few youngones behind Eric now, most of them with brown or black hair. Muppets all had brown or black hair, it would've been way easier to find her if she didn't dye it.

"Pffft, yeah. You've got a lot of people, don't you?"

There was only three of them in the DTs. Anything's a lot compared to that.

"Well, yeah. Five. With the keyboards."

"Hehe, yeah. Keyboards are actually cool, man, you know. In a way…" I could tell that he meant "Not in the way ye use them", but it didn't matter, cos I'd a little flashback then to when we were all in primary school, and Eric was best pals with Rob Carroll, and they'd both got Duran Duran pencil cases, with fellas wearing make-up on them, and everyone thought they were steamers with each other, and it made me feel a bit better about him standing there, acting better than me, the cunt.

"Course they are. Pink Floyd, 2 Unlimited, Duran Duran. Listen, I've to go back to the lads. Catch you later, man." I didn't give him a chance to answer me. I slapped him on the shoulder, still smirking about the pencil cases, and went back in. I could hear Harta squealing and squawking away up on the mic. He wasn't as bad at singing as Eric, but that wasn't saying much.

Back at the lads, Brillo was there and Richie's girl, Dearbhla, too. She'd probably been there for the whole time, but I hadn't clocked her before. I gave them all a nod, and looked over Brillo's shoulder to see how busy the bar was. I wasn't gasping, but I'd nothing to do with my hands. I sparked up a fag instead.

"Ah, the L.V. What'd you think, anyway?" Brillo was like someone that didn't belong to us. Or to anywhere. Auld man in a youngfella's body. He was all right, really. I'd been over to his house and stuff, on the Ennis Road; his Ma and Da were old, like most rich kids' Mas and Das. No idea why, but they always were.

"What did I think?"

"Yeah! How'd you think it went, like, squire? Good vibe off the crowd? Nice acoustics?" I swear he didn't have a clue what he was talking about sometimes. He just knew the right words to make it sound like he did.

"Ah, yeah. Suppose. Sound all right to you?" The Southern Comfort was hitting me now. That always happened – you took a break from sinking drinks for a small bit, and you felt the last one kick in on its own. Didn't feel too bad. Wasn't getting dizzy or anything. I think I was just a bit high from the gig.

"Aw, yeah, squire. Sounded tip top from down here. Few bum notes from The Edge there, but-" He gave Ian a little dig on the arm.

"Fuck off Brillo; you big spa, you." Ian was langered.

"It's *Boxer*, squire."

"Cunter, more like," said Niall. He looked funny, he'd probably smoked a spliff. His eyes were weird.

"Yeah, yeah, Bigfoot. I liked the bass, though. Well done you. This time next year you might have a go at using the bottom two strings as well, yeah?"

I sniggered a bit at that. It wasn't even fair; Niall was decent at playing, but slags weren't ever fair, and they didn't have to be true to get a laugh. That's why clever people didn't win slagging matches in school. It was always the cheeky lads with the most friends that got the best of you. Mob rule, as my Da said.

"It's over there by the amp, Brillo. Anytime you wanna pick it up and give us a solo, just let us know, yeah." Niall was so big that, even when he was saying something to you with a smile, you thought he might knock you out. He wouldn't, though. Gentle giant, as my Ma would say.

"Nah, I'm more the brains of the operation, squire."

"You've the brains of a Down Syndrome, you gowl. You wouldn't even have the brains to *play* Operation." Richie'd come back from the bar with pints and bottles. Dearbhla turned around and looked at him all lovey dovey. She probably liked her fella being a rock star now.

"I'm fucking brilliant at Operation, kid. Ask my Maw and Paw. Won every game last Christmas."

"Fair play. I suppose you've loads of practice with a tweezers, mind. From finding your mickey."

Niall was a funny bastard. I wondered what time it was. Harta's lot were still up, but he looked sweaty and bollixed. He'd probably have a plan for after. There wasn't no clubs on that we could all get into. He'd usually got a plan though. He was Harta. Time for another Hudson Blue at least, before the lights came on. I looked over at the bar, to see. One of the youngones serving was a pure ride altogether. When I was queuing up I remembered I'd wanted to ask Brillo about Áine, but he hadn't shut his gob for long enough, and now he was over there, and I wasn't gonna lose my place at the bar. I'd ask him later. In a bit. If I remembered. It didn't matter anyway, cos I'd seen her. She was grand.

"Right, so. What's the scala?" Harta slapped me on the back. We were outside, after closing. There was a fair crowd, still. No Termights tonight for anyone to be going off to; that was only Fridays. Baker Place was probably on, that was always on, but I couldn't remember if it was dance music on Thursdays or not, and Baker's was usually shit. The bouncers were easy though, so you'd end up in there sometimes If you got stopped going in somewhere else.

"I dunno, pal. You're the man with the plan." I was nearly out of fags. Someone else'd probably have some.

"D'ye wanna come to a house party, so?" He was licking the edge of a skin. I didn't know if there was gear in it.

"Is there a house party?" said Ian. He could barely stand up by now.

"Ehhhhhhh, there's always a house party. Or a house, at least. And it's always a party once I gets there. Ye all coming?"

I looked around at who was left. All the lads from the band, a few of Harta's, and Richie's girl. No Ciara or Bríd, but I saw them earlier. Everyone nodded or said yeah. I zipped up my tracksuit top up, it was getting chilly and I'd no coat, and I'd left my beanie at home. We were a bit down the road when I saw Áine, standing on her own. I'd forgotten all about her; I was polluted. I told the lads I'd be back in a sec.

"Hello…"

"Oh. Hi." She looked at me like she'd never seen me before, but she was probably just smashed.

"How've you- how's things? I saw you earlier, like. Then I…"

"You did?" She blinked at me, looked down at her feet, and then back at me again.

"Yeah! When I was up singing!" I was nearly thinking it wasn't even her now, but that was stupid. She looked the same, except for the hair. Or did she? I was hammered. So much free drinks. Shots and everything.

"You were up singing?" She looked surprised, nearly. There was a few youngones looking over at us. Probably her friends. They were talking, but I couldn't hear what they were saying.

"Yeah. I was with the - so… what's been going on, anyway?"

She was still looking at me like I'd two heads.

"Huh? Ah, nothing, really. Just out with the girls. Came in to see the gig, like. Maire's cousin is in one of the bands."

"Oh right." So was I, like. She was supposed to interview me for the Leader about it. I was very confused, now. I could hear one of my lads shouting over to me, probably Harta. To get a move on. I was busy, though. They could wait on a second.

"Yeah. So you were in the first band, was it?" This was mental now. Was she taking the piss out of me? How wrecked had she been the other night that she didn't remember shifting me, or doing GBH with me, or-

"Yeah. Supporting."

"Oh yeah! You guys were great, actually. I liked that one you did- ah, the REM one. The slow one, with the organs, was it? You were playing the acoustic guitar for it."

"The Sweetness Follows." This was just mad now. I dunno what I was feeling. Hurt? I wasn't hurted. I didn't know her; I wasn't mad about her or anything. I didn't care about her. I'd only met her once. Twice, now. And she wasn't really being a gowl to me. She was being nice, sort of. She was nearly flirting with me. But it was like she didn't even – the lads were calling over louder now. And her lot were coming over to her.

"Yeah, that one. You're a great singer, like." She was a bit closer to me now. I could smell the perfume off her. It wasn't the same one she had on before, I didn't think so anyway.

"Cheers. So…" What was I supposed to ask her? Did she run away, was she kidnapped? Why didn't she know who I was? I felt like an eejit, a bit. She was pure gorgeous. She looked different though. It was the hair. And… something else.

"So… what's your -"

"How'rya? Sorry to interrupt…" There was another girl there now. One of hers. She was talking to me. I blinked at her. Harta was saying something across the way, and pointing up the road.

"Er, hi?"

She sniggered, and put her arm on Áine's shoulder.

"C'mon you. We've to get a taxi."

Áine looked at her, then at me, and then back at her again. I could see the lads walking away now. All the lads, except Brillo, who'd disappeared off somewhere, probably. Still hadn't asked him about her. Kept forgetting. Too many random people talking to me all night. Too pissed to think properly. Didn't matter now, cos I'd found her.

"What?" She said it nearly angry, like you'd say to your Ma if she came in to wake you up in the morning when it wasn't school.

"C'mon! You fool. Say goodbye to your… friend, hon. We've to go. Sorry now, love." The last bit was to me. I just shrugged. I'd no idea what was going on anymore.

"Gimme a minute!" She pushed yer one's hand off her and moved closer to me. I looked at the friend like to say sorry, or I dunno, and she gave me a half-dirty look.

"C'mon! Will you just- can *you* tell her?"

The lads were a fair bit up the road. Áine's two other friends were walking over to us now.

"All right! All right. Jesus Christ… Am, bye then. Nice to meet ya!" She leaned into me and gave me a kiss on the cheek. I wasn't expecting it. She smelled half nice and half of booze. Then she turned away and walked off. I stood there for a few seconds, wondering what just happened, then I booted up the road after the lads.

"Who was that, you bollix?" said Harta, slowing down for me to catch up.

"Ah, just some – some bird." I couldn't be arsed telling him the story now. She'd just confused me more than anything. But I was glad she was safe.

"They're all just some bird to someone, sham." He passed me the arse off a one-skinner.

The party was an actual party, when we got there. It was up in some flat belonging to someone Harta knew, but he knew everyone. There was decks and speakers - music pounding through the place when we walked into the big sitting room. Dance music, so there was definitely pills going around. I'd been to things like that with Harta before, but the lads hadn't. They were langered though, and you can fit in anywhere when you're langered. We walked through, following behind Harta like he was the leader, and he was saluting everyone there like we were in Goodfellas. I didn't really know any of them, but I recognised a few heads from Quin's and Termights. A few metallers from outside Todd's, a few rides from around town. There was a mad smell of gear. We kept walking til we were out in the hall, where it was quieter. Harta stopped, turned around, and looked at us with a big grin on his face.

"What are ye doing, lads? Mingle, will ye? Don't be following me round like I'm the Pied Piper, sham. Fucking… I've things to see, people to do, like."

"Ah now. Shur aren't you our glorious leader, shur?" Niall was nearly too tall for the ceiling in there.

"I'm no one's leader, pal. I'm a lone wolf."

"You're a lone gowl, is what you are." It was Ciara, behind him. Bríd as well. I saw both of them when we were up on stage, but not when we came down. I didn't think about it at the time, cos I was looking for yer one.

"Ladies!" Niall went over and hugged the two of them at once with his big long arms. I gave them a salute each. Some other youngone came up the hall and pushed past us. The jacks must have been down the end. I looked behind me and only Richie and Dearbhla were still with us. Ian and Tim must've gone back into the big room. Mingling.

Later on, I ended up on a couch, with Ciara. No funny business or anything. Not yet anyway. You never knew with that one. She was talking about the battle of the bands. We'd stole some booze out of the fridge. There was a load of bottles inside, all cold, and a few slabs on the floor next to it, warm. We took a couple out and put a couple in; that way it nearly wasn't stealing.

"I honestly think ye could win it."

"Ah, here." We were all right, especially tonight, but she was getting a bit carried away.

"Ah here, nothing, Jon. Don't be giving me the false modesty now at all. Ye were brilliant."

"Cheers, like. But we're not as good as the DTs."

"Pffft. Fuck them. They're good, like. But they're only pricks. And he can't sing a note to save his life. You're way better than him. The crowd will love ye way more, trust me." It was pure nice hearing stuff like this, but she was langered. You couldn't take it too serious. Still, it felt good, a bit.

"Yeah, it's not the crowd that decides it though, is it?"

"Isn't it?" She was nearly finished her Bud.

“Nah, it’s judges, like.” I’d asked Tom Fitz; his sister was the bar manager in the George.

“Yeah, well the judges’ll still listen to the crowd, like. If ye were as good as U2 and no one clapped, shur ye wouldn’t win, would ye?”

“S’pose not… I dunno. I think it’s like, a few categories – technical ability, originality, maybe there’s one for what the audience thinks, yeah.”

“Well, look so. They’d beat ye easy if the technical bit was just about instruments, but if the singing is included in that, shur his voice is so fucking bad, ye might draw with them. Then all ye’ve to do is beat them in one of the other things.”

“Well…” She was making some sense, but I still didn’t believe it; not really. We were only together a few weeks.

“Seriously! Look, Ian’s not the best in the world on the guitar, but he’s not terrible either. There’s no way in fuck he could be as bad at playing as Eric is at singing, right? Niall’s actually good at the bass. Richie’s a natural at the drumming. I wouldn’t believe for a second that he’s only after starting, would you?”

“Nope” She was right about that, definitely. Some youngfella with long hair went past us, looking for something. Skins, probably. Or his hole. I gave him a nod.

“And Tim, well, shur forget about Tim for a minute.” She laughed, and I did too. Tim was just Tim. No one cared about the keyboard player. He’d been great on *Sweetness Follows*, though. I remembered seeing Áine in the crowd. And then how weird she was outside.

“Not interrupting anything, am I?” Brid squeezed in between us before we could say if she was or she wasn’t. She’d a flagon of a cider with her, half gone. She was half gone too, from the looks of her.

“He wishes!” Ciara said, laughing. Bríd laughed too. I rolled my eyes at the both of them.

“I think I remember that wish came true a couple of months ago, love.”

Me and Ciara didn’t look at each other after she said that. We never talked about the times we shifted each other.

“Aaaaaaaanyway, next question. Chaaaaaange the subject. Do ye want a yoke?”

I perked up straight away. A yoke’d be great; nice auld pill, to celebrate the gig. I’d only done one Saturday night - *that* night, but that was a while ago now. I’d still get a buzz off this one.

“Yeah! Sound out, Brid.”

“How ‘bout you, Ciar?”

“Hmmmm, yeah. I’ve got an interview tomorrow, though. I don’t want to be coming in all on a comedown.” Ciara was a great one altogether for grabbing a summer job. I never needed to, my Da usually threw me a few quid without telling the Ma. And the Ma did, without telling the Da. Or sometimes I went busking with Harta or Niall.

“Ah, go on. You can have a half, shur.”

"Are you just having a half as well? Cos I'd need to split one with someone. I can't just buy half a pill. They don't sell halves, do they?"

"Ah, well you have half, I'll have one and a half then?"

"One and a half, for yourself, Brid? Will you be okay with that?"

"I dunno. I've only really done halves, or one. Won't make that much difference, shur."

"Why don't we all have a half?" I said, getting bored already.

"That's still an odd number, though," said Ciara, looking annoyed at me.

"Right, well how many yokes do you have, Brid?"

"None, yet."

"None?" I blinked at her as if to say "What are you on about?"

"Well, yeah. I've to – we've to order them."

"Order them? Off who?" Ciara said. Someone was playing the Prodigy on the decks. I was wishing I was already up on a yoke now. The Prodigy sounded rapid when you were buzzing. That music was made to be listened to on drugs. When you weren't, it was like being stuck in Tropics or Doc's.

"Joan, who does the tickets in Baker's. She's going for some, in a minute, like."

"Yer one who was Miss Limerick?" She was a massive ride. Pure gothy looking for a beauty queen, but still.

"No, that's her sister, Jean. Joan is the one with the red hair."

I didn't think I knew that one.

"Ginger girl? And she works in Baker Place?"

"No, not ginger. Dyed red, like red the colour. Like the buses in England."

"Oh right, yeah. That one. I know who you mean now." I didn't, but it didn't matter. Ciara took a purse out of her bag and went through it for notes.

"Listen, I'll pay for one, and I'll take half, and we'll see how it goes. Is fifteen all right?"

"Fifteen, yeah. I mean, she's probably gonna get 'em for ten, but fair play, she's the one taking the risk, isn't she?" Brid took the cash off her and turned around to me. I'd probably just about fifteen on me, but it meant I'd have to scobe fags off people for the rest of the night. No booze needed though. Everyone always said yokes were better if you went on the water instead. Everyone was sound when they were buzzing, so people'd easily give me fags later, even if I didn't know them.

"There you go."

"Cheers, Jon. Ye were great tonight, like."

"Oh thanks. Sound. Go on, then."

"Go on what?"

"Go on and get us some drugs, like. Chop chop."

"Shut up, you lala." She thwacked me across the back of the head when she stood up, I wasn't quick enough to duck. When she was gone, Ciara turned to me.

"Right, so. Come on and we mingle."

"But we have our own couch, man! Someone'll nab this if we get up."

"Jesus, shush, will you. When you have your yoke, sitting down'll be the last thing you want to do." She was right, too. Even if you didn't like dancing, being up on an E made you wanna get up and shake your stuff, as my Ma would say. Sitting in comfortable couches was for later, when you were on a scummy comedown. I got up. Head felt a little dizzy from all the booze and excitement. And the night hadn't even started yet. I took a couple of fags out of the box in my jeans, and handed one to her. I thought I'd none left, but there they were.

"For me? Sound."

I gave her a light. She giggled when she saw me putting my hands around the lighter, even though we were inside and there was no wind. I always done that, and she always laughed at me for it.

Time must've flown, cos it felt like only a few minutes between Bríd leaving us at the couch and her coming back with our yokes. I was still with Ciara, in the big front room, watching people dance and having a sneer.

"Delivery for Mr Musgrave? Sign here, please."

Brid popped it into my hand. No need to cover up what we were doing. We weren't in a pub or a club. I put it straight in my mouth and washed it down with some flat Bud. We'd robbed one more each from the fridge, but we'd been nursing them, waiting for the pills to come.

"Will the lady require a half measure this evening, or is it the Full Service?" Ciara looked at Bríd for a second, then at the pill in her hand, then back at her again.

"Feck it. You only live once." She threw it into her gob.

"That's the spirit, love. Back the neck." I offered her my Bud, but she'd a white plastic party cup full of something, and she finished it off in one gulp. Still half swallowing, her eyes went watery, and she pointed over to yer man on the decks.

"Let's see if that twat has anything decent in his record box."

Me and Bríd nodded at each other, and followed her over. People were a bit wrecked, I kept banging into them, but I didn't care. I'd be where they were in about a half an hour. It felt like I could already feel myself coming up, but that was bollocks. It was on the way though, as long as she didn't get us duds. We got to the decks just as Ciara was striking up a chat with yer man. He'd a knacker's baseball cap on, and a Man Utd shirt. He was looking at her like she'd two heads. I tried to listen in over the noise coming out the bass speaker beside them.

"Got anything decent, like?"

"Haha, what's decent to you, love?" I couldn't put an age on him, cos he was tall and skinny, but he was definitely older than us.

"Anything! Beatles, Stones, Bowie, Velvet Underground. Anything, really." She was nearly screaming into his face now, but he looked like he was used to that.

"Am, I don't think so, sorry. I usually only bring rave, cos people'd be on yokes, like. Nobody'd ever ask me to play no metal, like." He was changing songs while talking to her. He put on *On a Ragga Tip*, by SL2. Sort of thing I'd normally think was shite, but if you're coming up on a yoke, it's just right. I wasn't though. Not yet.

"The Beatles aren't metal, shur." I couldn't see Ciara's face, but I knew she'd be giving him one of her looks, with the raised eyebrow and the witch's eyes. Richie's Da said she'd be able to kill all the weeds in his garden with one of her looks.

"Ah, you know what I mean, though. Quin's music, Termights, all that stuff."

"You mean good music?"

"Hahahahaha! Yeah. Shur all music is good to someone. Know what I mean, sham?" I just plays to the crowd like. I d'mind what no one listens to, man. S'all good. Peace and love, like. You know what I mean, baby?" He was off his face. I could tell from the way he was talking. You were pure nice on yokes. You couldn't argue with no one. We'd probably have world peace if yokes were legal and everyone took them. But then everyone'd be on comedowns, and maybe that'd be when the fighting happened. You can't cheat nature, like. Can you? I looked at Bríd for the answer, and then I realised I hadn't been talking to her at all, I was just talking inside my head.

"I'm off to find the bog, Bríd."

"Oh okay, sweetie. Tell us where it is, when get back, yeah?"

“Yeah, sound.”

As I passed them on the way out, I saw Ciara taking a CD case out of her handbag, and yer man the DJ looking at it funny, but smiling at the same time. And chewing. Choongums. I didn’t have any. I wondered if Ciara or Bríd did. If they didn’t, one or two of us could snake off down the shops for some. If we asked around, people’d probably want fags or water. We could make a shopping list. People on pills never ask for their change, same way people on Speed always forget whose tenner they were all snorting with, and it just ends up getting left on a table. If there was enough change between all of them, we could probably scab the price of ten fags out of it. Or twenty, maybe. I got to the bathroom just as some youngone was coming out. She was gorgeous altogether – like a little blonde fairy. She looked really embarrassed at me, and pushed past me down the hall. I went inside and locked the door.

After about two seconds I copped on to why she was mortified. She’d done a really stinky shit in there. It was all gone, flushed, but the smell was still there. It always surprised me that birds could do smelly shits. Pretty birds, really. If a youngone was a bit of a Ten Ton Tessie, you’d expect her to do big fat, smelly brown ones. Cos she’d be eating rubbish all day, and big dinners, and drinking Coke. But some gorgeous little ride? I think in my head they just done something different instead of shitting. What that was, I’d no idea. I looked into the bathroom mirror at my pupils. Were they massive big, or just normal size? A bang on the door took the heart out of me.

“Hoi! You in there! Open up!” I recognised the voice as a voice I recognised, but I couldn’t think whose it was.

“Eh, who is it?”

"Who is it? It's the Wank Police. We got a complaint about some activity in this area."

Harta.

"Screw you, copper! You'll never take me alive!" I picked up a bar of soap and threw it at the door. It made a nice thumping sound. My face felt hot now.

"Sir, please. Put down your weapon."

"You put yours down too, copper. Or I swear to God I'll-" I could hear my blood rushing through my ears now.

"My weapon is still in its holster, sir. You're going to have to trust me here."

"Trust a copper? Never! Where's my helicopter?" I wanted to breathe in a really deep breath, but the smell in there was rank. My eyes were jittering and stuttering when I looked around the bathroom. I was coming up big time, the first rush. It couldn't have even been twenty minutes. That was mad.

"Just open the door, Jon, will you? I'm dying for a slash, man."

I twisted the lock and as the door swung in and Harta came through, it was like all the music came with him, like a big wave that the surfers get up on. It just flowed in, like it was a real thing you could touch and feel. I actually could feel it though, even if I couldn't touch it. It was pouring into me, through my ears, and filling me up like blood. Into all my veins, and filling up my lungs and then I clocked what it was – *Oh! You Pretty Things*, by Bowie. Ciara must've made yer man put on her CD. Sound as a pound. Harta was behind me now, langer out, no shame.

"You all right there, man?" I'd the door still open cos I didn't wanna be away from the music.

"Me? Yep. Tipping away." I couldn't hear any pissing.

"Sure you're all right, like? Need a hand or something?"

"Haha, fuck off. Naw, I just did the thing." He done a big gear smoker's cough, hocked up a bit of phlegm and spat it into the water.

"What thing?"

He zipped himself up and turned around to me.

"The thing where you're on yokes and you're drinking and you think you need to go for a piss, and then you get to the bog and nothing comes out. Jaysus, what's the fucking smell in here, man? Did something crawl up your arse and die?"

"Ah, that wasn't me. It was yer one."

"Which one?"

"The girl. She was in here before me, like."

"Don't be stupid, bud. Girls don't shit."

"They- are you on a yoke?" Looking in his big saucer eyes answered that for me, straight away.

"Course, man. You?"

"Yeah, just necked one about… a few… a while ago." I'd no watch on me.

"Nice one! Have I been buzzing with you before, man?"

"I dunno. I don't think so, man. A smoke, maybe. And that acid that time, remember?"

"Hahahahahaha, yeah. When your skin turned into the carpet and the clock kept making you jump, was it?" I should have got mortified by that, but I wasn't. Another sign that I was coming up. You just felt good things on a yoke. No bad things. No afraidness, or jealousness, or anything like that. It was pure rapid like that. He was talking about the first time I done acid, with him and a load of his proper druggie friends. They'd all been pure cool with it. I'd gone into some mad hippy trance, where the floor was breathing, and the patterns from the wallpaper and the carpet were going on my skin. It'd been my first time though, and I done two whole tabs. I was pretending the whole time that I'd done it loads before, to impress the other fellas. So, when they decided after Baker's to get some more, I was off my face completely, but I went along with it and took another one. I didn't come down until about three days after it.

"Yep. Good times, man. Good times." I'd a gawmy looking grin on me, and I caught myself grinding my teeth. I wondered was that what that song *Teethgrinder* by Therapy? was about. Harta was beaming too.

"I think you might have come up, bud."

"Just a bit, yeah… fuuuuuuuucking hell." I took a massive deep breath; I'd been in there long enough for my nose not to smell the shit anymore, even if Harta still could.

"Mon we go listen to Bowie, sham. Before yer man starts playing Jason Donovan."

Off we went. *Fame* came on, she must have given yer man a 'best of' CD, cos that wasn't on Hunky Dory. The little tiny parts of the song you never normally noticed where really clear now. Every little note came across the room from the speakers and into my body. I started dancing while I was walking, just from the hips down. I rooted around in my pocket for my last few fags. Harta was shoving an open pack of Wrigley's under my nose.

"Sound out."

"No problem, brother. Here, gimme one of those straights and I'll do up a J."

I slid the most broken fag out of the pack and gave it to him. He only needed it for the tobacco. A girl walked past that I didn't know, and she was gorgeous. They'd all be gorgeous tonight, even the ugly ones. Ecstasy was like a magic trick that made you only see the good stuff in everyone, for a few hours. These were way different to the ones I got off Dara last week. I got a small guilty feeling inside, and I didn't know if it was cos I hadn't paid him back, or cos of Áine. It couldn't be cos of Áine though, cos she was all right. I was talking to her earlier. She was fine. I got a mad happy feeling thinking that. I bit into the choongum and rolled it round my mouth. When I took a big deep breath again, all inside my nose was minty, and it felt pure rapid. These were really strong. I was gonna ask Bríd what they were when I found her. I hadn't even looked at the pill before I necked it.

It was a great idea; taking a pill. Perfect way to celebrate a brilliant gig, and Áine being safe, and everything going right again. I'd been worried. Not cos I was mad about her, or cos I knew her enough to really care about her, but just cos I was… connected to it, and that wasn't a good thing. It was all over now. She'd been pure funny with me though. Didn't recognise me at all, unless she was messing with me, and if she was messing with me, it wasn't like it was a funny joke. There was no punchline to it. She'd just buggered off home, or to get a taxi. She looked pure different with the different hair, the more I thought about it. It wasn't like she looked like a different person or anything. Just… older. Women were funny like that, though. The stuff they done with make-up and hair and high heels and bras was like magic sometimes. They were rapid though. I could never be a steamer, I'd say. Women were brilliant. Real ones and the ones on telly and the ones in skin mags and blue movies. They were lovely. I'd started thinking pure funny. Like, really upbeat, if that was the right word. It was the drugs. I'd no watch so I didn't know when I took the pill, but it can't have been too long ago. I was all over the place. I'd already thought I came up, earlier. Or was it? I'd no idea. You came up a few times though, in waves. A youngone went past with Fuck Me boots on and I wanted to tell her how lovely she was. I didn't even wanna get off with her. I just loved her, and her shiny brown legs. These pills were rapid. I wanted to find people. Not even people I knew. Strangers would be grand, as long as they were on yokes too. People not on yokes would be no use. It didn't even have to be birds. Lads would be fine too. I loved everyone now. Not in a steamery way, just…

"Hi." Some youngone was in front of me now. She was pure gothy, but not with the white make up. Just stripey tights and all in black, and a corset that sucked her in at the middle and made her chest look big and gorgeous.

"Hello." It was gonna be a long night. In a good way. My face felt a bit warm, and I wanted to smile. My lungs wanted me to take really deep breaths, but not cos I was out of breath or wheezing; just cos breathing felt nice, and the air smelt really good. My muscles felt loose and stiff at the same time, and my toes were tingling and wriggling inside my tackies. I was glad I'd got the choongum off Harta now, cos I didn't even realise how much I was grinding my teeth until I did realise it, and after that, I forgot it again. They were good pills. So far, anyway.

*****

A few hours later, I was coming from one bit of the flat to another when I went past a window and heard voices outside. Outside the window. And we were on the second floor. I must've been imagining it. I was having a great laugh, buzzing around, talking to strangers, and to people I knew. Some of the strangers were people I knew now, that was how it worked. There was nothing like it. I went over to the window and the voices got louder. It was open, I only noticed when I got right up close, cos my eyes were gone wonky from the drugs – I still had the jitters in them – it was weird, but it was good too, cos you knew you'd come up, and you knew you weren't coming down . I climbed out through the window without even checking if I was climbing out into to nothing and just falling down into the street below. My feet touched some ground nearly straight away though, there was a roof out there, and a mad smell of hash. Everyone looked around at me and smiled when I came out. They were smiling, but a bit shocked too. Probably cos when you're off your face, you forget little things, so they probably forgot they were on a roof, and that people could come through the window to join them. I took a quick look around the gang that was there, saluting all of them even though I didn't really know any of them. There was flagons of cider and cans of Carling on the go, but I could tell straight away that everyone out there was buzzing. It was like a radar in your head that finds other people on pills in a party, cos they're the best people to be around. Áine gave me a nod and a big smile when she saw me. I gave her one back. I was already sitting down and lighting a fag when I realised how mad that was. I looked over again to check that it wasn't me hallucinating off the yoke. It wasn't. It was her. She looked different again; different to the night down in Catherine Street when she went missing. If I didn't know better, I'd almost have sworn she was a different girl altogether.

Six

I woke up with a crick in my neck. I must've slept funny. My arm was around the pillow, like I'd been hugging it. It was too early for me to be awake. But, the way the sun was shining through the curtains, it might have been late. I'd no watch, and the alarm clock radio was flashing at me; that meant the power must've gone off in the night. My Da walked past the door.

"Are ye gonna get up or what? Or are ye having a bed-in, like John and Yoko?"

My mouth was pure dry when I tried talking.

"What time is it now, shur?"

"Time for you to get a watch." He said that every time. It still wasn't funny.

"I have a watch. It's just… somewhere."

"That's a great place to keep it. Go on. It's nearly one o' clock."

"One o'clock!?"

"Yes, Jon."

"In the day?"

He done one of his pure dramatic sighs.

"Yes, Jon. In the day." He walked away, muttering something. I shook my head and rubbed my eyes, trying to make the sleepiness go away. Then I remembered all the stuff with Áine; only she wasn't Áine at all – that was the mental bit - she was *Caoimhe*, Áine's big sister. Brillo said there was two of them, back in Termights that night – the Shaughnessy sisters - but I'd forgot that. My teeth and my jaw were sore. Probably from all the choongums and the grinding. I tried thinking back through the night; it was pure fuzzy, but it started coming back. The gig was brilliant – we were really good. Then I met Caoimhe in the street, but I thought she was Áine then. She went away to get a taxi, she said. Me and the lads went to that party, and I took a yoke, and Áine – I mean Caoimhe - was there again, out on the roof. She went to the taxi rank, she said, but they met some other youngones they knew, and them youngones were going to a party, and that party turned out to be the same one I was at.

I ended up shifting her, after talking to her for a bit out on the roof; both of us were off our faces on yokes. And she gave me her phone number, and I gave her mine, I think. By then I knew who she really was. Cos everyone kept calling her Caoimhe, and no one called her Áine. I must have put two and two together. Being on pills and all loved up like an eejit probably took the shock out of it; I couldn't remember exactly. They looked the same. And different as well. That was why I got confused when I saw her, in the crowd, and outside the pub. That was why I thought she was her. Cos it was Áine on my mind all the time. And it was Áine I thought I was looking for in the pub. So it was Áine I thought I found, when I found her. Anyone could've made that mistake, I thought. It was still mental, though. Like something out of a stupid film, although in a stupid film, they'd be twins or something. It was lucky I didn't say something stupid earlier on, before I knew, or the cat would've been out of the bag. Asked her where she'd run off to. Or if I called her Áine. I hadn't though, cos I'd have remembered that. Cos the shit would've hit the fan, as my Da would say. And later on, when we were in one of the bedrooms shifting and smoking and chilling out, she told me all about how her sister was missing, and everyone was looking for her. Said she done it all the time, went missing. She said she'd turn up eventually, even though this time was longer than any of the times she'd gone missing before. She said she wasn't that worried about her, but that might have just been the Es talking. Her friends came in and found her after a while, to take her home before the morning, cos of her parents and stuff, and how they'd be sitting at home, worrying, cos of Áine. It was grand; we weren't doing anything when they came into the room. She was just lying into me, coming down off her yoke, and I was staring into space, thinking how mad everything was.

I got up to find clothes. I'd slept in my jocks, but I didn't remember taking anything off. I didn't remember coming home either, but I must have, cos I was here. Someone gave me another E, out on the roof. Not her; someone belonging to her, or belonging to someone else. It was still all fuzzy. I'd an awful feeling in my chest. Like I was dreading something. I wasn't, though. Except ringing her, maybe. I shifted the sister of the missing girl, and she'd no idea I knew her sister, or that I'd met her that night, and gone away with her, and God knows what else, too. What if me and the Caoimhe one ended up going out with each other? Was I supposed to just lie forever about it? Was it really a lie if no one could ever find out? In the middle of last night, it all seemed pure simple, and not complicated, and easy. It was like the most natural thing in the world, cos we were floating on yokes and everything made sense, and nothing was bad. Now though, in the morning, it felt different. Not like a bad idea exactly, just not the good idea it was the night before. Didn't seem worth the hassle now. I needed some fresh air, and a fag.

Downstairs was quiet, and I robbed a Granny Smith out of the bowl on my way past the kitchen table. I didn't know where I was going yet, but out of the house was a good start. Wasn't too long before I was in town, walking up William Street. I'd money left from last night, somehow. I gave Bríd the money for the first yoke, I remembered that clear. Bríd or Ciara; one of them, definitely. The second one must have been free though. That always happened – people who've yokes on them, for themselves or to sell, take a couple and get loved up and start handing them out for nothing. Bad enough if they're your own stash; but, if you were selling, you'd have got a load on tick from a dealer, and you'd have to bring him the money after you'd sold them. So, if you'd been handing them out for free like a hippy all night, you were screwed. Dealers who gave out bags of Es on tick weren't usually nice people, and you couldn't avoid them, either. They'd always catch up with you, sooner or later. "Don't get high on your own supply", Harta always said. He did, though; he was an awful man for it. He'd never been in proper trouble for it though. He'd more lives than a cat, that fella. His luck might run out some day, though. Everyone's did, eventually.

I ended up in Catherine Street later. Just walking and thinking, and not noticing where I was going. The brick arch in front of me gave me the chills. I didn't know why. Nothing bad happened there – it was just that it reminded me of her now, and she was still missing. Down the alley I could see big bins and stuff, and a few cars. There was another way to get in, over on Roche's Street. We'd gone in this way, though. I couldn't remember what way we came out. I was shivering a little bit, even though it was warm. I thought about walking down. Cos maybe it was like in films, where yer man would go back to the scene of the crime and he'd get these mad flashbacks. Like that film Manhunter, where yer man could see into the brain of the killer, and look at stuff through his eyes, if he just went to where the guy killed the families. It was too bright out and I was too sober to walk down there now; someone from an office or a flat might shout down to me and ask me what I was doing. And anyway, it wasn't a crime scene. She was just missing.

I felt a thump in my chest. If I was still seeing Caoimhe when Áine came back, Áine'd tell her everything – she'd tell her we shifted, that I was the last one who saw her before she ran away, all that stuff. The second she found out about us, or saw me with her sister somewhere. That was a big problem. I needed to tell yer one Caoimhe first. Had to be done, if I wanted to keep seeing her. It was that, or just ignore her and not call her or see her again at all. Forget it ever happened. I could do that. She was just a bird, like. I was around the corner on Roche's Street, thinking over how I was gonna manage telling her, when I saw him. Shane Collopy, from down our place, coming out of the other way in to the alley. What was he doing there? Weird. I stood into a doorway for a second, so I could see him, but he couldn't see me. He walked down the road and turned down onto O'Connell Street, then he was gone.

I thought about going back to the alley, to see what he'd been up to, but there was no point, really. He'd probably been just having a piss. I walked out over the bridge after a bit, trying to figure out how I was gonna tell Caoimhe about Áine - or what I was gonna tell her about Áine. I didn't even know myself what there was to tell. I couldn't leave it too long, though, I didn't know when the other one was gonna show up. I had to ring her anyway though, cos she'd gave me her number, and it was usually you that rang the girl, not the girl that rang you, if you wanted to see her again. I did wanna see her again, but it was complicated now. I'd be better off just leaving it. Cos either Áine was gonna come back and I was gonna get in a shit load of trouble I didn't want, or she was never gonna come back, and I'd have to keep a big secret from someone. Probably better to just forget about it. She was only a girl, even if she was a ride. Plenty of more fish in the sea.

I was half way through eating a rake of toast a few days later when the phone rang and my Da said it was for me. First thing I thought was it was gonna be Caoimhe. I still hadn't rang her. And Áine was still missing, too. The Gards were still asking people to come forward with any information, but it wasn't the first thing on the news anymore, if they even bothered mentioning it. Which was mad, I thought, cos she was still out there, somewhere. It was like people stopped caring after a while. After it wasn't news no more. I was only thinking about Caoimhe a few minutes before though, and people always rang you when you were thinking about ringing them. It wasn't her, though.

"How'rya? It's Tim."

"How's it going, man?"

"Grand. Listen, can ye practice today?"

"Ah, yeah. What time?"

"Fourish." That was ages away yet. It was only two now, about.

"Four, so. At Richie's, yeah?"

"No, at mine today…"

"Yours? What's going on, like? Shur isn't Richie's drums over at his?" We hadn't done a practice in Tim's for yonks. Not since we got Richie.

"Nah. His Dad dropped him off here a few minutes ago. They're having something done to the shed, so they've to move everything out. Painting it, he said. Richie didn't want to put the drums back up in the attic again, so he asked me if he could leave them here, and the amps too."

"Is my amp at yours too?"

"Yep. And your mic. All present and correct, like. Safe and sound, says you."

Felt weird they were moving my stuff around without me being there. Or without asking me.

"So…"

"So, well I said if we've all the gear here, and Richie's here, we might as well have a jam or something, yeah?" I rolled my eyes at him saying 'jam' like that, but he couldn't see me over the phone.

"Er, right so, sound. I'll see you in a couple of hours then, I suppose."

"Grand. See you then. Ciao." He hung up. Lads weren't like women on the phone. We just said what we needed to and put it down. My Ma could sit on the stairs for hours nattering about nothing, usually to someone she'd only talked to the day before. Clodagh was the same. They were like a different species.

It was a pain in the arse that they'd moved all the stuff over to Caherdavin, but there was plenty of time to walk it. Bit of a practice would be good, anyway. Or a jam, as Tim would say. The more we got in before the Battle of the Bands, the better we'd be, and I was starting to think we might do good in it. We wouldn't win, but we might do all right. I'd a good feeling about it. I wasn't looking forward to going to Tim's. His Ma looked at me like I was something the cat dragged in sometimes. Still, Richie'd be the new one today, so she might save her dirty looks for him. Especially since he was from down our place too. Snobby, she was, probably. It wasn't even that you *had* to meet her - we went around the back, not through the front door. She'd always come out though, in the middle of the practice, to say hello. Really though, she was checking that her poor little innocent Timmy wasn't getting corrupted by the rest of us – with our drinking and smoking and drugs, and all the other things she just assumed we did. I mean, we did do them, fair play, but still. Pure snobby.

Walking up past the shops by the Gaelic Grounds I heard someone whistling. Not a tune, a scobey whistle, to get your attention. I squinted over through the sun and saw two youngfellas. Pair of heads, from the clothes they'd on. Not from around there. The bigger one whistled again - definitely at me now. They saw me seeing them, so I couldn't pretend I didn't and just walk on; I had to go over. I put my hands into fists, just in case. Didn't matter that it was broad daylight, or that it was in a nice place like Ashbrook. People from nice places were even more bound to walk past and do nothing if you were getting a beating. They'd think it was none of their business.

"C'meeriwantcha a second," said the bigger fella. The younger fella had hair like an afro, even though he was white. Everyone was white in Limerick. Except the lads who owned the Chineses. The bigger fella was a bit fat, with a round face; looked like he was gonna be much fatter when he was older. I squinted again, it was hard to see in the sun, but I thought I might know them. I was sizing them up; I could've beat up either of them on their own, but together would be a different story. And anyway, one of them might have a blade. When I got over the road I recognised them. It was the Gollies. Seán and the other one – the one who actually looked like a golly. Seán didn't look like a golly at all, but they were brothers, so. I didn't know much about them, except their Ma read the Tarot cards for people who came to the house, and all the kids were supposed to have nits. Especially the curly fella, cos my Ma said it was harder to get nits out of curly hair with the fine comb.

When we were younger and people were working out who could beat who in a fight (like, if you could beat Liam Griffin and he'd already beat Alan Powell, then you could beat Alan Powell; there was no need to fight him to find out) no one could place either of the Gollies, cos they never fought anyone on their own. One of them always backed in for the other, like a tag team. And, if that happened, you were allowed to have one of your friends back in for you, that was only fair, so then it was two on two, and no one really knew who'd beat who when it was over, so you couldn't tell. And they'd always get beat anyway, cos Seán was a year older than Golly, but if he was fighting someone his own age, their friend who backed in would be that age too, so it'd be an unfair fight.

"Well, man." Seán looked at me like he kind of knew me, but he didn't as well. He probably didn't cop on cos we were on the Ennis Road, so he wouldn't be expecting to meet someone from our place. Golly didn't say nothing, he just stood there with a little sneer on him.

"Well," I said, looking at neither of them, but keeping the head up, so I didn't look frightened or anything. My uncle Frank taught me that one. It didn't feel like they were gonna jump me. Not so far, anyway. I kept my hands in fists anyway. I'd go for Seán first, try and knock him over with a punch. Always go for the big guy first, and the others will shit themselves. Frank taught me that one too.

"Have you a spare fag for a joint, sham?"

"Ah, yeah. Yeah, no probs. Hang on there a minute. I'll just…" I was talking too much. Sounded nervous. You couldn't sound nervous around scobes. They'd think you were afraid, or weak. And, even if they weren't thinking about jumping you in the first place, they might change their minds.

"Sound, man. Here, I know you, do I?"

I looked at him while still fiddling in my pockets for the fags like an eejit.

"Ah, yeah. Sort of." I got the box out, finally.

"You live in Thomondgate, don't you? Crossroads?" He was nearly smiling. That was good.

"Yeah, well, sort of, more up near Feehan's shop." We weren't Crossroads, but we'd the same red brick houses and they were built the same time, so it was all the one. We definitely weren't Kileely.

"Right, yeah. Cosgrove, isn't it? Jon Cosgrove?"

"Musgrave. Jon though, yeah." My voice sounded pure posh to me; probably cos I was on my way to Tim's, getting ready for his Ma. Or it was all in my head.

"Musgrave, that's it, yeah. Clodagh Halligan's your cousin, isn't it?"

"Yep. I lives next door to her, sham." That time my voice went so Limerick I sounded like one of the fellas who ride around on the horse and cart selling coal. I'd overdone it.

"Ah yeah, sound. Lovely girl, Clodagh. Sound out." He said *sound*, but the look on his face told me he meant she was a ride. I was used to people thinking that, though. She was, but I didn't think so, cos that'd be rank.

"Yeah, she's a gas woman all right." Clodagh being my cousin got me out of a fair few fights and beatings over the years, fair play. She knew all the heads in town, and they all must've liked her, cos I only needed to mention her name and I was safe.

"Yeah. Yeah… lovely girl, like." He'd the look in his eye there again, like he was thinking about riding her. I gave over the fags before he said anything more about her.

"One or two do you want?" I said. The other fella still hadn't said a word. He was like one of them little sidekicks the school bullies have in comics.

"Shur one'll do. But we'll take two maybe, just to be sure." Typical knacker, chancing the arm. I didn't care, I'd to go in a minute.

"Help yourself, man."

"Sound. Stay for a smoke?" *Shite, anyway.* I didn't have time for one. I'd to get to the practice. It was bad form to turn one down, though. I knew that from when I'd go getting gear up in Weston with Harta. If you bought a ten spot or an eighth and the dealer said will we have a smoke off it, you sat down and had a smoke off it. The worst thing you could do was say no, or say you'd somewhere to be. I learned all that off Harta. He was an expert in not getting killed in Weston by now. I wondered what to say, and then the little fella gave Seán a nudge in the arm.

"What's wrong with you? I can offer the man a toke, it's my fucking gear," Séan said. The younger Golly's face was all red, and he looked like he was gonna cry. His brother looked at me, and I remembered I was supposed to be answering him.

"Ah, I don't wanna start a fight, lads."

"Pffft, you're grand, sham. Wouldn't be much of a fight anyway. I'd pan this little faggot out with one dig, wouldn't I? C'mon, I'm not taking no for an answer boss, step into my office."

Now I couldn't say no. There was still plenty of time until four though. It'd be fine. We walked across the road, to behind the shops and the little AIB. There was never no one around back there, just deliveries in the morning, and people taking rubbish out after the day was over.

We were still smoking about an hour later. It flew by. The stuff they were skinning up with was pure strong, I was high as a kite.

"The hell is this again?" I held the joint in front of me and squinted at it. My eyes were watery from all the smoke, probably bloodshot too. I was wrecked.

"It's pure bud."

I didn't understand.

"Yeah? It's pure… what?"

"Bud."

"Yeah?" My brain was all jumbled. Nothing was making sense.

"Yeah, shur." He looked weird. The roots of my hair were all hot and my face felt melty. He passed the joint over to Golly, but I couldn't look at him with his high forehead and his curly mop full of nits and lice cos I didn't wanna be thinking about them walking around on his scalp and spitting out little eggs. I itched my own hair, thinking about it, then I stopped, in case they figured out what I was up to. No one was saying anything, and the quiet felt really long, and sort of loud, even though there wasn't any sound. I wanted someone to say something, but I didn't want it to be me. It wasn't – it was Seán.

"Pure bud." He was on this again.

"Huh?"

"The thing you're smoking, sham. It's not hash."

I got mad jolt in my heart, and my guts felt watery. What was he after letting me smoke? Heroin or something? Crack? I was screwed. This was pure illegal. Hash was illegal too, but you could go to jail for-

"It's bud, sham. Weed. It's the plants, the flowers, the leaves, the bud, bud."

I tried to make the words into something I could understand, but it was too confusing. My ears were ringing a bit. I kept hearing church bells far away, but they were happening too much to be real ones. Real ones only happened every quarter of an hour, I thought.

"What?"

"The joint, man. It's pure bud, not hash."

"But is it still… cannabis?" The little gap there, when I was trying to think of the right word, felt like it was two hours long. I wasn't even sure if it was the right word. The more I thought about it in my head, the less it sounded even like a real word anymore. I just said it anyway, to stop the quiet.

"Hahaha, listen to him, Gol. You're mad out, all the same, sham."

I nodded at him and tried to do a smile. I wasn't sure what I'd said wrong. I didn't know if I was in trouble now or not. I didn't know anything. Golly laughed too, but he didn't say anything. He passed me over the joint, but I didn't want it. I couldn't say no though, or they'd laugh at me again. Normally I wouldn't give a shit, but I was getting a bit paranoid, so I did. I never got like this after a smoke. Now I knew how Richie felt. I wasn't having a whitener, though. It was just… strong. I stopped thinking the word 'whitener' in case thinking about whiteners gave you a whitener. I didn't know why it would but it felt like it could and Jesus, I was wrecked.

"What about yer one anyway?" said Séan. I knew straight away who he meant.

"Which one?" It might have been someone else, not her. The bells were going again, nearer this time. I couldn't make out the tune they were playing. Something we used to sing in school or mass when we were small.

"The youngone gone missing. One from Castletroy. Mad, like. Disappeared off the face of the Earth, like."

"Uh, yeah. Mad stuff." This was the last conversation I wanted to be having, but I couldn't tell them that. I couldn't tell them anything, in case they -

"Saturday night, warn't it?" He passed Golly the joint. It was all brown looking near the top. The smell off it was something else.

"Hah? Yeah, sorry. She was out in town. Never came home." It was freaky talking to them about it, but I guessed everyone must be talking about it now. There wasn't much else going on. They didn't know she was my – that I – I stopped thinking, cos it was getting too hard to. And cos I thought if I thought my secrets too loud, they might be able to hear them. The bells were there again.

"Yeah, yeah. We were out that night, weren't we Gol?" He looked at his brother, and the brother gave a nod. He'd a mad load of freckles – if you got far away from him enough, it looked like a tan. I looked a bit closer at him, and it looked like they were moving around his face, so I looked away quickly again. The bells were doing a Christmas song, even though it was August. I didn't know which one.

"Yeah?" I didn't tell him I was out too. Not that it'd matter. Everyone was out on a Saturday night. There was nothing weird about that.

"Yeah, no. I mean like, we were round the place."

"What place?" He'd lost me now, but it might have just been the weed. I was thinking fuzzy.

"Well, they said in the paper the last time anyone saw her was in… Catherine Street, like. Some fella said he clocked her going down there after two in the morning, remember? From the clothes they said she was wearing. Said it was definitely her like, he thought."

"Oh right, yeah." That was all news to me. I hadn't really looked at the paper in a few days. I was afraid to, for some reason. It was like… it was like I thought if I read too much about it, I'd remember something I didn't wanna remember. That thought'd just come to me now though, cos of being stoned. I didn't know it before. Weed was like that, sometimes. It opened your mind, Harta said. I felt funny, and not in a good way. The song was 'O Come All Ye Faithful'. I smiled when I figured it out, then I stopped straight away, in case someone saw me.

"Yeah, well me and Gol were up near there, in a house party, like. We didn't even go up til after one, so we might have seen her ourselves, if we were looking out the right window or something, d'you know what I mean, sham?"

"Yeah…" I didn't.

O come all ye faithful

"Shane coulda seen her, like," said Golly. The real Golly. First time he'd said a word since I met them. My blood went cold when I heard that name. I tried to keep it together. I wanted to ask him something, but Séan got in there first.

"What you mean, like?"

"Shane Collopy." His voice was nothing like I thought it was gonna be, before I heard him. He looked like he'd have a squeaky little voice. But it was pure deep.

Joyful and triumphant

"Yeah, what about him, like? You know Shane don't you, man? From Canon Breen? Big scar on his mouth?" said Séan, to me.

I nodded. I wanted to see where this was going. Or maybe I didn't. Second time in one day, he'd come up. Something weird was going on.

"Yeah, well, 'member we were there at the party, like?" I looked at Golly again, with his big deep voice, but I looked away before I saw anything moving on him. I could hear my heart inside my ears, pure loud.

"Yeah…" Séan looked like he didn't know where this was going at all. He'd a strange smell off him too – half BO, half feet.

Come ye, o come ye, to Be-eth-le-hem

"Well, he *disappeared*, like. He was there when we came in, and then everyone was looking for him, cos he'd the yokes. Remember? He'd a bag of 'em. People wanted to tap a few off him, cos it was late then."

"Right…" said Séan. He looked like he was hearing all this for the first time, same as me. I felt like I was gonna burst from not knowing what was coming. I got pure para again, in case they'd realise or notice, but I didn't even know what I was feeling, so they couldn't have, I didn't think.

"So, yeah, bout half four, everyone's raging there's no yokes left, and they've their money and everything, like – not trying to scab one off him, or get one on tick."

Come and behold him

"Hang on now a second. Where was I?" Seán was licking his lips, and looking at him doing it made me lick mine. Then I stopped, in case -

Born the king of he-e-avan

"You were upstairs getting your hole, you gowl."

"Oh. Oh yeah, fair enough." Séan's smile was so big it nearly made me smile too, but I wanted to hear what happened with Shane. I'd the worst feeling ever now. Something bad was coming. I didn't know what it was, but it was too much of like, a coincidence. Why was he down that alley today? What was going on? There was a reason Golly was telling us this. I was sure of it. And I wanted the bells to stop for a second, so I could think.

O come let us adore him!

"So, yeah, about half four, sham, in walks Shane. And we're all hanging like, climbing the walls, getting ready for the comedown. No pills left. No nothing left, only a bit of hash. Looking at the curtains, like you do, sham, thinking about the light coming through them in a bit and bringing everyone's buzz down. You know what it's like, like. So, he comes in, and everyone's all:

"Where the fuck've you been, man?"

O come let us adore him!

"And what did he say?" said Séan. He'd different hair to Golly – pure straight. You wouldn't know they were -

O come let us adore hi-im

"He didn't say nothing."

Chri-ist the lord!

"What?" I said. That couldn't be it, surely. The noise of the bells stopped. Like someone'd put their fingers into my ears, or shoved my head under some water. I'd to remind myself to take a breath.

"Naw. He just… people were fucking hopping, wanting pills off him, but he didn't even talk to them, sham. He just took the bag of yokes out of his pocket and threw it on the counter."

"What, he just gave 'em away, like? Didn't ask for no money?" said Séan, finishing the end of the butt. I didn't want any more of it. I was done.

"Ah, no. It's Shane Collopy, like, man. People just put the money in the bag for him after he went away. They know better, like, than to be trying to burn him."

Séan nodded, and so did I, but I think I just nodded cos he did.

"Where did he go to?" Séan said. My head was pounding from thinking now, and I didn't even know what I was thinking. There was something wrong though – something wrong – something not right - with that Shane fella, and it'd something to do with what happened to Áine. It had to. There's no way it didn't. It was too much of a –I felt like I was swaying, and I was gonna fall over. He was in Catherine Street. He was at the alley. It wasn't a coincidence at all.

"He just went upstairs and panned out in one of the bedrooms. One next to you. I didn't see him again, really."

"Jesus, Gol. The things I misses when I'm off riding, hah?" He was laughing. He thought the whole thing was funny. I didn't think it was funny at all. My brain was gonna explode with all this new stuff in it.

"I know, like. What you think, though? Do you think he *kidnapped* her, like?" said Golly. I wasn't sure if he was messing or not, but I looked at Séan like he'd all the answers. He *had* kidnapped her. It was all pure clear now. But why would he do that?

"Well, I doubt it, like."

"Why?" said Golly. I wanted to know too. I sparked up a normal fag. I'd nearly forgot that I smoked.

"Well, did he have her with him when he came back to the flat like?"

"Oh. Naw." Golly went red and looked at his shoes.

"Exactly, you spastic. He was on his own. Where was he hiding her? Up his jumper? Don't be telling me any more stories, will you? Wrecking my head and I trying to enjoy an auld smoke."

He laughed, and Golly joined in, and I forced myself to smile with them. Séan was right. Even if Shane did go off, he came back on his own. – she was missing; she wasn't dead. It was still weird, me seeing him there, then running into those two, and hearing that story. But it didn't mean nothing, really. I was just stoned and paranoid. I was putting two and two together and getting five. Shane didn't take her. Then I'd an idea.

"Here, that flat ye were in?"

"Yeah, bud?" Séan answered me.

"On Catherine Street?"

"Yep. Well, sort of."

"Sort of?"

"Well the flat looks out onto Catherine Street, like. But when you've to come into it, the door is kind of on Roche's Street, see?"

"Kind of?" I knew what was coming.

"Yeah, you've to go down a little alley to get in."

I could hear the lads already when I turned into Tim's road. They were playing *When I Come Around*, by Green Day. I'd walked around in circles a bit before I found the right street name. I must have been still a bit wrecked, even though Golly's story shocked me out of it for a bit. I couldn't hear the bells anymore, at least. I was nearly normal, I thought. Until I walked through the door of the shed, and they saw me, and no one stopped playing, and no one looked at me. Then the para came back full, and suddenly I was gasping for something to drink. They were already half way through the song. Maybe three quarters. Waiting for them to finish it felt way longer than that, though. There was still no one looking at me. I didn't know what to do. I didn't wanna look at them now. I'd nothing to do with my hands either. The song wouldn't stop. It just kept going. I felt so weird. I'd to get out of there. I turned around and walked back out again, feeling in my pocket for my fags. I was really thirsty now. The second I got out the door the music stopped; not cos it was the end, it just stopped like they'd stopped on purpose. Richie was the last to notice, so I could still hear him for a couple of seconds, playing on his own. It sounded pure odd. Then someone said something into the mic.

"Oi!" It was Ian. I turned around, popping a fag into my mouth and lighting it. I looked at him like to say "What?"

"Nice of you to join us, like." He sounded a bit angry. I didn't know why. I didn't answer him. I wanted to, but the words felt all jumbled up in my head.

"Where were you?"

Again, I wanted to say something, but it was like my brain was telling me not to; that if I said anything it would come out like gobbledegook, and they'd *know*. They'd know what, though? My brain wasn't talking sense.

"Ah, I got held up," I said, finally.

"For an hour and a half?" It was Tim talking this time. He couldn't be right. It couldn't be half five already. I wasn't with the Gollies that long. But maybe I was. I'd no watch, and neither did either of them – I asked them a few times.

"Ah, yeah. Sorry, like." I turned the palms of my hands over and done a face. I didn't know what his problem was; they were still well able to practice without me. I was just the singer. They were the ones playing all the music. They didn't need me to hold their hands for them. I wanted to say all that to him, but I didn't wanna start an argument. Ian looked like he was raging, though.

"Yeah, well I've to fucking go at six, so." His eyes were bulging. He must've been waiting ages to have this go at me, and he was having it now. I seriously wondered if he was gonna trying and have a scrap with me in a second. I'd have battered him, like, but still. What was his problem?

"Oh. I didn't know that, like, sorry. I just… I met a few lads. I…" I didn't know why I'd to explain myself to him. But I did, sort of. And anyway, it wasn't just him I kept waiting, it was the rest of the lads too, even if they weren't getting their knickers in a twist at me. I couldn't believe how long I'd been behind that shop. It was mental. *Time flies*.

"A few lads? Here, are you drunk or something?" He was starting to piss me off now. He didn't wanna start pushing my buttons.

"What? No. Who are you, my Da?" I stood up as tall as I could, sort of to remind him he shouldn't be starting something with me.

"For God's sake, lads, let's just get on with it, yeah? Forget about it. He said sorry, Ian. Just leave it, like. We haven't enough time before you – before you've to head off," said Richie; he'd come out to us from inside the shed. Tim was still standing behind his keyboard, looking down at his feet. Niall was sitting on his amp inside, tuning his base with the sound down, or probably just pretending to, cos he didn't wanna get involved.

“Yeah, and whose fucking fault is that, like?” Ian said, but he said it walking away, like a chickenshit. If he’d said it into my face, and maybe gave me a little shove, I’d have probably knocked him out. So, it was good that he didn’t. I went inside to my mic. The tension was horrible, and so was the rest of the practice.

Ian went away at six without so much as looking at me. The whole thing was a disaster. I was sitting around the corner from the shed after, having a fag. The others were packing up inside. I was thinking about Shane Collopy, and if he’d anything to do with Áine going missing. I knew he didn’t, though. If there were cops from a TV show investigating the case, there was more evidence for *me* having done it than him, in fairness. Except I knew I hadn’t done anything. He hadn’t either though. He was just coming out of that flat when I saw him. Probably dropping off drugs. Or picking some up. He was dodgy, but he wasn’t some sort of kidnapper. That was ridiculous. Áine was probably okay. And, if she wasn’t, it wasn’t someone our age who done anything to her. People our age didn’t kidnap people, or murder them. Not like that, anyway. You heard of youngfellas in Southill or Moyross stabbing each other, but that was gangs; lads jumping other lads. They weren’t real murderers. Richie came over after a while and asked was I walking out home, so I walked out with him. He didn’t say much on the way. He was very quiet sometimes.

Seven

A couple of weeks later, Áine still hadn't come home. I was just coming in the door from an early practice at Richie's, and I heard the Ma on the phone, doing her posh voice, like she done when she was phoning my school.

"Actually, no - would you believe it, he's just walked in the door now."

I looked at her like to say "Who is it?" and she mouthed something I couldn't make out. I shrugged at her and made a face.

"Hang on there now, Caoimhe. I'll hand you over to him." She looked at me like the cat that got the cream. I panicked a little. There wasn't time to tell her to say I wasn't there. *Shite, anyway.*

"Hello?"

"Hi, Jon."

"Hey." I was trying to come up with the story on the spot. It was so long since I decided I wasn't gonna call her, I'd forgot anything I was planning to say if she rang me.

"How are you?"

"I'm... I'm grand." I wanted to ask her the same back, but I didn't know what she'd say. Her sister was missing. I hadn't called her after shifting her. Whatever she answered, it wasn't gonna be good.

"So… you never rang."

I said the first thing that came into my head.

"Yeah. Yeah, I'm sorry. I lost your number." It was nearly true. I threw it away about a week ago, so I wouldn't change my mind. It was all too much hassle. I was either gonna be seeing her, and her sister would show up and make me look like a bastard and a liar, or Áine would never turn up, and I'd have a new girlfriend that was sad all the time, and needed help, and I just didn't know her long enough for that. That was what I decided, even if it was selfish.

"You did?" She sounded okay about it. She didn't sound like she thought I was lying anyway.

"Ah, yeah. Must've come out of my jeans or something. After the- " I looked around to see if the Ma was hovering around, listening. She was gone. "After the party, like."

"Ah. I did wonder, but… I dunno."

"You dunno what?" I felt like shit now. I'd forgot how nice her voice was, too. I didn't know her long enough to say I missed it, but it was good to hear it again.

"I just thought maybe you didn't like me?"

"Ah no, I did. I do." I wasn't planning on saying that, but I was picturing her now, and remembering how nice looking she was. I hadn't shifted no one since her. I didn't think that was on purpose, but…

"Hah! Okay, well that's good. Listen, do you want to go for a coffee?"

"Okay, yeah. Yeah, when, today?"

I'd decided not to call her back, cos if she wasn't around, I wouldn't be thinking about the Áine thing all the time. I was getting good at not thinking about it. It was nearly like it'd never happened. Not her going missing; me meeting her. Being the last to see her, and all that stuff. It was driving me mad before. And all them crazy ideas I had about Shane Collopy too, even though they were just bollocks. I'd actually run into him a good few times since, pure randomly, like, and I didn't get the bad feeling from it anymore. I was free of all that now; better off. But I still said yes to meeting her, for some reason. I think it was just cos she was nice to me when I was expecting her to give out to me. I hoped I wasn't making a mistake.

*****

I ran into Harta, later on, after I walked Caoimhe up to her bus home. He was in Cruise's Street, scooping up all the coins off his guitar case, after busking. It looked like he'd done all right. He'd flat cap on, with a peak. He looked like a train driver out of a cartoon.

"Ah, just the man," he said, filling up his pockets with the change.

"The man for what?"

"Quick pint? Up in The Still House, or Tom Collins's?"

"Ah, no. I've been drinking all day, like." I could've drunk more, but I'd have to go home at some point, and I couldn't be falling in the door.

"A smoke?"

"Where?" A smoke would be grand.

"Marie's?"

"Yeah? Sound."

Marie was this mad one with straggly hair – I couldn't say what age she was at all, but she owned a house, so she must've been old. Harta crashed there sometimes, and my Uncle Frank had a room there too, when he wasn't down in Cork. Harta called it a home for waifs and strays. She didn't charge a full rent or nothing; Frank said you could pay her in hash, or by cleaning the place, or cooking dinner. She was sound like that, he said.

When we got there, it was him that opened the door, not her.

"Aboy the head, Jon. Well, Dom?" He'd a smell of gear off him, and his eyes were a bit bloodshot.

"All right, Frank?" I said, following Harta in the hall. We went into the sitting room. It was full of smoke, no sign of Marie. There was music on the stereo. I kind of recognised it.

"Who's that?"

"That's The Dead, man," said Frank. We sat on some bean bags that were on the floor. There was no three-piece suite – Marie was a pure hippy.

"Bit of Jerry and the lads, like," said Harta. I'd no idea what he meant.

"Ah, okay." I squished down into my bean bag and leaned back.

"Here, listen," said Harta, rooting through a pile of CDs next to the speaker. "C'mere and I tell you – I was thinking the other day, when yer man was playing the organ, like."

"Playing with his organ, was he?" said Frank. He was doing up a massive doobie. Probably seven skins in it.

"Haha. You know what's worse than having lobsters on your piano?" Harta said, picking up the album he'd been looking for.

"What's that?" I said.

"Having crabs on your organ," said Frank. I didn't get it, and then I did.

"Chalk it down. Listen, Jon: D'you like the doors?"

"The doors?" I looked over at the sitting room door. There was nothing special about it.

"No, the band, you spa. Jim Morrison, and all that," said Harta. Frank nodded and finished up licking the joint closed.

"Ah, no, I – I don't think I've heard any of them." I hated when Harta asked me about music, cos he was into all weird old bands, and I never knew them.

"Ah, you must know The Doors, Jon. *Light My Fire*? *Riders on the Storm*? *Break on Through*? Jaysus, have I taught ye nothing, boy?" said Frank. He'd a Cork accent, cos he'd lived in Fermoy for years, even though he was from here.

"Ah… maybe. I dunno. Stick 'em on and I'll see, shur."

*****

The fag on the way into town tasted pure weird, cos I'd brushed my teeth three times and used mouthwash. It was mad how much you cared about your breath when you were sober, when most of the shifts you had you'd be drunk, your mouth was stinking of beer, fags, and sometimes sick. I was just assuming we were gonna shift, but we probably were. Why else would she be ringing me and asking her to meet her? Unless she knew something about – nah, she couldn't. I looked up at Penney's clock while I was crossing over to Todd's. Ten minutes early. I could have another fag as long as I'd a choongum after.

She looked gorgeous, even if she was ten minutes late. She wasn't done up like for a nightclub, but she was way too good looking for a pot of tea in Bewley's.

"Hey. Sorry I'm late. Bus was late."

"Hi. Nah, you're grand." I gave her a quick hug and a kiss on the cheek.

"Where are we going then?"

"Quin's." Frank always said women liked it if you made decisions about what ye were doing, and he was right about most stuff.

"Do Quin's do coffee, or are you trying to get me drunk?" She winked when she said it.

"We'll see. Come on." I touched the back of her elbow and pointed her the right way. She'd really classy clothes on. A summer dress with polka dots on in, and a high collar. No fake tan, no tits hanging out, no skirt up her arse. But you could still see she'd a rapid body. Posh ones always dressed like that. Leave something to the imagination, as my Ma would say. It was better anyway. When you were going with some girl who dressed like a slag, you were always getting into scraps with fellas trying to come on to them in front of you, or the fellas started fights with you cos they thought they could rob the girl off you. Wasn't worth it.

We got the stage thing for ourselves, cos it was the daytime, and it wasn't the weekend. She'd a tea, I'd a coffee with fresh cream on the top. I liked coffee like that. The coffee my Da drunk at home was rank, and we'd only milk usually. Tony was behind the bar. He gave me that look you give someone if they're with a ride, when he took the money off me. She *was* a ride, too. No beer goggles now. No yokes, loving me up.

We hadn't said nothing about Áine on the way down. That was weird, and I wondered was it cos I didn't bring it up. Or maybe she was glad I didn't bring it up, cos it must have been all anyone talked to her about now. I was definitely glad she wasn't bringing it up. She was sitting across from me, instead of beside me. I always done that when there was a table and chairs. If there was a bench or a couch, you could sit next to each other.

"How's your band going, anyway?" She took a load of sugar in her tea.

"Good! Getting much better, like. Doing the Battle of the Bands next week." Felt like it'd come around really quick, but we'd been practicing loads, and we were sounding rapid now. All of us.

"Oh, yeah! I remember you saying. Got a name yet?"

"Yeah..." We couldn't agree on one, so we all put a name in a bag, and got Ciara to pick one out. Tim's one won it.

"Ooh. What is it?"

"Er, *Crane…*" I still wasn't used to it.

"Crane? Like, Frasier Crane?"

"Hah, yeah." Everyone kept saying that.

"Why that name, then? I mean, it's cool. But why Crane?"

"Am, Tim picked it. The keyboards guy. It's to do with someone in a film." I'd listened to him explaining, but I wasn't really paying attention. I just thought it sounded okay, and it didn't sound stupid. You couldn't go far wrong with one-word names. Oasis, Pulp, Nirvana, Metallica.

"Oh, like Marion Crane? In *Psycho*?"

"Yeah, actually. That's who he said. Tim, like." I'd never seen it. It was in black and white, it must've been ancient. Old horror movies weren't scary at all, you just laughed at them.

"That's cool. She's like, the original *MacGuffin*." She was just stirring the tea, I hadn't seen her drink a drop. I was waiting for the cream to cool down the coffee, then I'd probably drink it all in one go, like I always did.

"The what?"

"You know, the MacGuffin. Like, in a film, where there's a mystery and stuff – or well, any film. Sometimes there's like this thing, or this person – like a plot device - to distract you, so you're on the wrong track, and…"

"Yeah?" No idea what she was going on about. She was clever for a girl, though. Really clever for a ride. They were all clever up in Laurel Hill, though. They done all their subjects and their exams in Irish. Except English, probably. They were all rides too, as well. Most of them.

"Yeah, so in *Psycho*, Janet Leigh plays Marion Crane. And, when people went to see it in the cinema, they thought she'd be the main character – cos she was really famous, right?"

"Yeah. Yeah, she was." I'd never heard of her in my life.

"But, it starts off with her stealing money - $40,000, so you're like "Oh, she's a baddie". Actually, the money is the first MacGuffin, if you think about it. They both are, cos people are looking for them both, and that's what kind of drives the story along? Anyway, then she's driving off somewhere, and you don't know if she's going to get caught, and she runs into her boss at the traffic lights – and he's the one she stole from, right? So, you're thinking "Oh my God, she's nabbed!". But she gets away. And then, of course, Norman does her in, in the shower. And that's only about a half an hour into the film, isn't it? So, you were sort of fooled into thinking she was the important thing. Cos her name was on the poster and stuff."

"Yeah?" I understood like ten per cent of what she'd just said.

"Yeah, have you not seen *Psycho*, Jon?"

“Ah, I might have. I can’t remember.” I didn’t wanna look stupid in front of her.

“Jesus, Jon. It’s a classic. You should see it. I have it on video. Come watch it with me sometime.”

“Haha, okay, yeah.” That was an invitation. I felt good until I remembered who she was, and who her sister was, and all the other things I’d forgot about.

“I’ll hold you to that. Want a drink?”

“What? I have one.” The cream was melted in now, so I took a sup. It was just right, so I gulped more of it down.

“A real drink, I meant.” There was a bit of a crazy look in her eye. It reminded me of someone else; couldn’t think who.

“Ah, I’m a bit broke – I thought we were just going for coffee, you know?” I felt my cheeks get a bit red.

“Pfft. Don’t worry about that. Shur I’m loaded, these days. Perks of the job when your sister’s the missing girl in the news. Mum and Dad constantly throwing money at me, like it’s going to make things better. What do you want?” That was the first time she’d mentioned it, and I didn’t even have a chance to say anything back now. That was who she’d reminded me of – Áine. I realised it when she was talking now. I shivered a little, but it wasn’t cold in there.

“Are you sure?” I felt lousy, letting a girl pay for my drinks. I could get her back another time, though. It felt like there was gonna be a next time. She was sound out, as well as being a ride.

"I am, but if you don't hurry up and tell me what you're drinking, I might change my mind. I'm a complicated woman, Jon. You'll find that out, soon enough." Sounded like she thought there was gonna be a next time too.

"Okay. Hudson Blue."

"I'm sorry?"

"Hudson Blue. Cider. Pint of it. Ask Tony at the bar, he'll know. Er, *please*. Thanks."

"Hudson Blue, coming up. Here, help yourself." She slid a box of fags and lighter across the table to me. Her fingernails didn't have polish on them, but they were still shiny.

*****

The Doors were class, all the same. Harta was right, we could easily do a few of them songs, if we learned them quick enough – the keyboards would sound rapid altogether.

"See Jon, this one – I mean, everyone knows it – everyone knows *Light My Fire.* But, imagine that sound, at the battle of the bands. That'd fill the place up, like. And no one'd be slagging ye for having keyboards then, sham. They'd be nearly jealous of ye for it. What you think?"

"Yeah. Yeah, I know what you mean. I like the other one too, though."

"Which one, *Riders on the Storm*?"

"Yeah. Class, that is."

"It is, yeah, but *Light My Fire* is the one that'd blow them away, like. It's pure upbeat, and have ye a slow song already?"

"Yeah." *Sweetness Follows* was probably staying in the set; everyone liked it too much, and so did we.

"Well, there you go. One slow one is enough, you don't want to be boring them. Specially if they've a few pints in 'em."

"Yeah. You're right. I know this one. This one's in *The Lost Boys*, isn't it?"

"Yep. There's a load of their ones in films, like. Have you seen the Doors film? With Val Kimmeler?"

"No. I haven't, no." I'd heard of it. I wasn't old enough to go see it when it was out, and I'd no idea what it was about back then, so.

"Ah, it's class. Your man is the spit of him, like. The fella off *Top Secret,* it is, but you wouldn't recognise him in this. He looks exactly like Jim."

"Who's this, boy?" Frank came in from the hall, with a can of Smithwick's.

"*The Doors*."

I know that, you bollix. I meant who're ye talking about? Looks like Jim? Jim who?" Frank started up another joint. They'd loads of hash. Looked like nearly a quarter. Big block of it, covered in clingfilm.

"No, the film. Val Kimmeler."

"Val Kilmer."

"Yeah, that's the one."

"Class movie. That's Oliver Stone, like. He did *Platoon*. And *JFK*. And he wrote *Scarface*. Val Kilmer is brilliant, boy. He's married to Joanne Whalley-Kilmer. You seen *Scandal*?" Frank knew loads about films. He'd nearly every video under the sun in his house down in Cork.

"Nope." I remembered the poster – some ride of a woman, naked, on a chair, but you couldn't see nothing. It was an 18s. I couldn't bring them home, even if I got served over in Video Vision, cos the Ma was pure strict. Just for sex and tits and stuff. She didn't mind the violent ones, like Arnie. They'd blues and all over there, next to the bookies. They'd tell you to fuck off if you tried to get one of them out, though. Blue movies were even higher than 18s films.

"It's all right, like," said Frank, breaking off a big nodge from the block. Another song came on the stereo. I really liked them, now. I'd have to scobe the CD off Harta when I was going away. Niall loved them, I remembered him saying. He'd love doing the bass on that one, *Break On Through*, it was called. The singing sounded easy, too. Wasn't like Queen, where you'd nearly need to be an opera singer to hit the high notes. It was pure manly singing too. You couldn't imagine a gay fella singing something like *Light My Fire*. He was pure butch sounding.

"Any tit in it, sham?" Harta stood up and skipped through the CD until he got the song he was after.

"Loads, shur. It's about the Profumo Affair, isn't it?" said Frank. Both of us looked at him blank.

"The perfume of what, sham?" Harta sat down again on his bean bag. The song sounded good. They all sounded good, I thought.

"It's about hooring, boy," said Frank, rolling his eyes. He was nearly ten years older than us – than me, anyway. He couldn't expect us to know everything he knew, like. He was sound, though. The Ma was a bit funny about me hanging around with him – he was sort of the black sheep of their family - but she was ancient compared to him. She was like 36 or something.

"Can't go wrong with a bit of whoring. Listen, Jon, this one's called *When the Music's Over*. Absolute choon, like."

I'd already guessed it was called that, yer man Jim Morrison had said it so many times already. It was good, though. Long, but good. Too long to play in the battle, but I was already picturing it as one to finish on, when we started getting our own full gigs. The hash was really mellow – not too strong, nothing like the weed stuff the Gollies had a couple of weeks ago. It'd been a brilliant day. I was feeling pure good.

*****

We were on our third lot of drinks. I'd just enough to pay for the second ones; she told me not to worry, she'd get them, but I put my foot down, otherwise I'd have felt pure shitty. She was on the vodka and lime.

"So, are you going to talk to me about my sister then?" She said it out of nowhere, and I got the thump in my chest again.

"Huh?"

"Oh, you know. My sister. The famous one. The one who's missing, and no one ever shuts up about."

"Oh, right. Yeah…" I didn't like the tone in her voice. It was angry, not sad, but it still made me feel like I didn't know what to say.

"Sorry. Sorry, Jon. It's not your fault. I actually… this is the first time in weeks I've been able to feel a bit normal. Last time was probably that night I – the night of the party. Even then, people were all *Áine this* and *Áine that* at me, but still. I met you, that was good."

"It was, yeah." It really was. I'd been an eejit not to ring her. But I'd my reasons as well. They just didn't seem like good enough ones when she was actually here in front of me.

"And then you *lost* my number, of course."

I felt my face going red again.

"I'm sorry."

"Pffft, it doesn't matter. I didn't ring you either, in fairness. Mum went apeshit when I came home from that night anyway, cos I was supposed to come back straight after the gig thing, but obviously I didn't, and I didn't ring them to say I'd been staying out, and blah blah blah, so… I mean I was basically grounded after that. Like a child. Cos of *her*."

“Hmmmm.” I didn’t know if I was supposed to be joining in. I couldn’t, anyway. What was I gonna do, start calling her missing sister a gowl?

“I’m sorry. I’m being horrible, aren’t I?” She drunk down the last of her vodka. It wasn’t really the last of it, it was nearly full before she necked it. I was gonna have to be careful with her, she was a bit wild.

“No, no. No, you’re not. Really.” She was, kind of.

“No, I am. It’s fine. I’m just under a lot of – people don’t realise that – Áine is… look, she’s no saint, right? I love her, cos she’s my sister, but she’s always been a pain, and she’s always been their favourite, and she’s always got away with murder, you know? You know what it’s like.”

“Yeah. Yeah, I guess so.” I didn’t know, cos I’d no brothers or sisters. But I wanted to agree with her.

“I know it’s like, really serious that she’s still missing. And I know it’s not like the other times, when she just like, disappeared off with some older fella she shouldn’t have been with, or off to a music festival, or whatever, and came home a few days later saying sorry and stuff – I know it’s different now. And I know they’re going through a really hard time over it, at home. But… I’m still *here*, Jon. *I’m* not gone. I just wish they’d treat me – I just wish everyone would treat me like I’m not… invisible. I’m invisible to them; to all of them. Until they need to talk about her, then they can suddenly see - I’m sorry. I’m a bit drunk.”

“It’s okay.” She’d been talking really close to my face, and my hand was on her leg. I didn’t really think, I just kissed her. And she kissed me back. It wasn’t the first time – we were together at that house party. It was the first time today, though, so it still felt a bit like it was the first time. She was a nice kisser; I'd forgot that about her. The material of her dress felt nice – I'd my hands on her back, not feeling her up or nothing, but I felt the strap of her bra under there, and that gave me the horn a bit. When we stopped, I opened my eyes, and looked at her face. She was pretty. Really pretty. Not just in a good at doing make-up way. She fixed her hair, then she looked at my glass, and said,

"Same again?"

*****

"Jaysus, you kept that quiet, anyway."

I was telling them about seeing Caoimhe earlier. I had to tell someone, I was pure excited about it. Giddy, as my Ma would say. Harta kind of knew who she was, cos he'd seen me with her at the party.

"Kept what quiet?"

"Doing a line with her. How long ago did that start? Three weeks, is it? Must be."

"What? No, I only met her again today, like."

"Again after what, the party?"

"Yeah." I passed the joint over to Frank, who was listening, but not really listening, cos he'd no idea who Caoimhe was, in fairness.

"Yeah."

"Jesus, that's playing it cool, sham. Or was it her playing it cool? Did you not get her number or something?"

"Ah, I did, I just - It's complicated."

"Complicated, yeah. Well, to be honest, I'm just surprised you saw her again, like."

"Why? What's wrong with her, like?" I got a little jolt in my stomach when he'd said it. He didn't even know her.

"Ah, nothing, like. It's just-"

"There's nothing wrong with her, man. She's gorgeous, like. You seen her. And anyway, you can talk. What was that yoke you were hanging out of that night yourself?"

"What? Sarah?" said Harta, looking confused. Frank was listening to us a bit more now, when it looked like we were gonna have a fight about something.

"Yeah. That one. Head like a melted welly on her, like. If I'd a caravan full of mickeys I wouldn't let her look in the window."

Frank burst out laughing at that one. I stole it off Adrian Buckley though – that prick - so I couldn't be too proud of it. But he didn't know that.

"Haha, naw, Jon. Lovely looking bird, your Caoimhe. I was just saying I was surprised cos you don't normally ever meet any of them again. Fuck 'em and chuck 'em, that's you. I swear to God, Frank; your nephew – he's the Don Juan of Crossroads. Leaves a trail of broken hearts behind him, so he does. Broken hearts and broken hymens."

"Yeah, so I've heard, like. Gets that from our side of the family, definitely," said Frank, cracking open another can. He hadn't offered us any, but I didn't want any, so it was grand. I was enjoying Harta saying those things about me – cos, even though it was slagging, he was still saying good things. There was no shame in it. I was well toasted now. I'd have to scobe some of this gear off Frank when I went home. It was daycent.

"Must have fucking skipped a generation when it got to you then," said Harta, ducking the swing Frank took at him before Frank even thought about swinging. Then, to me:

"Ah, it's great though, Jon. Can't imagine seeing you with a girlfriend, like. Holding hands in Quinnsworth. Going over to her place for dinner with the parents. Going into H. Samuel's for an engagement ring, sham. You're gonna love it, boss."

"Fuck off, you." The weird thing was though, when he was saying those things and I was picturing them, they actually felt good. I could imagine them, and they weren't scary or nothing. They seemed like things I'd like to do; even the getting engaged thing. The hash was stronger than I thought, definitely.

"Yeah, Jon. Be good to see you have a bit of love in your life, like," Frank said. "I might want some love in my own life too, to be honest. Tell us, has she any sisters?"

My happy little stoned bubble sort of popped then, and it was good that it was my turn for a toke, or I might have started spilling stuff I didn't really wanna spill.

*****

"See, I don't know how I'm supposed to act, Jon. I don't even know how I'm supposed to *feel.* Do you know what I mean? I mean, there's no instruction book for it…" We'd been there a good while now, it was filling up a bit, but still kind of quiet.

"Am, I… I think so, yeah." I didn't know how to react to her when she talked about Áine. There was no instruction book for that either.

"You don't. Of course you don't; no one does. I do love her, Jon. She's my sister and everything. It's just… well I just thought she was up to her usual shit. I thought she'd come home, you know? But now it looks like – well, it doesn't look good, does it?" She looked sad. She was even pretty when she looked sad. Some people were just good looking, full stop. I felt bad thinking about her like that, when she was upset, but I couldn't help what my eyes saw, or what my brain thought.

"You never know, though. She might-"

"We do know though, Jon. Usually. With things like this. I saw it in a film once – I saw it in lots of films – If they don't get the person back in 24 hours, they're usually-"

"That's just in films, though." I hadn't touched my pint. It must have been number four. I wished I'd eaten something now, my head was a bit dizzy, especially whenever I stood up to go to the bar or the jacks.

"Yeah, but they don't just make films up out of thin air. They do research – they ask people. It's more than likely true. They must ask the police and stuff, before they put it in a film. I'm just… *worried* isn't the right word. But it's something like that. I don't think she's coming back."

"Ah, don't say that." She'd no idea. No idea that I wasn't just some new fella, listening to her, in a pub. That I was actually… part of it. Kind of. I hadn't done nothing wrong, apart from maybe the lie to her, but I hadn't done anything bad. Not to Áine. But I was still part of it, and she didn't know, while she was saying all this to me. And I couldn't tell her. Probably not ever. Unless Áine did come back…

"I don't want to say it, but it's probably true. It's just – it's been so long now. So long for us to just know… nothing. And that's the hardest part. If she had – if they found a… if we knew something, then at least we could start… getting over it, you know? But we don't, so we can't. And all that's left is… well, waiting."

"But you could be waiting for something good," I said, playing with the hair behind her ear, without really thinking about what I was doing. She shuddered a bit, like it was the wrong thing, so I stopped. When I took my hand away though, she grabbed the fingers, and held onto them. Her eyes had tears in them. I felt helpless. I wanted to fix it for her – make it all right. All of this was really knew to me. I'd never felt like that about anyone – not someone in my family, not one of my friends, no one. It was crazy. I barely knew her.

"That's really nice of you to say. And yeah, I hope so too. But we've got to be real. It's been weeks. If she's somewhere, just staying away on purpose, surely she's seen the papers, heard the news on the radio and stuff? She knows what Mum and Dad are going through. Surely she can't hate them that much? They're twats sometimes, like, but they're okay, Jon. They're not the worst. Not by a mile."

"So there's been nothing at all?"

"Well."

"Well what? Was there something?"

"I don't know really; if it's something, I mean. But there's been these… these calls."

"Calls? Like, phone calls?"

"Yeah. Sort of. I don't know how long for. But, the other day, I picked up the phone, and there was someone on the other end – I could hear them breathing. Not in a pervy way, like. Just so I could tell they were there."

"And who was it?"

"I don't know. They didn't say anything. I had a weird feeling. But, I dunno, really. It could've been anything. And, the thing is, I thought it was a one-off, but when I mentioned it to Mum and Dad, they went all funny."

"Funny?"

"Yeah, I can't really put my finger on it, but it was… it was like they were hiding something. I asked them if they'd had calls like that too, and they said no, but…"

"You didn't believe them."

"Yeah. Well, they looked at each other for a second before they answered. Just for a second, but I spotted it. It was like they were-"

"Checking with each other?" I knew what she meant. My Ma and Da would do that sometimes. Like, getting their story straight. They done it lots when I was around ten and started asking if Santa was real. I could picture it exactly when she said it.

"Yeah. Checking. It was weird."

"They probably just didn't wanna worry you, or something." It was the best I could do. And it was probably true. I got a bit of hope from it, though. Maybe she was okay, and she was just sort of ringing home, to hear someone's voice. That happened in films. It might be what was happening.

"Yeah, I suppose. Sorry for being such a downer, by the way."

"Don't be stup – don't be silly. You're grand. I understand. I think you're doing really good. I dunno how I'd deal with – I dunno how I'd cope."

"You don't have any sisters, do you? Or brothers?"

"No. It's just me."

"Is that good? I mean like, I know you can't compare it to anything, cos you only know what you know, but… do you miss it?"

"Miss it?"

"That's the wrong word, isn't it? Sorry. When you see other people having brothers and sisters – when you saw it when you were small, and on Christmas and stuff – did you think: *I want that*? Or were you like: *thank God I'm an only child*? Sorry, it's just it's interesting. Áine's only one year younger than me, so I've never really known what it's like to be the only one."

I'd to stop myself from saying "Except now". I'd no idea why something that lousy even popped into my head. That was horrible. And anyway, there'd been phone calls. They were probably from Áine. She was probably okay.

"I'm not sure. I dunno any different, like. I've only ever been the only one. Other kids are jealous of you like, like you said, at Christmas, cos your Ma and Da don't have to share out the money between loads of ye, so you get more stuff. But, when you're small, you think it's Santa anyway, so that doesn't even be a thing you think of, you know?"

"Yeah, I getcha. But did people call you a spoilt brat, like?"

"No, I don't think so. But… maybe they did, like. On the sly."

"I think they might have, haha. I mean, no offence like, I don't know anything about you in that way. For all I know, you could have got the bag of cinders every year. But I think children do that. I think it's a *defence mechanism*. I don't even think it's the kids themselves. I think the kid says "But how come I only got two Transformers and Jonathan Goodison got a car he can sit in with an engine, and all the Transformers, and a bike too?", and the parents have to say "Well, he's a spoiled brat." Or, if the parents aren't twats, like, they'd say "Ah, but that's because Jonathan is an only child, and he has no brothers and sisters, so his Mum and Dad buy him extra stuff, so he won't be so sad on Christmas, for not having any brothers and sisters. You wouldn't want to be like him, would you? With no brothers or sisters to play with? You'd be so lonely."

"Is that what they say?" I'd no idea. I was always Jonathan Goodison in that story, whoever he was.

"Yep. And we all nod our heads, but secretly we're like: I don't care about being lonely, Mum! I want a car!"

I laughed, and she laughed, but we both knew that she'd rather have her sister back right now than any present anyone could give her. But we didn't say that. We just lit up another couple of fags, and she leaned into me, and I played with her hair, cos that was okay to do now.

*****

"Seriously?"

"Absofuckingserious…lutely. Honest to God, boy."

Frank was talking to us about stuff. Computers, mostly. He knew loads about everything; I liked talking to him, even though the Ma would call it him filling my head with nonsense. She didn't know the half of what he was like, though. He carried a knife and everything – a cool Rambo one, with a compass in the handle, and you could screw it apart and there was stuff like waterproof matched in there – for survival.

"So, like, the one in *War Games,* where he uses the phone line to… hack into the games place, and the government and stuff," said Harta.

"Yeah," said Frank. He'd moved onto vodka and Coke now, he was a devil for the drink, my Ma said. She didn't know he smoked gear; she'd have had kittens.

"You have one of those?" I'd been to his place in Fermoy, but I'd never had a go on his computer, I didn't think.

"Well, like, that came out in 1982. My modem is a million times better than that. It's 28k."

"What? That's not even half a Commodore 64," I said. His modem sounded shite.

"No, that's kilobytes, you spastic." Frank got a bit shouty with drink in him, all the same. He was harmless, though.

"Yeah. And what's yours?"

"Kilobits."

"Oh right, yeah. Beg your pardon, like, *Uncle Frank*. Imagine the cheek of me, getting them two mixed up!" I stuck my tongue out at him to let him know I was only codding him.

"Seriously, though. What's the difference?" Harta had loads of computers, but he didn't have an IBM Compatible like Frank's. None of us did; they were too dear, and the graphics were shit, and you couldn't play games on them. Not the games like for the Amiga or the ST, anyway.

"Ah it's hard to explain. One's RAM, the other's to do with sending packets over a network, like."

He'd lost me now.

"Packets of what? Batchelor's Cup-a-soup?" said Harta. He'd robbed a bit of vodka off Frank. I wasn't having any, I was grand for now with a smoke.

"Information. It doesn't really matter. It'd be too hard to explain it all to ye. It's too complicated, like. Even I don't really understand it fully, like."

"Jayus, Jon. Even he doesn't understand it fully. What hope would we have, sham? Ah, Frank, you know I'm only blaggarding you, sham. Go on, tell us about this *inter-thing* anyway."

"Right, well. You know the way yer man in *War Games* can talk to another computer, using his modem?"

We both nodded. I liked that film. Yer one in it was a ride.

"And you know the way the computers in an office, or in your school, probably, are all hooked up with cables, and then that last bit of the cable goes into the printer, so no matter what computer you're on, the printouts come out the same place?"

"Yeah, sort of," I said. I hadn't ever thought of how that worked until he explained it just there, but now it was pure obvious.

"Right, well that's a sort of *network*, got it?"

"Got it."

"Now, imagine if, instead of that cable going into the printer, you brought it back across the room and stuck it into the first computer…"

"Right…" I was trying to keep up, but the brain was tired and stoned. Maybe it needed some vodka to make me clever again. I looked over to see how much was left in the bottle.

"Well, that's a different sort of network. That's a *Local Area Network.*"

"And what does that do?" said Harta. He'd took over the rolling.

"Well, see, they're all connected now. Like a hub. Like a hive, you know, with bees or wasps?"

"Yeah", I said, wondering was there other hives. I couldn't think of any. Ants didn't have hives. They had… something else.

"So now, you can send messages between them. Like, if there's eight PCs in a circle, you can sit on PC1, write a note to someone on PC8, send it down the wire, and they'd get the message, nearly immediately. How mad is that?"

"If they were in a circle, wouldn't PC1 be next to PC8 though? Couldn't I just nudge yer man and tell him the message with my mouth?" said Harta. Frank looked confused.

"Well, yeah, but that's not the – look, imagine that hub, though – that network of eight computers aren't in the same room anymore."

"Why, did someone rob them? That happened in our school. I heard it was DuDu Mac and them – fellas from the Island Field," said Harta, holding in the giggles. He was some tool.

"Feck off, you. Anyway, imagine that the eight computers are all in different rooms. Or in different schools. Or in different countries. And, instead of the wire looping around the room to connect them, what's connecting them is the phone line in the wall – the one that goes under the ground, all over the country. All over the world. *Now* think of how cool it would be for someone – for someone in another country – on another *continent*, like, to send a message to you from their computer, and it just appears on your screen. Like magic. That's what the future will be like, lads. Doesn't that blow your minds?" He sat back, looking pure satisfied.

"You mean like in that film, *Jumpin' Jack Flash*?" said Harta, not looking impressed.

"Oh yeah, that does happen in that, doesn't it?" I said. It was always on Sky Movies, that one. The black one from *Ghost* was in it.

"What?" said Frank, looking for something down by his feet.

"And anyway, shur if we're all connected by the phone lines, why would be sending letters to people down them, Frank? Why wouldn't we just phone them? Your future sounds shit, sham," said Harta. It did, in fairness. If you were gonna send anything down the phone lines with a computer, you should have been sending something decent, not letters. I wondered to myself if they'd ever be able to send blue movies down there, cos then you wouldn't have to worry about getting ID'd in the video shop.

*****

It was still lovely and bright and sunny out when we left Quin's. It was her idea, she said go get some cans and sit in the sun somewhere. I'd no money left, so I was grand with that. I let her do the going into Fine Wines; cos, even though I was taller than her, girls looked older. They just did. And if they were pretty and yer man behind the till was some awkward yoke, he'd never ask for ID. He'd be too busy trying to lickarse her. We went down by the Dublin Road, to the canal. It wasn't the nicest place to go, and people'd be walking past with their dogs, or just off for a walk, but no one gave you any hassle. I used to go there with my Da when I was small.

"What's your favourite smell?" Caoimhe'd picked a place for us a little bit down the bank, with some rocks for us to sit on. Better than a bench, cos auld ones liked sitting on benches, and if two teenagers were taking up a bench, drinking cans, and the auld ones had nowhere to sit, one of them might call the Gards, just to be crooked.

"Smell?" She wasn't talking about anything before that. It was just out of the blue. I cracked open a can of Linden. She'd got herself some Budweiser.

"A smell. Like, I don't mean Lynx, or a perfume. A smell that reminds you of something. Like, when you smell it, you get all… happy? D'you know what I mean?"

"Kind of, yeah." I'd run out of fags. She'd some, but I was waiting for her to take them out of her bag before I scobed one off her. I was enough of a charity case today without being cheeky on top of it.

"I like arcades," she said.

"Arcades?"

"Yeah. Not like, all of them. Well, maybe all of them, actually, but – I like the smell of whatever it is you smell when you go into the arcade. At the seaside, like. And I like how it's always kind of dark in there, even if it's sunny outside. I love that little change. And that bit, when you've begged your Mum for some 10ps and you can't wait to get in and have a go on Double Dragon, or Street Fighter. It's such a brilliant feeling. And that arcade smell makes me feel it. Do you think I'm mad now?" She'd such a great smile, especially the smile when she was laughing.

"Nah, I know what you mean. It's like the pub smell. When you get in the door of the pub it smells like-"

"Fags and beer?"

"Haha, yeah. But it's a good smell to me. And it's other smells too, sort of clean smells?"

"Yeah, cos everyone's had a shower and done themselves up, and there's loads of perfume and body spray, right?" she said, opening her can. It fizzed a bit too much, cos of the walk down, and she got suds on her fingers.

"Exactly. And cos – if you smell that smell, that means you're in, like. The bouncer didn't stop you for ID. It's like that smell is the smell of…"

"Success?"

"Yeah, I suppose. Success. And good times."

"Good times. Same with the arcade one, for me. Even if I go past one of those slot machine places in town here, that you're not allowed into, cos they're over 18s. And they've no video games in there at all, I'd say, just poker ones and one-armed bandits, and boring stuff like that. They still have that smell. You definitely think I'm mad now, don't you?" The sunlight was all golden now, where we were sitting on the bank, and it was making her even more gorgeous than normal. I was turning into an awful auld sop, all the same, cos of her.

"No! Not too mad. You like video games?" I didn't know girls liked games. I never saw any of them playing them when I was in the arcades in Kilkee or Ballybunion. Lads played the games, youngones just hung around wearing make-up and looking to get asked away for the shift.

"Yeah, course I do. They're deadly altogether. Have you got a Mega Drive?"

"Naw. I've an Amiga. I might be getting a Super Nintendo, though. They've got *Football Champ* on that. I seen it in that video shop in town, the one where you can rent out games."

"Pffft. SNESs are shite, like."

"They're not. They've better graphics than Mega Drives. You ever seen *F-Zero*?"

"The racing one? It's all right, yeah." She lit up her fag and gave me one. She didn't smoke as much as me when she was drinking, so cos they were her fags, I'd to wait longer for one. It didn't matter. She liked video games. That nearly gave me more of a horn than what she looked like. Girls never liked the stuff we liked. They only liked shite stuff, like going shopping, or watching *Dirty Dancing*. Except maybe Ciara and Bríd. Them two were okay, for girls.

"Sound, thanks. Yeah, It's rapid though. I played it loads of times in Roche's Toy Shop. You couldn't have a game like that on Mega Drive. Mega Drive can't do 3D."

"Yeah, it can! What about *Thunder Blade*? Or *Road Rash*, or *Space Harrier*?" She knew loads about games. It was mad.

"S'pose. Not the same, though. It doesn't have the special chip thing in it." I couldn't remember what it was called, but they were always going on about it in *C&VG* and *Ace*. I read them when I was over in Richie's, usually. I bought *Amiga Power* myself.

"Chip, schmip. The Amiga's good though. My e- I mean, someone I used to know had one of them. *First Samurai* is brilliant. *Speedball 2,* as well. 'Ice cream!'"

"Haha, yeah." I'd heard her nearly say 'My ex' there, and it made me feel pure jealous, even though I'd no idea who she was talking about, and we'd all got exes. Well, except me. I never had relationships. I liked shifting a new girl every time. The lads gave me a slagging over it, but they were just jealous, as my Ma would say. This was the second time I'd been with her though, so…

"So, are girls not supposed to like video games then?" She put her hand on the back of my hand, and done a pretend sad face at me.

"Ah, no, well, I've just – I just never met one that did before."

"Well, you've met one now, haven't you?" She took my hand into hers and gave it a squeeze. Her skin was pure soft and I could feel the shininess of the backs of her nails.

"Yeah. Crazy stuff." I finished my Linden, cos it was getting lukewarm in the bottom of the can.

"I know, right? Next we'll be wearing trousers, and wanting the vote." She'd brought herself right over in front of me now – eyes looking into mine, and I could smell her hair, and see little drops of wet in between the tiny gold hairs on her arms. The back of her neck felt really cold. Her lips were all spongey and perfect when I shifted her. She'd sort of clamped her two legs around one of mine, and the heat coming off her was something else.

*****

"Seriously though, what's the scala with yer one anyway, Jon?" Frank was out in the kitchen doing something. Me and Harta were listening to The Doors again. He found another CD, a live one this time. They were even better live than they were normal.

"Ah, I dunno. She's great, like." I thought we'd already had this conversation, but you done that when you were stoned – went round in circles.

"You riding her yet?"

"That's for me to know and you to find out." I didn't even like him saying that about her, even though he wasn't saying anything, really.

"That's a no, then. She's a fine looking thing though. Is she sound, like?"

"Really sound, yeah. She's clever too, like."

"Pffft. What's she need to be clever for?"

"I dunno, like. She just is. She likes films and stuff – she's mad into them. And video games as well."

"Video games? Jaysus, did you check down her knickers to see she isn't a man?"

"Haha, yeah. Very good. No, she's all woman." I'd been in her knickers a bit earlier on, but I wasn't checking anything. I got a bit of a horn remembering it.

"Well that's something, says you. You gonna see her again?"

"Of course, yeah." I definitely was. We'd said.

"Fuck. Must be love. What are we gonna do with you at all, Jon?"

"Ah, fuck off. I think this might be-"

"The beginning of a beautiful friendship?"

"Yeah, something like that. She's cool, man. I like her. A lot." I got a funny feeling saying it. Not a bad one – a good one, like you'd get off taking a yoke.

"Gaaaaay."

"You're gay."

"Touché."

"Touche-gay. What's this one again?"

"*Roadhouse Blues.*"

"Ah yeah, I heard it before, earlier, on the other one."

"Much better live, isn't it?"

"Yeah. Much better." I was wondering would they have a book of sheet music in Savin's for The Doors. They probably would. They'd everything in that place.

*****

"What's yours then?"

We were lying back on the grass after the shifting. Well, I was sitting up a bit, and she was lying into me, her head just under my nose, so I was getting all the good smells off her.

"What's my what?" I was trying to drink my can without moving her, I'd to put it in the other hand. It was warmish now, from the sun, but I didn't care.

"Favourite smell, you mong." She'd a lovely giggle.

"Ah, let me think." I nearly wanted to say "You", or something else clever and nice like that, but I'd feel a bit stupid, even if it was true right now. People didn't say stuff like that in real life.

"Take your time. Get me a can out, will you?"

"Sure. Ah, grass."

"Grass?"

"The smell of it." I opened the Bud for her and gave it into her hand. It didn't fizz up, cos they were lying in the bag for a while.

"Like… cannabis?"

"No!" I'd only ever smoked that kind of grass once, with the Gollies the other day, behind the shop. And that smelt rank.

"Oh. Just *grass* grass. I getcha. How do you smell grass? Are you like, on all fours, smelling it, like a cow?"

"Haha, piss off. No, I mean when it's cut."

"Oh! Yeah, that's a nice smell. Unless you have hay fever, I guess. Any particular reason for that, or do you, like… just love grass?" That giggle again. I liked the way it made her jiggle on my lap. I liked loads of things about her that I'd never thought about anyone else. The sun was really boiling now, even though it was the evening.

"Yeah, am. Well, no."

"Jon?" She turned her head a bit, so she was nearly looking at me, but not quite.

"Yeah?"

"I think there's a story heeeeeere…" She moved herself again so she was more squished into me. I'd been on the horn for ages now, even though we'd only really been shifting. I hadn't tried doing nothing serious with her yet or anything. But I definitely wanted to. Maybe in a bit. Or another day, if she didn't want to today. I didn't mind. I'd wait, if it was for her.

"Am. Hmmmm." There was one, but I didn't really wanna tell it to her. It was a bit of a weird one, and I didn't want her to think I was, well… weird.

"Go on. You can tell me. I'm your – you can tell me."

I ignored what she'd nearly said, even though it made my heart go a bit thumpy. Was I wanting her to say 'girlfriend' there? I'd normally have run a mile if someone was talking like that after me only knowing them for – but I supposed I actually knew her ages now. I just hadn't seen her for a lot of it.

"Okay. Right, well. So, a long time ago."

"In a galaxy, far, far away?" She'd to move herself a bit again, so she could drink her Bud without headbutting me, and I'd a weird feeling, like I didn't want her to go anywhere, so I squished myself into the back of her again.

"Shush. Anyway, we were all about ten."

"Who's we?"

"Ah, me and some lads from down my place. You don't know them."

"Ah, but give them names, Jon. Otherwise I can't picture the sceeeeene." She sparked up a fag and gave me one. We'd only had about three each since we got down there.

"Cheers. Okay, it was me, Dara, Joe, Alan, and Martin, I think." I was trying remember if Richie was there, but I didn't think he was.

"Okay. And you were all ten?"

"About ten, yeah. So, it was the summer, and we were all play – we were all hanging around down the Distillery."

"The distillery? What were you doing, making whiskey?"

"Haha, no. It's just the name of a place in Thomondgate. I dunno why it's called that. Anyway, shush and let me tell the story!"

"Ooh. Yes, boss." She gave my leg a squeeze, a bit too close to my langer, and I nearly forgot what I was gonna say.

"Yeah, right, anyway. So, they'd been cutting the grass down there, the Corporation had-"

"The grass! Now we're getting somewhere!"

"Caoimhe!"

"Sorry!"

"So, there was loads of cut grass, right? And we were down there, being ten like, and piling it all up, making it into forts and tunnels and stuff. And we were just sitting around, and these two youngones came over. I think they were from around there – from the Distillery houses."

"Ooh. And were they hot?"

"Eh, they were like eight or nine. But pure cheeky."

"How do you mean?" I liked her voice. The top of her head was real close to my mouth and I just sort of kissed her on the white bit of her scalp, without even thinking about it. She made a 'Mmmm' noise and pushed into me a little more.

"Like, they were brazen. They were talking about shifting and all that, and asking us about langers. About *our* langers, like. Swear to God."

"Jesus! The little trollops."

"I know, yeah. So anyways, they start asking do we wanna play *Catch a Boy, Kiss a Boy* with them." I felt weird, and wondered if I should keep going. I felt like I could tell anything to her, though. It felt okay.

"Fucking hell. And they were *eight*?"

"Ah, I'd say they were more nine than eight." They weren't, but it made it sound better, I thought.

"Oh right. That's *fine* then, isn't it?" She giggled again, and drank some more beer. She was running her hands up and down the leg of my jeans, not in a horny way, she was just doing it cos I was there. It still felt good though. "So, did ye?"

"I well, I was, like – I didn't know if we should, like. I'd never gone away with – I hadn't kissed a girl, yet. Dara definitely had, cos he was Dara, but I knew Joe hadn't. And I didn't think either of the other fellas had either, like."

"Awww. Poor little innocent Jon." She'd turned around a little more to face me while I was telling the story. I liked looking at her face. And the rest of her.

"Eh, whatever, I was ten, like. Anyway, so Dara said yeah. And then Alan did, so I thought I might as well, like."

"Of course, like. That was just good manners, wasn't it?" She stuck her tongue out at me in a messing way.

"Haha, yeah. But Joe didn't wanna at all."

"Which one was Joe?"

"Ah, just some fella. I didn't really know him. He was always more friends with Richie and them."

"Richie from your band?"

"Yeah. That guy. So, Joe went home, all huffy like, and we all called him a steamer – not to his face, cos he was a big bastard, but when he was gone, definitely. You know how it is. And, when he was gone, the rest of us played."

"What, *Catch a Girl, Molest a Girl*?"

"Hahahaha. No. Jesus… it was them trying to catch us, so…"

"Oh. Fair enough then. I think that one's legal."

"It was all legal! We were only messing around, like. There was no – it was pure innocent." I knew she was only playing with me, but I said it anyway, just in case.

"Hmmmm. I'd say it was, yeah. Did you get caught? By the girls, I mean. Not the Gards."

"Haha, stop it. Nah, I got away all the time. They were too slow."

"Yeah. Eight year olds are the *worst* at running, aren't they?"

"Nine!" She was really funny. I couldn't believe I hadn't rang her back after that first time. I'd been missing out on all of this.

"Of course. And tell me, was one of your lads really bad at running, all of a sudden? Did one of them get caught way too many times? 'Fell over' a lot, like?"

"Yeah! Dara. How did you know?"

"Women's intuition, hon. And tell me, did Dara grow up to be an absolute perv?"

"Haha, yeah. I think he already was back then, to be honest." Dara was a horndog, everyone knew that about him. He was into blue movies and skin mags before anyone I knew.

"Thought so. He'll probably end up being a serial killer someday. So, is that the end of the story?"

"Ah, yeah, well." I wondered should I end it there. She could tell there was something else though, the way she was looking up at me.

"Jon…"

"Okay, fine. The next day we all went up again. Well, me, Dara, Martin and Alan. No Joe. He was like, out with us over it. He got pure pissed off and stuff. But we just called him gay and carried on, like. You know the way it is."

"Yeah." She rolled her eyes at me, but she smiled after it, so it was okay.

"And, this time, we waited around, like – obviously waiting for them youngones to show up."

"Very youngones."

"Shuddup. Anyway so, we waited ages, and we got bored of piling up the grass and making forts. And the grass was gone a bit shitty by then. And we were gonna go home, cos we'd only really come to play the game. All the rest was just pretending, in case someone saw us and wondered what we were doing, like."

"Of course. The old rock solid alibi. And tell me, if you didn't get caught the first day, why did you go back?"

"What?"

"If you weren't… getting anything out of it, why did you come back the next day?"

"Ah, cos I was ten? I was bored? Nothing else to do?" That wasn't the whole story. The truth was I was kind of jealous of Dara and the lads, even if them girls were a bit too young for us. I was the only one apart from Joe that hadn't done anything. And the lads were giving me a bit of a slagging too for it, saying I was gay like Joe. And it annoyed me, cos Dara was one thing, but the other two – they'd got their first shifts now, before me. I didn't like them having something I didn't have. That was why I went back. But it didn't feel like a good idea to tell her that, so I just said what I said.

"True. Go on, anyway. Actually, reach around and get me another can. Have I one left?" She'd two left. I opened it for her, to save her shiny nails.

"Okay, so, just as we're about to go, one of them turns up. On her own."

"On her own? Did the other one throw herself in the Shannon the night before because of the trauma, yeah?"

"Hahaha, stop it. No, she just said the other one was… busy, I think. I can't really remember. It was a long time ago."

"Your Honour…"

"Haha. Very good." I was crazy about her already. I'd forgotten about the Áine stuff, until I remembered just then, so I tried to forget again, so it didn't ruin everything.

"So, did you play anyway? Catch a… whatever you called it."

"No. We just, well, we were all just chatting away, really. And then she sort of came up with… she said that we-"

"Uh-oh…"

"No! Am, she wanted to go away with us. All of us."

"What, like a gangbang?"

"No, you gowl. It was just… ten year olds."

"And an eight-year-old."

"Nine, probably."

"*Probably*. And did you? Did all of you?"

"I think so. I suppose so. I didn't – I can only remember what I did."

"What do you mean?"

"Like, she took everyone away, one by one, just over to some little wall thing. And then we all came back, after two minutes or whatever. I think Dara tried to stay a bit longer with her, but she wasn't having any of that."

"Sensible chi- sensible girl. So. What did you do with her? Or do I want to know?"

"You know what, I actually didn't really shift her at all."

"You didn't? Or you're just saying that now, in case I call the police?"

"Haha, no. I just went over with her, and she was like, okay then. And I got a funny feeling about it. So I sort of done this weird movie kiss thing?"

"Huh?"

"I like, almost picked her up, against the wall. Cos I was tall even then, like. So I lifted her shoulders a little. And I kissed her on the lips, with my eyes closed, but not a shift. Not French kissing. Just on the lips, for a really long time, then I stopped."

"You are the most romantic child molester ever, Jon. Show me!"

"Haha. Show you what?"

"Show me your movie kiss. Unless I'm too old for you, like."

"Hah, shag off, will ya?" It was all only messing, no matter what Caoimhe said to me, I felt okay and good. I could never ever imagine having a fight with her or anything.

"Oh, please! I want to know how it felt. For her, like. What was her name?"

"Ah, Carrie. I think."

"Okay, I'll be Carrie, you be you. Here. Use this bit." She took me over to a broken bit of wall on the bank. It might have been somewhere people got changed for swimming, back in the old days, by the look of it. I went with her, just to make her happy.

"Right then, do me like I'm eight, Jon." She was hilarious. I couldn't keep a straight face long enough to get ready for the kiss. I stopped laughing eventually, then I just sort of lifted her up, under the arms, and kissed her on the lips, mouth closed, for about a minute. It felt silly, but it was still a kiss with her, so it felt good as well. I put her down, and we both opened our eyes.

"Well, now. If I was an eight-year-old slapper called Carrie, I'd have given you at least nine out of ten for that."

"Haha. Thanks? I think…" I walked her back over to our stuff. I liked holding hands with her. I normally hated doing that stuff with a girl.

"I'll tell you what, Jon." She took a fag out, passed me one, and lit hers up.

"What?"

"I'll never be able to walk past some cut grass again without feeling like a sex case. Cheers for that."

*****

"So, are ye right for the battle thing then? When is it?" said Frank. He'd been making some food for himself. Uncle Ben's boil in the bag rice and curry. It smelled rank, but I still wanted some, cos of the munchies.

"Saturday."

"This Saturday coming?" He was talking with his mouth full. My Ma would've gone spare. She grew up with him though, so she was probably used to it. He was ten years younger than her, so she probably gave him an awful time when they were small.

"Yeah. There's a sort of sound check thing early on, then the gig is on in the night. You gonna come along?" He came to one of our gigs before, when we'd Tom O'Neill on drums for the night. We were a bit shit back then though.

"Yeah, shur. Why not? You going, Dom? Are yere lads in it too?"

"Hah? Yeah, no, I'll be there. Are we in it? The battle of the bands? Will you go away, will you." He made a face.

"What? What's wrong with a battle of the bands, boy?

"Ah, nothing. We're not a band, anyway. We only plays other people's stuff, like. Jon and the lads writes their own songs and everything, don't ye?"

"We do, yeah." I was looking at him pure suspicious, like he was gonna say something slagging, but he didn't. I was probably a little bit para. It was good hash, but I'd had lots of it. Was nearly time to go home anyway. I could've stayed over; Marie was sound like that, but I didn't wanna get any hassle off the Ma. It was safe enough to walk out the road from there anyway, even in the dark. Limerick wasn't as bad as people from other places made out. You were grand, usually.

"I know that, boy. I seen them play a few times. Haven't seen ye with the new drummer yet though, have I? What's he like?"

"Richie? He's sound out."

"No, I mean what's he like on the drums, you eejit."

"Oh right, yeah. No, he's good. He's very good, actually." Richie was nearly getting to be the best one in the band now. Apart from Niall, maybe. And me.

*****

"Okay, this is me, then," said Caoimhe. I'd walked her up to outside Roche's stores; where you'd get a bus out to Castletroy. It was still early, but she'd said she'd be home for her tea to the Ma and Da.

"Oh right. Well…" I wasn't sure what to do. It'd been brilliant, and I didn't want her to go. And it wasn't a date we were on. We'd already gone away with each other loads, so this wasn't that bit you see in the movies where people are mad nervous thinking is there gonna be the first kiss. We were well past that bit. I'd fingered her and everything, down by the canal.

"I assume we're doing this again, yeah?" She said it, so I didn't have to be the one to now; that was handy.

"Of course, yeah!" I meant it too. I wasn't just doing the thing where you agree just to get rid of them. I almost nearly couldn't wait to see her again. And not just cos she'd let me drop the hand on her either, even if that was kind of rapid.

"Haha, I like that you're not one of those 'Play it cool' guys, Jon."

"Huh? Oh right, yeah. No. No, I'm not." I was until today, but I didn't tell her that, obviously.

"Shit, that's it."

"What?"

"My bus – the University one. I have to go, sorry! Call me later? Or tomorrow?"

"Ah, yeah. Later, definitely. Or tomorrow." I wanted to call her the minute I got home, to be honest. Maybe I needed to start being the play it cool guy again, in case she thought I was a sap. She wouldn't, though. I knew that already.

"And you've got my number, right?"

"Eh, yeah." I didn't look her in the eyes, in case I gave away that I'd lied about it before. Even though I sort of thought she might already know, and she was just fine with it now.

"Good. Don't *lose* it. Okay, I've gotta love you and leave you." She kissed me on the cheek, and ran over to the bus before yer man closed the doors.

"I won't."

I waited for her to give her money over, get in her seat, and give me a wave as the bus drove off. It was still early and I was buzzing from all the booze still, so I went up Cruise's Street to see was there anyone around.

*****

It was a bit cold walking home from Marie's so I put on my jacket. I'd been carrying it all day, when it was too warm to wear it. But it wasn't too warm now. I was freezing my bollocks off.

I was out of town and over the bridge fairly quick. It'd been a rapid day – the time with her, and the smoke with the lads, and listening to The Doors and all that. I was properly stoned, and that made Limerick feel a bit scary, walking through it. When I was pissed I could go through town while World War 3 was going on and I wouldn't notice it, cos drink was like that. A smoke was different, though. I kept seeing fellas in doorways that weren't really there, or seeing things moving out of the corner of my eye. I knew it was just the hash though. It wasn't real. I'd be home in a minute, eating Taytos and Penguin bars anyway.

Coming down across from Frazer's into the big alley where all the back gates where, I did actually think someone was following me, though. Like, a real feeling. I didn't look behind me, I sped up my walking. I could hear someone, though. Someone huffing, like they'd a smokers cough, and they were trying to keep up with me. I got to the Kellys' house in the Square, and I swung around, pure dramatic, to see could I catch whoever it was. There wasn't no one. I was just being para. I'd been pure convinced of it though. I was nearly sure that it was real. I only had to go past the green now, and turn up by the way to Feehan's shop, and I'd be home, so it didn't matter anyway. I walked quick, even though there was no one after me. Wouldn't do any harm, I thought. Just as I got in the side gate, I heard it again. The huffing. I'd it closed behind me already, though. So I went in the back, through the kitchen. My Ma said something sarky to me when I went through, but I wasn't listening to her. I went up to the box room upstairs, where we kept all our spare stuff, and I kept the light off, and snuck over to the window. There was no one down there. I'd just been para, definitely. Then, as I was about to get out of there, I saw someone walk out of the alley next door to us, and flick his fag butt onto the ground, making a load of orange sparks. I couldn't make out who it was, in the dark. I kept squinting at him, but it was no use. A youngfella, not a man. Tallish. Normal clothes. Black baseball cap on. It probably meant nothing. I was just being para. I wondered would it be too late to phone Caoimhe, or would it be too soon, cos I'd only been with her a few hours ago. I decided I was a bit too stoned still, since I was imagining boogymen following me home, trying to kill me, so I just got some munchies from the kitchen and went to bed.

Eight

The next few days were brilliant altogether. Everything was really coming together; with the band, with me and Caoimhe, with everything. I was on top of the world. Áine still being missing was the only thing that was wrong, but I was even sort of getting used to that, kind of. Or I was getting better at pretending it wasn't happening. Anyway, nothing's ever completely perfect. Not in real life, anyway.

Me and Niall were in Savin's on Monday, down at the sheet music bit. Yer man behind the little desk was a bit queer, in lots of ways. I knew him to salute, but he made me feel weird, the way he'd look at you.

"There's your boyfriend, Muzz."

"Piss off, will you."

"What's wrong with you? Don't fight it, man. Let the gayness flow through you. It's the 90s, man. It's legal now and everything."

"Can we just get the thing?"

"The *thing*? Is that what you're calling it now? His thing, is it? His big hairy mickey, rubbing off you in the cinema. Spunking all -"

"Nailer…"

They'd every sort of music in books there, but you'd to get the right instrument as well as the right songs. That's what Niall said, anyway. I couldn't read music, I only looked for the chords. We needed one that had piano, or organ. The chords would be in them ones too; in little boxes over the lines with the notes. Ian could work out the lead by listening to the song himself. I'd made a few tapes of the CD for all of them the other day, except Niall, cos he already liked The Doors.

"That's the one," he said, pointing at a book down near the bottom. It was black, with yellow writing.

"Is it?"

"Yeah, shur. I've the album of it myself. Or you could get *that* one there."

"Which one, now?" I could see yer man coming out from behind his counter; he'd be over to us in a minute, asking if we were "all right". I shuddered, nearly.

"That one. Best of The Doors. *Light My Fire* is on that, and *Break on Through*, like."

"Cool. We picked which one we're doing yet?"

"Nah. I want *Break on Through*, I think Tim wants the other one though, so."

"Why d'you want that one; cos of the bass, yeah?" There was a cool bassline in it, to be fair.

"Yeah, it's rapid, isn't it? Did you know there was no bass player in The Doors?"

"How wasn't there?" I'd heard the bass player on their songs. I wasn't deaf. Yer man was hovering now, right behind us. He gave me the willies.

"Ah, it was all on the organ like. Ray Manzerik played the treble with one hand, bass with the other. There was two keyboards on it, top and bottom."

"Are ye okay there, lads?" said yer man. He sounded like a girl, but not really. Girls didn't make your arsehole close up when they talked to you.

"I'm grand, yeah. How about yourself?" said Niall, turning around to him with a big grin. He was about a foot and a half bigger than the other fella.

"What? I – I mean, did ye need any help there? Are ye looking for anything in particular?" He was just sort of… slimy. I couldn't put my finger on why he creeped me out. It wasn't even that he was a steamer - I didn't even know if he actually was one. He was just like… when he talked to you, it was like a slug walking over your hand.

"No, we're just looking," I said, wanting him to go away from us. Yer man looked at me for way too long. Then he licked his lips really slowly, and said:

"Yeah. Aren't we all? Anyway, give us a shout if you… if you *need* anything, yeah? Thanks, boys." He walked back over to his desk. I shivered, he creeped me out so much.

"I think you've pulled there, Muzzo. Wanna borrow a few johnnies? And a tub of Vaseline?"

"Fuck off."

*****

"Can you make your way up to me, if I give you some directions?" Caoimhe rang around eleven in the morning. I'd been washing the car to make a few quid off the Da.

"Yeah, I'd say so. I'll just get the same bus you do, yeah?"

"That's the one, yeah. The *Ollscoil* one, outside Roche's. That'll *almost* bring you to my avenue, but I can tell you the rest if you have a pen and paper handy."

"I do, hang on a sec. And they're both gone? For how long, like?" She'd a free gaff, she said. I hadn't seen her since the last time, at the weekend, but we'd been chatting loads. My Ma didn't know what to make of it. I could tell by how she'd look at me when I came off the phone. I didn't say nothing to her, though. She could take a long walk off a short pier if she thought I was telling her anything.

"Well, Mum is at her sister's - she won't be back until tomorrow afternoon, and Dad's at a conference, but he said he might be back this evening. I think he's just bullshitting me though, to stop me planning any parties. You know how it is."

"I do, yeah." I did, from the movies. My Ma and Da never went off anywhere and left me on my own. And, if they did, they'd send Clodagh in to check on me, like I was fourteen or something.

"I don't think he'll be back at all, though. And if he does come back, you can hide in under the bed or something."

"Oh, so we'll be in your bedroom then?" I liked the sound of that.

"We will not! I'm not one of your slutty eight year olds, Jon." She was never gonna let me live that one down.

"Haha, piss off."

"No, now. You can come around. You can have a cup of tea. But you keep your hands to yourself, and you can go home after *Coronation Street*."

"It isn't on tonight, though." It was Tuesday. That was only on Mondays and Wednesdays; the Ma never missed it.

"Look at you. Brains as well as good looks. Where did I find you at all?"

"In Denmark Street, I think." *When I still thought she was her sister*. That was one of the maddest nights ever, in fairness. And she'd no idea.

"Aww! It's so sweet that you remember that. Careful – if you don't watch out, you're going to get a reputation for being an old romantic, you know."

"Nah, I'm from Thomondgate. We don't have romance here, like."

"Oh? What do you have then?"

"Stabbings, mostly. And hard drugs. Er, *sham*."

"Mmmm, such a bad boy, Musgrave. My bit of rough."

"Yep. That's me." I didn't know if I should have been offended by that, but I wasn't. I liked everything she said to me, or about me. Maybe I *was* getting soft. I didn't care.

"You're the Mellors to my Lady Chatterley."

"Yeah…" I had no idea what she was on about, but her voice was really nice. I'd have listened to her reading out the phone book.

"Anyway. Pen, directions, bus, get here. Chop chop."

"Yes ma'am." I was bursting with the excitement. It was gonna be rapid altogether. No parents, all day. And all night, maybe.

*****

"You know I never actually mentioned what a good job ye did with the painting, Rich. It's so… exactly the same fucking colour, like. Well done," said Niall. We were at practice, on Wednesday. We'd dropped off the music to everyone the night before. Yer man in Savin's let us do photocopies instead of buying the book. Turns out he was actually sound. It was a pain in the arse going around all the houses. Made me wish we all had Frank's thing he was talking about, for sending letters to computers with your phone. I'd finally thought of something useful to do with it. Fair play.

"Yeah, my Dad and his brother did it. He says it's a different shade. It isn't though. He's a spastic." Richie was doing something with a twisty bit on the side of one of his drums. Tuning it, maybe. Drums could go out of tune, Frank said.

"Ah, he's all right, your Da," I said, putting my stand up tall enough to reach my mouth.

"He's a pain in the hole," Richie said, and I didn't argue with him, cos everyone's Mas and Das were pains in the hole, to them. Tim suddenly blasted out the intro to *Light My Fire,* all on his own. We stopped talking and looked around at him. It was spot-on, he didn't miss a note.

"Jaysus, Timbo. Where did that come from?" said Niall.

"I stayed up learning it last night. What do you think?" He was being all modest, but he must've known how rapid it sounded.

"Fucking amazing, man. Do the rest of ye sort of know it?" I said. I hadn't got the words off by heart, but I had my sheet.

"Ah, I know the chords. I can nearly do the lead, but that doesn't matter for now," said Ian. Niall put the strap of his bass over his shoulder and plugged the lead into his amp.

"Yeah, I'm good to go as well, man. And I can do this too." He played the hook from *Break on Through.* That sounded decent as well.

"Right so. Who's counting us in? Richie?" I looked over at him.

"You can do it if you like, Muzz." He hardly ever called me that. I leaned into the mic.

"One, two, three, four!"

*****

Her house was massive. I found it easy from the stuff I'd wrote down off her on the phone. I got off at the right place too, or it would've taken me all the way out to the college. UL was only a proper University for a few years. It was called the *NIHE* when I was growing up, and auld people still called it that, or they just called it Plassey, which was the old name for Castletroy, Frank said. Caoimhe's house had mad big gates and everything, and a big long pebbly driveway. They were open, so I could just walk straight in. I seen a keypad thing there though, and a speakerphone, from when they'd be closed. Pure posh altogether. They must've been loaded.

I rang the bell. It was musical. Classical or something. I knew it, but I didn't know what it was called. She took a while to come to the door. Probably cos the house was so big.

"Well, hellooooooo." She looked gorgeous. She'd a glass in her hand, with something in it, and ice.

"Morning." I looked her up and down. Shoes with heels on them, Jeans with flares, a stripy top, and a sort of red thing around her neck, like a kerchief from Scouts. She looked French, kind of.

"Come in, come in. Sorry about the state of the place." She took my hand and kissed me on the cheek. She smelled a little boozy, and like perfume as well.

"Are you kidding? It's spotless, like." You could've ate your dinner off their floor, as my Ma would've said.

"Eh, yeah. Dolores was here yesterday, but…" We walked in through the hall. Their stairs was wooden and varnished; no carpet. I wondered had they just got rid of the old one and were waiting for the new one to come.

"Who's Dolores?"

"Oh, she's our housekeeper," she said, like that was something normal to say. Pure posh altogether. I felt like a knacker, nearly.

"Ah, I getcha. Fair enough." I tried to make it sound like it was no big deal. Like everyone had a housekeeper.

"Oh God, sorry. I must sound like such a posh fucking twat. I'm having some gin and tonic, do you want some?"

"Eh, yeah, I suppose so. Thanks." It was a bit early, but what the hell. We went into their front room, or one of their front rooms. The couch and chairs were all black leather, and the coffee table was a massive glass thing.

"Come through to the kitchen, the ice is in there."

"Grand." I followed her in, watching her arse move from side to side in the jeans. I was getting the horn already. It was gonna be some day, all the same. She'd a glass on the counter already for me. She stuck it into a bit on the front of their big metal fridge-freezer – the sort of one Frasier has in *Frasier* - and ice cubes came out. I tried not to look too impressed by it, I was already feeling like a right pooro. She got a bottle of Schweppes's out of the fridge part, and started pouring gin into the glass for me.

"Say when…"

"Ah… when." I never understood that thing, cos I always wanted to say *now*, or *stop*. Saying *when* didn't make any sense. She poured me a large one anyway.

"Good boy." She filled it up with the tonic water, and I wondered should I have asked for lemonade instead, cos tonic water was rank, but I didn't wanna look like a gowl, so I just left it go. I took a sip. It tasted good and horrible at the same time, like all spirits did.

"You never sláinted me!" She done a face, but she was just messing.

"Oh right. Yeah, so. Cheers." I clinked her class. Her chest looked massive in that top. Girls' chests always looked bigger in the summer, for some reason. I wasn't complaining.

*****

"D'you remember when we used to climb up here when we were small? When we weren't allowed to, like?" said Richie. We were sitting on the roof of his shed, Wednesday night, drinking some Linden Village out of flagons. His Ma and Da were off at some do.

"Yeah. What were we doing? Looking for ghosts?" My cider was warm, but at least it wasn't flat.

"Haha, probably. Remember we made those tapes?" He picked up a bit of muddy dust and threw it down into the garden. Their dog looked up, all confused. We could see him, but he couldn't see us. You could see all the Square from up where we were. Well, most of it. Joe Mac's house in the middle; the back of the Kellys, whose little kid got killed years ago, the Buckleys who'd a deaf boy, Gar; the Gollies and their Ma who read people's fortunes; the Powers on the corner, with their one ride daughter and one fat ugly one. And the green in the middle, but no one was out playing on it.

"Oh, Jesus, yeah. I found one of them one time." I sparked up a fag. I didn't offer him one; I remembered, this time. More for me, anyway.

"You did? When?"

"Ages ago, now."

"Haha! Mortified. What did we sound like?"

"Gowls."

We were weird kids, me and him. We got really into spooky stuff one Halloween. Drawing pictures; big ones, on these big sheets of paper my Da had in the shed. They were orange, not white, but we were only drawing in biro, so it didn't matter. We'd draw skeletons and vampires and ghosts; both of us drawing on the one sheet. We'd go into the library and find books with Irish ghost stories, and see if there was any ones about Limerick. There wasn't any really, not about the city, more just about places out the country. Like Adare and all that. Except the one about Drunken Thady and the Bishop's Lady. That was a scary one, and it happened just down the road. We used to go down to Thomond bridge to see the scrape marks where the fingernails had dug in. My Da said those marks were only from something when they were building the bridge, hundreds of years ago, but we didn't believe him.

We used to walk around at night, looking for spooky things and bats and ghosts, and frightening the shit out of each other. And Richie'd this ghettoblaster thing that could tape tapes, so we used to make our own little radio shows about ghosts and stuff. We'd do stupid American voices for some reason, and listen back to them, thinking we were pure cool. It was when he was about ten and I was about nine. Whenever there was sweets out that had skulls or coffins, we'd go down the shops and buy loads of them. And Richie got the Ghost Castle game for his birthday; we loved playing that. We were an awful pair of eejits, but we were only small. Pure innocent. It felt like a million years ago now.

"Rich?"

"Yeah?"

"What's the story with that Shane guy?" I dunno why I brought it up just then, but it popped into my mind, thinking about the old days.

"What Shane guy?"

"Collopy." I had way more left in my flagon than I thought. It was cos the bottle was brown, and you couldn't see the label either. I took a long swig while I waited for him to say something.

"Eh, him? He's… I dunno, man. I haven't talked to him in ages, like. Not since – not since I started going to Ardscoil, like. Long time ago." He wasn't looking at me when he was talking; just staring down into the garden. I didn't know if that meant something or not.

"Why's that then? Did ye just… drift apart or something, like?" I knew it was more than that, but Richie was tricky to get stuff out of sometimes. Ciara said that about him to me too, so I wasn't just imagining it or nothing.

"Ah, er, I dunno. I suppose so, yeah. You know what it's like. You start going there, and everyone's different, and… and like, you don't really talk about no one back home to them lot, cos they're all pure snobby and stuff, and they'd think you're a knacker, yeah?"

"Yeah. Yeah, same here, like." People from Ardscoil didn't know nothing about the worser parts of Limerick. They just thought they did, even though they'd never even been there, and that was annoying. I'd got in a fair few fights in 1st and 2nd Year. Just with people being pure ignorant and stuff. It stopped after a while, though. Same as anything does.

"Yeah, and, I got friends with new people there; and with people I used to know from JFK, and it was like, well… I changed?" His face looked saddish.

"Yeah, I suppose. I get you, sort of. But like, Shane and them - when I remember it back, I remember you were hanging round with that lot for ages, and sometimes you'd be hanging around with me, and sometimes you wouldn't. But like, at some bit, you stopped." I was thinking about the time five years ago. It was still clear, though. I still remembered it, cos of lots of things.

"Stopped what?" He took a big swig out of his cider. He was ahead of me, cos I could see the ends of it, under the sticker, when he put it down again.

"Just… stopped hanging around with all of them. Dara, Shane, Joe, Der- well, not… Anyway, you started calling up for me. And you'd be talking to me about your missus, and you were always like either up at mine, or off around with her, and you weren't ever with them again. Like, all of a sudden, nearly."

"Oh right, yeah. Yeah, that's true…" He was looking into the garden again.

"So… did something happen?" Lots of things happened back then. Lots of things in Thomondgate, in one week, but that's not what I meant.

"Happen with what? With who?" He was looking at me again now.

"With Shane. And Dara. And Joc. I mean, I know something happened with, well, you know what I mean. But, why weren't you palling with the rest of them, after that summer? Was it just the Ardscoil thing, or…" I didn't know if he knew what I was getting at. I didn't even know what I was getting at. But there was something there, I knew it. Something *off* about it, that he wasn't saying to me. Something he'd never said to me.

"Eh, I dunno, Jon. It's a long time ago now. I don't think it was anything that like, happened."

"No?" I didn't believe him. At all. But what could I do? Torture him to get the truth? I necked back the last of my cider. I wanted another fag.

"Yeah, no. You know what I think it was? I think I just grew out of them. Or I grew up, and they didn't. Does that sound stupid to you?"

"Naw. Makes sense, sort of." It did. And he was going with yer one back then as well, and she was older than him. Maybe that was just it, and I was the one being stupid.

"Yeah. I mean, you seen them yourself these days. Around. They're still the same as they were back then. And I'm… well, I'm different. And so are you." He looked pure wise when he said that, like he was 20 years older than he really was, I thought.

"Yeah, I suppose. But Shane, though…" I gave it one more shot.

"Yeah?" He looked like he was tired of me asking him stuff, but he didn't look cross.

"Do you think he's… dangerous, like?" I didn't know if that was the right word, in fairness. I didn't even know why I was asking about Shane, cos the youngfella had never done anything to me. I'd just got some shite in my head about him back when Áine was missing first. But he'd shag all to do with that. I knew that now. But, still…

"Dangerous? How'd you mean, like?"

"I dunno. I never knew him, like – I never hung around with him when we were small. But I remember everyone thinking he was a hard man and all that, and then like… and how did he get that scar?" I'd asked people before, but everyone said different stories. Most of them were just guesses.

"How am I supposed to fucking know, Jon?" He said it like I was accusing him of doing it or something. He looked… offended, nearly.

"Er, I don't know. You used to know him, like. I was just wondering if-"

"Look, I don't know anything about Shane Collopy now. I used to know him, and he was a wanker. And, if he's anything like the rest of them round here, he's not gonna have changed much. He's still probably a wanker. And, is he dangerous? Well, he's one of the Collopys, so what do you think? They're scumbags, man. I wouldn't wanna end up down a dark alley with any of them, like. Would you? And, the scar thing - I dunno, bud. I heard he fell off his bike. Any more questions, like?" I couldn't tell if he was angry at me, or just a bit drunk. So I left it.

"Heh. Naw, you're grand, Rich. Will we get another couple of bottles?"

"More? What time is it?"

"Ah, it's early still." I'd no watch, but Quilty's offie didn't close until eleven.

*****

"A *treehouse*?"

"Yeah, it's just out here, down the bottom of the garden. I can't believe I haven't told you about it before. Come on!" Caoimhe took my hand and dragged me with her through the really short grass. Their back was massive, and full of perfect looking flowers. They must've had a gardener. As well as Dolores, like. There was no way the Ma and Da kept it all that nice. Especially since both of them worked, like she said. The Da was a professor in UL, or something like that. The Ma had her own shop in town, selling clothes for tall people. And fat people, maybe. I couldn't remember exactly. It was more like a tree *cabin* than a tree house. It was massive, and long. Between two big trees, with poles in the middle, to hold it up.

"Jaysus."

"It's cool, isn't it? Dad built it for – He built it years ago, when we – when I was little." Her voice cracked a little. I knew it was cos she was thinking of Áine, but I didn't wanna say anything about it.

"It's amazing, like." We were standing under it now. There was a little ladder to go up, into a square hole thing.

"Wait til you see inside. Come on." She climbed up first. I waited, cos it didn't look strong enough for the two of us to be on it at the same time. She shouted down behind her:

"You're not looking at my bottom, are you, Jon?"

"Ah, no." I was, of course.

"No? Why not? What's wrong with it?" She was up now, looking down at me through the hole.

"Er, nothing. It's lovely, like. You've a great arse." I was a little bit drunk. Gin on an empty stomach.

"You say the most romantic things. Come on, up you get."

It was amazing in there. They'd plugs in the wall and all. A telly, a video player, a couch-looking thing.

"Wow."

"Yeah, I know. Here, did you want to watch something? Wasn't it *Psycho* we said?" She pointed to a shelf behind the TV with a rake of videos on it. It was like being in Xtra-Vision. She really was mad into films.

"Ah, yeah. It was." I didn't really wanna watch something. I wanted to get her on the couch and do all sorts of stuff with her. There was no Ma and Da around. We could do anything. But I didn't say that, cos there was no hurry, and I wanted to make her happy. I really did.

"You don't sound too enthusiastic. Here, have a look through those. I've got… something for us." She moved the little round table in the middle over to the side, and got down on her hands and knees. I wondered what she was up to.

"Okay, yeah." I looked at the names of the films. They weren't in any order, really. *Soylent Green, Friday the 13th, Angel Heart, Chinatown, The Crying Game, Jacob's Ladder*, and *Psycho*, of course. I'd only heard of some of them. I looked back at her. She was taking one of the floorboards up. Her arse looked even better than normal the way she was bending.

"See anything you like?" she said. She probably meant out of the films, though.

"Ah, yeah. Few good ones. What you up to?" The one *Angel Heart* looked like the best one. I seen the trailer for it on Sky Movies, but I'd never watched it, cos it was an 18s, and the Ma said it wasn't suitable, and my telly in my bedroom didn't have the cable on it, so I couldn't watch it on the sly.

"Me? Oh, nothing. Just ah, getting us some treats to have during the movie." She winked at me, and held up a small baggie of white powder. My heart did a little jump, cos I kind of guessed what it was.

"Is that…"

"Speed, yeah. It's good stuff too, trust me. If there's one thing my sister is good for, it's that she knows really good dealers. This is quality fucking shit, trust me." She looked a small bit sad when she mentioned Áine, but she said 'is', not 'was', and that made me feel kind of better about it.

"Heh, yeah." I almost nearly said something I shouldn't have – about Áine, and the GBH, but I stopped myself, thank God.

"Right then. Pick a flick for us, and I'll rack them up." She put an album cover on the table – the *Nevermind* one, with the naked baby – and started chopping up powder with a bank card. The two of them weren't anything like each other, really. But then, in some ways, they were.

*****

"So, when exactly did we lose you to the Dark Side, you big mush? *So* disappointed in you, Jon. Me and you - were the last ones left, like. And now, well…" She was only messing, Ciara was. I knew she was happy for me, and I could take a slagging off her anyway, cos she was sound out.

"Ah, I dunno, like. What can I say?"

I was actually beaming. It was Thursday already. We were in the Supermac's in town. It'd been a rapid week. Especially the Tuesday. And I'd been to the cinema earlier, with Caoimhe. We went to see *Natural Born Killers*. It was an 18s, but they didn't say nothing to us going in. It was brilliant altogether. Yer man Robert Downey Junior was in it. He wasn't normally in cool films. I hadn't seen him in anything in ages, really. Woody from Cheers was in it too, but he looked nothing like him, so Caoimhe was the one who had to tell me who he was. We didn't even shift each other for most of it, cos it was so good. And she loved movies anyway, so I wasn't really expecting to get much off her during it. And I didn't mind either, cos there was no hurry. I'd see her again soon. It was hardly like that was the last time she was ever gonna be with me. We were going with each other properly now. The battle was in two days as well, so there was lots to be beaming about, not just her.

"You disgust me," she said, making a slurping noise with the straw in her milkshake.

"I am pretty disgusting, in fairness." I'd got a Fish Box Meal. I liked the chicken boxes, but sometimes I was in the mood for fish. No one else I knew liked them. It wasn't even real fish. Well, not fresh fish anyway. It was nice, though.

"Yeah, but normally you disgust me in more interesting ways. Now you're just… gay." She was nearly finished her food. She was just picking greasy chips out of the bottom of the box. The ones that were hiding under the chicken at the start.

"Love you too."

"Haha, naw. I'm made up for you, really I am. When are you seeing her again?"

"I saw her today, like."

"Yeah, I know that; you said. Is she coming on Saturday though? Do I get to meet her?"

"Yeah, of course. Didn't you meet her at the party, shur?"

"Hmmmm, no, not really. I looked out on the roof at some point and you were eating the faces off each other. I didn't like to interrupt." She winked at me. I didn't remember too much about a lot of that night.

"Yeah. We were probably busy, in fairness." I was grinning again. Even thinking about her made me happy. It was pure weird. But I liked it.

"Jesus, will you stop with the fucking smiling, you spa? I'm not used to it off you."

"Ah, fuck off. One day your prince will come, love."

"Pffft. Unless you literally mean Prince, I'm grand." She finished the last of her shake. Women loved Prince, for some reason. Even white women. He was going away with Kim Basinger and everything, when she was making Batman. I read it in the News of the World magazine. He was only a shortarse and all. He must've had a langer like a horse.

"How about Michael Jackson?" When we were growing up, girls used to have posters of him on their walls. Clodagh had a *Bille Jean* t-shirt; she got it done in that metaller shop in Williamscourt Mall; they printed anything you liked in there, as long as they had it. It didn't have to be off a metal band or anything.

"Eh, maybe a few years ago, like. When he still looked…"

"Black?"

"I was gonna say *human*…" She put her coat on, and leaned over into my box to see was I finished my food yet. She was right, all the same. He'd gone pure weird looking since he came back with *Bad*. His music wasn't any good either now, really. But the videos were still brilliant.

*****

"I'm a fucking heartless bitch, Jon." She'd tears in her eyes, nearly. Or they might just have been watery from the drink, or the speed. I couldn't really tell. She was sniffling too, but that could've been the drugs as well.

"You're not. You're not at all. I think you're – I really like you." I was feeling things I didn't really understand. It was like – her being sad was making me sad. And I wanted to stop it. I wanted to fix her, to make that feeling go away. And to make her better, cos I-

"You shouldn't. I'm horrible." She picked up her glass to drink out of it, but it was empty. That was the third time she'd done that. We'd watched the film – *Angel Heart* – It was pretty mental, especially the end of it. I didn't see that coming. Then we'd had a bit of shift, and a bit of a chat, all drugged up of course, and then she started talking about Áine, and that was how we'd got here.

"No. No, you're not." I still had some in my glass. I wasn't bothered about it, though. I wondered should I give it to her. But maybe she'd had enough.

"You don't even know me, really." When she said that, it made me feel bad. Hurt, nearly. It wasn't true. Or, it was, but I still didn't like it.

"I know you enough. I know you enough to know you're… great. You're amazing. I've never met – I've never known anyone like you. You're – you're lovely." I wasn't lying, or telling her what she wanted to hear. I wasn't like that with her at all – the way I'd be with other youngones, just telling them some bullshit, so they'd shut up and let me carry on getting what I wanted. I meant it. I cared about her. She was different. She was special. Her face went a weird kind of sad looking – like sad mixed with happy.

"Thank you…" She put her arms around me and held on to me tight, for really long. And I liked it. I didn't want her to stop. Her skin was warm, and the smell off her neck made me feel really good. I didn't know why a smell would make you feel nice, but the smell of her did. I started to stroke her hair, and I could tell she liked that, cos she made nice noises, and she squeezed into me a little more. I looked over her shoulder at the table, and the wrap of speed on the record cover. I wondered what time it was, cos it was still bright out.

"I… I'm really glad I met you, Jon." She looked up, into my eyes. I wanted to kiss her, but I didn't wanna stop looking at her. I could've looked at her face forever, like. I'd never get bored of it.

"Me too. Me too." I put my fingers through the hair behind her ear. My heart was going ninety, and it wasn't even the drugs. She was better than drugs. She closed her eyes for the kiss, and I did the same. We stayed there for ages, shifting each other, not coming up for air. Every second of it was brilliant. I forgot everything else in the world – the good stuff and the bad stuff, when we were like that. It was like nothing I… I wanted to stay like that with her, there, and never do anything else or go anywhere else. This was what people were on about when they wrote them songs about love that I never really got before. This must've been it. I must've been – I had to be -

"Jon?" Her voice took me out of my little dream, but not all the way, cos I loved her voice as much as I loved –

"Yeah?" I was breathing heavy, like I'd just finished a race or something.

"Let's go to my room."

*****

"All right then, Crane. Show me what you got," said Bríd. She was sitting in a chair in Richie's shed. It wasn't her first time coming to a practice; she used to come to Tim's yonks ago. It was her first time here, though.

"Sure," I said. It was Friday, the battle was tomorrow. I'd asked her to come over, cos we were ready now, and I wanted someone fresh to hear us – to hear the whole four songs. We started with *Light My Fire*, Tim and Richie started that one on their own, together. I watched her when they kicked it off, her eyes went wide, and she started grinning. That was what I'd been hoping for.

We pulled off all four songs without any fuck-ups at all. We didn't even stop or chat away in between. It was like a proper rehearsal. Pure professional. Everyone was buzzing after we finished on *Sweetness Follows*. We were ready, I thought. And the rest of them thought it too. I walked over to Bríd after I turned my amp off. I tried not to look too big headed, but I dunno if it worked.

"So?"

"Are you kidding me, Jon?" Her eyes were kind of light brown and green at the same time. Nice looking. She was a nice looking girl, really. Apart from the curly hair.

"What?" I pretended I didn't know what she meant, but I knew she meant we'd been brilliant.

"Pfffft, ye're amazing. Seriously like, not just cos I know ye. Not just cos you're my friends, like. Ye are seriously good. Seriously. I think ye might win it!"

"Ah now, steady on, like." We weren't gonna win it, but we were gonna do a hell of a lot better than I would've thought if you'd asked me a month ago. We weren't gonna win it, but people were gonna be impressed, like. Chalk it down.

"Honestly, unless fucking Pearl Jam themselves turn up, I think ye're gonna be the best there," said Bríd. She was touching my arm. It was really funny how, since I had an actual girlfriend, stuff like that didn't mean nothing to me anymore. A few weeks ago I'd have been thinking 'Hey, hey. What's the story here, like?" Not any more though. It was pure strange. In a good way.

"You know the DTs are in it, right?"

"Ah, fuck them," she said, rolling her eyes. I remembered she used to go away with Eric, and he'd dumped her, I heard. So she was probably a bit biased.

"I heard you already did, like. Well, a third of them, anyway."

"Oi! Piss off! I didn't do nothing of the sort, you wanker." She pushed me in the chest, messing. I believed her too, but only cos I'd asked Ciara had she rode Eric, and Ciara said no, and Ciara would've told me if Bríd told her, even if Bríd had told her not to tell anyone. Cos you couldn't trust no one, really. That's just the way it was.

*****

"What was that?" Caoimhe's voice was the first thing I heard Wednesday morning. I'd no idea where I was, and my head was pounding.

"What was what?" I looked around the room, half-awake. It was messy, compared to the rest of her house, but that wouldn't have been hard.

"Shhhh, will you a second?" She looked scared, nearly. I wondered what time it was, and how long we'd slept in. It was really sunny out, even through the little crack in the curtains.

"Okay, sorry." I listened to hear what she was hearing, but I couldn't hear nothing.

"No, it's okay. You're okay." She squeezed my leg under the quilt covers, to make me feel better. I'd my jocks on, I wasn't naked. I must've put them back on after we'd – I heard the noise now. It was a car.

"Shit," I said. "Who's that?"

"I don't know. It might just be a parcel or something; a delivery. Mum's not back until later on – and Dad said, well, he said he might be – listen, you have to get dressed. Quickly. Really quickly! I'm sorry. But you have to. They'll kill me. They'll – just…"

"It's okay. I'm on it, I'm on it!" I hopped out onto the floor in my bare feet and looked around the room for my stuff. My heart was going ninety again, but not in a good way. The car noise outside got closer, and then it stopped. I pulled my jeans on as fast I could, but it felt like I was taking ages.

"Shit. Shit, shit, shit, shit." She was panicking, but she wasn't getting dressed herself. She'd no bra on, and she was covering herself with the quilt, like one of the women in a James Bond film. I found my top hung over the post thing at the end of her bed, and pulled it on over my head. I couldn't see my tackies anywhere. A car door opened outside, and then slammed again. It sounded really, really near. Her bedroom must've been at the front of the house.

"What do I do?" I didn't know, myself. In the films, they'd climb out a window, but I couldn't do that, cos it sounded like her Da was right outside, or her Ma; whichever one it was. Or they hid under the bed, but her bed was really high off the ground for a bed, so I reckoned you could see straight under it from her bedroom door, if you were one of her parents, or anyone else. Even though she'd joked about me hiding under there, yesterday on the phone.

"I don't know. You need to hide. You need to – okay, okay - the wardrobe. Fuck, fuck, come on. Quickly!" She sort of pushed me off the bed, and I landed on my knees. But I spotted my tackies from down there, so it was nearly a good thing. There were really loud footsteps outside now. I was glad we'd closed the curtains, cos we were on the bottom floor, I remembered, and her Da might have been able to look straight in.

"Oh God, I'm sorry!" She whispered it, nearly. I was panicking as much as she was now. I grabbed the tackies, and went across to the wardrobe.

“You’re grand. It’s fine.” I opened the door and squeezed in between all the hangers of clothes. It wasn’t tall enough for me to stand up straight it, so I slid down the back wall and sort of half sat, half squatted, holding my tackies, and my breath as well. There was no noise from outside. Just her, breathing. We’d had such a great day. And night – Jaysus. I’d gone all the way with girls before, but it’d never been anything like that. And it wasn’t the booze, or the speed. It was the – the music off the doorbell made all the quiet go away. I heard Caoimhe doing something – maybe putting on a dressing gown or something. Then I heard her feet on the floor, and the bedroom door opening, and then nothing, for a good while.

I was trapped in there, really. There was no way I could stick my head out and see what was going on, cos I’d no idea who’d be out there when I did. I had to stay put, until she came back. I wasn’t too uncomfortable, but I was trying to stay very still, and I was worrying one of my legs would get a cramp in it, and when that happened, you’d no choice – you’d to sort it out, or your whole leg would go all numb, and that was one of the worst feelings ever, and you’d to lie down and get someone to push your toes back for you, like we did when we were playing soccer. If that happened, I’d have to come out of there, and then I’d be –

“Hello.” Caoimhe opened the wardrobe door, with a big mad smile on her face. She was wearing a silky looking nightie thing. There was no one else with her.

“Hi.” I started pushing myself back up the wall behind me, cos I could still get a cramp if I wasn’t careful.

“It was the fucking postman,” she said, holding her hand out to help me up.

"You're joking." I started laughing a bit too much, but that was the nerves coming out. I looked at her again. She was so fucking beautiful it nearly hurt me to see her. It'd hurt me more not to, though. Way more.

"Nope. But, yeah. Probably better if you do get yourself out of here, while you still can. Cos next time, it won't be the postman, you know what I mean?" She looked sad. I liked the way she was moving her fingers on my wrist. I liked everything she did to me.

"Oh, okay. Like, now? Will I go now?" I probably looked sad too, but that was grand. I liked showing her how I felt. There was no need to play it cool. She wasn't like other girls. She wasn't like anyone.

"Hmmm, let me see." She pulled me in close to her, and I could smell the smell off her neck again, but it was even better now. My lips were about a millimetre away from the skin on her shoulder, and all of her felt pure hot. I moved my fingers down all the way from her neck, over the silkiness of the thing she was wearing, right down to her backside. I was nearly bursting out of my jeans from how much I –

"Yeah. Maybe another half an hour, yeah?" She gave me a really cheeky look, and walked me over to the bed. I wanted to say something smart and funny and romantic, maybe, but I could barely even think of any words, she'd me so… whatever you'd call the way she made me get.

"Yeah," I said, finally, in nearly a whisper. She laid back on the sheets, and put her hand on the neck of my t-shirt to pull me in to her.

"Or *maybe* an hour…" she said, closing her eyes for the kiss. I'd have stayed a lot more than an hour, if I could. There was nowhere else I wanted to be except with her.

*****

"Okay, these are fucking strong, man." I'd only had a handful of the mushrooms off Harta. They looked pure weird; nothing like the ones we'd pick out the country ourselves, in November. They were black, with long tops. The ones we normally got were sort of grey, with little nipply heads.

"Told you. Direct from the 'dam, bud. Quality merchandise." His friend had brought them back from Holland on the boat. You could just walk into a shop and buy them over there. He had to smuggle them in his bag, but it was grand, cos Harta said sniffer dogs were only trained to find hash and real drugs. Mushrooms just smelt like… mushrooms.

"I can *see* the music, like." We were in Marie's, on Friday night, in the spare room he stayed in. The stereo up there wasn't as good as the one in the front room, but she was down there now, with her friend English Bob, so we went upstairs to get out of their way.

"That's nothing, man. I can *smell* it." It was darkish in the room, and Harta was smoking a fag. The orange tip of it was doing trails in front of him, and I could see a little green dot following the orange one, even though it wasn't really there. Pure trippy. There was no curtains, so the streetlights were coming in from outside, and it was making everything look weird and rapid and scary and good.

"What does it smell like?" I could feel all the ridges on the tips of my fingers, and I was feeling them with the ridges on the tips of my other fingers. I tried counting them in my head, but I kept forgetting what I was doing.

"Avocados." Harta's voice sounded weird, like it was doing an echo, but the echo was happening before he said the words.

"I dunno what an avocado smells like, though."

"Of course you do. It smells like this music."

"Ah. I see. Well that's just… that's just common sense, isn't it?" I said, feeling a sort of rush in my head and my chest, and the skin on my face starting to get hot.

About a half an hour later I was really regretting taking them mushrooms. I was locked in the bathroom in Marie's. I'd locked it myself, like. Someone hadn't locked me in there. The bathroom downstairs, past the kitchen, with the bath in it. Not the one upstairs that was just a toilet. I dunno why I'd come down there, but I had. I was standing in front of the mirror, looking at my own face. Always a bad idea. My skin looked green and yellow. I started moving my mouth, and I could hear my tongue, really loud. I moved the rest of my face, and it was like it had joints in it. Like I could move bits of it I normally wouldn't have been able to. And I could hear it. I could hear the bones of my skull, moving around under the skin and the flesh.

I got away from the mirror and sat down on the toilet. That was a bit better. I closed my eyes, cos I hadn't liked what I seen in the mirror, so maybe not seeing anything would be good. But when I closed them, I still saw things, cos mushrooms didn't play ball with you at all. They didn't go by the rules, cos they were just craziness wrapped up inside themselves – inside a food. But it wasn't really like food. I wouldn't ever have eaten normal mushrooms, in my dinner, or in a soup. They were horrible things altogether.

It was all black first, though, when I shut my eyes. Not really black, kind of purply, but still empty. Then I started seeing the numbers. All different numbers, green and yellow and purple, just written on the black, like someone was using outer space as a blackboard, and using light as some chalk. It was maths. There was equals signs and pluses and multiplied bys – everything. I wasn't good at maths, or science, or… equations. That's what they were – equations. That was the bit of maths I really wasn't good at. But I wished I was now, cos my brain was telling me this was important. My mind was saying to me that these were the answers. The answers to everything. Not like, to the things I was wondering about – what was going on with me, what'd happened to Áine – none of that stuff. That was just Me Stuff. These were the answers to the whole of life, and universe, my brain said. All I had to do was look at them, and take them in, and work it out. Solve for X. Or Y. Or for A, B, and C. For all of them, and then I'd know the answer to everything. And when I came out of this trip, I'd be – well, I'd be a genius, like Einstein, or yer man Stephen Hawkings, who looked like a spastic but was actually the cleverest man in the world. But I wasn't the cleverest man in the world. I wasn't even the cleverest in my class in Ardscoil. Especially not in maths. I was only doing Ordinary Level for my Leaving Cert next year. I was pure stupid.

Every time I thought a bad thought like that about myself now, my emotions went right down, and I felt like I could cry. And when I thought a good thought, like about Caoimhe, and shifting her, and riding her, they went crazy up and up, and my heart went so fast I was afraid it was gonna kill me. And when I thought about the maths, and how I needed to solve the problem, and I couldn't, I just felt like I couldn't breathe, like I'd asthma, and I wanted to stop feeling that feeling, so I tried to take control. I tried to choose what I felt about.

So I thought about Caoimhe. I thought about her gorgeous face, and how soft her skin was, and how great her lips felt when were kissing. How nice it felt when her fingers were on my skin, when her breath breathed on me. How nice it was to get the first smell of her whenever I met her, and how much just being near her made me on the horn. And I thought about all the things we'd done the other night – stuff I'd thought I'd forgot, cos of the drink and the drugs. And I could see pictures now, like a movie – clear as day. I saw her, gorgeous, naked. I saw her face down there, between my legs. My langer in front of her lips, all stiff and rock hard. It was so clear it was like I was there myself, inside a movie; inside a 3D movie. But it was a movie where I could feel the feelings and smell the smells, as well as seeing and hearing. It was better than any movie. When her tongue licked up and down the whole length of my yoke, I felt every bit of it. When she put all of it into her mouth, I could feel all of the hotness and the wetness. When she stopped for a second, and smiled, I could feel the love inside my heart. When we started doing it for real, it was like I was there, taking her knickers off real slowly, touching the skin on her stomach, the way she was flat and round there at the same time in a way that I thought was so gorgeous – it was like I was watching a repeat of Tuesday night on TV, except I wasn't watching, I was in it. When I took the knickers off over her ankles and kissed down the insides of her legs, I could feel everything, and smell everything – she smelt so good down there, better than anyone I'd ever done that with. And she even tasted good, cos I was tasting her again now. And I could hear her too – groaning and moaning, and telling me not to stop. And when I was finished on her with my mouth, and she begged me to put it inside her, I heard that too. And I felt it – being in her, all the way. So warm, and wet, and a perfect fit.

And it wasn't even a movie anymore, it was more like a time machine, cos I was back then, on Tuesday, and back there, in her bedroom, and it was real, and I felt it all again, and I did it all again, and when I was inside her, and moving, and she was moving with me, I leaned down to her face, and I kissed her, and it felt like we weren't even two people anymore; it was like we were just the one thing, just like it had felt on Tuesday night. And when we finished, for the first time that night, and I was panned out on top of her, breathing,

I told her I loved her, and she said it back to me too. And I meant it, and she did too. The same as we did on Tuesday.

Nine

"Okay guys – the drummers, especially – listen up! We're gonna just use the one kit for the sound checks, like we told you during the week. Same kit we'll be using tonight. The one from the… Delirium Tremens? Am I saying that right, or do I call you the DTs? Either's fine? Okay. Cool, cool. Just checking. Great name, by the way, guys. Christy Moore's an absolute legend. Aaaaanyway, the rest of you: if you've brought your amps, you can use them now, but for tonight we'll probably use the best ones we have. Saying that, if you've brought a good one, we might ask you to leave it up there, just so we get the best possible sound - all right guys? Cool, cool. Uhhhhh, what else… We've got a PA here, and monitors, but - singers? I know you might be a bit fond of your own mics, but I'd much prefer if you used the ones we have up here. They're like 400 quid a pop; they're *Shure* dynamic ones– the real deal - so I'm pretty … *Shure* they're gonna be better than the ones you have. Haha, sorry about that one. Right. Has anyone got any questions?"

No one said anything. There was barely any of us there yet, in the Glory Hole. It was the daytime. Some of our lads, the DTs, a few youngones and youngfellas who might have been in other bands or might have just come along to watch. It was a half hour before we'd been told to show up for sound checks or roll call or whatever this was. Yer man with the microphone looked around, shrugged his shoulders, and put it back in the stand. There was no reason for him to use it. We'd all have heard him fine if he just talked normally. Me and Ian and Tim were sitting at one of the round tables, with all our gear. The fella hopped down off the little stage and came over to us.

"Hey guys, you get all that, yeah?"

"About the drums? Yeah, I think Richie already knows, cos he didn't ask anyone to give him a lift with his kit, like," I said, looking him up and down. He'd a sort of Hair Metal do, and blue John Lennon glasses. He'd tight jeans on, and sort of young clothes, but you could see wrinkles on his forehead, and crow's feet around his eyes.

"Awesome. Yeah. Good, good. Who's Richie?"

"Ah, he's our drummer?" I was annoyed now that I'd lugged my mic and my stand with me, but they might let us leave them there til tomorrow if we asked later. They'd be safe enough in a pub overnight, I thought. The place would be locked.

"Riiiiight, of course, yeah. Hey, you'll like this one - what do you call a guy who hangs around with musicians?"

"A drummer?" That was the oldest joke in the book. Brillo was always saying it.

"Oh. You know that one, then? Cool. Okay, okay, okay. Here's one: how do you know if a lead singer is outside your front door?"

I didn't know that one. While I was thinking, a voice behind me said:

"He doesn't know when to come in!" It was Richie. He'd no gear with him, just a pair of sticks.

"This guy gets it, am I right? Hahaha." Yer man was some tool. We nodded at him like you'd nod at your English teacher when he was trying to make a joke or be cool. Richie sat down next to me.

"Who's this fella then?" He said it like yer man wasn't standing two feet away from him.

"I'm Jed, man. I'm sort of running the show today, for my sins, heheh. Are those sticks I see? Are you Richard?"

"I dunno, man. Are you my mother?" said Richie, squinting at him. Tim sniggered into his hand.

"Huh?" Jed looked a bit confused.

"Richard is what my Mam calls me, bud. It's Richie. Nice to meet you though… *Jed*." He put out his hand and Jed shook it, still looking a bit not sure of him.

"Great to meet you. Great to meet all of you. Is this the lot then? Nice tight four piece?"

"Ah, no. One more to come." I didn't know where Niall was, but he was usually late.

"Ah, a five piece. Rare, in this day and age, man. Wicked. What's in the box there, sir?" said Jed, looking in Tim's direction.

"Er, a Yamaha SY85."

"Yeah? Strange place to keep a motorbike, isn't it?"

"What?"

"Hahahahaha, your faces, guys. No, man, it's cool. I know what that is. It's a synth, yeah? *Rare* to see a rock and roll band with one of those, guys. You *are* rock and roll, right?

You're not gonna be doing any Technotronic covers, are you? *Pump up the jaaaaam, pump it up*. Hahahahaha. I'm just kidding, don't worry. No, synths can be cool. Roxy Music, the Floyd, Kraftwerk. Looking forward to hearing you guys play, really I am. What are you called again?"

"Crane," said nearly all of us together.

"Like Frasier Crane, yeah?"

"Yeah," said nearly all of us together, but a bit quieter. Tim rolled his eyes, probably cos no one ever asked was it like Marion Crane, off *Psycho*.

"Cool name. I suppose most of you have heard of a little group called Finding Stephen, yeah?" He looked very pleased with himself. Everyone sort of shrugged or shook their heads.

"Eh, haha. Funny. Yeah, no, seriously; I don't think it was before your time or anything. I hope not, anyway, hehe. Way to make a dude feel old, guys ."

I nodded at him, looking at the wrinkles again. He'd a t-shirt on that said *Dead Head for Life*, whatever that meant.

"Yeah, we had a *few* hits, to put it mildly. *Dream Maker*, *Rock the House*, *Alison's Afterglow*?" He looked funny. Sort of hurt. I felt bad for him, so I said:

"Oh yeah! Finding Stephen. I remember now. Yeah. Ye were… *good*!" I nudged Richie, and he nodded, a bit too much, so it looked fake. Poor Jed probably didn't notice, though. He was too far up his own arse.

"There you go. Jesus, had me worried there for a sec, guys, hahaha. Thought I'd lost my mojo," he said. His face had gone a bit pink. I was thinking of The Doors. *Mister Mojo Rising.* I'd been listening to them loads. Especially the live ones. And *The American Prayer*, which was goodish, but a bit weird as well.

"No chance of that, I'd say, Jed. Who could forget Finding Stephen, like?" said Richie, keeping a straight face, and kicking me under the table. I wanted to giggle, like we were in school.

"Phew! Hehe. No, yeah, we had an EP hit the Billboard Top 200 in the States as well for a while. Amazing times, man. They loved us over here too, of course. Clare FM still play our stuff a lot. Well, on Tuesday nights anyway. They've a lot of love for us over there. *Gotta whole lotta loooove*. Classic tune, that. You guys like Led Zep, no?" He didn't talk like a real person. He talked like someone *playing* a person like him, in a comedy.

"Of course!" said Richie. I didn't know he did, but maybe he was bullshitting.

"Cool, dude. What's your favourite LP of theirs?" He said *LP.* No one said LP anymore.

"Ah, not sure really. Maybe *Led Zeppelin 1*. Or *Led Zeppelin 2*. Or… *Led Zeppelin 3*?"

I sniggered out loud, and they both looked at me funny. Then I realised that was what they were actually called, and Richie wasn't making a joke. I felt a bit stupid. Then Jed said:

"All good choices, yeah. I like *Houses of the Holy* myself."

"*The Song Remains the Same*? Great tune, that one."

"Yeah, dude. I should've known you'd be the one into them, here. Drummers always love Led Zep. Our sticks-maestro, Billy Galvin? Yeah, he's really into them. John Bonham was the man, man. Absolute genius, God rest his soul." Jed was Richie's new best friend now. That might be a good thing, if he was one of the judges. He hadn't said if he was; he just seemed to be running the show. It was funny how he called Richie a drummer, too. He'd been a drummer for like a month. Apart from that Sexton's thing.

"Yep. You just couldn't replace him, like. They had to split up when he died. Couldn't go on."

"True, true. Do you remember at Live Aid, when Phil Collins played drums for them?"

"Ah, no. I don't think so," said Richie. They were boring me now. I didn't give a shit about drummers. And I thought Phil Collins was a singer anyway. Maybe they meant a different Phil Collins. They must have. I couldn't remember Live Aid. Well, I could, but I was only small. I was probably out playing when it was on.

"You're probably a little too young, dude. Yeah, he played in the Wembley one, then he flew over on Concorde to America, and like, Led Zep had got back together – just for that show."

"Mad! Were they any good, like?"

"It was fucking terrible, man. It was so bad, right, that Robert Plant and Jimmy Page – they actually took Bob Geldof and Harvey-"

"Back in a bit. Going to the jacks," I said, before I fell asleep listening to the two of them. No one answered me anyway. I walked past some long-haired youngfella with a Flying V guitar, tuning up. I didn't know who he was. The side of his face was like a pizza from all the pimples. He looked like he needed a good scrub.

"Well, how's you?" Steve Clarke was in the jacks, having a piss. He was the bassist for the DTs. I knew him from school as well. He was in Maths with me. And English

"Grand. Yourself?" I'd needed to go more than I thought. It was coming out of me like a horse.

"Eh, I'm cool, man. Ye in this thing tonight then, yeah?" He'd bad skin, even though girls thought he was a ride. It was probably from his big greasy fringe. Fringes gave you spots, if you didn't keep them clean.

"Yeah. Ye are too, yeah?"

"Yeah, man. Why not, like? We just… well, we get to play with the Cranberries, like, so it's worth a go, yeah?" He said it like they only had to turn up to win. That was probably true, but he was still a prick for it.

"Yeah. And loads others there, isn't it? The Stunning, The Blissful Martyrs, The Hitchers…" I couldn't remember who else. I zipped myself up and went over to the sink. I wouldn't have bothered if no one else was there.

"Yeah. I don't give a shit about any of them, really. But it might be a laugh. Few drinks in it, yeah? For the sneer. Catch you later, man." He didn't wash his hands at all. He just pushed his fringe back with them. No wonder he was such a greaser.

Back at the table, Jed was gone, but Niall was there.

"Aboy the head, Muzz. How was the jacks? More than three shakes is a wank, you know that, yeah?" He had a pint. None of the rest of us had gone up and tried, even though the bar was open.

"Bit early for that, isn't it?" I said, even though I wanted one now too.

"Ah, shur it's nine o'clock at night somewhere in the world, Muzz."

"It's nine o'clock in the morning somewhere too," said Richie. Couldn't argue with that.

"Any news on when this is getting started?" I said. We only had to do one song, then we could go until later on, they'd said.

"Ah, he said not long now. He'll call us all out when we're up," said Tim. He was looking at the sheet music for *Light My Fire*. I didn't know why. He was brilliant at it already. And that wasn't the one we were doing, anyway. We wanted to leave that as a surprise, for tonight.

"Cool. Who are that lot?" I nodded over to some lads at another table. All dressed like metallers. Yer man with the acne was part of them. He was sitting with them now.

"Ah, that's Abortion on a Crucifix", said Niall, half laughing.

"Abortion on a Crucifix? Jaysus. What do they play then, smooth jazz, is it?" said Richie, raising his eyebrow in that way he always did. I sniggered.

"Nah, I'd say they do hymns, like." I looked over at them again. Their bass player had a bass with no head on it. I was wondering how you'd tune that.

"They're from Clement's, I think. They used to be called Fuck the Virgin Mary, but they'd to change it, cos yer man who owns the Pike Inn wouldn't let them put it on the poster," said Ian. He'd a tracksuit top on that had big 70s collars on it. Probably got it in The Edge.

"Ah, yeah. Fair is fair. Better off going with something a bit more *family-friendly*, yeah?" said Niall. He was nearly finished his pint already.

*****

By the time we were on stage that night, kicking off our set, I was feeling great. Our sound check had gone fine – I'd screwed up the lyrics a bit, but that was cos of pints on an empty stomach, and me and Caoimhe and Harta had been to the Chicken Hut since then, so I'd plenty of soakage in me now. We were doing *Sweetness Follows* first – the same one we'd sound checked with. There'd been hardly no one around then, so it was grand. The crowd in there now hadn't heard us do it already today. All the other bands had done their checks too, and there was honestly none of them I thought were any better than us, really. Except the DTs, and they'd sort of cheated, cos they did one of their originals, and it was one with no singing on it, so we were ragin', cos we were wondering what yer man Jed was gonna make of Eric's voice. But we'd find out that soon now, anyway. They were on after us, for their first two songs. All the other ones had already done two.

"*One two, one two.*" My voice was coming out clear, and having the monitors on the floor really made the difference. I'd noticed that earlier. I could hear myself really good off them. There was a mad blast of church organs behind me. Tim had his amp up too high. I done a little chuckle into the mic, sort of to get the crowd on our side straight away. It was jam packed. Saturday night, busy pub, Expo weekend, and Jed had put us on late – second on the bill, as Nailer said. After Eric's lot played next, everyone else would do their second two songs, so us and the DTs would be doing our other ones around half ten, quarter to eleven. Everyone in there would be plastered by then, which might be good or bad. I wasn't gonna be drunk, though. I was pacing myself, after earlier. I felt pretty straight.

"This one's called *Sweetness Follows*." I could nearly feel Tim smiling behind me, cos I hadn't said *The*. He started the keyboards, and we got a few cheers before I'd even started singing. I looked down at Caoimhe. This song made me think of her. It was sort of our song, nearly. I was singing it the first time I saw her, in McDaid's. And, I didn't really understand what the lyrics were about, but something about the name of it fitted us. You could barely hear Ian on this one, cos I was playing the rhythm on Harta's acoustic again, but the bits he was doing were actually really cool, if you listened properly. When we finished it, the whole room went mad. I'd to stop myself from grinning like a spa, cos that wouldn't have been cool, and I was supposed to be cool, cos I was the singer. Singers were always cool. Even Jarvis Cocker was cool, and he was sort of a nerd. I gave Caoimhe a little smile, before Niall started *Nicotine Buzz*, and we were off again. Jed was at the side of the stage, wearing his John Lennon shades, moshing away like a metaller. He was all right, him. I was starting to like him a bit.

I got down off the stage after, and Caoimhe nearly knocked me over with the hug.

"Oh. My. Fucking. God. You guys were amazing! *You* were amazing. Oh my God!" she said, after she stopped squeezing the life out of me.

"Ah, now," I said, but I sort of agreed with her, a bit.

"Well done guys," said Ian, slapping me on the back, like he was my coach, or my Da or something. I didn't know what to make of that youngfella sometimes.

"Yeah, lads. Fucking brilliant stuff. Specially you, Timbo," said Niall, who'd a full pint already, like magic. I looked at poor Tim, who had a head on him like he was Bono now. He'd been brilliant, though. The keyboards were the loudest bit of *Sweetness Follows*, so if he'd made a mistake, everyone would've heard it. He didn't, though. He was bang on.

"Lads, ye were all great, honestly. These guys are gonna have to do something special to beat ye. Swear to God," said Bríd. Her and Ciara and Caoimhe and Dearbhla were all sitting in together, thick as thieves. Girls night out. Caoimhe was dressed really muppety – combats, long-sleeved t-shirt, and a black Green Day hoodie. She still looked cute as anything though. She'd have looked good wearing a bin bag, as Harta would say. I heard a mad buzz come out of one of the amps behind me – the DTs were plugging their guitars in. Then Eric's voice:

"Hey. We're Delirium Tremens. This is one of our own. Yeah…" I squatted down next to Caoimhe, cos I'd no chair at the table they were on. The DTs' first one was the instrumental from earlier – they didn't even tell us what it was called; I wondered did the other two come up with the idea to do one with no singing – cos they must've known Eric was shit, they couldn't not know. No matter how good friends they were. And I wondered if their other original was gonna have no lyrics either, cos then they'd only have to do two songs where Eric ruined everything by singing. He was already on the guitar solo now, and people had their jaws on the floor all around us, he was so good at lead. I wondered did they know *I am the Resurrection*, cos if they did that tonight, with the six minute solo at the end, we'd have no chance. They finished up their first one and I clapped along with everyone else. Well, I made my hands do the clapping thing, I wasn't actually making the noise, cos fuck them.

"Wonder what's next?" Caoimhe whispered into my ear. She'd her hand up the back of my t-shirt, and it was tickling me a bit, but it felt good as well. The smell of her made me feel pure calm sometimes, and pure excited other times, even though it was the same smell.

"Bout to find out." I nodded at the stage, where Eric was in front of the mic stand, so he was gonna sing on this one. Hopefully it'd be *Into Your Arms* by the Lemonheads, cos I'd heard them do that one a while back, and he was awful on it. Like a cat getting raped with a nailgun, Harta called it. He started by himself, on the guitar, and I knew the tune, but not the name of it, off the top of my head.

"Nirvana..." said Caoimhe. She was right. I knew it now, it was *Lounge Act*. I got excited a bit, he'd never be able to sing that prop-

He stopped playing before the rest of the song started. I looked at Niall, and he shrugged at me. Then the drums went mental. I knew that beat too, but it was from a different song. What were they up to?

"Huh?" Caoimhe said, but I didn't know what was going on either. The bass kicked in and I recognised it now. Eric leaned into the mic:

"Monkey see, monkey do…"

They'd changed from doing *Lounge Act* to doing *Stay Away*, for some reason. Or maybe it was some joke they were doing. Either way, it was bad for us. I looked over at Ian and he looked worried. *Stay Away* wasn't really a proper singing song. It was all low in the verses and screaming in the chorus. Eric could probably pull that off. I listened to him. He was pulling it off. Bollocks, anyway.

*****

Everyone kept trying to buy me drinks while we were listening to the other bands and waiting to go on again, but I was trying to keep it sensible. The DTs had gone down really well, even though Eric sort of screeched too much in *Stay Away*. The others were all right – Abortion on a Crucifix were just… the best thing about them was their name. And some of the rest of them, well they were just the usual normal boring stuff everyone did. And their originals all sounded like songs I already knew, in small little ways. Like when you'd watch the Eurovision, and nearly every song sounded a bit like Abba. There was none of them we had to worry about. It was one of those times I'd actually have liked to ask Brillo what he thought, but he wasn't coming – he'd his girlfriend's birthday to go to, out in her house. He was coming to the Expo tomorrow though. We all were going to that, cos of the Cranberries and the Stunning, and cos it'd be a mad laugh. We didn't think we were going cos we were playing. We weren't gonna win now. They were.

"Who are they again?" asked Ciara, sitting onto my knee for a second. I'd scobed a chair, and I wasn't moving out of it til I had to go up on stage again, or til my bladder exploded.

"Ah, I think they're called Thumb. Or Numb." I couldn't remember, but it had a B at the end of it, definitely. They were four pure serious looking youngfellas altogether. You'd think someone was after stealing their packed lunches, the faces on them.

"Or Glum," she said. There was a smell of Black Jacks off her again. And vanilla.

"Haha, yeah. Have you seen Caoimhe?" I'd lost her somewhere – she might have gone to the bar after coming back from the toilets, but it was black with people in the place now, you couldn't see no one, cos of everyone.

"Is she not there?" Ciara looked down, and I looked where she was looking. There wasn't anything there though.

"Where?"

"Joined to your fucking hip, like." She winked at me and stuck out her tongue. I jerked my knee up to try and make her fall off, but she gripped onto me like I was a horse.

"Very good. Seriously though, have you-"

"Jesus Christ, thank God you're back," said Ciara, over my shoulder to someone. I felt fingers on the back of my neck, and I knew who it was from the smell.

"Why, was he missing me? The poor misfortune…" Caoimhe leaned in over my shoulder, and I felt her lovely soft chest against my back; even through all her muppety gear.

"Fuck off the two of ye, like," I said. I gave Ciara a little knee up the arse to give her the hint that she should get off my lap and let my actual girlfriend sit there. She understood me straight away, fair play to her.

*****

We were up now. The last lot had been absolute shite – The Climbing Vines, they were called – so terrible I was actually worried they might have ruined the crowd for us. They had barely got a clap when they came off. I was fixing the stand, cos yer man the singer had been a dwarf compared to me. Definitely not too tall to be a rock star, him. Niall put his arm around my shoulder and took me away from the mic so he could say something and not have the whole pub hear it.

"Listen, don't worry, man. They're gonna love us even more now. You good?" He slapped me on the back, too hard as usual.

"I'm good." I took a sly look at the crowd; most of them were chatting, a few were looking up at us.

"Let's do this." He sort of high-fived me, but it wasn't up high, it was in the middle, where a handshake would be. A *middle-five*, maybe.

We'd dumped *Promqueene*, cos it was too like *Nicotine Buzz*. Same amount of chords, same sort of guitar and stuff. We were doing one I wrote called State of Grace instead. There was no keyboard for it, so we'd hooked Tim up with another electric guitar, to make sure we were nice and loud, and so Ian could play the lead without it sounding all empty up there. Richie tapped us in, and I took the mic out of the stand. It had a soft start, then it got heavy. Kind of like *From Despair to Where*, by the Manics, but I hadn't even heard that one when I wrote it, so it wasn't a rip-off. Ian started finger picking real quietly, and Tim did one soft strum, with no distortion pedal. Sounded good so far.

"I'm wanting you to know that I... am fine." I heard Richie do those cymbals that were the really quite ones, that sounded a bit like waves.

"I've got to tell you what it is on... my mind." Another strum from Tim, and a bit of lead from Ian. It sounded rapid. One or two soft beats on the toms from Richie. I could see Caoimhe smiling up at me. It gave me a good feeling in my chest. The crowd were quiet, but that was good. Them talking would've been worse, cos you'd hear it, we were playing so soft.

"Let me take you to my fav...ourite place." Nailer wasn't due to come properly in for another bar after this one, but he was hitting the one note every time Tim strummed, and it sounded brilliant. One more line and then it'd go mental.

"God knows you keep me in a staaaaaaaaaate" Tim's kicked his pedal. Richie's cymbals started getting louder. Ian used his fingers like a capo and ran his plectrum over the tightest part of the strings, right next to the pick-ups, like at the start of *Supersonic.*

"Of............" Niall's bassline came in, Ian stuck his pedal on and dragged his fingers all the way along the fretboard. His amp let out a scream of feedback. We were nearly there. I was bent over my mic, ready to throw my head back when the heavy part happened. Just. One. More. Word:

"Grace." Tim's pedal kicked in again, like a motorbike starting. Nailer came in loud and fast on the bass, Ian screeched out a bit of lead, and Richie fucking exploded behind me on the drums. Nearly straight away, there was people up the front, moshing. We'd chose the right song.

Two and a half minutes later, I was sweating like a bastard, and everyone in the crowd was clapping and cheering. It was a short song, but there was a lot squeezed into it. That was another reason we chose it, cos *Light My Fire* was so long. Richie and Tim started that up now, and I had another look into the crowd. Everyone was facing us now, even the people queueing over at the bar. Maybe we did have a chance. I listened for my bit, and came in on time. I felt a bit like my hair should've been longer for singing this one. Or I should've worn some leather pants. It didn't matter. I sounded good enough. We sounded good enough. We sounded great.

*****

Half an hour later, we were waiting for them to do the scores. The DTs had gone on after us, and I wasn't really sure how they'd done. No one else out of our lot was sure either. They'd done another one of their own, another one with nearly no vocals. It had a bit of singing, but only for a few seconds near the start and the end, and all the rest of it was guitar solos and stuff. And they were good at that, but I honestly felt a bit bored listening to them. So did Ciara, she said.

For their other cover, they did *Creep* by Radiohead, and I was delighted about that, cos there was no way Eric was gonna be able to hit that high note – he was gonna mortify himself. But, when they got to that bit in the song, he didn't sing anything at all, they just did the solo, and sort of added their own bits to it, showing off again, so there was no part where he sounded really shit. That's when I knew we weren't gonna win it. Bríd and Caoimhe were still saying we had a chance, and Harta was saying fuck the DTs, but they were all only being nice. We'd lost, but it was grand. It wasn't like we'd embarrassed ourselves. And I could get pissed now, so that was good.

“What are we doing later, sham?” said Harta, squatting down next to me and Caoimhe.

“Hah? Later? Like, going out, you mean?”

“Yeah. Ye going upstairs?” He was smoking a rollie. It wasn’t a joint. You couldn’t get away with a joint in Quin’s, let alone the George Hotel.

“Eh, Tropics? I dunno about that, like.” I never went there, it was all chart shite and knackers.

“Ah, it might be a laugh,” said Caoimhe. Ciara nodded at her. Niall leaned into the table from where he was standing.

“Upstairs, is it? With all the slappers that go in here? Load of minkers in hotpants and belly tops, all pissed out of their heads, is it? Sounds fucking amazing. Count me in!” He was such a pervert.

“I’ll go,” said Ian. Tim nodded too. Richie and Dearbhla were up at the bar, but the way things were going, I figured they’d say yes too. I shrugged.

“Right then. Suppose we’re going to… Tropics.”

“Ah, Jon, it’ll be a laugh if all of us go up there, yeah?” Ciara said, waving the smoke off Ian’s fag away from her face, even though she was smoking herself.

“It will. And I’ll be there, won’t I? And that’s all you need, like,” Caoimhe said, giving my knee a little squeeze. I rolled my eyes and nodded at her like I was giving in, but she was right. Anywhere would be grand if she was there.

“Aw, shur will you look at ye two, *god bless us and save us*,” said Harta, squeezing my cheek like I was a baby. I got hold of his skinny wrist and crushed it until he let go. Then I said:

“Listen, you. Any chance you can get us some yokes?”

Before he got a chance to answer, someone started talking over the PA. It was Jed.

“Okay, okay. Hey! Shhhh, everyone. Thanks. Thanks. Shut up, now. Yeah.” A few people in the crowd shouted out stuff, but I couldn’t hear them.

“Is this the results?” said Caoimhe. I shrugged at her, but it probably was.

“Okay, guys. First off, thanks to everyone for coming along tonight and supporting the Battle of the Bands. Sorry, the Paddy Expo Battle of the Bands, here in the Royal George Hotel. Gotta keep the sponsors happy, am I right? Yeah. Yeah, anyway. Me and the other judges have finished our… *deliberations*,”

“What’s that mean?” whispered Niall.

“It means shut the fuck up,” said Ciara, looking pure serious for a second. Jed went on:

“And we’re happy to say, we have a winner for you.”

There was a little bit of me that was hoping, but that was stupid. We’d done good, but they’d won. Caoimhe squeezed my arm, all excited.

"So, we'll call out the top three, in reverse order, yeah? Can I get a drum roll, please? No? Place is full of drummers, and I can't get a – oh, hello. What's your name? What? Derek? Derek, it is. Which band are you from, Der? The Escrows? Good name. Good name."

Some youngfella from one of the other bands had run up onto the stage with a pair of sticks. Richie and Dearbhla had managed to get back to us through the crowd. She was a lovely looking youngone altogether, but I didn't know her, really. Jed was still going on:

"Anyway, yes. Now we have Derek, from the Escrows – ye didn't win, by the way, Derek, sorry…"

The crowd all went *awwww* at that. Pure lousy. I giggled, even though I was dying with the nerves.

"What? It's the truth! Tough crowd, ye are, guys. Anyway, in third place, with a score of 23 out of 40, it's…"

I nearly closed my eyes. I knew he was gonna say our name. I could feel it in my bones. Third wasn't too bad. But that meant there was two bands better than us, and I couldn't –

"Numb!" The crowd did a load of whoops and cheers, even if they didn't know who Numb were or like them. Everyone was well pissed by now. It was after eleven. I looked across at Niall to see what he thought, but his eyes were glued to the stage.

"Yeah, well done, guys. One for the future, I think. Yeah? Okay, okay. Next, in second place, with a score of 34 out of 40, it's… Hmmm, well this is a surprise."

It had to be us. Hopefully. I didn't know now, all of a sudden. It was like I thought we were brilliant a few minutes ago, and now, I had no idea if we were terrible or not. I didn't even hear what Jed called out, I was thinking so much, but everyone in the crowd around us went sort of mental. There was even a few people booing.

"What? I missed that. What did he say? What did he say?" I asked Caoimhe. Everyone else at our table was either staring at the stage or standing up now.

"He said the DTs!" Her eyes were nearly bulging at me. It was so loud in there now I couldn't even think properly. Jed came over the speakers again. What the hell was happening? Numb weren't even that good. And none of them bands were better than the DTs. It was a fix or something. I tried to hear Jed.

"All right, all right, all right, guys. Settle down, settle down. Just the one more name, then we're done, yeah. And ye can all get back to… whatever it is you're doing."

I was looking around the room now, for Eric and Steve and the other fella, Tony. I wanted to see what they thought of it. I'd have been going mental if I was them. I couldn't see them at all, though. Their table was empty.

"Okay, okay. The winner of the 1994 Paddy Expo Battle of the Bands… three hundred pounds prize money…"

I'd forgot that bit. Not that it mattered. The whole thing was a fix. Jed was probably in on it too. I'd almost nearly started liking him and everything, the prick. I looked around the table for someone to eye, but they were all looking at Jed. Caoimhe was frozen stiff next to me, mouth open, like a cartoon.

"… and, of course, playing tomorrow in the main event, with The Hitchers, Blissful Martyrs, Something Happens, The Stunning, and *your* very own Cranberries, is…"

"Come on to fuck, will ya?" shouted someone in the crowd. Loads of people laughed. No one on our table did. Jed looked down at his piece of paper again, but he obviously knew who it was already. He was just making it dramatic. I just wanted it to be finished, so I could get pissed and talk to Harta about some yokes.

"Crane!"

I shrugged, let out my breath, and thought "Well thank fuck that's over." I turned around to Caoimhe, who sort of screamed into my face. Everyone at the table was jumping around like Ireland had just scored at the World Cup. I'd no idea what was wrong with them. About two seconds later, the penny dropped, and I realised it was us he'd said. I still wasn't used to that name. We could hardly change it now, though.

*****

"IDs there, lads. Please", said one of the bouncers. He looked like the neck of his shirt was too tight on him. His face was as red as a baboon's hole.

"Ah, what? We just won the Battle of the Bands!" said Tim, before any of us could stop him. I'd never heard anyone sound more fifteen in my life. He was polluted.

"The what? Lads, I don't give a shit if ye just won the bobsled in the Winter Olympics. *IDs. Now*. I won't ask ye again." He looked like he could kill you stone dead with one of his fingers, in fairness. I started doing the thing where I went through my pockets to look for my ID, but there was none in there; I knew that already. Niall showed his crappy UL one, the one with his brother's photo on it.

"What's this? You out in the University, are you?"

"I am, yeah."

"Hmmm, really? What are you studying out there, pal?" said the other bouncer. He was more ratty looking. Skinny, with a pointy face.

"Ah, Biochemical Engineering," said Niall, without missing a beat. He was good, considering how pissed he was. I was still pretending to have lost my ID, even though no one was looking at me.

"Jesus, that sounds a bit hard," said the red-faced fella. He looked like the 12 Times Tables would be hard for him, though. That's probably why he was a bouncer. The rest of them were here with us now – Richie, Ian, Tim, Ciara. Bríd had to shoot off home, she said. Harta was gone to get the drugs. Dearbhla and Caoimhe were in the jacks. They'd be here soon, hopefully. We'd stayed for another drink downstairs, and then headed up.

"Ah, tis all right, shur. You just need a particular… what's it called?" Niall screwed up his face like he was trying to remember something. I was wondering was he taking the whole act a bit far, but he was doing grand up to now.

"Mindset?" said yer man. The rat-faced one turned around and started letting other people through from the rest of the queue, to get things moving.

"That's the one, yeah. Mindset."

"Yeah, so. Tom, isn't it?" That was Niall's brother's name. He was tall as well – I remembered him being in Ardscoil.

"What? Oh right, yeah. That's me. Tom. Tom O'Neill. That's what they call me. Yeah. Tom." He probably should have stopped talking there. Ciara went past me and showed her fake ID to Rat Face. She got in, no problem. Ian went through too, even though yer man took a long few seconds squinting at the shitty Rail Card, before letting him go on. I was standing behind Niall, and Tim and Richie were behind me. It was like we'd our own queue, for some reason.

"So then, Tom…" He took Niall's card and put it against his chest, so you couldn't see the writing anymore.

"Yeah?" said Niall. They were nearly the same height as each other.

"Tell us, what's your star sign?" said yer man, big grin on him. Fuck it anyway, I'd forgot that they used that one to catch you out. Everyone learned off their fake date of birth, but you'd only know what star you were, off the top of your head, for your real birthday. Niall took a few seconds, and the rest of us held our breath. Then he put on this perfect Jim Morrison voice, and went:

"I, am a Sagittarius. The most *philosophical*, of all the signs…" I nearly burst out laughing. The bouncer didn't get it, obviously, cos bouncers in Tropics wouldn't be listening to The Doors. But Sagittarius must have been the right one, cos he nodded, gave Niall back the card, and shooed him in the door. I'd stopped pretending to find my ID now. I was coming up with some story, cos I was next. I had no story, though. Yer man looked at me, I looked at him, and he just went:

"How'rya? Go on in, you're grand." I couldn't believe it. I'd to stop myself turning back to Tim and Richie and grinning like a spa. Then I remembered Tim had been the one complaining, so he must've had no ID himself. Fuck it anyway. I couldn't do nothing to help him, though. He was on his own. I just hoped Richie had some, and that Caoimhe didn't have no hassle getting in. If she didn't get in, I'd just leave, and go off somewhere else with her. But I didn't know how I'd know if she did or not. I gave yer one in the ticket box a full fiver, not four quid, cos no one had given out concessions downstairs. They should've been letting us in free really, but we could hardly start complaining about it. And we'd just won £60 each. I just felt lucky I'd got in. I wasn't gonna push it.

About 20 minutes later and no sign of Richie, Tim, or Caoimhe. Dearbhla either. I was ready to go, when in they came, with Jed, of all people. Caoimhe ran straight over to me when she spotted me. I was really happy to see her. I gave her a massive hug, and a big long kiss on the lips.

"Helloooooooooo! Did you miss me?" She'd totally different clothes on – a black dress with a high neck, but a really short skirt-part. Legs up to her neck, as Frank would say. Her and Dearbhla had changed in the toilets; that's why they'd gone in there.

"I did!" I had, even though I'd only seen her a few minutes ago. It was weird. Everything felt a hundred times better when she was with me, so it felt a hundred times worse when she wasn't.

"Good! I missed you too. Let me tell you the story anyway!" She was so gorgeous; not just cos of the sexy dress. She just… was.

"What story's that?" I saluted the rest of them over her shoulder, so's not to be a gowl. Jed gave me a big cheesy thumbs up. He looked smashed. I liked him now. He'd given us top marks in the judging, he said. We'd got 35 out of 40.

"Oh, the one where none of us could get past the bouncers, and then good old Jed came along to the rescue, and got us all in. For free!" She'd the best smile ever – even her teeth were beautiful.

"For free? Fuck's sake, ye jammy bastards, ye. First round's on you, then, love."

"Haha, fair enough. Have you-" She got cut off by Niall, who'd been up at the bar.

"Jaysus, Muzz. Have you seen the amount of *fanny* in here tonight?" He'd a long-sleeved t-shirt on, with a big green symbol thing in the middle, and the word *Subvert*. It might have been a punk thing. I hadn't asked him about it.

"*Dude…*" I looked daggers at him and nodded my head to point out Caoimhe was there.

"What? Oh! Right. Sorry. Beg your pardon, m'lady. What am I like at all? Eh… Muzz, have you seen the amount of *vagina* in here tonight?"

Caoimhe burst out laughing.

"Listen you, he's brought his own vagina with him tonight, okay?" She wagged her finger at him. She'd nail polish on; light pink-coloured.

"Haha, I know, I know. We're not used to it, Caoimhe – this one, having an auld ball and chain, like. Still, well done to ye. Both of ye. Now, if ye'll excuse me, there's a youngone over there with a skirt on that's the size of a belt, and she's dying to have my babies. She just doesn't know it yet. Cheers, ears." He put his glass up, but we'd no drinks, so he just pretend-clinked the air, and wandered off over to the dancefloor.

"Heh, sorry about him," I said, putting my hand on the bottom bit of her back, just over her *bottom*, as she'd call it.

"Niall? Ah, he's harmless. I mean, he's not harmless to that poor girl in the tiny skirt, but… He's lovely, Jon. All your friends are lovely. Honestly. I really like them."

"They're all right, I suppose. Now, about this round."

*****

"How do you do it?" It was later on, and Ciara had come over to me on the balcony thing that went around the upstairs bit of Tropics. I was looking down at the dancefloor, watching Niall throwing shapes and trying to go away with yer one in the skirt. It wasn't working so far.

"Do what?" I was waiting around for Caoimhe. She'd gone to the bar cos she was faster at getting served down there. Girls always got served quicker, especially good-looking ones.

"The way you just – we're in here, on a Saturday night, right? And there's all these *hot* looking girls, wearing pretty much fuck all, yeah? I mean, super-hot, Jon."

"Yeah…" I didn't know where she was going with this, but it was all true so far. I was seeing could I spot herself downstairs at the bar, but there was too many there to make her out.

"Yeah, and I've been watching you all night, and you seriously haven't taken your eyes off that girl."

"What girl?" I got annoyed, cos I hadn't been looking at no one.

"Caoimhe, you dick." She punched me on the shoulder, messing.

"Oh! Oh right, yeah." I understood her now. Niall was moving in for the kill downstairs. Yer one was tiny. He could've picked her up and taken her home in his guitar bag. He'd probably have to club her over the head first though, the way it was going.

"Seriously, it's amazing. I've never seen you – I've never seen *any* guy act like that. I'm almost… jealous."

"Jealous?" I looked at her funny. I didn't know what she meant. She didn't fancy me or anything. Except maybe when we were both drunk and desperate.

"No, not like that, you spa. Don't worry, Jon. No fear of you there, like. I just mean – that thing that you've got. With her. It's… something else. I wish someone would look at me the way you look at her. Ugh, I'm making myself sick now." She was smiling. You didn't see that a lot, she normally just looked sarky.

"Ah, yeah, I… I suppose so?" I wasn't sure what I was meant to say to that. I liked what she was saying though. It made me feel good. Not even embarrassed; I didn't give a shit about being embarrassed now – not about Caoimhe.

"Hold on to her, Jon. She's making you a…. a better person." She gave my arm a little squeeze.

"Hah, yeah, maybe." It wasn't even a maybe. She was. I'd never been this happy, and it was all cos of her.

"Ooh. Speak of the devil. I'll leave you guys to it, yeah?" She nodded over my shoulder, and I turned around and saw Caoimhe with our drinks. Bottles of Miller, cos it was packed in there now, and bottles were easier to carry through a crowd without getting spilt, she said.

"Ah now, you don't have to go." I was just being polite, obviously. But I liked Ciara, so it wasn't like I wanted to get rid of her either.

"No, no. I'm grand. I'll go find the others. Anyway, once she gets over here I'll be invisible in about 20 seconds, so…" She was still smiling, she didn't mean nothing bad by it. And it was true, in fairness.

"Hey! What are we talking about, then? Hi, Ciara," said Caoimhe. I felt her fingers go into the back pocket of my jeans, and she handed me my bottle.

"Hi! Oh, just love's young dream, like. I like your dress, by the way. Anyhoo, I'm gonna make like a tree and get out of here. Have fun, you two. Don't do anything I… you know the drill. Mwah." She wandered off towards the stairs. I watched her go, and then I forgot about her straight away, and Niall and the one in the skirt, cos my Caoimhe was back.

*****

Harta had basically disappeared. It was only me, Ciara, and Caoimhe who'd given him money, so it wasn't like he'd a bomb of it on him, and it wasn't like everyone was coming over every five minutes asking me where he was, but it was still annoying. The club was gonna be on for an extra hour, cos of the bar extension, so he might still show up, but it didn't look like it. He'd no Jed to get him past the bouncers, either, and he looked like a right hippy for this place, even though he was older than all of us. He'd gone off to some flats somewhere, he said. Down the back of Henry Street. He'd took a loan of my jacket and someone else's hat, cos it was cold outside. He said they might ask him in for a smoke down there when he was buying the pills, but he wouldn't be too long. He fucking was, though.

Ciara hadn't said much about it; she was talking to some girl I didn't know, in one of the booths inside the chillout room. They were looking very friendly though. I kept seeing her touch yer one's leg. Maybe she did swing both ways. Everyone else was just getting drunk, and me and Caoimhe were sitting on one of the nice couches, next to some youngones who looked way too young to even be in there. One of them looked about thirteen.

"Ooh, the slow set!" Caoimhe said, nudging me with her shoulder. We'd been shifting away like kids at a kiddie disco. No shame, as my Ma would say. The dress was making it pretty easy to do stuff as well, but I was trying to be careful not to be too obvious, cos I didn't want no one going past to see us and think she was some sort of slapper.

"Yeah, the *erection section*." Tropics was sort of like a kiddie disco anyway – just with real booze instead of lemonade. They played music from the charts, and old ones from the 80s and the 70s – all pop, though – and about three times a night they'd put on a few slowies, so you could take a youngone up for a dance, and get your hole. *Always* by Bon Jovi was on. The video for that was full of rides, but it still was a shite song. Bon Jovi weren't real rock. They were gay. Guns and Roses were much better.

"Are you not gonna ask me, then?" she said. She was drinking a bottle of Bulmer's now. With a bendy straw that she'd robbed off the bar.

“Ask you what?” I was looking at the kids next to us out of the corner of my eye. They were being so rowdy and loud that they were annoying me now. They were gonna get thrown out if they didn’t watch it. I’d no idea how they’d even got in. But maybe those bouncers were perverts or something. Most bouncers were.

“To dance!”

“Ah… this is shite, though, I said. She liked Belly, and Janis Joplin, and L7, and stuff like that. There was no way she was into Jon Bon and the lads.

“Of course it’s shite; we’re in Tropics, and it’s the slow set. What do you want, *Suzanne* by Leonard Cohen?” She gave me a wink and pushed my chest. She’d done her make-up again the last time she went to the jacks. She looked perfect, but she’d have looked perfect to me even if she’d no make-up on. And that wasn’t even a lie.

“Well, yeah, no, but… at least something decent, like.” The song ended downstairs and a new one came on. It was all bass at the start. I knew it, I just had to think a bit. Then the next bit came in, and I got it. *With or Without* you, by U2.

“Aha! I think God was listening to you, Jon. This decent enough for you?”

“Ah, yeah. Yeah, I like this one. Sound.”

“Come on then.” She sort of had to climb over me to get out from behind the table. She felt nice on me, and she smelt lovely. I could’ve just stayed like that with her, but she wanted to have a dance, and I liked making her happy. I grabbed a hold of her hand and took her down the stairs with me. I heard someone smash some glass upstairs while we were on our way down. Probably them kids. We found a spot on the floor and she put her arms around my neck. There was something about the song that made everything happening feel rapid. Like we were in a romance movie, and this was the bit near the end, where they played a mushy song, and everything worked out perfect. Even though we were really sort of only at the start of everything, not the end. But it did feel perfect. I closed my eyes and kissed her, and it was even better than perfect.

We stayed on for the next song, even though it was Celine Dion, and it was awful, but we didn't give a shit. I'd have stayed up for another one too, if the fast music didn't come on after. When we were walking back off the floor, dodging eejits on their way up to dance to N-Trance or whatever crap it was, she leaned in and whispered:

"You're the best thing that's ever happened to me, Jon. Honestly, you are," and it didn't even sound stupid, cos I felt exactly the same. I thought about saying something back, but the music got too loud, and I didn't wanna shout in her ear, so I just squeezed her hand, and kissed her on her forehead. Anyway, I'd plenty of time to say stuff like that to her. And not just tonight; for a long time after it too. I wasn't going nowhere. And neither was she, hopefully.

*****

"Laaaaaaaads! We're playing with The Cranberries!" It was after two now, when Tim came crashing into our couch upstairs, nearly knocking all the bottles off the table. He was the most langered I'd ever seen him. He didn't get out much, as Frank would say.

"Ah, we are, yep," I said. I'd sort of almost forgot about it, I was so wrapped up in herself.

"Imagine that, like? We didn't even have a Richie four weeks ago. Now, look at us, Muzz!" He'd a smile on him like a six-year old going to see Santa in Todd's. I liked the way he said *a Richie* instead of saying *a drummer*, but maybe I was just langered myself.

"True. And we beat that lot as well." Eric and them had been mortified. Sore losers. Jed told us they'd got up and walked out after he'd said they were second instead of first. They didn't even know we'd won it, I'd say. They didn't even stay for that. I wondered what they'd think when they found out. Probably be raging. That was annoying. It wasn't like we'd cheated or anything. We won fair and square, as my Da would say.

"The DTs? Course we did, Muzz. We're better than them. We're better than… *everyone*, like." He was drinking alcopops, it looked like. Such a lightweight.

"Ah now, we're not better than *everyone*, like."

"We are! Well, we're not better than Nirvana. Or Pearl Jam. Or Green Day. Or U2 – did you hear them playing U2 earlier? I was like "They're playing U2! Fuuuuuuuuuck!!!! – but yeah, okay, we're not better than *everyone*. But we're better than all the bands that were in that battle, aren't we?" Tim's eyes were so big and mad I nearly thought Harta had shown up after all and given all our yokes to him. He hadn't though, the prick. He was still on the missing list. I'd have words with him tomorrow.

"You definitely are," said Caoimhe, drinking her cocktail, even though it looked like it was all just ice left now.

"Caoimhe! Hi! Your dress is… nice. Did you like us?! Did you like *Light My Fire*? That was me, that was!" said Tim. I was struggling not to laugh, cos drunk him was really funny – he was so different to normal him.

"Ah, I think the other boys helped too, Tim."

I looked at her while she was talking. She was so gorgeous, even at two in the morning, with about ten drinks in her. And she wasn't just gorgeous. She was sound as well. And cool. And she loved video games. And she loved, well, *me*. I felt really lucky.

"Pffft. Yeah, okay. I *suppose* they might have, like. Still though, I was good, wasn't I?!"

"You were *great*, Tim." She said it like a Ma would say to her kid about the drawing he brought home from school. She was only messing though – he'd been rapid, we all knew that. He'd probably won it for us.

"Thanks! I've to go now, lads. There's these women walking around down below, right? And they're from Bacardi – they actually work for Bacardi - and they've these backpacks on, and the backpacks have guns attached to them, with hoses, so they look like the guns from *Ghostbusters*, except they don't shoot lasers, they shoot Bacardi, right? And they're wearing hotpants, and belly tops, and boots, and they're all rides; and if you're nice to them, they sit you down on the stage bit, and you lean back like you're at the dentists, and open your mouth, and they squirt a load of Bacardi down your throat. And Jon?"

"Yes, pal?"

"I have been nice to them *many* times tonight. Soooooo many times. Anyway, lovely seeing ye, lads. Bye!" He got up and ran off, like a kid in a playground running over to the swings. Caoimhe looked at me for a second, then she burst out laughing, and so did I, and we went back to our snogging. I'd given up on Harta at this point. It didn't matter anyway; I was already too happy and loved up. No need for any yokes. They'd have been wasted on us. You couldn't get any higher than we already were, just from each other.

*****

I fell asleep at home nearly straight away after my head hit the pillow. I was exhausted, from the day, and all the drink. Whatever it was, I woke up at half five in the morning, the digital clock with the red numbers said. The house was dead quiet. They were both asleep by now. My Da with his eye mask on to keep out the sun in the morning, and the lamp at night when my Ma would be reading one of her Roddy Doyles. My Ma with her earplugs in, to keep out Da's snoring, but not the alarm in the morning. There'd be no alarm today though, cos it was Sunday. The Expo. We were supporting The Cranberries, in Arthur's Quay Park, cos we'd won. I'd forgot that. It was amazing.

I tried not to move too much, cos that was the best way to get back to sleep after you woke up in the night. Don't move too much, don't think too much, don't say anything. I'd no one to say anything to, anyway. I stayed pure still, even only breathing when I remembered I needed to. I wanted to turn over, but I didn't. The skin on my legs and my belly felt like there was little pins pricking them. Frank told me once that that was your brain checking that your body was asleep before it started dreaming. It pricked you, and made you wanna scratch and turn over. If you ignored the feelings, after a while, your brain would think you were out cold, and you'd start dreaming while you were awake. You could control your dreams then, he said. I wondered was I awake-dreaming right now – if us winning the battle was just a dream, if Caoimhe was, if everything good that had happened was. The room wasn't dark anymore, it was kind of getting light, cos it was the summer. I was warm, even without the covers. I'd my eyes open, but I was falling asleep again, it was working. I dunno if they closed on their own, or if I closed them, but in the end I must have drifted off, cos it was the real morning, and I couldn't remember any sleep. I felt brilliant. I was so excited about everything that was happening today I was nearly bursting. I was so happy, it felt like I was on a yoke or something. And then I went downstairs and heard the news come on the radio, and everything went to shit.

Ten

"Gardaí investigating the disappearance of Limerick schoolgirl, Áine O'Shaughnessy, say they have recovered the remains of a young woman in a city centre location. The identity of the body has not yet been confirmed, but a spokesman from Henry Street station has said investigators are not ruling out foul play. We'll bring you more on this story as soon as we have it. This is James Kehoe, for Radio Limerick One, in Limerick."

I felt like I was gonna faint or black out. I got this mad dizzy feeling in my head. I put my hand behind me to grab onto the kitchen counter. My Ma looked at me all funny.

"Are you okay, Jon?" Her voice sounded weird – like I'd my hands over my ears and I was listening through them.

"What? Yeah… yeah, I'm fine." I wasn't fine. I was struggling to keep standing up.

"Are you sure? Look at him, love – he's white as a sheet…" She said it to my Da, but he was in the sitting room, watching something on TV. He couldn't see me. Or hear her.

"What's the matter, Jon? Was it the radio, was it? Jesus, did you know that girl? The one who's missing? Is that what it is? Jon? Talk to me, Jon!"

"What? No. No, I – I didn't – I'm just going up to my room for a bit. I'll be grand. Just feel a bit sick. That's all." I needed to get out of there. I was hoping my legs didn't collapse underneath me, going up the stairs.

"Your bedroom? Jon? Sick? Come here a second, please. Have you -" I was already halfway up the stairs.

"I'm fine, Ma. I'm grand, I'm fine." My feet were like bricks. I fell onto my hands twice going up the steps. My room was on the left, but my stomach decided I was going right. I just about managed to lift the seat before I puked my ring up into the bowl. It was all watery stuff, no food. The back of my throat was burning, and the smell of the puke going up my nose made me throw up again, straight away. She shouted up after me:

"Jon! Are you all right up there? Answer me, Jon!"

"Yeah! Yeah, I'm… I'm fine, Ma. I just… have the runs." It was the best I could come up with. It'd stop her coming up the stairs anyway. If she thought I was puking she might wanna know why.

"Ah, Jesus. Well close the fecking door then, will you? And Jon?"

"Yeah?" I was croaking more than talking now. The smell of vomit was burning my eyes and making them water.

"Put some Toilet Duck down when you're finished. Right around the bowl, do you hear me?"

"Yeah…"

"What did I say then?"

"Toilet Duck. Round the bowl. Make sure." I spat out the last of the stringy spits and reached over for some tissue to wipe my mouth, and around the edges of the bowl, where I'd missed going in. Da was saying something downstairs – wasn't sure if it was to me or to her, but I closed the door anyway, and I couldn't hear either of them after that. I finished up in the toilet, gave it a second look to see if I'd cleaned off all the sick, and went straight into my room. I pushed my tackies off my feet, got on the bed, and stared up at the ceiling and the glow in the dark stars and moons I stuck up there when I was small, even though it wasn't dark. I wasn't small anymore, but right now, I felt very, very little. Caoimhe's hoodie she'd given me was there on the chair where I'd taken it off last night. Cos Harta'd took my Leeds Utd jacket with him and not come back. She didn't need hers, cos she got straight into a taxi outside back door of the George, where the cab rank was, in Shannon Street. I put it up to my face, and the smell of her was still on it. It smelt like she was nearly there with me, and I felt a bit better, but I still felt awful too.

I put the tips of my baby fingers all the way into my ears, so I couldn't hear any sound at all. Not my Ma shouting up to me, my Da muttering, or the radio. It was so quiet I nearly felt safe. I closed my eyes real tight. My breathing started slowing down, but I could still hear the sound of my pulse, inside my ears. Everything that was good had just got really bad. I had to think about what I was gonna do, but I couldn't.

I had to phone her. Their family would've heard it well before they put it on the news; that was how it worked. Or how I thought it worked, anyway. They could've known all day yesterday, but she was with us; with me, so they'd have had no way of getting hold of her til she went home. I wondered why she hadn't phoned me last night. But maybe they hadn't told her til the morning. It'd been late when we went home, anyway. I must have been up in the room nearly an hour. No one came up to check on me. Then I heard the engine starting up outside, and the front door shutting, then the doors on the car.

Downstairs, there was no one around. A note from my Ma on the table; it said "Gone to get the shopping", but my Da wasn't around either, so he must've drove her. I went over to the phone, nervous, and just sat down, looking at it, like that was gonna do something. I had her number. I knew it off by heart now. I couldn't pick up the receiver. I wanted to have a fag while ringing her, but I couldn't, not here. I'd just have a quick one out the back, and come back in and phone her straight after, I told myself. I was halfway through the second fag in no time. I was pure stressed. I'd sparked the second one off the first one. It tasted like air, or nothing at all, cos it was too soon after the last one. Waste of a fag.

Back inside, I must've dialled the number about 20 times, and hung up before it even started ringing on the other side. I was chickening out big time. I just didn't know what I was supposed to say. If things were different, I'd be straight on to her, and I'd know exactly what to say. She was my girlfriend, and she needed me; and even though I hadn't had girlfriends before, I usually knew what the right thing to say was to people. But things weren't that simple. I had this secret, and the one person in the world I wanted to tell it to, I couldn't. And that made me feel like a liar whenever I talked to her about Áine. It wasn't fair at all. And now it was worse. I pictured her, sitting at home, probably crying, waiting for me to call her. I couldn't just leave her like that. I swallowed all the spit in my mouth and picked up the phone again. My heart was pounding now, pure fast, waiting for the rings.

I got the engaged sound. Of course it'd be engaged – everyone they knew must be trying to get through. Their little girl had just been found dead. It was definitely her, too. It must've been. It couldn't be a different girl found dead, and Áine still missing at the same time. That was too much of a coincidence, and Limerick wasn't that big. There wasn't dead bodies found here every week. Not of kids anyway. It'd been a long time since that had happened. And when people were missing and they find a body and it's on the news, even when they didn't say the name, it was always them. They'd to wait, for some reason, before they said it. I didn't know why. It was her. It was Áine. The Áine who was supposed to interview me for the *Leader*. The Áine I met next to an alley in Catherine Street that night, and got up to God only knows what with. The Áine whose sister I was going out with. Who I was in love with. For a second I thought I was gonna puke again, but it went away. I tried to get through again, for the fifth time. Still engaged. It was no use. It'd be like that for ages, unless I got lucky and got through between the calls. But I'd have to be very lucky to do that, and it felt today like my luck had ran out. I needed to get out of the house for a few minutes. To clear my head.

"Aboy the head, Jon."

I was on my way down towards Pa's when I ran into Dara, sitting on the small wall next to his place. I hadn't seen him since the night Áine was – since that night. I remembered I hadn't paid him. It'd been weeks now. A month, pretty much.

"Hey, man. How's it going?" I was thinking did he remember giving me them at all, now. He mightn't.

"Grand, shur. Haven't seen you in yonks, sham. Have ye that money for me at all?" Bollocks anyway.

"Ah… might do, actually. Hang on and I see now. What was the damage, anyway?" I wondered if he'd ask for the full whack, now he wasn't loved up no more. If I paid him on the night it'd probably have been two for a tenner, and I'd have no debts to settle with him.

"What was it, two?" It wasn't a real question. He knew well it was two. He was seeing if I'd chance my arm and say it was only the one.

"Yup. That's the one."

"Eh, call it fifteen, yeah?" That was fine They'd have cost fifteen each, on a bad night, off someone I didn't know. Supply and demand, as Frank would say. I didn't care now anyway. My mind was on other things.

"Oh, sound. Here. Sorry about the shrapnel." I gave him a tenner and the rest in coins. I'd a bit more, from the prize money, but I didn't wanna let him see the twenties, in case he upped the price. Not that I really gave a shit now.

"Ah shur no bother. Money's money, sham. Listen, d'ye hear about yer one?"

"No. Who?" I knew exactly who he meant, of course.

"That youngone that went missing – Blondie one, Castletroy or somewhere like that. In all the papers?"

I thought about Caoimhe at home, thinking I'd forgotten her, or thinking I didn't know yet.

"Oh yeah. Awful, isn't it?" I didn't know what else to say. That was the sort of thing people said, though. Mas and Das.

"Yeah, sham. Poor misfortune. Listen, I'm after hearing from my Da that it was a *murder*."

"What???" The word made the blood inside me turn into ice. They hadn't said anything like that on the news. I'd listened to the whole thing. No one said *murder*. I felt dizzy again, and my heart went ninety. Dara's Da would know, though, and he'd hardly be telling lies. He was a Gard.

"Yeah, that bit wasn't on the news. Probably be on there later. It was murder though, swear to God. Strangled to death, she was, he says. Fucking mad altogether, sham."

"Jesus." I wasn't able for this. I was barely getting my head around her being dead, and now he was saying this to me. My legs started to go again, so I put my hand on the wall. I didn't think he noticed me acting funny. If he did, he didn't say anything about it.

"Yeah. She was out in town. Same night I met you inside in Costello's, wasn't it? That was when it happened, they think."

"Yeah? Did they do the *Time of Death* thing?" I dunno why I asked him that, it wasn't the movies. They didn't know stuff like that in real life, I didn't think.

"Hah? What? I dunno, no, I just – that was the last time someone saw her. Above in Catherine Street."

He didn't mean me, he meant yer man the Gollies told me about, but I still felt para. Murder. Strangled. It didn't feel true. She was fine when I was with her. And Caoimhe said she was ringing their house. Or it might have been her, she didn't really know. But it wasn't her. She was dead. And now she was after being murdered. The whole thing was messed up. I wished this was one of Frank's awake-dreams, but I knew it wasn't.

"Oh yeah, I suppose so. Listen, I've to head off."

I think he said something back to me, but I wasn't listening anymore. My head was wrecked. I didn't even know where I was going. I got this feeling like I just wanted to keep walking, forever, until I was away from everyone, and everything that was happening. Nothing made sense. But everything did as well. Cos now it didn't matter about Shane coming back to that party without having her with him. Cos he'd killed her. And I couldn't tell anyone. I couldn't tell the Gards now. Not when she was missing all that time and I didn't say nothing. Not now she'd been murdered. It'd be me they thought that done it, not him. No one was gonna believe me now. I wanted to collapse on the ground, but I couldn't do that – Dara was still there behind me, and there was youngfellas on the green, playing Headers and Volleys. I kept walking. I was pure tired, and it was dead hot out. I turned down by Pa's shop, to take the long way into town.

I wondered did Caoimhe know. Not about Áine being dead; of course she'd know that by now. But about the murder – all the details. Any of the details. She mightn't. She was only still a kid really, to them; the Gards might have just told the Ma and Da, if it wasn't all on the news already. Give them time to let the kids know themselves. It wasn't *kids* no more, though. It was just one kid. That made me feel sick again.

I had to decide. I could go back to the house and try to ring her again. Or, I could go to the lads, like I was supposed to, in Arthur's Quay Park. Our sound check wasn't until five o'clock, maybe half past, but there was stuff on all day, and Jed told us if we came early we could hang around, meet the bands, have a few free drinks and stuff. None of that was as important as calling her, though. But I didn't know if I was gonna get through. Everyone was gonna be calling their house. It was gonna be a circus over there. Maybe I should go to Castletroy myself? I knew the house now. I couldn't just show up there, though. Not without calling her first. Maybe she was trying to call me; I wasn't at home, so how would I know?

I needed to get my head straight. I needed to breathe. I needed to have a cigarette. Then I'd go back home, and check if there was any missed calls. And trying ringing her again. Or maybe wait a while, in case she called me. It was a nightmare. I'd been so looking forward to today, and now it was all going to shit. At least it couldn't get any worse, I guessed. I hoped not, anyway. I couldn't find any wood to touch, so I crossed my fingers and went up the path past the soccer field, on the way back to mine.

Inside, I checked the phone to see if she'd called. The star sixty-nine thing. It said someone had called, but it wasn't her number. I didn't know it. Must have been someone for the Ma or the Da. I hung up and rang her house. Engaged. And again. Engaged again. After the third time that I put it down, it rang on my end. I grabbed it, cos I knew it was her.

"Hello, Caoimhe?"

"Jon? Is that you?" It wasn't her voice. It was a man.

"Ah, yeah. Who's this?" I was in no mood to talk to someone else now, and they'd be blocking the line if she wanted to call me.

"It's your Uncle Frank, boy." Frank. What did he want? He never called this number; he didn't like talking to the Ma. She was always giving out to him about his life, or about hanging around with me.

"Frank? What's up?" Maybe he'd heard about Áine. They all knew she was Caoimhe's sister – him, Harta, the boys in the band, Ciara and Bríd. I'd said to them all not to bring it up around her, though. That it wasn't something she liked talking about, or something like that. And they all did what I said, in fairness. Up to now, anyway.

"Ah, I've some bad news, boy. Sorry." He definitely had. Weird of him to call me about it, but nice too, I thought.

"Yeah. Yeah, it's terrible, isn't it?" I was wondering what they'd be saying when they found out the whole truth. About what Dara had said.

"Oh, so you know? How do you know, like?" He sounded a bit confused. I didn't know why.

"Ah, the radio. Same as as – hang on, Frank. What's your bad news?" I got a nasty feeling, not for the first time today.

"About Dominic, like."

"Harta? What about him?" My head started spinning again. I needed to sit down, but there wasn't a chair near me. I squatted down on the floor instead.

"Oh, right. You don't know, then." Now he was the one confusing me. The spit in my mouth went a funny taste, like what happens just before you get sick. Something terrible was coming. I could feel it in my bones.

"He got jumped last night. We don't know what happened, but he was *stabbed*, Jon. In town. The Gards brought him in to the Regional around midnight. He's in intensive care. They won't let us in to see him yet. He's not woken up."

"Jesus…" I nearly dropped the phone. That was why he never came back. I'd forgotten all about him with the rest of it. What the hell was happening today? Why was everything going so wrong?

"I know, boy. Listen, his Mam and Dad are out there now. I only know cos your cousin Fiona gave me a ring this morning, like she does sometimes, and she was talking about working last night, and she says something about a fella being brought in stabbed. And she said she knew him from seeing him busking in town, like. And I knew it was Dom. I just knew it. Was he with ye last night?" Fiona was a nurse out in the hospital. She was nearer Frank's age than mine. I didn't really know her now, not since we were small.

"Yeah. Yeah, he was at the battle. He…"

"I thought he was. Cos she said he was wearing a white Leeds jacket. And I thought, he supports Liverpool, like. That's Jon's jacket. You're the only one in Limerick I've ever seen with one of those, like. Can spot you a mile away with it…"

"Yeah. Yeah, he went off to – he was cold. You know, cos he's such a skinny fu - I gave him my jacket after the pub. One of the lads gave him a beanie hat. He went away around twelve. Twelve midnight." I was trying to hold it together, but I was struggling. I lit up a fag. If they came back and caught me now, I'd just tell them to shut up. I didn't care anymore.

"Oh right. Well, listen, I dunno what else to tell you. They'd no clue who he was in the Regional until Fiona talked to me, so I told her where he lived, and they were able to look up the number for his Mam and Dad. I'm going in to see can I see him now, but they probably won't let me. But I'll have a try anyway. Fi might pull a few strings for us, you never know. Will I give you a ring later at home, or would you be coming out yourself, or what is it?"

"I... I don't think I'll be here. I have to – some other stuff's happened too. And I have to go play in the park." I wasn't making much sense; I could hear myself like I was listening to someone else talking now.

"Go out playing? In the park? What?" He probably thought I'd gone mental. He wasn't too far wrong, though. I was losing it.

"No. No, not like that – we've to do the gig, for the Expo. We won the thing last night, so... And there's another thing."

"Ye did? Jayus. Yeah, I'm sorry I couldn't get to that, like. I was in Fermoy, only got back this morning. Thumbed a lift up, like. Jesus, well, that's good. Well done, like. What's the other thing?"

"Sorry?"

"You said there was other stuff. Listen, don't worry if you can't come out. Like I said, he's not awake yet, and they won't be leaving anyone in who isn't family, so." His voice got quieter at the end, like he took his mouth away from the phone. I wondered was he at Marie's now. Was there someone else with him. I didn't know the number for her place, so it could have been the one that came up when I checked for missed calls. It was an 061 one, anyway. I couldn't remember the rest of it.

"Áine. Caoimhe's sister. The missing one. The Gards found a body last night…" It wasn't getting easier the more I said it. Or the more I thought it. It was getting worse. I needed to get off the phone and try calling her again.

"Oh Jesus, Jon. I'm sorry. Has it been on the news, yeah? Course it has, sorry, I'm being thick now. I haven't even listened to the radio today. I've been caught up in all this, like. I didn't know. How is she? I mean, sorry; obviously she's not good, but how is – did you talk to her, boy? Is she there with you now?"

"No. No, I can't get through to her house yet. I've been trying…"

"Oh. Yeah, shur it's probably gone mental over there. Would you not take a trip out to the house, no?"

"I… I've never been – I haven't met her Ma and Da, like, yet. So…" I wasn't sure what I was trying to say. It was hard even to get words out now. I was picturing Harta in a hospital bed now, all covered in bandages and tubes. Beeping noises in the background. It was pure clear, like a movie in my head.

"Ah. Yeah. Not the best type of, ah, introduction, no. Still, listen to me – she's gonna need you now, boy. Even if you don't go out there, you need to talk to her. And she's gonna need you lots after today as well. It's not gonna be easy, like. You okay? You think you can handle it, like?"

"Yeah, of course." I didn't think I could, but I was gonna try, for her.

"You love her, don't you?" It sounded strange coming out of Frank. He didn't normally say stuff like that. Not to me, anyway.

"Yeah. Yeah, I do." *More than fucking anything*, I thought. More than I could ever even try to explain to him, or to anyone.

"I could tell, boy. That's good. That's good for her. You're gonna be lots of help to her. And don't worry about it, like. When you love them, it just comes naturally, shur. Take it from your auld Uncle Francis, boy. I've been around the block a few times." He sounded really kind. I was glad I'd talked to him, even if he'd brought bad news with him. My Ma didn't get him at all. I wished she was here now to hear him.

"Yeah. I think I'll be okay. Listen, I need to get off the phone. I need to-"

"You need to call her, of course, I know. Listen, whatever you do, look after her. And shur look after yourself too. Is it Arthur's Quay Park ye're in today, boy?"

"Yeah. Yeah, if I even get there."

"Ah, you will. Don't worry. You'll be grand. I know you've shit on your mind and you've all sorts of things going on, but you'll get through it. You can do all the things you need to, just take them one at a time, yeah? When are ye on stage, so?"

"Am, I'm not sure. The Cranberries are on about half nine, and there's three or four bands on before us, so…" I felt nearly ashamed talking about the stupid gig with all this happening, but he'd asked me.

"So around six, maybe? Listen, I'll try get in to see ye, and hopefully I'll have news about Dom then. Good news, please God. I'm gonna let you go now, right? You go talk to your woman. Tell her everything's gonna be all right, even if you don't think it is. That's what she needs to hear from you, boy. Take it from me."

"Okay, yeah. Thanks, Frank." I was thanking him for letting me get on with calling Caoimhe, but as well for the things he'd said. They'd really helped me. He was a good guy. I'd make the Ma understand that, someday, I told myself in my head.

"Not a bother. Take care of yourself, pal. I'll see you soon."

*****

"Jaysus. Are you all right, Muzz? How's Caoimhe doing? Where is she?"

Niall was the last to come, as usual. I was in Quin's with Tim, Ian, and Richie. I'd come into town after giving up on getting through to her, but I was still gonna keep trying. There was phone boxes everywhere, and I'd money. We'd been talking about it all, me and the lads. They hadn't known about Harta. They did now.

"Ah, she's at home. I dunno how she is, I can't get through, man."

"Fuck. Did you want to just go, like? Out there? She's out in Castlecon- Castletroy, I mean, isn't it? Did you want a taxi? I'll chip in, like." He was sound out, Niall.

"Ah, no. Listen, I'll just keep trying. And we've the gig." I felt like a gowl saying that. The gig wasn't as important as her. But the lads were important to me too. And at least the gig was something to focus on; that's what Richie had said a minute or two ago to me. Something normal to think about in the middle of all the madness, he said.

"Okay. Okay, so. Whatever you think's best, Muz- *Jon*. We'll back you up, like." He said it like I was gonna have a scrap with someone, and they were gonna jump in. They probably would, though, in fairness. Most of them. I looked at Richie just then. He looked miles away.

"Okay then, lads. My round. What's everyone drinking?" said Tim, and we all told him, and Ian went up to help him bring them back from the bar. Tony was on today, so we'd be grand getting served. I waited for Niall to be sitting down, before I told him what had happened to Harta. It was gonna be a long fucking day.

*****

I'd tried ringing Caoimhe a whole load of times by the time we were over in Arthur's Quay at four o'clock. I hadn't even got the ringing sound once. I was so frustrated. I thought about Frank's yoke where you could send letters to people's computers in a few seconds. It didn't seem so stupid now. It would have been really handy today. I just tried to keep my chin up and concentrate on the gig. The park was mad today – full of carnival stalls and jugglers and people selling candyfloss, but I wasn't interested in any of it. I didn't wanna have fun. We were over by the stage with Jed. There was a massive ice box thing there, full of cans. He was telling us to help ourselves.

"Yeah, anyway. What a night, guys. I didn't even know ye were gonna win, by the way. Scout's Honour. I just did my voting, and Tom and Mark and Joanie did theirs, but it was Peter from the bar who added them up, like. We didn't get to see. Then he gave me the envelope with the winners in it, and well, the rest is history, yeah? Amazing stuff. Those other guys, Jesus. They did not take it well, did they?"

"Heh. No. Fucking pack of steamers," said Niall. Every one of us looked depressed, but he was doing his usual thing of trying to keep everyone up. He was feeling it too though, inside. I knew that. He was very fond of Harta. And of Caoimhe too, even though he'd only met her the once. I opened one of the cans, cos they were free for the bands. I could see one of the Hogan brothers, from the Cranberries, across the other stage, chatting up some youngone. I didn't really care. Meeting famous people was the last thing on my mind now.

"Haha, naw they were okay guys. Until they lost. Prima Donnas, I guess. But, I mean, he must know, right? That he's terrible at singing? How could you not know?" said Jed. He was wearing a t-shirt that said 'Shit Happens' on it. It was the right day for that t-shirt, definitely.

"Ah, maybe not. Maybe it's like when you've BO, and you can't smell it yourself?" said Niall, sparking up a fag. The stink of the smoke made me want one too.

"True. Good call. Maybe it is," Jed said, then he sniffed his own armpits. Half as a joke, but probably half to check for real, in case Niall was being sly. Someone on the stage behind us was doing a *one-two, one-two*. It was a woman's voice. Or a girl. We were going on in a couple of hours. We were kind of the lowest on the bill, but only for bands. There was all school choirs and dance groups going up there for the first few hours, and that was gonna start soon. Some fella walked past on stilts, juggling pins. I looked up to see his face, but the sun hurt my eyes and I had to look back down. I felt someone touch me on the back, in the way people do when you're upset and they're trying to make you feel better. It was Tim, coming back from somewhere. I thought about how funny he'd been the night before, and that cheered me up for a few seconds at least.

*****

"Well, squire? Long time, no see. How are you holding up, Maurice? I heard ye'd a bit of bad news." Brillo had come out of nowhere, about two minutes before we were due on.

He'd his missus, Aisling with him. She was over by the front of the stage, with a load of girls. I wondered which bad news he meant, there was so much of it.

"Ah, yeah. It's been pretty fucking grim, like." I'd had a lot to drink, but I was sober, I thought. You needed to be in a good mood for drink to make you merry. If you were in a bad mood it was supposed to make you worse, but I didn't feel worse. Probably cos I couldn't.

"How's yer man, Harta? Any more news, like? Fucking awful doing, he got, I'm after hearing. Fucking Limerick, what?" He was wearing a white Paddy Expo t-shirt. Loads of people were, they were giving them out free from the stage, and over where you came into the park. He'd it on over a rugby top, so it looked like he had a collar on it.

"Ah, no. My Uncle said he might come down and let us know, but I haven't seen him, like." I was looking over his shoulder at the lads, who were already on stage. I'd have to go any second now. I looked behind me at the crowd. There was loads here now, even if they weren't all sitting down to watch the stage.

"Oh right, yeah. Sound. And listen and I tell you, what about yer one?"

"Yeah, I – I've to go up, Bril- Brian. We're on in a second."

"Of course, of course. But, listen. I haven't seen you in yonks, like. I didn't know you were seeing yer one of the O'Shaughnessy's – Caoimhe. How mad is that?" He'd a big surprised look on his face. I didn't really know why. The lads were tuning up. I needed to go.

"How mad is what?" I said it, but then I started to realise what he meant, even before he told me.

"Well, like – remember I set you up to go do that interview? Remember? And then yer one goes missing, and now she's, well – And then I hear you're doing a line with the sister, like? How'd that happen? Small world, like, isn't it? I was saying to Aisling that-"

"What did you say to her?" I was panicking, suddenly. I'd forgotten. No one knew I'd met Áine that night, so no one could connect me with her, really, except Áine herself. So, no matter how bad I felt today, at least I'd been feeling that now Caoimhe wouldn't ever find out I knew Áine first, and we'd never have to have that talk, but now I realised that Brillo could fuck everything up. He could say something to someone, or to her, even. And she'd ask me why I hadn't told her about the newspaper thing. She'd think I'd kept something from her. Not the thing I really had, but something, and that was nearly as bad. And his girlfriend, well – she went to school with Áine. She might know Caoimhe too. What was gonna happen when they went back in September? Or, what was gonna happen at the funeral? What if they talked? I didn't need this now. I could hear someone shouting my name from the stage. It sounded like Richie.

"To Aisling? Nothing, like. I was just saying how funny it was that you didn't know who either of them were that time I asked you, and now you're going away with the other one. And you were supposed to-"

"I've got to go, Brian. I'll talk to you in a bit. Listen…" I had to say something. I didn't know what, exactly, and I didn't have time to think, but…

"Yeah, Maurice?" He raised both his eyebrows. He'd a little mole on his forehead I'd never noticed before.

"Do me a favour. Don't say nothing about that interview thing to anyone else, yeah?" If I was trying not to sound dodgy, it wasn't working. Richie was doing rolls on the drums. We'd already done our sound check, it was all good up there.

"Huh? Why not?"

"Just, it's hard to explain, just don't bring it up, yeah?" I wished I could find some magic words to get him to play ball, but I couldn't explain it without telling him why, and I was never gonna tell anyone that. I couldn't.

"Okay, Jon. If you… if that's what you want, like. Why, though?" He was looking at me pure suspicious now, but I didn't have time for this. I heard Niall warming up his bass with the hook from *Break on Through*. I had to go.

"Just because. I don't want things to be… I'd just prefer if you kept it to yourself, yeah? It's nothing, really." It wasn't nothing. It was something. Everything had gone to shit already today, and this was another thing that had come out of the blue that might end up fucking up everything. But if I could just get him to…

"Consider it done, me old china plate. My lips are sealed, yeah? It was only an auld – I just thought it was funny, like. Funny *peculiar*, not funny *ha-ha*. But yeah. Forget about it."

"Thanks, man. I appreciate it." There was still her to worry about – Aisling, but like Frank said earlier – one thing at a time. Caoimhe wasn't here. She wasn't gonna meet either of them today. I could deal with it tomorrow. I *would* deal with it tomorrow. Just not now. *One thing at a time*.

"No bother. Go on, break a leg, squire."

“Cheers, man.” I left him and climbed up onto the stage. Jed was up there, holding the mic. They’d given us six songs worth of time. I needed to forget about everything else for the next 20 minutes, and just get up there and give them a show.

*****

“Ah, man. That was amazing, boy. Something else, ye are, I swear to God.” Frank was the first person I saw when we came off the stage after *Light My Fire.* We’d done brilliant. I was buzzing. I caught the can of Heineken Niall had threw over to me from the box and opened it. I didn’t even like Heineken, but it was free. Frank was saying good things, but there was something off about his face. I got a really bad feeling again.

“Thanks, man. So, what’s the story. Is he okay? Did he wake up?” I’d seen Uncle Frank half way through the last song, but he might have been there for the whole set. It’d nearly put me off remembering the words, thinking about Harta, but I’d got through it.

“Ah, yeah, hang on. Come over here with me a second.” His face went pure serious. My guts dropped, and my heart felt like it was sinking. I didn’t wanna know what was coming next. I didn’t want him to say Harta was –

“Right, so. Listen. He’s awake.”

“Oh, God. Oh fuck, thank God for that.” I nearly wanted to hug him for telling me that. Still, he didn’t look happy. There was something else.

“Yeah. Yeah, it’s good. The doctors say he’ll be okay. He’s out of the woods, they said. Superficial wounds, they didn’t hit nothing important, he was lucky, like.” All of that was good. The feeling in my stomach wasn’t going away, though.

"That's great. Sorry Frank, I feel like… I feel like I wanna cry, you know? But in like, a good way. I'm just so-"

"Yeah. Yeah, I know what you mean. But, here. There's something I need to tell you. Something Dom said."

"Yeah? What?" The inside of my throat went really dry, but I couldn't even take a sip of the beer, cos I felt like my whole body was frozen stiff.

"He told me – he said that the guys who jumped him, right? He said they weren't after him, Jon."

"What do you mean?" Of course they were after him. Hadn't they nearly stabbed him to death? How could they not be after him? I didn't understand what he was saying at all.

"Well, he said that – it's a long story, but he said two things that were important. Two things that he wanted me to tell you. Cos you need to know."

"What? Why do I need to know them?" I felt really cold. Even though it was still boiling out. I'd the shivers, like I needed to put a jumper on.

"He said that when they were stabbing him, right, they were saying someone else's name. Like, to him. They were saying it like that was his name, do you know what I mean?"

"Ah, kind of?" I was wondering why he said *someone else* instead of just saying what name it was. But there was something inside me that already knew the answer to that. All the noises from the rest of the park sort of got quieter, like the whole world was holding their breath, waiting for Frank to say the next bit.

"They were calling him… they were calling him *Musgrave,* Jon. They were calling him your name."

I couldn't move now at all. I my foot felt really wet, and I looked down and saw I'd dropped the can, but I couldn't remember dropping it. I was dizzy, my brain was going ninety, I didn't know what it all meant, but I did as well.

"Jon? Jon, are you okay?"

"I… I'm – Frank?"

"Yeah?"

"What was the second thing? What was the other thing he wanted me to know?"

"Oh. Sorry, yeah. Well, when he was on the ground, just before he passed out, he heard them talking, right? They must have thought he was dead, he said. Cos they were saying stuff about him like he was. Talking about him in the, er…"

"Past tense?" I felt like I was in a dream now. A really bad dream that I couldn't wake up out of. Even if I held my breath and counted to three, like they said you should.

"Yeah, but it isn't just that. They were arguing. They were saying how they'd killed the wrong guy. And Jon?"

"Yeah?" There was nothing he could say now that was gonna surprise me or shock me. I was gone way beyond that today.

"He said one of them was called *Shane*. Maybe Shay, but one of those, definitely. Does that ring a bell? Jon? Shane, or Shay? Jon?" Frank was sort of moving side to side for some reason. Then he went up in the air, like he had a parachute on in a movie, and he'd just pulled the string. I didn't realise until they woke me up that he hadn't done any of that, and I'd actually just fainted.

*****

"Hello?" I couldn't believe I'd actually got through.

"Oh God. Jon! I'm so glad to hear from you. I've been- well, I called you earlier, a few times, but your Mum said you were out, and then I remembered about the concert, and I then I didn't know how to get to you, and they – they won't let me go out – they wanted me to stay here, and… I'm sorry I missed it and stuff, it's just…"

"Jesus, don't be stu- don't be silly. The bloody gig doesn't matter, Caoimhe. The gig is nothing. Okay? It's you that matters. You're all that matters to me, you know that, right?"

It was after ten o'clock at night when I finally got hold of her. I was over the road from the park, in the phone box. The Cranberries still hadn't been on yet. Everyone had been doing long sets, cos the crowd was massive, and the Expo guys didn't mind, Jed said. I'd been drinking. A lot. And there'd been gear. And someone had a wrap of speed too; one of the lads from The Blissful Martyrs. I was off my trolley, but I was trying to keep it together so she wouldn't notice. I hadn't been having a good time or anything, I was doing it to blot everything out of my mind. But it hadn't worked. It was dark out. I was completely para now, cos of what Frank had told me about last night, and what Harta said. Someone was trying to kill me. He'd even given me his hunting knife. The one with the compass on top. I had it in my pocket, in case they – in case someone tried to come after me again.

"Thank you. I love you so much, Jon." She sounded like she was crying. She sounded really sad, but her saying that still made me feel really good. It did every time she said it, but especially now, for some reason.

"I love you too, babe. Loads, I really do."

"I wish you were here."

"I can come, if you want? I can get a taxi or something."

"Would you? I mean, I dunno if they'll – I don't know if my folks will let you – if they'll say it's all right. I might have to ask them or something. It's really bad here though, Jon. It's so… sad. You know? I wish I could come to you."

"Yeah. Well, listen, I'll do whatever you want, honestly, you decide."

"Thank you. I'm really tired. I've been – they were up when I came in last night. Sitting in the living room, with the lights on. I thought I was in trouble or something first, but then I saw the Gard in my Dad's armchair, and there was another one in the kitchen, making a pot of tea, and I just knew. I knew it was about Áine. I… oh, God, John, do you know what they did to her?"

"Yeah. Yeah, I do. I'm so sorry." The Gards had told the news people it was a murder now. Frank had told me that, he'd heard it on the radio in the hospital. So I didn't have to pretend I didn't know.

"Why, though? Why would someone do that to – look, I know I've been horrible about her, Jon."

"Ah, you haven't." I wanted so much to be able to be there with her right that minute, and hug her, and hold on to her, and make it better. I felt helpless, like I couldn't do nothing.

"I have, you don't have to lie. But, Jon – I did love her. She is- she was my sister. And she didn't deserve this. No one deserves that. To be… what they did to her. I can't even think about it. But it's all I can think about. It's there when I close my eyes. It won't go away. And I'm so tired Jon. And I've been drinking all day, and I haven't eaten a thing. I'm ready to collapse. Seriously I am. But I don't want to go to sleep. Cos I'm afraid of what's in my head. I'm sorry, I'm being stupid."

"You're not. Listen, if you're tired I can just – I can come tomorrow. In the morning, after you've had some rest. Maybe ask your Ma or Da for some Valium or something? You need to sleep, Caoimhe. Or you'll go mad, trust me." I wanted to see her, but what I wanted wasn't the most important thing now. I loved her. She was the important thing.

"You're amazing. Is that okay? Are you sure? Do you mind? Cos like, I might be no use to you tonight, come to think of it. Even though I really, really want to see you now. I really do. But, you're right. I need to sleep at some point. And I… well I don't want you to come all the way out here and I just end up conking out, and you're left awake, with all these strangers, do you know what I mean?"

"I do. I know exactly what you mean. It's okay. I just want you to be okay. I can wait til the morning. I can. Honest." I could wait forever for her, if I had to. But tomorrow would be long enough.

"Okay. I'm just so – what am I going to do, Jon? How am I gonna… I just wish I knew who did it, you know? Because…" She stopped. I felt myself getting angry. Not at her. I could never be angry at her. I knew exactly who I was angry about, and what Frank told me had made me ten times more angry. I was ready to blow.

"Caoimhe?"

"Yes, baby?"

"If I was able to find out who did this to her… If I knew, for sure, who it was. And I could get them, yeah? What would you want me to do with them?"

"What – what do you mean?" She sounded confused, but something else as well. I couldn't place it just from her voice. I'd have to be looking at her, maybe.

"I just… you heard me. Just imagine for a second that I've got… a way of finding out who – who did this to Áine. Would you want me do something to them?" I hadn't even told her about Harta, let alone about him being stabbed cos someone thought he was me. Cos Shane thought he was me. I wouldn't have even known where to begin, in fairness. It was too mental, even if I'd been straight and sober.

"Like what?" She was asking, but she knew. I knew her enough now to be able to tell from her voice. She knew.

"Do to them what they did to her?" I meant it. My hand went down to the knife in my pocket, and it gave me a weird feeling. Not good or bad. Just… something.

"Jon, I…"

"I need to know, Caoimhe. I need to hear you say it." It was all talk, maybe. I didn't really know anything for sure about what happened to Áine. But Shane tried to kill me last night, even though he got the wrong guy. Why would he do that, unless he knew that I knew it was him? There too much there for it not to be him who killed her. I didn't care how drunk I was now, I was right about him.

"Look, I don't know how – what is it you know? Has someone said something?"

"Caoimhe, Caoimhe, Caoimhe, please. Never mind all that. I'm asking you, as someone I love, and someone who loves me: Would you want me to?"

"Jon I don't want you to get into trouble. Even if you did know – I just, I don't want to lose you. What is this all about? You're scaring me, Jon." That was the last thing I wanted to do.

"No, no, no, no, no, no, no, no, shush. It's okay. It's okay. No need to be scared. Caoimhe, listen to me now. I'm not trying to scare you. I love you. I just… I wanna fix this. I wanna… I wanna promise you something.

"What do you want to promise me?" She sounded so sad still, I just wanted to make her better. I wanted to make the bad stuff go away.

"I promise you I'm gonna find out who did it. And I'm gonna kill them. For Áine, and for you." My voice was slurring. I sounded langered, I knew that. She probably thought it was just the booze talking. She probably just thought I was saying something to make her feel better. She didn't know I was already halfway there. She didn't know I already knew who he was, and all I had to do now was find him. He didn't know that either.

*****

It felt like the day had lasted about 48 hours, but I wasn't tired. The speed had helped, but I was already wired cos of everything else that had happened. I stumbled over across the road after saying goodnight to Caoimhe, and I love you, and I'll see you tomorrow, and all that stuff. I was at the bit where you could see both of the ways into the park from the one spot. I was going in the one next to the back of Roche's Stores, not the other one. And then I saw him. It was dark, but I saw him. Shane. Just strolling out the other gates, down across from the back of the shopping centre. He was on his own. He was walking on his own. The fella who needed a gang to back him up all the time. The fella who needed two other guys with him to jump Harta and stab him like cowards. He was all by himself. No one to protect him. It'd just be me and him. One on one. I watched him walk until he was nearly out of sight, but I knew where he was going. He was going home. Well, he thought was, anyway. I felt the knife again, and took a really deep breath. My nose was sniffly from all the speed. I wondered what he'd been doing in there, but nearly everyone from Limerick had been in there at some point that day. He didn't need a reason. Unless he was in there looking for me. I wondered about all the times in the last few weeks I'd seen him in random places I went. I wondered if he'd been -

"There you are, man! Fucking hell, where've you been? Thought you'd done a runner or something, like. We're all inside. Cranberries will be on in a minute, man. Still plenty of free booze left. We're hanging with the lads from The Hitchers. Come on in, like." I recognised the voice behind me straight away, and I got an idea. Maybe it didn't have to be one on one? No one ever said revenge had to be fair, did they? I didn't have to give him a fighting chance. He hadn't given Áine one.

Eleven

"Come on!" I said. Richie was as fucked as me. I'd had too much of everything. Drink, smokes, speed. Way too much. All I wanted to do was find Shane.

"I'm coming! Hang on, where am I coming to?"

"Jon?" He sounded a bit lost.

"C'mon, man. Come on." I was raging. Not at him, just raging. It'd been too long. I'd waited too much now. We had to do something. Well I had to, but Richie was gonna help. I knew he had it in for Shane too. Something went on between them two, years ago, but he wouldn't tell me. It was something serious though, I knew that for sure. That's why I'd dragged him off with me from outside the park. He was the only one I'd have brought with me to do this. And it had to be now, or I might never have the balls to do it again. I was off my head, he was on his own, and I'd promised her.

"Up here. Keep going, man."

"Yeah, but fucking… ah, now, seriously. Where we off to? Dearbhla's back in – Jon?"

I blinked at him and shook my head. Not shaking it at him; I was trying to shake the thoughts out. Or the booze. I wanted to be langered, though. I didn't need a straight head for this. We went up the stone steps onto Sarsfield Bridge.

"Come on to fuck, will you?" I pulled on the sleeve of his tracksuit top to hurry him up. I could see someone in a white t-shirt right down the other end of the bridge, near the traffic lights. It had to be him. That was what he was wearing.

"All right! All right. Jaysus, cop on, will you?"

He was going too slow. Or I was going too fast for him. I needed to go fast though, or I was gonna lose Shane.

Everything made sense now. I remembered, but I didn't remember. But I what I could remember was enough. It was him; it was Shane. He'd killed Áine. He was there that night. He disappeared from that house party. The youngfella of the Gollies said it. He was there, at the alley, after me, and Áine never made it out of there alive. She never made it out at all. That was where she died; strangled, by him. I didn't know why. I didn't need to know why. I just knew he done it. I couldn't go to the Gards. Not now. Too much time had gone past without me saying nothing to them; or saying nothing to Caoimhe. It'd look pure dodgy; I'd look pure dodgy. They'd think I done it. But I didn't. It was him, and I was gonna make him pay for it. And for poor Harta, too. I wasn't thinking straight, but I was as well. He was after getting away with murder. Real murder, and no one should get away with that. It wasn't right. You had to pay for what you did. He'd nearly murdered Harta too. And I'd told her – Caoimhe – I'd promised her I'd get who done it.

"Jon?" Richie was gasping for breath.

"Come on, Rich, keep going."

He said something else, but I didn't hear him. I couldn't see the white top anymore, and that meant he'd turned down to the right, towards Thomondgate, not gone straight on up the Ennis Road. It was definitely him, then. We just needed to go faster. He'd hear us, of course, when we got closer. We couldn't sneak up on him by running, I knew that. It didn't matter, though. I was done sneaking now; he could hear us all he liked, it wasn't gonna help him. I tried to run a bit quicker, but my lungs were bollocksed from all the hash and fags, and the cider and beer was sloshing around in my guts. The speed was giving me energy though. I stopped for a second, leaned over, and puked up a load of hot sick all over the path. We were near the end of the bridge. I puked again, less of it coming out, cos less of it was in there. I felt pure rough.

"You okay, man?" Richie was behind me, breathing like someone having an asthma attack. I tried to remember if he'd asthma, but that was someone else. Harta, maybe. Or Bríd. My head was spinning too much to think about things.

"Yeah, I'm fine. Keep going, I'll catch you up." I was bent over now, could barely move. But I needed to move, or Shane was gonna get away. I felt like crying, but I wasn't sad. Just angry.

"Keep going where, man?"

"DOWN THE FUCKING STRAND, RICHIE." I shouted so loud an echo came back off somewhere, or it might have just been in my head.

"All right, man. Calm down. What strand?"

I didn't know if he was being crooked or just stupid. I didn't care. I got myself back up and started running again. My guts were sore inside, like I'd food poisoning, or cramps, like you'd get from eating wild apples when you were skinning orchards.

"Just fucking come with me." My own voice sounded funny to me. Like it was weak, or I was sick. I felt the tears coming down my face, even though I wasn't crying. It must've been from puking. I was around the corner and onto the strand. I was nearly afraid to look up in case Shane was gone, but there he was – far away, but still there. We could catch him still. I tried to run faster, but I was already going as quick as I could. Richie'd stopped asking questions now, thank God; he was keeping up with me okay.

I really was gonna kill him. I realised it properly then, when my head went a bit clear. The puking or the running – one of those'd sorted me out – I was thinking straight again. We were gonna catch him, and I was gonna stab him with Frank's knife, and I wasn't gonna stop until he was dead. I didn't wanna kill someone. I didn't wanna go to prison, or to court, or anything like that. But maybe I wouldn't. Maybe we could just put him in the river when it was over, and never tell anyone about it. I could trust Richie. He wouldn't say nothing to no one. I felt calm, once I knew what was gonna happen. They were crazy thoughts, but I believed them. And I meant them. He'd killed Áine, for no reason, and he thought he'd got away with it. He hadn't any mercy for her, why should I have any for him? He'd tried to kill Harta – tried to kill me, really. It was… justice. Justice was gonna be done. I looked to the side at Richie. Maybe I didn't need to have brought him at all. Shane had turned again after Munchin's church, but the fence and the wall were low there, so I could still see him heading up the hill. We were so close.

"Jon?"

"What?" I didn't have the breath to be running and talking at the same time.

"What are we… what the fuck are we doing?"

"Just keep going, will you? Just keep following him!" I pointed up at Shane, who was nearly at the Golden Gate Chinese now. We'd followed him too far into Thomondgate. That place opened til one in the morning, there'd be people there. The street after it was quiet enough, though. If we got to him before Frazer's pub we could still get him. I tried to run a bit faster. Richie said something else to me, but I wasn't listening.

He was walking fast. Or we were running slow. I couldn't tell. We should have caught him already, but I'd stopped a good while when I puked up, so he got a real head start on us. He must have heard us by now. I'd have heard someone running after me like that, late at night, in a quiet street. He hadn't even looked around. It was weird. I didn't care, though. It was good. He'd no idea what was gonna hit him. We were nearly behind him. I suddenly had a panic about what we were gonna do when we caught him. We were too far into Thomondgate to just jump him. Even if there was no one in the street, people lived there. They might look out their windows, or open their doors. They mightn't, though. Sometimes people didn't wanna get involved. You'd no idea what the story was, sometimes. You didn't know if the person getting jumped was innocent or whatever. Maybe they deserved it. And what if you went out to say something or to break it up, and someone pulled a knife on you? It wasn't worth it. I felt my pocket for the knife. I got a sick feeling in my throat thinking about it – about stabbing someone – but it was him I'd be stabbing. It'd be different. Cos he deserved it. I was close enough to him to touch his shoulder now. I got the weirdest feeling – not like anything knew the feel of – it wasn't an afraid or a guilty one. It wasn't a good or a bad one. It was just a feeling. Richie's breath wasn't beside me anymore. I looked around quickly and saw him bent over, out of breath, gasping. He wasn't looking at me. I turned back to Shane and grabbed onto the back of his t-shirt. He let out a really weird sound, then he fell onto the path. We were about ten feet away from Frazer's, I'd just got him in time. Richie was shouting something, but the rage took me over now – I couldn't hear him. Shane was wriggling under me and making funny noises again – not words, just sounds. Just really stupid sounding sounds. Something was wrong, and I didn't know what. I was on his back, half holding him down and half trying to turn him over. He was screeching now, like a little girl, and the weird feeling was in me again. Something wasn't right at all. I got all of my strength and managed to roll him over on the ground so I could look him in the eyes. Richie was right next to us now, gasping, and saying something frantic. I looked down at Shane and brought my fist up, ready to smash his face in. Except it wasn't his face. It wasn't him at all. I felt Richie grab me from behind and pull me off the youngfella, who was still making the awful, weird noises. I shook Rich off me and tried to focus my eyes on who it was in the white t-shirt that we'd followed all the way home. It was dark, but I could still see the face. It was Gar Buckley. The deaf kid from up next to Johnsey's shop. That's why he was making weird noises instead of talking. That's why he never heard us coming.

I couldn't say anything to him. I wanted to say "Sorry", but I couldn't say anything. And he wouldn't have been able to hear me anyway. I squatted on the ground and sparked up a fag. I could hear Richie trying to calm the poor youngfella down and get him up off the floor, but I dunno if he was doing any good. We'd fucked up. We'd lost him. I felt bad about knocking poor deaf Gar over and nearly smashing his face in, but that didn't matter. He'd get over that, it was just a stupid mistake. I pulled on the fag like there was something inside it that'd make it all better, but nothing would, now.

We'd blown it. I'd blown it; Richie didn't even know what we were supposed to be doing. He must have been pure confused now, thinking I'd brought him all that way to jump some poor deaf youngfella. He was gonna ask me questions. I didn't care. It was all gone now. It was over. The chance was gone. There hadn't even been a chance. Not really. I felt like shit. I was still raging, but I was numb too. Sometimes you got so angry that you couldn't even feel anymore. I couldn't get up. My legs didn't wanna work. Everyone was still back at the park, but I was near my house now, and I didn't know which one of them I wanted to go to. It wasn't like Caoimhe was there, anyway.

We walked back towards the bridge, up Clancy Strand again. Neither of us said anything for a bit, and when someone did, it was him.

"What… what just happened, man?"

I didn't look at him when I answered.

"I don't know."

"Ah, no, man. Really. Why did you want to – why were we after that poor youngfella, like? A fucking deaf kid. What did he do to you, like?"

"Nothing!"

"Then WHAT? Tell me, Jon, will you?" His mouth was screwed up all angry. I half thought he was gonna take a swing at me.

"Okay. Okay then. Hang on. Gimme a second."

I took a big breath. And then I told him all of it. Everything I knew, about the whole thing. I didn't care anymore. And it came out easier than I thought it would. It felt okay to tell him. It nearly felt good. It must've been relief, from having so much secrets. I told him about meeting Áine that night. And how I couldn't remember how I got home, or how I'd left her. I told him how I heard from Brillo about her going missing, and how I didn't know if I should tell anyone I'd been with her on that night. How I'd been scared that people'd think I done something to her. That the Gards would think I done something to her. I told him about the two Gollies, and Shane going missing that night from the flat. I told him how I met Caoimhe, and how I thought she was Áine. And how we'd got together, and I didn't tell her, even though I wanted to. I told him about this morning, and the radio, and Dara telling me about the strangling. I told him about Harta, in the hospital, and what he said them fellas had said who jumped him.

Even while I was telling him, I realised that I'd never really wanted to tell Caoimhe the truth. I was only worried about her finding out about me and Áine by herself, and me being caught. I felt like that when we thought she was alive, and just missing, cos I knew when she came back, it'd all come out. That was the only reason to tell her. Cos I didn't wanna lose her. I didn't wanna lose what we had. It was like she said – the best thing that ever happened to me. I couldn't lose that. I couldn't live without that. I just couldn't. But I'd never told her, cos I was afraid of what she'd say, and what would happen to us.

And when I found out she was dead this morning, and there was no way of Caoimhe finding out, I stopped wanting to tell her. It wasn't guilt – I didn't feel guilty about anything I'd done; it was just worry, about her catching me out. And me losing what I had with her, because of it. I didn't want that. We walked slow. There was no hurry now. I took out another fag.

"Gimme one of those, will you?" said Richie, looking pure serious.

"Ah, Rich. You gave up, man. Seven months now, like." I didn't wanna start him on them again. That'd be lousy.

“Yeah. And I’ll give up again tomorrow. Just gimme one, now, yeah?” He looked… different. Not angry or sad, just different.

“Okay, long as you’re sure.” I handed one over, and he took it, but I nearly didn’t let go of it for a second or two.

“I’m sure. Now, listen…”

I listened, and we walked some more, and Richie smoked, and he told me the whole story about what happened with them five years ago – with Paudie, with Dermot, with all the lads, and with Shane Collopy. And then I knew everything. I knew why he hated Shane, why he stopped hanging around with him after that, why him and Joe weren’t pals no more, and how Shane got that scar on his face – that was the craziest bit. I was shocked, by all of it, though. I’d never known a thing about any of that. No one did, apart from their little gang; and the Gards, I supposed. I’d so many questions I wanted to ask him – about Paudie Collins, about Marion, about Dermot Mac, about big Joe, and about Shane Collopy. But I didn’t wanna interrupt him just yet. So I let him talk, and I let him smoke my fags, cos he probably needed them, telling me all that. We were still talking and walking when we saw Shane come out of the alley, up the strand. He was doing his zip up. He must have gone down there for a piss. He looked very shocked to see us. Or to see me, anyway.

“What the-” His voice sounded small. Weak. I didn’t move. Richie sprang at him like a tiger, and knocked him over onto his back, back into the alley.

“You fucking prick, you!” Rich was on him, holding his arms. Shane was trying to wriggle out of it, but he’d been winded. I still couldn’t move.

“Jon. Jon!”

"Wh- I..." I didn't know what to do, but I couldn't just leave him do it by himself – that's why I'd brought him in the first place. To help. Now I had to help him. I ran over, even though it wasn't really running, cos my legs were like lead.

"Fucking... get off me, you gowl. What're you doing?" Shane had mad wild eyes on him. I could smell the booze off him from here, but I might have been smelling it off myself.

"Jon. Fucking... help me, or something!" Richie was struggling to hold him down. He was gonna get up in a second. I thought about the knife, and then Shane headbutted him, full force, in the face.

"Aaaaaagh, you cunt, you!" Richie rolled off him, holding his nose. He was pumping bleeding. Shane got up and ran towards me. I had to do something. I didn't know if he was gonna come at me or try to get past me. He was in my face in two seconds. He took a swing at me, and I ducked it. I punched him in the gut as hard as I could, and he went falling backwards.

"Hold him, Rich!"

Richie just about got up in time to catch him falling. His nose was a mess from the headbutt, there was blood all over his face and his tracksuit top.

"Get the fuck off me! What the fuck are ye doing? I'll fucking kill ye!" He was talking the talk, but Richie had a good hold of him now. Arms under his armpits, like in a half-nelson. He couldn't move. I punched him as hard as I could in the face. I heard something crack, either his nose or my finger, I couldn't tell. He screamed, like an animal. We needed to get him away from the road. The alley was between some of the big houses they had down that strand. I didn't know what was down the end of it, but it was dark, that was all that mattered.

"Go back!" I said to Richie, pointing into the dark. He was looking at me really strange, through all the blood and snot. He looked scared. He wasn't the only one. I was scared too, but I had to keep going. The alley was grassy, not tarmacked. You could see marks in it where people had drove their cars down it.

"What the fucking… let go of me, South! Let fucking-"

"Shut up!" Richie said, and started dragging him back more, on his heels. Shane was trying to dig into the muck with his shoes, and when that didn't work, he was kicking out, but Richie had him good. I followed them into the dark, my heart going ninety.

"Hold him for me. Hold him, Rich." I punched him again. This time it didn't hurt my hand, or it did, but I'd gone numb or something. I did it again. And again. Then I gave him a few in the belly. Richie was nearly falling over, trying to hold him, every time I let off a punch, but he still had him. I knew what I had to do next. I took out the knife. Richie's eyes went like saucers when he saw it.

"Jon! What the hell? Ah, no, Jon. You don't want to-"

"Shut up, Rich." I looked down at the blade in the dark, with the moon making it shine. My blood was thumping in my ears now. I felt like I was going on stage or something – the way you didn't know if you were nervous or excited. I looked at Shane, and he'd gone real quiet. Like a rabbit in the headlights, as Frank would say. I thought about him, earlier, giving me the knife. To protect myself, he'd said.

"Jon, look. I know what you're thinking, man. But you can't- you can't… do this. I know he did what he – I know you're hurt. But this isn't – this isn't the way, man. Put it down, like. Put it down. Please." Richie looked like he was gonna cry. He looked really small and young. Like we were ten or eleven again. Just for a second.

"Ah, don't. Come on. Please, I'm begging you," said Shane. I looked at his face. The scar. It made him look scary normally. Now it just made him look weak. I was full of something. Hate. And sadness. I felt so sad for poor Áine, and what he'd done to her. I felt sad for her being left there in that alley. For weeks. All on her own. No one with her. No one who loved her knowing where she was or what had happened to her. Cos of him. And Harta, in hospital, nearly dead, cos of him too. And now Richie was telling me not to, and Shane was saying "Please". No. Fuck that. I knew what I was gonna do. What I had to do. What I'd promised I was gonna do.

"Get out of here, Rich." I looked at the knife when I said it, not at him. I didn't wanna look at him now.

"What?" He barely said it. It was like a whisper.

"You heard me. Let go of him. Get out of here. Go home, or go back to Dearbhla. I don't care. I'll handle it, yeah?" I walked closer to them, but I still didn't look at him.

"But, Jon, please. Don't do – let's just go, yeah? Come with me. It'll be fine, yeah? We'll go back to the park. Frank's there. Or we can – we'll get a taxi to Castletroy. Go see Caoimhe, yeah? She'll be delighted to see you, man, she-"

"RICHIE, GET THE FUCK OUT OF HERE, NOW." This time I looked at him, cos I needed him to know I was serious. Shane wasn't saying nothing. He didn't know what was going on. I didn't care. He wasn't gonna matter soon.

"Okay. Okay, I'll go. But… don't do something stupid, Jon. Please? Promise me? Just don't - "

"GO!" I pointed the knife at him. I didn't mean anything by it, I just did it. He took his hands off Shane for a second, and Shane wasn't expecting it, cos he hit the ground. I moved like lightning, to get to him before he could get up and make a run for it. I was on him in a second, my knees on his chest, holding him down. I didn't look at Richie, I was keeping my eyes on Shane. The look on his face was pure terror now. I put the blade under his chin, to make sure he didn't get any stupid ideas.

"Go on, Rich. I'll see you later, okay?" I said it pure calm and quiet, cos I felt nearly calm now. I felt like I was in control.

"Okay. Okay." That was all he said, then he walked out of there and left us on our own. Shane suddenly came to life and started screaming after him:

"RICHIE! RICHIE! COME BACK! Don't leave me with this fucking cunt. He'll kill me! He will, he'll murder me! He'll murder me, Richie, he's a fucking- " I slammed my elbow into his jaw to shut him up. I still had the knife on his throat. We were on our own now.

"Okay. Okay, listen. I fucking know everything about you, Shane," I said, pushing the blade into him a little more, til I saw a bit of blood come out. It was black instead of red, in the dark, but it still sort of shocked me.

"You… you, what? You know about me?" He'd stopped trying to wriggle out from under me now, probably cos of the knife.

"Yeah. I know what you did. I know you jumped Harta, and you stabbed him, or you got one of your scumbags to do it." Saying it out loud made me even angrier, and I wanted to just shove the knife all the way into him now, and get it over with, but I didn't.

"I dunno what you're talking about, sham!" he said, but I could tell he was lying. He was crying now, like a weakling. Loads of tough guys were just weaklings. Just bullies, who were no good without their boys to back them up. It was just me and him now, though. He wasn't so tough now.

"You fucking do, you liar. You thought you'd fucking got me, but then you didn't, yeah? You knew you didn't, cos you said it. And he heard you."

"Who heard – what are you on about?"

I slammed him with my elbow again. I wondered how many of those he could take before I ended up caving his skull in. I might find out yet.

"Harta! My friend Harta. Your boys jumped him last night. Thought he was me, cos of the jacket. And cos he'd his hair up inside the hat. That was it, wasn't it? Ye didn't know he wasn't me, from the back, and ye jumped him – the lot of ye, fucking cowards."

"Listen, man. You've got the wrong guy here, like. I dunno your friend. I dunno what you're talking-"

"DON'T FUCKING LIE TO ME." I punched him full force in the nose, and it crunched when I broke it. He let out a scream so loud my ears started ringing. I kept holding him down and I pushed the knife in a little harder. I needed to say more. I needed to get it all out. And I needed to hear him admit it. Admit all of it.

"You killed her. Four weeks ago, in town, down that alley. You killed Áine."

"No…"

"You fucking did! Don't lie. I left her there – I… she was okay. And you – you came into there – I don't know why, but I know… I know you were there. I know you were at that party."

"What fucking party? What are you-" He stopped again, cos I pushed the knife in more.

"You know what party. In Catherine Street. Or Roches Street. You were there. I know you were, the Gollies said you were. They told me. And you… I don't know, you found her there, and you attacked her, and you strangled her, and you just left her there. And I don't know why. You're just… sick."

"I'm sick? I'm sick? YOU'RE THE FUCKING SICK ONE!" He shouted it so loud that he nearly knocked me off him. The knife came out of the skin under his neck, but I still had it. I still had him. But something was wrong. I got feeling in my stomach that was worse than anything, and at the same time, I sort of recognised it. I'd felt it before. I looked down at him and his scarred face and thought about Richie's story. Bit it off him, like a wild dog or something. I was gonna do much worse to him tonight. I was gonna make him suffer.

"I… I'm the – what do you mean?"

"It's you. It's fucking you, you psycho. Why'd you think we jumped you – your bud who we thought was you? Why'd you think I've been following you and stuff? The fuck is wrong with you, sham? Get a grip!" His whole face was covered in the blood from his nose now, all black in the moonlight – his eyes were the only bright parts.

"I don't…" Something was really wrong. I felt like the bottom was dropping out of my stomach. And he *had* been following me; all those times I seen him. And that time outside my house. Was that him? But why? The fuck was wrong with *him*?

"Fucking… look, I dunno what the fuck you're playing at, sham. But I'm not the sick- I didn't- why don't you KNOW?" The way he said the last word made my blood go like ice.

"Why I don't I know what?" I felt it now, inside me. The truth, about everything. It had always been in there, I knew that now. But I didn't have it in my head, as words. I needed him to say it.

"That you're the one who killed her?"

The second he said it, I knew it wasn't a lie. But I didn't know how. I looked down at him again, like that would give me the answer. And it didn't.

But he did. He told me everything. About how he was at the party that night. About how he was pilled up and coked up, and horny as fuck, he said. And how he'd seen this fella and youngone come down the alley together. How he watched them shifting each other. And how they started doing a bit more than shifting, and how he was off his face, and how watching them was giving him the horn, so he snuck downstairs and hid behind some bins to watch them going at it, and maybe play with himself a bit. No harm in it, he said. Just a bit of fun. He told me how the sex they were having was really rough, and she was screaming her lungs out, and then the guy was sort of choking her, and she was screaming some more. How he sat there, behind the bins, watching them, wanking away, til they were finished. How he didn't know he'd just watched someone get strangled to death, until it was too late for him to stop it. How he thought the girl had just passed out drunk or something, and the guy had just left her there, like a dickhead. He told me how he waited a while, and then went over to have a look at yer one. Maybe to feel her up, or have a look up her skirt while she was passed out. Maybe to wake her up and try it on with her, cos shur why not, he said. How he realised she was dead then, so he went out into town for hours, looking for the fella, but he couldn't find him, so he came back and covered her body up with some old tarp and some black sacks, and shoved it over into a corner, cos he didn't wanna call the Gards, cos he was so off his face. How the next day he realised he couldn't call the Gards, cos he was from a family that were always in trouble with the law, and if he'd admitted he was there, they might have tried to fit him up for it, cos they all hated his family – especially him and his brothers. How he wanted to phone in anonymously, but he couldn't even do that, cos he remembered when he was younger, Colm Mac, Dermot's brother, made a fake bomb threat to Gards from a phone box in town, but they still caught him and arrested him for it. How he'd found the O'Shaughnessy's number in the phone book, and rang their house a load of times, but he chickened out from saying anything, in case someone found out it was him ringing. He told me how he didn't know who the guy was in the alley, but he knew his face from somewhere around, and he knew he had a white Leeds jacket on. He told me how he'd seen me walking through Thomondgate with Richie one day, and he started to think I might be the guy, cos I was the right height, and the right colour hair, and maybe the right face as well, even though it'd been dark, and he'd been off his face. How he started following me, to see if there was any clues, or if I gave myself away, cos he was mad into detective books and TV shows, even though he hated the Gards. He told me how he knew for sure when he saw me wearing the

Leeds jacket walking home from Marie's that night; the night I thought someone was following me. He told me how he'd seen me with Caoimhe, and he found out from someone that she was the sister of the girl that got killed, and he decided he was gonna do me in before I could kill her too. How he was only trying to protect the poor girl from the same thing happening to her. But, of course, he'd got the wrong guy. And so had I.

*****

"Just… get the hell out of here." I took the knife away from under his neck, but I still held onto it. It'd been first thing I said in a good few minutes. I'd just been pure silent, taking in everything he said. Trying to hold myself together. Thinking what to do next.

"What?" He was still under me. Still covered in blood and snot now. I had to get off him to let him up, but I wasn't even sure if I could stand. I'd have to try, though.

"Just… go." I knew there was another way. I could just have stuck the blade into his neck and that would have been the end of it. But that wasn't me. I wasn't a – I couldn't do that. I stepped up off him, still pointing the knife at him, in case he tried anything smart.

"Ah, I…" He didn't take his eyes off me. I knew he thought I was gonna kill him now. I knew from the look in his eyes, and it made me feel sick. Not that I needed anything more to make me feel like that. I was numb.

"FUCKING GO! Before I change my mind." I jerked the knife at him, just to make him see I meant it. He got it. He started walking backwards out of the place, still looking at me, just in case. He thought I was gonna knife him in the back if he turned around. Cos he thought I was a murderer. When he got to the road outside, he didn't say anything, he just ran. I didn't know where to. Probably home. Maybe to get his brothers, to come back for me.

Maybe to call the Gards. I didn't care. I got up and stumbled a bit. I still had the knife in my hand, in case he came back around the corner or anything. I didn't know where to go.

I didn't understand anything that had just happened, but I knew it was true. All of it. All the memories of it had come back when he was telling me the story. It was like I was watching the movie of it in my head. It was the drugs. It was the GBH. I wasn't a murderer. I wasn't a killer. I liked Áine. I didn't like her the way I liked Caoimhe, but I wouldn't – I couldn't have done something like that to her if I wasn't – off my face? Insane? Harta had said the GBH made people sex mad, and that they couldn't remember stuff the next day. He never said if made them crazy, though. He never said it made you… I didn't know who the guy who killed Áine was, but it wasn't me. Except it was me, though. Whatever had happened, Shane's story was the truth. Mine had been the lie. He wasn't the bad guy. He was the MacGuffin, as Caoimhe would say. My chest hurted when I thought of her now. It felt like she was so far away from me.

Everything was over now. All of it was gonna be gone. It didn't matter if Shane Collopy didn't tell the Gards, or if he never came after me again – by himself or with his brothers or his friends. I knew. That was all that mattered. And it wasn't like before. It wasn't some little white lie that I was para about my girlfriend finding out. I killed someone. Murdered them. And it wasn't just someone. It was the sister of the girl I loved. The only girl I'd ever loved. And I'd told her I'd get who done it. I told her I'd kill him. I promised. What was I supposed to do now?

"Jon?"

I nearly jumped out of my skin. It was Richie, a little bit up the strand, walking down to me, pure quickly.

"Rich? How did you – where were-" I was so happy to see him and at the same time I wasn't.

"Ah, I couldn't just go, man. I had to stay. I was worried about you, like."

"Oh. Thanks, I guess." His nose was a bit bloody, but it wasn't as bad as Shane's had been. He'd live.

"Heh. Yeah man, I saw him – Shane. I saw him run away. I was over there, on the wall, keeping an eye out. I panicked, like. I thought he'd stabbed you or something, so I ran down, but then I – then I saw you. And you were – well, you're okay." His smile was kind of sad. I wondered did he know about what I done, and then I realised how stupid that was.

"Yeah. Yeah, I'm… okay." I'd never been less okay. I'd never felt so bad, and empty, and sad, and hopeless. It was all over. My life was over. Caoimhe was over. Everything was gone. I sparked up a fag. I'd never had one taste so good in my whole life.

"I'm glad, man. You had me worried. I didn't know you had – whose knife was that, anyway?" He didn't ask me for a fag. He'd probably given up again already, knowing him. He was better off.

"Ah, it's Frank's. He gave it me cos of what happened Harta. For protection, like." We were almost at the traffic lights on Sarsfield Bridge now. There was still loads of cars around, whizzing past us. Probably cos it was the Bank Holiday weekend.

"Jayus, yeah. Harta. It's been some couple of days, man…"

"Heh. It has, yeah." I was glad he was here, kind of. I wanted to be on my own, but I didn't as well.

"So, what happened?" said Richie.

"What do you mean?" So much had happened. In the last two days. In the last four weeks. In the last half an hour. It was too much.

"With Shane? Why did he – what did you do to him? What did he say?"

"Eh. It's a long story, Rich. I'm tired, you know? Maybe another time."

We were up on the bridge now. I could see Arthur's Quay Park, it was all still lit up. The concert was still going. I could hear Dolores O'Riordan singing. It wasn't one of the ones I knew by them – like *Linger*, or *Dreams* - but you could hear it was her from the voice. Everyone was over there, still. The lads, Frank, Ciara, Bríd. Just not Harta. Or Caoimhe. He was still in the Regional. I wondered if he was out of Intensive Care yet. I couldn't remember if Frank said he was. And she was still at home, with her family. It was painful to think about her right now. It felt like someone was stabbing me in the heart. I wanted to say so many things to her, but I knew I couldn't. I knew I wouldn't be able to look her in the eye, knowing who I really was now, and say – well, say anything to her. Even though it was ripping me to pieces thinking it, I knew I'd never see her again. I couldn't. Not with the things I knew. Not with the things I'd done. She was the best thing that'd ever happened to me. And I was the worst thing. She just didn't know it yet. And maybe she mightn't ever know. I hoped not. If there was a God, I hoped he'd see that I was sorry, and that I'd try to make up for it, and maybe he could stop her ever knowing about it, cos she'd been through enough. And maybe I was gonna hurt her again now, but I couldn't help that. I'd made her a promise. It was the least I could do for her to keep it.

I saw the truck coming way before Richie did; so, when he shouted at me to watch out, it was too late. That was probably what he'd tell people after; that it was an accident. He wouldn't have known I walked in front of it on purpose. It was over in a heartbeat. No pain. No nothing. Frank told me once that your whole life flashes in front of you when you die, but mine didn't. It was different for me. There was nothing except dark for a bit, then it got really, really bright. Then I heard a song, playing pure quiet - it had church organs in it, but I couldn't remember what it was called anymore. I couldn't remember what anything was called anymore. Everything was fading away. Then, there was a nice smell, but I couldn't remember what that was from either. The sort of smell that could make you feel pure calm sometimes, and pure excited other times, even though it was the same smell. Then I did remember - just for a second - and I was happy one last time. And then everything stopped, it all went black again, and it was over.

The End

Afterword

Well now. That was a thing, wasn't it? Hi, and welcome back to my career. It's been a while. Thank you so much for buying this book. Or, if you stole it, I'm sorry life is kicking you in the financial balls right now, and I hope it gets better.

It's been a long road to get here, from 2013. Literally everything about my life has changed, and most of it for the worst. But I'm here now. And I've written this, and hopefully in a few months' time, you'll be reading another one of these afterwords, because I don't plan on stopping now. Writing books has been my dream since I was way too young and stupid to write a book that anyone would want to read. Trust me, I found some manuscripts recently, and 19-year-old me was not Stephen King by a long chalk. That said, they were still better than all of the Fifty Shades of Grey books, so it's swings and roundabouts, really. I hope you liked the book, and the new characters; because this the start of a whole new universe, connected by the people, the places, and the stories of Richie, Harta, Ciara, Marion, and all the rest. At the time of writing, the next Boys of Summer book should come out in early 2017, it'll be called More Than Words, and I'll be taking you back to 1991, to have another look at Richie and Marion, but from a different angle, with a different story, and probably another crime of sorts. I've officially got my mojo back, so stick with me, please, and we'll have a hell of a lot of laughs, cries, and really unfair deaths. That's sort of my thing. Ciao for now, CW.

PS. If this was your first Ciarán West book, go out and find the other ones on Amazon! Unless you hated it, in which case, I'm sorry.

Acknowledgements

Oh my. There are too many people to thank, and all of you have names. And the thing is, when I start naming them, I'm bound to forget one. You always do. It's like trying to name the seven deadly sins, or the seven dwarves. Someone always gets left out. So, if you've ever helped me when I couldn't help myself, if you've ever loved me when I didn't deserve it, if you've ever thrown money at me, or put a roof over my head, or listened when I needed someone to listen, or talked when I needed someone to talk; if you've ever encouraged me when I was ready to give up, or stopped me when I couldn't stop myself; if you've ever been there when others left me, if you've ever walked away because it was the best thing for me – Thank you. I hope I can make you all proud of me some day. Until then, thanks for putting up with me. I appreciate it more than you'll ever know.

19581225R00205

Printed in Poland
by Amazon Fulfillment
Poland Sp. z o.o., Wrocław